# ALL WE *carry* HOME

Books by Nicole M. Miller

*Until Our Time Comes*

*All We Carry Home*

# ALL WE *carry* HOME

A POST–WORLD WAR II NOVEL

**NICOLE M. MILLER**

Revell
*a division of Baker Publishing Group*
Grand Rapids, Michigan

Published by Revell
a division of Baker Publishing Group
Grand Rapids, Michigan
RevellBooks.com

Printed in the United States of America



Library of Congress Cataloging-in-Publication Data
Names: Miller, Nicole M., 1986– author
Title: All we carry home : a post–World War II novel / Nicole M Miller.
Description: Grand Rapids, Michigan : Revell, a division of Baker Publishing Group, 2026.
Identifiers: LCCN 2026004061 | ISBN 9780800748340 paperback | ISBN 9781493455607 ebook
Subjects: LCGFT: Romance fiction | Historical fiction | Christian fiction | Novels
Classification: LCC PS3613.I5464 A77 2026
LC record available at https://lccn.loc.gov/2026004061



Cover design by Laura Klynstra
Cover image © Rachael Fraser / Trevillion Images

Published in association with Books & Such Literary Management, www.booksandsuch.com.

Baker Publishing Group publications use paper produced from sustainable forestry practices and postconsumer waste whenever possible.

26 27 28 29 30 31 32 7 6 5 4 3 2 1

To Bomp and Old Fat Grandpa,
whose legacies live on in the smiles,
laughter, and spunk of the Miller boys.
We love you and miss you both.

## Bedouin Legend: The Bloody Shoulder Arabian

Legend tells of a prince struck during a fierce battle. Through the chaos of war, his pearl-white Arabian mare returns the prince to his palace, saving his life.

Upon her master's recovery, the mare births a colt with a blood-red coloring upon its shoulder, identical to the blood from the prince that had fallen upon her own shoulder. It became a mark of destiny—of a great and courageous warrior spirit, imbued by the mare and prince and the mutual bond they shared.

The mark is revered and appears once in a generation.

# Prologue

## Warren

JUNE 17, 1945
BAD KÖTZTING, GERMANY

Oh no. Was it that time already?

The little gray mare bobbed her head, huffed, and pawed at the fresh straw in her stall. Her massive sides heaved, and her tail flicked as if she was in pain. She huffed again and stumbled, nearly falling to the ground in her stall. From what I'd seen of the other horses from Hostau giving birth, this didn't look normal.

I needed to find the veterinarian, fast.

I raced through the makeshift aisles of this former Luftwaffe airfield turned horse stables.

Mira was one of the hundreds of pregnant mares we'd had to transport, and we knew it was risky to move them such a distance so late in their pregnancy. I hadn't known anything about horses before my men and I tiptoed into Czechoslovakia and evacuated these horses so the Soviets couldn't seize them from the now-defeated Nazis. I was a city kid from Philly. I appreciated the history and tradition of my cavalry unit but had never expected to stand beside the beasts.

"Do you know where Dr. Baumann is?" I asked Eddie as I drew near him. Sergeant Eddie Moore was lanky and had laugh lines etched in his narrow face. He held two nails in his lips as he hammered a loose board on the ramshackle stalls we'd been patching for days.

He jutted his chin to the northern barns. "Has his hands full with a foal on the way."

My heart dropped. Mira didn't have much time.

The airfield spanned dozens of acres, and its pavement, metal buildings, and small pens were a far cry from the lush green fields of Germany, Poland, Holland, and Austria, where so many of these priceless animals had originated.

When I reached the air hangar that housed nearly a hundred gleaming white Lipizzaner horses, I spotted a few soldiers all gathered around one stall. "Hey, Doc," I said as I reached the stall. Inside, Dr. Baumann was bent over a white mare with a huge, heaving belly. A petite woman in a nurse's uniform crouched next to him.

Dr. Baumann exemplified the studious veterinarian, a short man with thick black glasses and a neatly trimmed beard. He was a local civilian who had served the Germans at Hostau and helped us greatly in our evacuation. No one knew these horses better.

The woman beside him I didn't recognize. She had wavy brown hair tied back at her neck, a straight, short nose, and lips that tilted up at the corners in a friendly, kind way. Her tan uniform sleeves were rolled up to the elbows.

"Mira is in labor," I said.

"Bad timing," Baumann said in his thick German accent. He wiped his brow with his forearm and turned to the woman beside him. "She's a first-time mother?"

I answered at the same time the woman did. "Yes." She caught my gaze with her dark brown eyebrows lifted in surprise.

The doctor nodded and motioned to the nurse. "Will you see to Mira?"

Something dipped in the pit of my stomach. Mira hadn't had a foal yet, and from what Dr. Baumann told me before, it meant she was at far greater risk of complications. What if something happened to her?

The nurse nodded and stood. Tendrils of her brown hair framed her face, and her pale blue eyes pierced right through me as she wiped her hands on a rag and picked up a medical bag. "Let's go."

I hesitated and approached Dr. Baumann in the stall. I leaned down to whisper as softly as I could, "Doc, with all due respect, I think Mira needs a veterinarian, not a nurse."

Baumann chuckled, but his focus remained on the mare before him.

The woman's uniform revealed her last name as Bryant and her rank as a senior ward nurse—a first lieutenant. She smoothed a hand over her uniform and smiled. Her eyes sparkled as she sized me up, and I realized with a twist of guilt in my stomach that she'd caught my statement.

"Don't worry, Captain Hayes," Baumann said. "I assure you, I'm sending the more experienced hands with you."

That loosened the knot in my stomach.

"Come on, Captain." Lieutenant Bryant slipped through the soldiers around us and walked with purpose to the barns south and east of this hangar. From her answer earlier and her direction of travel, she knew exactly who and where Mira was, which inspired confidence.

Was she the more experienced hands? This woman had to be all of twenty-five years old. Though she was slender and I guessed five feet, three inches, her pace left me in the dust.

I jogged to catch up.

"I'm sorry, Lieutenant." My mouth was dry. "I didn't mean to insult—"

"It's okay, Captain." The sun washed over her smooth skin as she looked over her shoulder. "You're not the first to underestimate me."

Her tone felt genuine and honest, which helped to unravel the coil of unease.

"Besides," she added, "I know Mira means a lot to you."

"You do?"

She smiled. "From what I hear, you're her person."

"Her person?"

"Some horses just have a person they trust implicitly." She pointed to the mess hall, which was along our way to Mira's stall. We gathered towels and a bucket of hot water and then resumed our original path.

"How is it you know so much about horses?" I asked.

"I grew up on a ranch. Gramps taught me every secret he knew about training them." Admiration and appreciation shone through her gaze.

Why hadn't I seen this woman around Kötzting before now? Surely the men would have been all abuzz about this pretty, blue-eyed nurse. I wanted to learn more, but as we reached Mira's stall our collective attention shifted.

Lieutenant Bryant set down her bag, studying the mare. She moved slowly into the stall and closed the half door behind her. Mira, a brilliant gray Arabian with chestnut speckles across her coat, huffed and stomped her foot, shifting her weight as if to lie down. She was one of so few horses to have survived the desolation of Janów Podlaski, the state breeding farm in Poland. If this foal didn't survive, there was every chance that the lineage, cultivated over hundreds of years, would become another casualty of this war.

Lieutenant Bryant rubbed the horse's neck and whispered softly. The mare's body and skin twitched as a contraction came and went and her sides rose and fell with each panting breath. "Why don't you come in and soothe her while I examine her?"

Mira nickered at me as I walked in and sniffed my pockets for candy.

"I still don't know why she likes me so much," I said as I scratched the horse's neck. "I know nothing about horses."

The lieutenant wrapped thin fabric around the base of Mira's tail, to keep the hair out of the path of delivery, I guessed. "She knows that you saved her."

I smiled and scratched under the mare's mane. "Honestly, I think she saved me."

Lieutenant Bryant held my gaze, her own sparkling in delight. "They have a way of doing that."

When we'd liberated Hostau stables, we'd discovered hundreds of Allied prisoners of war and nearly six hundred horses stolen from all over the continent. This was the goal of Operation Cowboy.

In the massive evacuation, I'd watched as one of the mares had fallen from the steep ramps we'd constructed for the few horses who were too pregnant to walk the distance to the Allied-controlled border.

We couldn't lose another.

After everything I'd faced and done in the past two years on this continent, these horses were the only bit of good in a mire of destruction and death.

Mira groaned and pulled free of us both, circling in the stall.

"This is progressing fast," Lieutenant Bryant said. "You were right to go to Dr. Baumann when you did."

She pulled me aside while Mira shifted, lowered to her knees, and fell to her side, her large abdomen protruding high and heaving with each breath.

"It's time." The lieutenant reached for her bag and the water.

"How can I help?"

She looked at me and grimaced. "Are you sure you want to? It can be quite an . . . involved process."

"I'm not going anywhere."

She knelt beside the mare, rubbing her neck and soothing her. Her touch seemed to instantly set the horse at ease. Was she this good with her human patients?

For the first time, a war wound didn't sound so bad.

She moved from rubbing Mira's neck to gently pressing on the horse's abdomen.

I stood next to the supplies, ready for her commands, and watched the woman, on her knees in the dirt and seeming not to care a lick, as she studied the horse with what appeared to be expert precision. Dr. Baumann had meant what he said.

She caught my gaze, and a flush filled her cheeks.

"Sorry to stare," I said, tipping a smile. "I promise, I was just looking at the horse."

"Have you used that line before?" She chuckled and kept running her hands over the horse's stomach. "I'm trying to get a sense of whether the foal is properly aligned—whether the head and front hooves are pointed downward or if it needs to be turned."

"Turned?"

She smiled, perhaps at the bit of panic in my tone. "Yes, it's easier before she starts pushing."

"How would one turn a foal?"

She angled her head, and the meaning was clear.

She wasn't kidding about this being an involved affair.

"You've turned foals before?" I asked.

"Yes, sir."

Perhaps it was the unique setting, but I wanted her to call me Warren. I realized then that I didn't know her first name. Nor did I want to breach the protocol we'd come to live and breathe all these years of service.

Mira snorted and screeched a guttural, painful whinny. She flopped and kicked, her back leg nearly clipping the lieutenant.

I reached for her as if I could pull her free, but Lieutenant

Bryant held up a confident hand. "Captain," she said with polite authority, "I've got this."

I sensed deep down that she did.

"Keep a hand on Mira to calm her," she directed, her head dipped as she listened intently through the stethoscope. After a few moments, she lifted the stethoscope. "The foal's heart rate has slowed. I need to get in there."

"Just tell me what you need, Lieutenant."

She stood and shook her head. "I'm not used to ordering a captain around."

"I doubt that," I fired back. She carried herself with a confidence that told me she was in charge whenever she needed to be.

She pointed to her bag. "Can you position that within my reach?" She settled behind the horse.

Over the next few moments, I watched her swiftly tend to the mare and unborn foal, never once showing uncertainty. She was quiet and efficient. Within minutes, the foal was turned, a nose and two tiny hooves emerging with each contraction.

The process seemed back on track, until all progress stopped. With the foal's head and neck free of the birth canal, the mare began to thrash and moan.

"I need you to help me pull." The lieutenant turned to me. "The foal is stuck at the shoulders."

Stuck? We had to do what? And if we failed? Terror shot through me at the thought. This was Mira.

I stood beside Lieutenant Bryant, and we each grabbed the tiny little legs of the creature so desperately trying to make its way into the world. A world of war and death and yet also life and even love.

There was no stopping now.

Lieutenant Bryant leaned against me, her arms and face close to mine as we braced to pull the foal during the next contraction. Though the smell of the animal overwhelmed me, I caught a whiff of floral shampoo. Lavender. It was enchanting.

"Be ready," she said softly. "Any moment now."

I uttered a silent prayer to God that we'd manage to save this little piece of innocent life among all that had been lost in the past two years since I'd landed in Europe. I'd watched too many of my men fall, and I'd taken so many lives by my own hand.

Perhaps that was why this woman, this horse, felt like a ray of light in my otherwise dark world. Saving the horses at Hostau had been our chance at redemption, a chance at hope for war-weary souls that had only faced death and destruction.

"Now!" she called out, and together we pulled firmly on the slippery, frail limbs. But nothing budged, and the contraction ended. "No, no, come on, mama," Lieutenant Bryant breathed. The conviction in her voice gave me chills. "Give us one more push."

I followed her lead, ready for the next opportunity to pull. Her levelheadedness reassured me, and I knew from the limited experience I'd had with these animals that the horses picked up on her energy, just as I did.

"One more time," Lieutenant Bryant whispered, almost as if in prayer.

The mare's stomach tightened, and we didn't even need to communicate—we pulled in unison, and in a rush of fluid and long legs, the little horse slid into the world. The smells of straw, sweat, new life buzzed around us. Mira snorted, looked behind her, and then fumbled to her feet.

Lieutenant Bryant held the foal in her lap. I handed her a wet towel on instinct for her to clean up the mess around the baby's mouth and nose. She did, and the foal snorted out the rest of the mucus and gave a high-pitched squeal as it started breathing.

The lieutenant smiled. "Well done, Captain. You're an excellent delivery nurse."

Adrenaline coursed through me, mixing with the relief of it all. "Good to know I have alternative career options after the war."

She laughed and ran the towel over the foal's dark gray hair.

"Is it a colt or filly?" I asked, unable to see as I backed away, allowing Mira to step forward and examine her progeny.

"A colt," Lieutenant Bryant said. "A little colt to continue the lineage."

And carrying on the lineage was what he would need to do. Most of the Polish Arabian herd had been destroyed in the blitzkrieg in 1939 or stolen by the Soviets later that year.

I reached down and helped Lieutenant Bryant to her feet as Mira began licking the colt's hair. We were no longer needed. The lieutenant accepted my help to stand, but her attention was so fixated on the horses that she remained tucked next to me.

I thanked God for this moment, the life that had begun anew, and the chance to have met this strange and delightful nurse who cared so deeply for these creatures.

She caught her bearings and seemed to realize our proximity. I stepped back, not wanting to make her uncomfortable.

"Nice work," I said lightly. "I'm glad you were here, Lieutenant."

Her gaze locked onto mine. "For Mira?"

"Of course." And so many more reasons.

"It's Eva." She handed me a towel to wipe my hands. "You can call me Eva."

"I'm Warren," I said. "But it sounds like you know me better than I know you."

"Everyone knows the leaders of Operation Cowboy," she said.

I was conflicted by the notoriety. I didn't want or need the praise, even from her lips. Every man in the 42nd had played his part. Colonel Kenneth Roland, Major Bret Conway. We had just pulled the strings and borne the burden if anything went sideways.

She turned to the colt. "What shall we call the little guy?"

I considered it, thinking of the men who had fought and risked everything to ensure this little life would be free. "What about Phantom? As an honorary Ghost Soldier?"

"Perfect."

As Mira licked the wet foal clean, a streak of dark red among the black-gray hair became visible.

"Is he injured?" I asked, pointing to the foal's shoulder.

Eva looked and stepped closer, stroking Mira's hip as if to set her at ease. The mare ignored her as she went up to the foal and brushed her hand along his body. Phantom looked up at her and brushed his muzzle against her cheek.

Eva's eyes shone as she stepped back beside me. "It's not an injury. It's a marking. I've never seen it. The bloody shoulder."

"That sounds awful."

"It comes from Bedouin legend." She turned to me and waved her hands in a flourish. "There's an ancient tale of how a prince's loyal white Arabian mare carries him all the way home after battle and then delivers a colt that bears the bloody mark that her injured rider had left upon her. It's the sign of a warrior, of good luck and great courage."

She put a light hand on my arm, as if I wasn't already enraptured by her words and the adorable scrunch of her shoulders.

"His coat will fade from dark gray to light gray and white, just like his mother's. This mark will stand out against the white hair like a badge of honor." As if her entire being hadn't been radiating before, she grew more passionate as her gaze pored over the foal. "This colt truly is special. I'll never forget him."

Neither would I.

She gathered her bag, and I picked up the buckets, stool, and rag and followed her out of the stall.

Phantom rose shakily to his feet, a thin body on willowy legs that didn't even seem capable of holding him erect. The baby wandered over to Mira and began to nurse, which seemed to set Eva further at ease.

"He's marvelous." She rested her arms on the stall and watched the mother and child.

I watched Eva and her intense gaze on the horses. I didn't want to interrupt, but I was so curious to learn more about this mysterious nurse. "Where do you call home, Lieutenant?" I asked, leaning my elbows on the stall.

"A tiny town out west that no one has ever heard of." She sighed. "There's no place I'd rather be on earth."

"Why is that?"

"The valley is hugged by mountains on every side, and the wildflowers paint the hills in the springtime. The sunrises over Beacon's Bluff—the land glows as if all the spoils of the gold rush were gathered in one place. It's heaven." Her face tipped upward, and her smile went dreamy before she gave her head a little shake as if to wipe away the image. "What about you?"

"Philly. No mountains or sunrises worth mentioning. But then, before the Army, I didn't much care to rise before noon."

She chuckled and then looked over my shoulder and straightened, the humor gone from her expression. I turned, my pulse picking up.

Nurse Sally Emerson raced up the aisle with a worried look on her face. "Eva," she breathed, then nodded to me. "Captain Hayes. A rogue SS band attacked a supply convoy, and we have dozens of critical injuries. Eva, we're shorthanded—"

Eva picked up her medical bag. "Let's go," she said.

Sally nodded, and the three of us strode quickly from the stables and toward the barracks and medical tent.

As Eva kept pace with me, she shook her head. "I thought there was an armistice."

"Not every German agrees with the ceasefire," I said.

"The convoy. Are they your men?" she asked.

I nodded. Lucky, Reid, and another dozen of the 42nd Reconnaissance Squadron. Though my pulse quickened and my heart thudded loudly, I kept my breathing calm and my mind focused.

There was no benefit to assuming the worst. Eddie had told me days ago that I needed to stop living on edge, always waiting for the next sniper around the corner. But this was a reminder of what we all still faced.

Eddie met me at the entrance to the hospital tent, his arms crossed, his face drawn. "No one was killed." He pointed to the nearest bed. "Lucky took the worst of it."

Eva was already there. The boy writhed and clutched his eye. She reached for his hand and put her other hand to his forehead. "Lucky, is it?" she said.

He grunted.

"Is that an ironic nickname?" she said with a smile. "Let me see your eye."

He moved his hand away from his face to reveal a deep gash in his eye.

"You are a lucky son of a gun," she said. "This is just shrapnel, not a bullet."

Lucky grimaced. "Am I going to lose my eye?"

Her lips pressed into a line, and she glanced at me. "Better than your life, soldier." After she drew a syringe full of morphine, she put a comforting hand on his shoulder. "Besides, fellas with eye patches are simply irresistible to us women."

Lucky calmed slightly. "Really?"

She injected the morphine. "Really."

Once the fervor had settled and the injured had all been triaged, Eva and Sally brought handfuls of soiled rags to the rack beside Eddie and me.

Sally was saying, "I know you're not on duty, so thank you for helping us."

"It's no problem." Eva brushed stray hair from her forehead. "I just wish I were here longer."

"You and me both," Sally said before she went back to her patients.

"Are you being discharged?" I asked, halting Eva's return.

"I thought you knew." She crossed her arms and stepped closer to me. "I'm on leave. I'm due back to my unit in the Philippines."

The air fled my lungs. "You came here on leave?"

"Called in every favor I could." She smiled. "I needed to see the horses after I heard about the rescue."

The Philippines. From internal reports, things were rough over there. As dire as the fighting had been here in Bavaria, we'd heard rumors of terrible casualties in the Pacific.

"When do you fly out?"

"Tomorrow morning."

Her words were a bullet that tore through my every expectation. I'd never encountered anyone like her—not among the dozens of debutantes that Mother had thrust upon me before I enlisted and removed myself from the Philadelphia matchmaking pool. Nor among the hundreds of Army nurses of incredible strength and valor. Eva Bryant was something else.

What woman used her leave time to act as a veterinarian to refugee horses and then jumped into the hospital ward without hesitation? The information was all too much, too fast.

She locked those dizzyingly blue eyes on me. "Will you look after Mira and Phantom for me?"

"I promise." I glanced at my wristwatch. "You going to stay here all night?"

She nodded and reached for another patient's clipboard.

"I need to check in with Colonel Roland about this attack," I said. "I'll be back before dawn."

"You know where to find me."

By the time dawn broke, the boys and I had surrounded and captured the German soldiers who'd attacked our convoy, but the morning flight had left long before I returned with the prisoners.

Eva was gone.

I walked up to Mira and Phantom's stall, and the sight of the colt comforted me, despite the deep ache of regret that I hadn't been able to bid Eva goodbye.

Any day, Eddie and the boys and I would be sent home. I didn't know what lay beyond these shores for me. There wasn't anything in Philly I wanted.

At the least, I'd honor my pledge to Lieutenant Bryant and do everything within my power to take care of these innocent, priceless refugees.

# *One*

## Eva

**APRIL 2, 1946**
**FRONT ROYAL, VIRGINIA**

The smell of gasoline from the distant motor pool, the rumble of Jeeps, and the troops bustling around the military base in Front Royal set me at ease as I awaited the start of the auction. This was familiar, yet my body ached and my heart cried out for the Oregon high desert I called home.

A hundred horses were on parade after their own long journey from Nazi captives to American spoils of war. Only a few would be up for auction, and there was only one I cared about.

One I'd had my eye on for almost a year.

The one I'd helped bring into the world. Memories of that little colt's birth—and the captain who'd helped me—had been the lifeline to help me through the worst days of all, my time in the Pacific Theatre during our most desperate hours.

After Japan's surrender last August, I'd remained stationed in Manila to help with the demobilization efforts and treat the soldiers who were too wounded to return home. All the while,

I'd been corresponding with every contact I could to learn of Mira and Phantom's whereabouts. The records surrounding the horses of Hostau were unreliable. I learned Phantom had been shipped stateside, due to be auctioned in Front Royal.

Mira, on the other hand, had seemingly vanished.

Gramps's letters had grown more dire in the past few months, and he'd confessed that the farm was not what it had once been. We needed horses to train and sell. He'd specialized in showing Arabians, and I knew that if we had Phantom at Birkstrom Ranch, we'd be unstoppable.

Upon my discharge a few weeks ago, I'd taken a global detour to German bases and French ports to look for Mira. I ran out of favors and time and hopped on a ship to Virginia, where I prayed I had enough in my pocket to bring this colt home and unlock a future for Gramps's farm.

It had been strange to be back in Kötzting without the men of the 42nd, most of whom had been discharged in 1945. Captain Hayes had been an unexpected complication to my first trip to Kötzting. Unlike so many of my fellow nurses throughout the war, I'd never dated any of the GIs. It was all in good fun, they'd said. A healthy distraction among so much darkness. Warren Hayes was the first and only man who'd made me reconsider my rule.

Perhaps it was for the best, though, that we didn't get the chance to say goodbye. He'd never come back to the hospital once he'd been pulled away. Maybe it was better this way, easier to live with a regret than a mistake.

What if he'd asked to write me? How would I have explained that I couldn't be involved beyond Kötzting? There was no future with me.

Phantom was all that mattered now anyway.

"Okay, ladies and gents, this horse here is a real special one." The booming auctioneer's voice echoed. "He's the son of the renowned Polish-bred Arabian stallion Wiraz and the mare Mira.

As we've said before, folks, there weren't many Arabians to survive the pillaging of Janów Podlaski during the Soviet occupation . . ."

The words faded away at the clattering of hooves on the wooden platform.

The young newborn of less than a year ago had grown tall, his coat a unique mix of dark gray, light gray, and a splash of chestnut-red coloring down his right shoulder—the mark of a warrior. He was big for a yearling—nearly full-grown and taller than most Arabians. His black nostrils flared and drew in the unique smells of the auction arena and hundreds of onlookers.

My heart froze, and I felt the awe of the crowd in the hushed moment of his arrival.

And then the stillness was shattered. Phantom struck at his handler with his front hoof. The tall man jumped out of the way, and in his moment of distraction, the horse bit his arm.

"Oh, that has to hurt." The auctioneer's deep voice held a grimace to it. "But I'm sure it's just a sign of that classic Arabian spunk. Let's start the bidding, shall we? Do I hear $100?"

I lifted my number. Apparently, so did another half dozen individuals.

"$100! $200! $300!"

I raised the paper number again.

A few bidders dropped out after $500, and then a few more dropped out after Phantom circled and bit the handler again. The handler limped away, passing the horse to a fresh victim.

What had happened to this poor colt? His eyes were wild, his body tense. The voyage to the States was long, and God knows the soldiers who'd transported him weren't all horse experts. Had he been mishandled? Despite the soldiers still using the cavalry name in battle, their horses had turned into mechanized Jeeps and tanks. Though some were still true horsemen at heart.

I wondered where Warren and his men were these days. If life after the ceasefire had treated them well. He'd promised to look after Mira and Phantom, but I'd heard that he and his men had been discharged not long after Phantom was born. I knew well that our hands were tied in the Army, and I only hoped he'd somehow found Mira.

"$1,500!" the auctioneer bellowed. "Now we're talking."

*No, no, no.* I only had $2,000 to my name. It was everything Gramps and I had scraped together, all we could possibly stake on this stallion to save the farm. I'd hardly made $1,000 a year during my time in the war and had mailed every cent to Gramps.

I held up my number.

"Back to the bidder over here," the auctioneer said to me. "For $1,600. What about you, sir?" He pivoted on the podium to face the other bidder, who was buried in the crowd and hidden from my view.

His number lifted into the air in agreement.

"$1,700," the auctioneer trumpeted.

I raised mine again, sweat beading on my forehead and my chest tightening. *No, please.* I needed this. I needed *him.*

Phantom whinnied and stomped as the handler led him off the platform and back to the stalls. As he faded from my view, so did any hope of seeing him again. The last of my bidding was nigh, and with a deep, stabbing pain in my gut, I knew how this would end.

"$1,800," I called out.

"$1,900," volleyed back the other bidder. I strained to see who it was. Could it be a fellow trainer who Gramps would know? The crowd was too thick, and the other party stood on the far side of the auction block. I was only five feet, three inches with heeled cowboy boots on.

"Over to you, miss." The auctioneer pointed his gavel to me, his piercing eyes locked on me through his spectacles.

I nodded, my final bid now out into the universe. Even if I tossed in the $50 that I had for the hotel and meals, there was no sign of the other bidder slowing down.

The fury of conversation around me blurred to a distant echo.

"$2,100 to the gentleman," the auctioneer said excitedly. "Yes!" He grinned wildly, clearly surprised to see the scrawny colt draw in so much. He swiveled to me, itching to raise the bid again.

I was done. I was out.

"Going once."

I gave a shake of my head.

"Going twice."

I'd lost him.

The slam of the gavel to its wooden base made me flinch.

"Sold! For $2,100 to the gentleman in the trench coat."

Again, the stark reminder slapped me across the face. Gramps and I were small potatoes in this realm. No matter his magic with training—the way he could turn a rotten old mount into a reliable partner—this horse show world was about famous bloodlines and deep pockets.

And yet, I still wanted their acceptance, still wanted to prove what we could do with the right horse and right chance. We had to, if we were to keep Birkstrom Ranch afloat.

Disappointment turned to bile in my stomach, and I feared losing my morning coffee and apple. I'd been counting on this for so long. What would Gramps say? "Chin up, honey. Something else will come along." That had gotten him to this point, and though I hadn't been home to see it yet, rumors had reached me that things were bad around the farm.

I slipped from the crowd and walked through the barn, desperate to see Phantom once more. There weren't any other Janów horses for auction today. The horses were too rare now, and I didn't know if the opportunity would ever arise again.

Those two weeks of leave in Kötzting, Germany, had been the sole bright spot in five years of utter devastation and death. To be a part of the regiment that had saved the horses from Russian and German capture. To help Dr. Baumann with dozens of foal deliveries. To help when that convoy was attacked and the hospital was understaffed.

When I reached Phantom's stall, as the bustle of noise continued at the auction block beyond, I pressed my hand to his nose and he sniffed me, as if remembering. The tension in his body eased.

"I'm sorry, boy," I whispered. "I hope we see each other again."

Phantom blew hot breath against my cheek through the bars.

Voices rose from down the aisle, and I turned as two other Arabian trainers approached.

"Jackson, Brunt." I nodded.

The men each tipped their caps to me.

"Howdy there, Eva," Brunt said.

I motioned to Phantom. "Were either of you the bidder?"

"No, and I didn't recognize the bloke." Jackson gave me a sympathetic smile. "Give Bill my best. I hope to see him in Scottsdale."

They kept walking past, and the weight of defeat bore down on me.

Gramps probably wouldn't feel up for a journey to Scottsdale for the big show. His voice had been frail and raspy the last time we spoke a few days ago, and he confessed that he'd been in and out of the hospital for months. I wondered what else he'd been hiding from me while I was overseas.

I needed to call him and let him know. He'd be waiting by the phone, no doubt, for the news. I put my hand on the broad forehead of the horse one last time. "Goodbye, Phantom."

At least I could always hold on to the memories of Germany and the dreams of what could have been.

I'd called in a favor from my former patient, an airman, who had promised to help me fly the horse home by Army plane. Now it would just be me and my barrack bag next to the empty cargo bay.

I slowly made my way down the street to my hotel. I stopped

at the telephone in the lobby and asked the operator to connect me to the farmhouse. The operator hesitated. "Miss, I'm going to connect you with the sheriff instead."

"What?" But she'd already changed the line.

"Eva, it's Sheriff Lowe." He drew in a ragged breath. "Where are you?"

"I'm in Virginia." Fear and knowing sliced through my gut and took the wind out of me. "What's going on?"

"We've been trying to reach you for days. Your grandfather collapsed in town and, well, you'd better get home quick."

## Warren

*Sold*. The word I'd been desperate to hear. I'd been prepared to spend anything to make it happen.

I had made a promise to look after him. I would honor that, no matter what.

I'd spent a year battling the Army's chain of command to purchase this horse, who had been deemed spoils of war when Poland didn't claim him after VE Day. Instead of buying him outright, I'd needed to participate in the auction, where no outcome was certain.

Now Phantom was mine.

Mira, however, was still MIA. Her records had been misplaced, mishandled, or were missing entirely. But I wouldn't rest until I'd tracked her down too.

A bald man beside me who had the sun-spotted, wrinkled face of a horse trainer clapped me on the shoulder. "Congrats on winning that colt. He has some spunk. Good bloodlines too, from what I know of the Arabian breed."

I knew that, and much more.

I thanked him and turned to look across the crowd to try to see who I had been bidding against. A woman, it sounded like, but the crowd was still thick, interest high over these unique horses from the war-torn lands of Europe.

Others came up, some who recognized me as a former captain in the cavalry—the captain who'd led the Ghosts of Patton's Army to save the captive horses of Hostau, Czechoslovakia. I'd never live down that *Stars and Stripes* article. I didn't want the publicity or fame. I just wanted to move on.

I responded to the comments and questions from the crowd around me, but I was itching to see Phantom. At least I could look after one of the horses that had changed my life, changed the course of the war for me and my men.

The horse that had introduced me to her.

After a few more handshakes and pleasantries, I strode with purpose toward the barn.

I wanted to see the horse that was now mine. The horse I had no idea what I'd do with. I couldn't exactly take him back to my lonely, empty apartment in Philadelphia. I hadn't grown up with horses, like many men in the cavalry had. Operation Cowboy was my boot camp in horse care.

Right now, I just wanted to get this horse somewhere safe. I'd contacted a stables on the outskirts of the city, purchased a truck and trailer. Kenneth Roland from the Second Cavalry would meet me there—he had a proposition he'd insisted talking about in person.

Through the crowd of spectators, I spotted a glimpse of Phantom and felt the flood of memories wash over me.

Memories of that dark-haired, blue-eyed nurse who knew more about horses than half my regiment combined. Our effort to help Mira bring the unique-colored colt into the world.

*"The sign of a warrior, of good luck and great courage."*

The spark between us had also felt lucky, perhaps even a once-in-a-generation type of pull.

Lieutenant Bryant had come to mind often over the past year—especially as the reports continued to bubble up about how horrendous the military campaigns of the Pacific had been. I'd never forgotten a moment of that day we'd spent together in Kötzting, and despite my efforts, I hadn't been able to track her down. She'd disappeared like Mira. Had she ever made it home?

"That's one fine horse," an old man said, pausing next to me and looking over Phantom from beneath his sweat-stained, tan cowboy hat.

I drew in a long breath. "I'm looking for a trainer, if you know of anyone." I knew I needed at least that much, given how violent Phantom had appeared on the auction block. The colt looked a bit worse for the wear from the year since I'd seen him. His eyes were wild, his mane tangled and tattered. I could only assume he'd been frightened and neglected in transit due to the chaos of the post-war shipments from Europe.

"I own and run a stables a few hours away." The man rubbed his cheek and looked over Phantom. He stepped closer, and at the same moment, Phantom lunged, teeth out, and bit the man's arm.

I winced.

The man cursed, grabbed the tender place on his arm, and fumed to me, "But I'm not accepting clients like this."

Taking care of this horse might not be as straightforward as I'd hoped.

The crowd around me looked on, but I didn't let their judgmental gazes distract me. Phantom was a product of war, and the terror and anger in his eyes hit me to the core. I'd seen it in some of my men after a rough campaign.

I had to find the right person to pull Phantom from this dark, broken place.

# *Two*

## Eva

**APRIL 22**
**BAKER, OREGON**

I checked the drip on Gramps's IV line. Again.

"Sit down, honey," Gramps mumbled from his hospital bed, peeling one eye open and grinning despite the pain that morphine didn't seem to touch. "You're not on duty anymore."

"Well, maybe I should be. They don't run a very tight operation around here." I crossed my arms and shot a glare down the long hallway of the hospital ward, which was vacant of all but a desk nurse at the entrance to the building. It was well past the morning shift change. "They're thirty minutes late for your next dose."

Gramps held up a large, wrinkled hand that was freckled and tanned from a life spent outdoors. I took his hand, squeezing it gently and smiling down at him with my most practiced bedside manner. Those hands had done so much in his life—carved the gates and barns of Birkstrom into works of art, sheltered animals and humans alike from the cold world.

"There are probably more pressing needs," he said.

The underlying message was clear. Some people had a chance of walking out of this hospital. And then there was Bill Birkstrom. A respected and beloved institution in the town but, with advanced lung cancer, a few days or weeks from his passage into the great beyond.

My stomach clenched and my chest tightened at the thought. I wasn't ready for this. I'd never be ready for this.

I'd returned from Virginia a few weeks ago after my fruitless attempt to buy Phantom at auction. I had hoped to pick up the life I'd led before, training horses, winning championships across the nation, furthering the sterling reputation of Birkstrom Ranch. Instead, I'd come home to find the stalls nearly empty, the buildings falling apart, and the property awash in debt.

And the man who'd adopted me at age six on the edge of death.

He'd hidden more than I could have imagined.

What if I hadn't joined the nurse corps? Would I have caught his cancer symptoms sooner, forced him to see the doctor? What if I had been able to save him, this man who had saved me?

"Honey, wipe that worried frown away," Gramps said, tugging my hands playfully. His thick, unkempt black hair framed his rectangular face, and wisps of gray hair dotted his bushy eyebrows. The eyes below were kind, perceptive, and creased from constant smiling. "You were telling me more about the auction when I nodded off. Restart that, would you?"

Those memories only sank the knife deeper in my heart.

"I can't. I'm so disappointed I couldn't bring Phantom home. The bloody shoulder mark, the perfect build. Such a fiery spirit." Never mind the recollections of Captain Warren Hayes. Those were just for me.

"Perhaps it's time to think about a different future for your life." His tone shifted ever so slightly.

I pulled up the chair beside his bed and sat down. "What do you mean?"

"Victor Merrick has been trying to buy the ranch for some time now." His eyes, dark brown and full of sorrow, fell to his lap. "With how much I owe, it might not be long before the bank takes it anyway."

"Gramps." The Merricks were the proverbial Hatfields if the Birkstroms were the McCoys. And I'd allow no future where they took over Gramps's ranch. "Quit saying such things."

"I don't want you burdened with the mess I've left. If I hadn't been so sick these past few years—" He broke into a wheezing cough. I stood to place the oxygen tent mask over his nose and mouth and patted his shoulder reassuringly. Once the fit subsided, he nodded his thanks. "I've left you the ranch," he said with a crackling, dejected voice. "I trust you to do what you think is best with it all. There's nothing much here in Baker for you anyway. Travel the world and find the love of your life."

Pain shot through my body again, and I busied my hands by refolding some of the clean linens at the table next to his bed. "I did travel the world. I love being here, at the ranch. I love the sunrises over Beacon's Bluff and the memories of all the horses we've saved."

"You'll be alone." He coughed once. "It means nothing without family by your side. Without love."

I glared at him. We'd had this discussion too many times to count. "You know how I feel about that, Gramps."

"I'd hoped facing death firsthand on the battlefield might change your perspective a bit." He pointed at me with a crooked finger. "That it would have shown you what matters in the end. You'll never be free if you don't let your parents' deeds go. You can't spend the rest of your life carrying their sins on your shoulders."

But Gramps hadn't seen what they'd done, the lives they'd destroyed.

"Where is that nurse?" I looked at my watch. "Perhaps I should go find her."

"Evelyn Christine Chalmers," he whispered commandingly.

I went still, my blood going cold at the use of my full name. My real name—not the name I'd put on my dog tags.

That name was poison.

"Gramps," I hissed. "Don't say that so loud."

For once, I was grateful for the emptiness of the hospital wing. No one had heard that horrible name—the daughter of legendary criminals.

"Listen to me." He took my wrist and covered my hand with both of his massive, arthritic palms. "I know I'm not your true blood, but I hope that my words mean something to you."

"Your words mean everything to me." A sob escaped my throat.

"Then hear me." His eyes glistened. "You're always holding so tightly to what you think you can control. You know what happens when a horse pulls and pulls . . ."

"The rope breaks." Dozens of horses that Gramps had cured of such a dangerous habit flashed before my eyes.

"So let the past go."

"I wish it were that simple." The world didn't work that way. No matter how much I wanted to erase my family's name from the headlines, the public still clung to it as if it were some sort of cosmic joke.

"The press, the gossiping crowds—they can't hurt you. You're not a helpless little girl anymore." He jerked my hands as if to jolt me from my thoughts. "You'll never have a husband or a family with that secret weighing you down."

I already knew this, and I'd resigned myself to that fate. It was what held me back from dating the way the other nurses did. There was no future with me.

Because I'd never reveal this secret.

In the quiet moments, I pictured life with others around me—children, friends, a husband. Dozens of animals, horses, and laughter. That was a life I'd never known firsthand, had only read about in novels. It was a life that belonged to others.

But Birkstrom Ranch? If I poured enough of my blood, sweat, and tears into it, perhaps I was worthy of that much.

If not, there was truly nothing left for me.

## Warren

Phantom and I burst out of the trailer, and I held tightly to the rope to keep him from bolting away. The horse pawed his front hooves and snorted viciously at the onlookers around us.

"You weren't kidding." Kenneth Roland—formerly Colonel Roland—circled us on the lawn of the sprawling stables outside of Harrisburg, Pennsylvania. Lean, with lines at the corners of his eyes and a slow smile, he'd be mistaken for Roy Rogers if he was wearing a cowboy hat. "He's impressive."

Kenneth, an experienced horseman, held his hand out and approached Phantom tentatively. The horse flared his nostrils and swung his hindquarters around to kick, but Kenneth anticipated the move and stepped free of the horse's range.

One of the stables' trainers approached hesitantly, took the lead rope from me, and led Phantom into an open pen.

Relief flooded me as someone more knowledgeable and capable took the horse. I hoped this time I'd find someone who would take Phantom and address his behavioral issues. We'd been rejected at three other stables so far.

The trainer in the pen pulled at Phantom's lead rope, but the horse reared and broke free as the metal clasp gave way. The man darted through the fence boards to get free of the charging stallion.

I pressed my hands over my eyes and sighed.

"I've seen a lot of horses," Kenneth said. "Never seen one quite this volatile."

His words carried weight for me. He'd been the mastermind behind Operation Cowboy and had even participated in the last of the mounted cavalry's war games before the war. Before the mechanized cavalry eclipsed all.

"Why do you think he's like this?" I asked.

Kenneth rubbed his face. "I did some digging on the shipping records after you called me. Sounds like Phantom was brought over when he was five months old, and separated too early from his mother in Europe. That means he wasn't weaned properly. He was isolated and never learned proper manners or herd behavior from other horses."

Just another war wound too deep to heal with a stitch or cast. I didn't have the first clue about how to right this wrong, but I had promised Lieutenant Bryant I'd look after him.

The memory of her long, dark brown hair tied up, her bright blue eyes focused on Mira as she had labored, filled my mind. The Army nurse who had called in favors to look after the Hostau evacuees. The faint smell of lavender. Almost a year later, the memory was so clear and the stirring in my gut still so strong. Wherever she was in the world, she'd want to know that this colt was safe.

"Most horses this bad are put down," Kenneth said softly.

"That's not an option."

"Well, we'll see what Stanton has to say." Kenneth nodded to the trainer. He turned to me with his gaze narrowed in the blinding sun. "I have something else I could use your help with. Were you planning on joining your family business back in Philly?"

"Not if I can avoid it." I wasn't sure what my future held. Phantom was the immediate distraction, but I had no desire to work for Continental Savings and Loan. "I'm not ready to leave the men of the 42nd behind. I just don't know what that looks like."

His eyes went bright with excitement. "Have you ever considered running for public office?"

The boys and I had bantered about the suits in Washington who had no clue what we faced in the field, but picturing myself as one of those suits?

"Hear me out," Kenneth said, holding up his hands pleadingly as if he saw my reticence. "I know the government isn't perfect, but what if we can make a difference at the national level—better benefits, more hospitals to support veterans. What if we can help avoid the next war?"

I wanted those things—and more. Though I wasn't entrenched in politics, I wasn't unfamiliar with how power worked. I'd watched my own father influence other businesses and public authorities alike with whatever means was best for the bank and his interests.

Despite that power in the hands of self-absorbed men, could Kenneth and I make changes for the better if we were a part of that system?

Kenneth's father and grandfather had both been senators in Virginia, his home state. He would be a surefire candidate.

"Pennsylvania's incumbent senator isn't popular," Kenneth said. "The analysts I've talked to say you've got a really good shot after all the publicity around Operation Cowboy."

That sent a shiver of surprise through my body. This wasn't the career I'd ever pictured for myself—but the military hadn't been either. After being discharged, I'd considered starting or joining nonprofits, businesses, even returning to the Army. Nothing seemed quite right. Nothing felt the way they had when I was truly in my element with the Ghost Riders, our mission clear and our path before us.

"You're talking about running this year?" I asked. "We're only six months from election day."

"Six months is better than six years from now when the seat will be up for grabs again." His jaw flexed. "You heard about James, right?"

The name hit me to the core. Of course I'd heard. One of dozens who had struggled to adapt back into civilian life, forget what he'd seen. What we'd been asked to do in the name of freedom. James hadn't been able to find a job, so he'd turned to the bottle and stayed there. He'd been drunk, fell onto the tracks accidentally. Or at least that's what I told myself. The train conductor hadn't even seen him in the darkness.

"I don't know anything about politics," I said.

"That's why I'll build you a team to help," Kenneth said. "You've got a good head on your shoulders, and you're a charismatic leader. You'll listen to voters and represent them well in DC."

"Elizabeth is on board with you running?" I asked. The sister of the embedded British Intelligence officer from our unit, Elizabeth was Kenneth's fiancée. He'd met her after the European armistice, and their connection had been intense and immediate.

He winced. "Though she doesn't understand the American political landscape, she's with me."

The idea bounced around my brain as Phantom paced in circles in his pen, stirring up dust clouds.

"Just think about it," Kenneth said.

"When do you need to know?"

"Yesterday." He smiled. "The longest I can wait is early August. There's a fundraiser with everyone in Philadelphia who you'd want in your corner. It'd be the prime moment to announce your candidacy. I have enough contacts to set you up with a campaign manager and crew. All we'd need is your shining smile and big, broad shoulders."

US senator. Serving in a suit instead of fatigues.

Father expected me to step alongside my brother William, marry a Vanderbilt or Rockefeller, and continue the family legacy. There'd be no helping my men from that position, other than approving a home loan. There was a place and need for that, sure. But I wanted to do more.

Phantom snorted and stomped up to the fence where the trainer, Stanton, watched and shook his head in defeat.

"You know," Kenneth said, straightening and then stepping away from the fence when Phantom raced past, "there's one fellow I've heard of in Oregon. It'd be a long drive, but his methods are supposed to be a bit unorthodox. He's known for taming the untrainable."

"Why didn't you mention him sooner?"

Kenneth blew out a long breath. "I didn't believe you when you said this horse was so far gone."

My shoulders sagged in frustration. "I guess orthodox methods haven't really worked out. How long will the unorthodox approach take?"

"I have no idea."

"What's this fellow's name?" I asked.

"Bill Birkstrom," Kenneth said. "He's in Baker, Oregon."

That town sounded familiar. "Eddie Moore lives in Baker."

"He'll know where to find Bill, then."

Stanton strode toward me, and I knew what was coming. Kenneth nodded his farewell, leaving me to fend for myself when Stanton reached me.

"I won't be able to help you." His hair was slicked back with sweat. "In fact, I want you to get this dangerous horse off my property."

"I'll leave with him first thing in the morning." I held up my hands to calm him. "Let me feed and water him here. We'll be wheels up at first light." Depending on how long I'd have to fight to get the colt into the trailer. My arms and back ached at the thought. I wasn't fully recovered from the last time.

"I won't have any of my men feeding or looking after him," Stanton said with flushed cheeks, a vein bulging in his forehead.

"I understand."

I was starting to believe there wasn't a man alive who could reach this horse.

Once the handlers and barn owner went away to their other duties, Phantom wandered over to me, his half-broken halter dangling on his head.

I slid it off over his ears, and he nuzzled me gently. "Why can't you be like this with anyone else?" Even these moments were rare. When I tried to load him into the trailer or into a stall, all bets were off.

I needed to get him to a barn where he was safe and I could visit from time to time. I didn't know enough about horses, nor would I have time for anything different down the line.

Especially if I seriously considered this idea of Kenneth's.

Senator?

"Come on, buddy," I said to Phantom. "I just need to know you'll be okay. I must do that. For her."

The horse rubbed his forehead up and down my arm as if nodding in agreement.

What was I even doing? I had no place watching after this horse, yet I couldn't forget my promise to her. I'd tried desperately to find Eva Bryant, but the records went cold after her discharge earlier this year.

To Oregon it was, then. Hopefully this Bill Birkstrom was all he was rumored to be. I'd drop off the horse, ensure he was properly looked after, and then begin the new chapter of my life. In public service?

Would I even be able to secure the nomination and votes? All I knew was that I'd give it a try. If it meant being a voice for my Ghosts even now that they were scattered across the States, so be it.

They'd given their all for me, and for God and country. I could do no less.

# *Three*

## Eva

**MAY 6**
**BIRKSTROM RANCH**

"Rumor has it you're broke, Eva. Why not make this easier and sell me the scraps of Bill's ranch now?"

Five years of blood and bullets, and this is all I had: a thousand acres of dilapidated fencing, a few broodmares, and a relentless neighbor determined to take it all.

*Gramps . . . why did you have to leave me now?*

Victor was a short, robust man with a permanent sneer, deep lines in his brow, and dark shadows under his eyes. Gramps had only been in the ground for a few hours and the vulture had swung in, picking through what was left of my life.

I dug my black heels into the soft ground outside my barn and clenched my teeth. I still wore the dress from my grandfather's funeral. I could still feel the reverend's hand on my shoulder and hear his words. "*You know, Eva, at most funerals, people say all sorts of nice things about the person we're putting in the ground. In Bill's case, everything is true.*"

How different Gramps was from this man before me.

"Get off my property or I'll call Sheriff Lowe," I said.

"Go ahead. Lowe was over for dinner last night," Victor sneered. "We're endorsing him in his reelection campaign."

Hopelessness washed over me. No doubt the Merricks were providing some sort of financial support along with their endorsement, which carried weight in the community. I was truly alone and a David to this Goliath, without a stone to my name, surrounded by sand.

"One more missed payment and it will be mine." His lips curled at the edges, and the sheen of sweat on his skin repulsed me. "How many horses do you have left to sell to scrape up a payment?"

None. I couldn't afford to lose the two broodmares I had, but neither could I count on the yearlong turnaround of purebred foals to sell. We hadn't had a winning stallion at Birkstrom Ranch for years, which meant no one cared about our stock. In the world of Arabian horse breeding, titles mattered more than anything.

I'd spent the two thousand dollars I had saved for Phantom on Gramps's medical bills and a casket.

Even with just the few horses we had, I had mountains of work to do in the few precious hours before the end of the day. The sunrise funeral had been small and quiet. Gramps, like me, had adored the pastel sunrises over the eastern plains, the Wallowa Mountains to the north. The wildflowers of spring painted the hills purple, white, yellow, and orange.

But it was now nearly noon, and there were still chickens to feed, a coop to clean, stalls to muck, wounds to tend, a goat to wrangle and milk, a few stall boards that needed fixing, a persistent leak at the water pump. Five years of neglect to patch.

Not to mention the equipment I needed to inventory and sell for a mortgage payment. I'd miss the tractor to plow the roads come winter, but I'd make do.

Had Gramps been right? Should I sell it all off and start somewhere else anew?

That thought caused my blood to run cold. No. This was my home, and the only piece of Gramps I had left. The place I'd found sanctuary twenty years ago. How could I abandon it to this man who only cared for money, power, and reputation?

My heart hammered as Victor tilted his head and inched closer. "You can't compete against me, girl."

"You haven't been a threat on the show circuit in years," I hissed back. "If it wasn't for the judges you have in your pocket, you'd have lost your own land decades ago."

Victor's wrinkled face flushed with rage. He clenched his fists at his sides, raising his right hand ever so slightly as if to strike me. Something in my words had struck a nerve, deeper than even I had intended to. He stepped toward me so abruptly that I stumbled back and slammed into the barn siding, knocking the wind out of me.

"You know, back in the day, we had different ways of getting things done." Victor leaned over me, propping his hand against the wall behind me. He smelled of alcohol and smoking tobacco. The animosity that radiated from him felt as dangerous as the Japanese forces that had surrounded us in the Philippines.

In that moment, I smelled blood, gunpowder, smoke, and death. Terror seized me, and I braced my foot against the barn wall, pushing myself up and Victor back a few steps. My heart raced and my head swam.

Victor chuckled and paced around me. "Bill isn't here to protect you anymore. Just sign over the land and I'll be on my way."

Memories from that Philippines hospital bubbled to my mind. Those times when the enemy closed in, when the sergeant next to me gave advice of how to fight once the ammunition ran out—that terror and adrenaline rose in me. I'd be ready to push back if Victor forced me to. I was alone but not helpless.

"Excuse me," a strong voice boomed across the yard.

Victor quickly stepped back.

I straightened, turning toward the unexpected visitor and savior. My thumping heart and raging pulse came to a screeching halt.

The square jaw, high brow, and firm mouth. The short, dark hair and stubble-ridden chin. Though he wasn't wearing Army fatigues, I could picture the name tag, rank, and stripes. As if a year hadn't passed from those moments we shared in Germany. His attention was narrowed on Victor as he walked closer, his fists tight.

"Captain Hayes?"

He froze midstep, his gaze swiveling to me. The intensity of his focus on Victor softened, and a different type of fire lit in his eyes. "Lieutenant Bryant?"

Victor rolled his shoulders back, glared between us. "We'll resume this conversation another time."

He turned toward the driveway, but as he was about to pass by, Captain Warren Hayes held out a hand to stop him. He towered over the elder man, and he pushed him gently in the chest, a subtle threat that made it clear to both of us that he had seen Victor corner me.

Shame and relief raged inside me.

"Is there a problem here?" Warren asked me. There was a fierceness to his expression that warmed me to the core and set me at ease. The fear and danger I'd been drowning in only a few heartbeats before was replaced by confidence that the captain of the Ghost Riders had my back.

I had no idea what had brought him here, but at least just for a few minutes I had someone in my corner, even if Sheriff Lowe and the rest of Baker County were in Victor's.

"No problem at all." Victor offered his signature grin and shook his head, which drew Warren's skeptical gaze to him. "Just a friendly conversation between neighbors." He then spat, "Captain."

Warren looked at me for confirmation, not taking the man at his word.

I just wanted Victor to go away. I nodded ever so slightly. I couldn't wrap my thoughts around anything else aside from Warren standing before me, half a world and hundreds of bloody days away from the airfield in Germany.

He looked exactly as I recalled, aside from the civilian attire and day-old stubble. His light green eyes were warm. Even without his stripes and pressed slacks, he carried himself with a straight back and an air of authority.

Warren turned to face Victor and lowered his voice. "I'd better not catch a whiff of another *friendly* neighbor conversation like this."

Victor's demeanor went stiff and cold, as if seeing something he hadn't expected in Warren's gaze.

I bit back a smile, thinking of all the soldiers I'd met over the past five years and the extraordinary bravery and strength I'd witnessed. Victor was nothing compared to the dangers that these soldiers had seen. Especially Warren, who had led his men behind enemy lines for two years.

On the other hand, Victor's money, his connections, the bank debt I faced . . . those were things that still scared me.

Warren dropped his hand, allowing my neighbor to flee without another word. Then he strode up to me, his presence soothing the gaping wound left from this morning's funeral.

His lips curled into a charming smile, and faint dimples appeared on his cheeks. His wrinkled brow smoothed as he took in my face. "I'm surprised to see you, Eva."

Shivers raced down my spine as he spoke my name. Of course I hadn't forgotten him or the time we'd shared in Germany. But he remembered me?

"What are you doing here?" I asked.

Excitement and playfulness took over his expression, and his shoulders lifted in delight. "Come see." He motioned for me to follow as he walked toward the driveway.

As we stepped into the sunlight, I was grateful to see my circular driveway empty of Victor's car. But the one vehicle there—a dust-covered, new Ford truck—had a horse trailer behind it.

A horse? Curiosity pricked at my limbs, and I ran to the domed metal trailer, stepped on the side fenders, and peeked through the open slats to get a better view of the horse. Inside, a gray horse paced the metal box with sweat coursing down his neck and haunches. Even without seeing the mark on his shoulder, I knew who it was.

"Phantom." The earth spun below me, my breath caught in my throat and my heart humming. I thought he'd been lost to me.

Like a lightning strike, the realization hit me.

"You were the other bidder," I said, standing on the wheel cover and looking down at Warren.

"Other bidder?" He looked up, using one hand to shade his eyes from the harsh sun. "You were at the auction in Virginia?"

How had we not bumped into each other? What might have been different if we had?

None of that mattered now. Through the narrow windows of the trailer, I studied Phantom. He looked thinner than when I'd last seen him. His eyes were wild and his nostrils flared as he paced the small quarters of the trailer, untied.

"What about Mira? Have you found her?"

"No." Warren's smile faltered. "But I'm working on it still."

"Me too," I said. "Perhaps I'll beat you to that one."

His eyes sparkled at the challenge. "You're on."

"What in the world are you doing in Oregon?"

"Kenneth Roland recommended I seek Bill Birkstrom. Isn't this his stables?"

I stepped off the side of the trailer and held back the tears that clawed at the corners of my eyes. "He is—well, he was my grandfather."

Warren frowned. "Was?"

"He passed away a few days ago." I motioned to my dress. "We buried him this morning."

Warren's shoulders sank. "I'm so sorry." The depth of his words went beyond feeling empathetic for a stranger. He pointed in the direction Victor had left. "Your neighbor came over for this friendly chat right after your grandfather's funeral?"

I nodded. That was what the Birkstroms and Merricks had done for generations. They threatened, they stole, and they passed the resentment on to the next crop of children. At one point, I'd hoped to break that cycle.

Other pieces slowly clicked into place in my mind. "If you were referred to my grandfather, that means no one else wanted to take him on."

"He wasn't weaned properly and then was isolated and neglected." Warren put a hand on his hip and ran the other through his hair. "He's actually quite dangerous."

A thousand thoughts crashed through my head in the same moment. This was my first and perhaps only chance at a client. This was also the type of horse Gramps and I specialized in. Or we had, five years ago before I shipped out. Phantom could be the sole redemption for the ranch and the remnants of Gramps's training program. His legacy.

If I didn't act quickly, I'd lose my chance, and I'd most certainly lose everything to the Merricks.

"I can train him." I knew I could. And the horse's physical prowess, renowned bloodlines, and unique marking were a recipe that could make him a superstar. "Give me a chance and he could be a national champion."

## Warren

National champion?

I could hardly believe that Lieutenant Eva Bryant stood before me. That this mythical trainer—my last option—had been her grandfather.

My mind raced, and my pulse hadn't calmed after seeing the neighbor towering over her and threatening her. I'd need to figure out more behind that story, but I only cared now that she was safe, the threat removed, at least temporarily.

For two weeks, I'd driven and thought about Kenneth's idea—and what I wanted in life. As I reached Oregon, I'd convinced myself that it was worth a shot—I'd run for the senator's seat and fight alongside Kenneth in his new crusade. I'd called him from the road to let him know, committing to this path. I had a mission once again.

Never would I have expected Eva to reappear in my life. I was grateful for this second chance.

Now we stood in the high desert of Oregon, the heat of the sun bearing down upon us. The farm was vast. A beautifully carved Birkstrom Ranch wooden sign hung above the driveway gate. The barns were weather aged and in need of fresh paint. The ranch house was small and ragged around the edges. Two horses grazed in a distant paddock, but there was no other sign of additional staff or trainers.

If Bill Birkstrom was gone, could Eva train the horse instead?

She'd been confident in the way she handled Mira in Germany and the way she delivered the colt. Dr. Baumann had spoken of her mastery—in animal husbandry. Everything was different now. Phantom wasn't the same horse he was a year ago. I bore the bruises and cuts to prove it. And over the past five weeks I'd owned him, I'd wondered time and time again whether I could even save him from himself.

Given Kenneth's recommendation, I'd pictured Birkstrom as a towering, strong man who would be able to subdue the rowdy colt. But Lieutenant Eva Bryant was nearly a foot shorter than me and a hundred pounds soaking wet.

I grimaced at my thoughts. Mother would slap my head for thinking such direct thoughts about a woman, but it was hard not to acknowledge the reality of the situation. Phantom was dangerous—I knew that for certain.

As if Eva picked up on the direction of my thoughts, she took a small step closer and held my gaze with a determined look. The fact that she wore her funeral dress and heels seemed to further emphasize her commitment.

"I can do this. You've seen my work before."

I held up a hand. "The past year has been hard on Phantom. He's not what you might recall."

"What have you got to lose?"

*You*, I thought.

"If you're here now, you must not have anyone left."

She had me there. And that knowing grin across her face was irresistible.

I looked around again at the flat property that seemed to go for miles. It reminded me of the devastated farms after the Nazis or Russians had trampled them and slaughtered their staff and horses.

Perhaps she needed this, especially after losing her grandfather.

"Gramps wasn't one to take on easy clients." She followed my gaze and grew serious. "He also took on any horse who needed help and didn't charge much of the client. Which is why, well, things are lean right now."

Her Gramps sounded every bit the opposite of my own grandfather: ruthless and cutthroat. I probably knew which of the two had more peace at the time of his death, but regardless, I wasn't sure I could just turn her loose with an erratic eight-hundred-pound animal.

What if my horse injured her? What if something worse were to happen?

The voices of my grandfather and father in my head chirped with all the things that could go wrong and what the headlines would say. How it would affect my chances for election or the stock price of Continental Savings and Loan. I hated those voices. I'd been able to drown them out while on the front lines, because so little mattered aside from the lives of the men around me.

"Please, Captain, just give me a few months to see what I can do with him."

Her tone was measured, professional. Still, I could hear the tinge of hope and desperation. Her voice from when we met rang in my ears. "*You're not the first to underestimate me.*"

Phantom kicked the metal of the trailer, shattering the calm between us.

I ground my jaw and shook my head. I couldn't. I'd need to find an old rancher somewhere to take the horse and turn him loose in a large pasture, safe from anyone or anything. Hadn't Phantom suffered enough with whatever had caused him to be so uncontrollable?

"What would it take for me to convince you to give me a chance?" Eva crossed her arms.

Phantom stomped and shook the trailer, and I let out a long breath. The horse couldn't stay in there for much longer. I'd already driven two days straight from our last stop in Nevada. I'd been feeding him and watering him inside the trailer, but he stomped most of it into the floor and kicked the buckets over. I needed to clean the mess inside, and I also needed a decent night's rest.

As I'd learned from Eddie and Kenneth in Czechoslovakia, horses needed to be loaded and tied carefully, differently from how cattle were transported and handled. That also put the handler in harm's way when the horses were violent.

"If you can get him out of the trailer without causing harm or injury to yourself or the horse," I said, "I'll consider a one-month trial."

Eva's eyes lit up. "Two months?"

"One month." I held back my smile at her tenacity. After the first experience at the stables that rejected us, I had decided I'd need to stick around for a while to know this was the right place for him. I needed to know he was safe and wouldn't risk him being mishandled. Not that I'd worry about that with Eva. "If it looks like you might get hurt, we shut that door and he stays in there, got it?"

She straightened and nodded. "When I show progress in one month, then we discuss entering him in competition?"

"No promises." Phantom was a long way off from any show horses I could imagine, and he was far too unpredictable to be around a crowd. Besides, my own timeline added further complications. Once August hit, I'd be too busy to come back to pick up Phantom, and hiring another person to do so could be risky.

She huffed a satisfied breath, then held out her hand. "Keys?"

I hesitated. "Keys for what?"

"Your truck." Her cheeks were rosy under the beaming sun, and her lips smothered a smile.

I handed her the keys, and she motioned me to stand aside. She went into her focused, silent mode, the way she'd been back in Germany when she was tending to Mira during Phantom's delivery. No wonder horses listened to her—she transfixed anyone and anything around her.

She slipped into the driver's seat, the twirl of her skirt catching the wind. She fired up the engine and then twisted to look behind her. She carefully backed the truck and trailer against a pasture with an open gate.

Clever. As I realized what she was doing, my arm ached. Why hadn't I tried something similar in the dozen barns I'd visited in the past month? Not one other trainer had even suggested this.

She parked the trailer in between the gate posts, opened the door, and ducked out of the way as Phantom burst out of the trailer. Then she closed the trailer door and the paddock gate behind it.

Phantom trotted and snorted into the air, kicking up red dust. I expected her to turn and gloat, but her gaze was locked on the horse. She went completely still, and her brow creased as she studied him.

I walked up to her slowly, watching her as she absorbed the state of the horse. While she was distracted, my mind wandered. I'd tracked down her hospital unit just before I was discharged. I knew she'd been in the Philippines, which had suffered some brutal battles in those final months of the war. Had she been safe? Or did she bear those silent, invisible scars we all seemed to carry home?

Perhaps I'd have the chance to find out now that she'd won our little wager.

I stood next to her along the fence line. "In Hostau, the trainers insisted we walk the horses into the trailers. I thought that's how it was done."

"That is customary for hauling horses, yes." She nodded. "Sometimes you have to work with what you've got."

"Now you tell me." I rubbed my arm stiffly, the crude bandage peeking under the sleeve of my T-shirt.

Her expression shifted to that of a combat nurse. She reached over, pulled up the sleeve, and peeled back the gauze that covered a long gash.

"Hey, wait," I protested. Her hands were smooth against my skin, and it took everything I had not to pull away.

"Who bandaged this?" She pulled back the entire wrapping. "This is atrocious."

"I did." I winced. "I didn't have many supplies on hand." Not to mention I was in a rush to get Phantom somewhere safe after being run out of Stanton's.

She handed back my truck keys. "Come to the house so I can clean this up. Then we'll firm up our training contract."

"You mean our one-month trial."

"I said what I said." She motioned for me to follow, leading the way to the ranch home and leveling a challenging smile back at me. "I'll have you convinced in no time."

# Four

## Eva

One month. Phantom. Warren Hayes, walking right behind me into Gramps's kitchen.

My kitchen.

I pointed him to the table and retrieved my medical bag. My head buzzed, my thoughts whirled. Phantom's poor condition. How to reassure the captain that I could handle this. Evaluating the cut on his arm that looked infected. So much to do, so much to process.

Warren paused in the entryway of the small house, looking at the photos and ribbons nailed to the wall in a cluttered, chaotic manner. I approached with my bag in hand and looked at the photo where he lingered. Me as a young girl and Gramps next to me in the show arena, his presence commanding. I sat on a white Arabian in a western saddle, with a big cowboy hat, brilliant grin, and grand champion ribbon.

"That was my first championship win," I said with a smile. "I was eight years old."

Admiration flashed in his gaze. "And that's your grandfather?"

I nodded. "That was his best broodmare, also Polish bred." The memories were sweet, but the loss of Gramps was still raw.

I went into the kitchen and set the bag on the table, and Warren followed. He lowered himself into a chair beside the table and lifted his sleeve over his shoulder. At least with this problem to solve, I could fall back on my training. I could almost hear the echo of artillery in the distance. Was I treating a fellow soldier or my new client?

It didn't matter. The gash was jagged, dirty, and inflamed, and I couldn't in good conscience just let him walk away in such a state.

Those piercing eyes shook me to my core, as if I were back in Germany, ordering him around as Mira gave birth. But I wasn't a lieutenant anymore, and he wasn't a captain. I was the trainer and owner of Birkstrom Ranch. He was my first—and only—client. His patronage and Phantom's success could save me from foreclosure, or worse, the Merricks.

I pulled out gauze, bandages, and iodine rinse.

"When were you discharged?" His gaze remained on my face, which affected me differently than the other soldiers who'd stared without reserve. It made my stomach flutter and my mouth go dry.

"Six weeks ago." I pushed back at all the memories that surged when thinking about the past year. The jungles and the mosquitos. The enemies at our doors and the smell of death in the air.

"You were in the Pacific until then?"

"Until mid-March, yes," I said. "Then I went back to Europe, searching for Mira."

"I heard things were bad in the Philippines." There was a catch in his voice.

My hands trembled the slightest bit. I needed to change the subject. "Tell me more about the past month with Phantom. Have you been trying to find a trainer this whole time?"

"Yes, though I would have come here much sooner if I'd

known Bill Birkstrom was your grandfather. I was hoping to find something a little closer to home in Pennsylvania."

I poured iodine onto the gauze and then pressed it to the wound, carefully scraping away the dried dirt and blood. "Who turned you down?" It was gossipy of me to ask, but I wanted to draw his focus away from me.

"Just about every trainer I came across. Greenly, Kellogg, Harding, Stanton."

I bit back a smile and ran a saline rinse over the cut. "How did this happen?"

"Well, we had to leave in a bit of a hurry from Stanton's place."

"Stanton's a good trainer, but he has a short fuse." I pressed the gauze to the wound to dab it clean and wipe away the ragged edges.

"I thought I could just overpower Phantom to get him in the trailer."

"And how did that work out for you?"

"I think you know." He flinched. "Turns out the metal doesn't give way when a horse slams you into it."

"Gramps always said that forcing a horse to do something was about as productive as asking a snake to fly."

"Sounds like a wise man."

"He was." I reached for my needle and catgut. "I'm going to put a few stitches in. Do you want a local anesthetic?"

He shook his head. "I'm fine."

"You're lucky to only end up with bruises and a cut. I've seen far worse accidents with a trailer."

"I thought we'd reached an understanding a couple times, me and Phantom," he said. "He spooks easily, retreats into that wild state. Kenneth Roland said he'd been ignored and mishandled since he left Germany." He winced slightly as I threaded two small stitches at the center of the bite. He looked at the wound and shook his head. "Tore up my favorite shirt too. That trouble-maker."

The admiration in his tone sent warmth all the way down to my toes. I put ointment over the cut and wrapped it. We'd need to talk business, and then I was itching to get back out to Phantom.

Something caught my eye at the edge of his shirtsleeve—another scar, still fresh. It sat next to one that was a few years old at least. A bullet wound.

Without thinking, I went to his other arm and lifted the sleeve, seeing similar fresh wounds. I lifted the back of his shirt and he protested, but I was too far into my training to stop. We didn't ask patients where they were injured in the heat of a battle; we just did our own observation and evaluation.

His back told me the story of his time in Europe and of the past few months. A web of soft, pale scars had long healed, but a smattering of fresh and aged bruises indicated just how rocky things had been with Phantom.

"All of this and you haven't given up on him?" I breathed.

He pulled away, lowering his shirt and catching my gaze. "I won't ever give up on him."

Lightning shot through my veins at the resolution in his features.

"You said it yourself when he was born," he said. "He's special. That once-in-a-generation mark and one of so few Polish Arabians left on the planet."

"I'm so glad you were that other bidder." Emotion cut off my words. "I thought I'd lost him forever."

A long pause stretched between us.

"I just wish I'd found you in Virginia," he said with a soft laugh. "It would have saved me a few bruises."

I set my bag aside. "We should probably discuss a fair monthly rate for training and boarding."

"Whatever you charge is fine." He stood, shoulders straight

like any soldier. "In fact, I'd prefer to pay a premium since Phantom is so volatile."

I wasn't going to take advantage of his generosity, but I had to keep the ranch afloat. It was my responsibility now.

I pulled out an old, blank contract that Gramps had used over the years and filled in the terms, then presented it to Warren, who signed it after a quick read.

"He's not the worst case I've seen." I crossed my arms and leaned against the countertop. "Will you be returning to Pennsylvania? How is it best to contact you?"

"I had thought to stick around for a while if you don't mind." He hesitated. "I'd love to learn a bit of this famous Birkstrom magic."

My stomach quivered nervously at that, but I didn't allow my face or body to flinch. I needed to keep him happy and engaged in the process. Besides, if he was here and saw Phantom's steady progress, I'd have more time and opportunities to convince him to enter Phantom into local shows and, eventually, the national-level competition.

"I'd figured you for a career Army man." I brushed a stray lock of hair from my face. "What are your plans after we get Phantom onto the national show circuit?"

He chuckled, admiring more of the trophies stashed all over the kitchen. "I have some plans taking shape."

I recognized dodging a subject, but I wasn't one to judge, so I didn't push it. "While you're in town, I'd recommend the Geiser Grand on Main. Betty Harrison will make sure you're taken care of."

"I appreciate that." He smiled. "Eddie Moore mentioned the same hotel, and I'm meeting him there for dinner later tonight. Perhaps you would like to join us?"

"Thank you," I said with a warm smile back. "But my only dress is dirty, and besides, I have a date with Phantom."

He looked slightly disappointed, though he nodded politely.

I rifled through my bag and pulled out a few extra gauzes and wraps. "You should change your bandage daily. I'll remove the stitches in a week."

He took the bundle from me and then followed me out of the house and toward the front pasture, where Phantom trotted along the fence line.

"What is your plan?" Warren asked.

Butterflies danced in my stomach as I remembered the dozens of times Gramps had cured a skittish horse using a simple but effective method.

"A bucket of water."

## Warren

"A bucket of water?" I repeated.

Sure, the horse needed water. But part of her training plan?

Eva grabbed a bucket, filled it at a pump next to the porch, and walked over to the pasture, where Phantom watched her with wild eyes. She went to the fence, but I kept my distance. I couldn't intervene. I needed to feel reassured that she had control.

Phantom raced up, bared his teeth, and then bolted away. She climbed through the wooden panels of the fence and stood there peacefully with the bucket of water in hand. The horse cantered in circles, came close, and tried to nip her, then raced off. At one point, he sniffed the bucket but didn't venture close enough to take a drink.

I realized what she was doing. There was no other source of moisture in the entire pen—no blade of grass, not even a puddle on the ground. In the high desert, it might not rain for weeks. The horse needed to drink from the bucket in her hands if he wanted to survive.

Could Phantom understand this? At least I knew she'd never risk his health.

Phantom ran past Eva another half dozen times, biting at her each time and narrowly missing. I clenched my fists to keep from vaulting into the pen to drag her out. This felt hopeless.

But the longer I watched, the more I noticed. She was calm and confident, walking toward him without cowering. I hadn't seen any other trainer move the way she did. Others had jumped in fear or puffed up their chests and tried to overpower the horse. Eva moved with the horse, not against him. It was a dance.

"The other trainers seemed to favor force," I said.

"Breaking horses just gives you broken horses." She glanced at me. "That's what Gramps said."

Confidence rose in me. Perhaps I had found the right place for Phantom.

Thirty minutes later, the colt took a step closer and brushed his lips against the water for a split second. My breath caught, and not even the wind seemed to stir before the horse took a deep drink and then ran off, nearly striking Eva with his back hooves.

Relief flooded my chest as she stepped out of the pasture, bringing the bucket with her. She set it down outside the fence and beyond the horse's reach and wiped her brow. Her black dress was now tinted with red dust, and her shoes were caked in dirt, her face flushed from the direct sun.

"We'll be the best of friends in no time," she said with a chuckle.

"How often will you do that?" I motioned to the bucket.

"Six or seven times a day until we're on sturdier ground."

Fear pricked at the back of my mind at the danger she'd face each time. I had to trust her and her family's methods. "That's quite the dedication."

"He's worth the time." Her eyes—those lovely, piercing, pale blue eyes—locked onto mine. "He could change the landscape of Arabian breeding in the States, especially with so few that survived the war."

The passion in her voice sparked a fire in my core, and I held back my urge to write her a blank check. I wanted this to work, and I wanted her to be successful in taming the defiant stallion. I only wished I had more time to see this through. In three months, I'd need to return to Philadelphia to formally begin campaigning.

"You're welcome to leave the trailer here in the driveway," she said. "You don't need to lug it around town."

"I appreciate that." I stepped toward the truck. "I'd better see about a room. What time will the training begin tomorrow?"

She smirked. "Sunrise to sunset, Captain."

I adored the way she still called me by my former rank, but I also longed for her to see me as a peer, not as an officer from the world we'd left behind.

I unhooked the trailer, bid her farewell, and drove back down the long highway stretch into Baker.

Main Street was lined with brick buildings, the street so expansive compared to the cramped streets of Philly. Handfuls of people milled about, and kids played in the residential streets a few blocks from the center of the town.

I remembered how fondly Eva had spoken of her hometown while we were in Germany, and now I knew why. It was quaint, welcoming.

A tall, white building on the corner of Main and Washington appeared, just as Eddie and Eva had said it would. The three stories of ornate, arched windows shone golden in the setting sun.

I pulled my truck along the street to park, grabbed my duffel bag from the floor of the cab, and walked wearily into the hotel lobby. Eddie leaned against the check-in desk and conversed with the older woman behind the counter. They both turned and smiled.

"Speak of the devil," Eddie said with a toothy grin.

Though Eva still used my former rank—as a joke, I was hoping—I was grateful the formality and decorum of the military were behind me. Eddie Moore and I had become fast friends, despite the pressures of our rank and the expectations therein.

I embraced my former sergeant. "Good to see you, Eddie."

Eddie pulled away and motioned to the woman in her late sixties with auburn-red curls, thick black spectacles, and heavy makeup on her wrinkled skin. "I was just telling Betty that we were expecting a war hero."

"Knock it off with that," I growled.

Betty wore a floral sundress and had long, bright red nails. She chuckled and held out a hand. "Betty Harrison, at your service, Captain Hayes."

"It's Warren, please," I said, irritated, though I smiled back. "Is there a room available?"

"Of course." Betty flipped a page on the notebook before her. "And for how long can we keep you in our humble little town, Captain?"

"A month, to start."

Betty made a soft scratch with a pen on the paper and then handed me a key. "Second floor, corner room for you, Captain. Bathrooms are communal on each floor. Restaurant is open until eight p.m."

I tipped my head in thanks, and Betty beamed.

A porter appeared and took my bag to my room. Eddie led me from the dim but lushly decorated lobby and into the center area of the hotel, where dozens of tables were spread out beneath the balcony of the second floor and a glass ceiling on the third floor. The art, carved wood accents, and chandeliers all betrayed the simple, quiet town that lay beyond these walls.

Eddie sat at a table and motioned to a waiter. I slumped into a chair, my body still aching from the injuries, two-week drive, and shock of it all.

Eddie grinned. "So, how'd it go at Birkstrom Ranch?"

I restrained the urge to reach over the table and punch him in the shoulder. "Why didn't you tell me that Lieutenant Bryant runs the ranch?"

"Well, I didn't know." He chuckled. "I only made the connection with her and old Bill Birkstrom a week ago when a buddy of mine mentioned he was in the hospital and had bumped into Eva. It's a small town, but I only knew her as the Birkstrom girl. Not a Bryant."

"Is she his daughter's daughter, then?" I asked, nodding my thanks to the waiter who brought us water and menus.

Eddie shook his head. "I'm not one to speculate, Captain. Bill didn't have any biological children. He never married."

Interesting. He was right, though. It wasn't right to gossip about Eva or speculate further. "Where are your children? Isn't your wife in New York?"

"Yes, Violet is in New York seeing to her mother." Something flickered in Eddie's expression. "The twins are at the house and promised they'd keep out of trouble. Peter got caught stealing again and was suspended for the last two weeks of the school year." He turned to the waiter. "Can we get a few beers?"

"Just water for me," I said.

"Oh yeah. I forgot you don't partake."

I was the odd man out in the unit. A few others didn't drink for religious reasons, but I had watched Father and William lean on their nightly whiskey to escape the emptiness of their days, and I'd decided long before I found my purpose in the Army that I wouldn't follow suit. Especially when their nightly whiskey became two, then three.

Unease pricked the back of my neck at the tone of Eddie's voice, the despair in his eyes. I'd seen the same shadow in my brother. And in some of the other men of the 42nd who had been deeply scarred.

"What about that job lead you mentioned when we chatted a few weeks back?" I asked. "At the paper mill?"

"Fell through." He took the glass of beer from the waiter and drank a long swig. The silence stretched between us, and everything unsaid hung in the air. We'd shared these moments before. The anticipation before an attack. The waiting after a sniper fired one shot as we tried to locate the source. The quiet after the firing ceased, when we had to count our dead.

"Something will come along," I said, but my heart wasn't in my words. I'd heard this too many times from my soldiers as I'd kept in touch with them in the past year. We'd all been so glad to be home, to touch American soil again. To be the few who'd defied the odds and made it home on our own feet.

Back in Kötzting, Eddie had told me that I needed to move past the anticipation of a sniper attack or ambush. Something told me that despite his advice, he hadn't quite rid himself of that reality either.

I wasn't sure I ever would.

"You should come out and see Phantom," I said, raising my glass of water. "Remind you of the good ol' days in Germany."

"I'd like that. I'd love to show Annie too. Think Eva would be okay with her coming?"

"I think so. Bring Peter and maybe he can muck out a few stalls to make up for the suspension. Might keep him out of trouble."

"Ha," Eddie huffed. "I wish." He stared at his hands blankly. "I will bring them out. I do miss the horses—the calm and clarity they bring. I think we need that about now."

He needed so much more, but at least I could start there.

# *Five*

## Eva

MAY 7

The smell of metal, gunpowder, and blood engulfed me. The floor of the 1930 Chevrolet sedan was hot, piled with dirt and grit from the dozens of states we'd driven through and left our mark on. I covered my ringing ears, the roar of gunfire nothing but white noise in the enclosed space. I pressed my forehead to the carpet as I wedged my six-year-old body between the seat and floorboards.

Bullet casings from the .45-caliber Thompsons rained down around me, each one hitting the carpet of the car and trailing a thin stream of smoke as I waited for death. The dozens that landed on my flesh left searing scars that would never fade.

The casings morphed into those of the .30-06 of an M1 Garand, the steady *crack-crack-crack* of eight rounds, and then the clink of the clip ejecting. They showered upon the ground—now the jungle dirt floor of my Army field hospital.

I woke with a jolt, the familiar bedroom of my childhood coming into focus around me in the early morning hour.

My heart pounded, my skin prickled with goose bumps and sweat. I kicked the covers aside, checking the wristwatch on my nightstand. Four o'clock in the morning.

Every day it was a nightmare of a similar variety. The voices might change, the setting might change. But death loomed. I was always helpless to stop it.

I ran a hand absently over the scars on my forearms. There was no use in trying to go back to sleep—and the prospect of working with Phantom and seeing Warren changed my focus instantly.

After a long shower, coffee, and donning my well-worn cowboy boots and slacks, I stepped out into the glow of the rising sun.

I collided with a tall figure outside my door. The man's hand was lifted as if to knock, and instead, he caught me by my elbow and kept me from tripping off the small porch. He had a bundle of flowers in his other hand.

"Whoa, Eva," he said smoothly.

"Keith Merrick?" My breath caught. "What in the world?"

I pulled from his grasp and straightened. A thousand memories shot through me. I hadn't seen him in five years since I'd joined the nurse corps, not since that night I'd told him my deepest secret and he'd told me he wasn't sure he could marry someone like me—someone whose name was so tainted.

The nightmare of the Thompson rounds hitting the floorboards flashed again in my vision, but I tamped it down.

As vivid as Keith's rejection had been, so were the times we'd played together as children, the moments we'd snuck away together. He'd been my closest friend until the war and my confession upended everything.

Keith looked like his father, Victor, but without the hard lines around his mouth and eyes. His face was narrow but chiseled and still boyishly handsome, his eyes a deep brown. His hair was honey blond and straight as it fell over his brow in a mysterious, brooding manner. There was a reason the girls in town had always fawned over him and battled for his attention. Except for me. I'd always had his attention and didn't know what to do with it.

The Romeo and Juliet of Baker County—until I'd so foolishly thought that young love would triumph over my parents' unspeakable sins.

"You look amazing, Eva." He scanned me. "It's so good to see you."

A lump of emotion rose in my throat—feelings I'd long since buried. I smothered it all back down to the same unending pit of self-pity that I refused to confront.

"These are for you." Keith held out the flowers and shoved his free hand in his pocket.

I clenched my jaw. I hated flowers, but I knew the gesture was meaningful. I took them and walked into the kitchen to put them in water, nodding for him to follow me.

He stepped inside, looking around as if waiting for Gramps to walk around the corner.

"Thank you," I said softly as I reached for a glass jar out of the cabinet and turned on the faucet.

"I've been wanting to see you since you got back." He stepped up to me. "Can we talk?"

The distance between us felt strange. Years ago, I would have been tucked against his side, completely twitterpated by him. Now, I saw life differently. "I have a lot of work to do this morning."

"What about your sunrise rides to the bluff? Can I come along?"

The reminder hit me to the core—yet another thing I'd lost in the mess I'd discovered when I returned to Birkstrom. I put the flowers in the water. "I don't have time for that anymore."

"Is there anything I can do?" He took my hands in his. I expected electricity but felt nothing.

"You can have a conversation with your father," I said. "He made his intentions very clear yesterday."

His eyes flashed with anger. "He promised me he wouldn't come by yesterday."

"He lied." *Again.*

"I'm so sorry." He shook his head, squeezed my hands. "I'll talk to him."

"I don't want to lose Birkstrom," I whispered.

"I'll do what I can to talk him out of this crusade." His voice went soft, reminiscent of that timid, frightened boy I'd latched on to in our youth. I was the runaway uncertain of this new home, and he was the boy terrified of his father.

Would the man standing before me be able to stand up to his father the way he never could as a boy?

"Eva, I need you to know," he said, "I messed things up all those years ago, but I missed you more than you'll ever know."

I pulled my hands free of his and crossed my arms. "Cheryl said you were keeping plenty busy with Millie." Cheryl Jenkins, the only other woman who showed Arabian horses in our area, had always been my source of gossip.

"I tried to move forward with my life, but it didn't work out at all with Millie." Keith flushed, then his eyes locked onto mine. "You've always been the girl for me."

*Just not my name*, I thought.

"I reacted poorly when we last spoke," he continued. "I was young and dumb."

No, he feared the truth of who my family was and what it meant to his reputation or family name if the word ever got out. I just couldn't see how he wasn't equally ashamed of who his father was.

It didn't matter, because I'd thought long and hard about those moments. In the long nights when I couldn't sleep or the quiet shifts at the hospital before the onslaught, I'd agonized over my first and only love who had turned on me. In time, I realized I couldn't blame him for how he'd reacted. In a way, his rejection reminded me of where I stood in this world.

I vowed I'd never tell another soul the truth. I'd never date or get married, not when that meant the same shadow of my own family cast upon someone else.

I could give my love to these horses, care for those who were in need. They didn't know or care about my identity.

"I need to get to work." I walked from the house, fleeing from the wave of sorrow that washed over me. Besides, Warren would be here any moment.

When I turned into the barn, the wisps of morning sun began to shine upon the rotted wood siding. The warmth did little to soothe the chill on my skin.

Keith followed. "We belong together, Eva. It just makes so much sense—and you know how much I care about you."

I grabbed a bucket, lifted the pump handle, and sighed. Nothing emerged.

"I can't talk about this right now," I said with a weary sigh. "If you want to help, do you know how to fix this pump?"

He shook his head. "I can send our new handyman, Jeffrey, over if you want."

"Don't bother," I said with a wave. "I'll figure something out."

What choice did I have? I was alone here, left to pick up the pieces of a shattered life.

## Warren

When I pulled into Birkstrom, there was an extra vehicle in the driveway, and my pulse raced.

Eva's neighbor. Again.

And so early? It was hardly six a.m.

My mind snapped into combat mode, into sneaking through the buildings unnoticed and cornering the opposing forces. But before I'd even left my truck, a tall blond man came walking out of the barn, brushing his hair back. This wasn't the same man as the day before.

I stepped in front of his path, and he drew to a stop. He looked up at me in surprise. "Who are you?"

"I might ask the same question," I growled. I stood several inches taller than him, and I channeled my best General Patton look of intimidation.

He turned back to the barn. "Oh, are you with the new set of hooves?"

"Captain Warren Hayes." I offered a hand in forced cordiality.

My rank seemed to have the desired effect. He went somber and his jaw flexed.

"Keith Merrick," he said, shaking my hand hesitantly. "I own the stables down the road."

I nodded. "I gave another man by the name of Merrick a very clear directive that there were to be no more friendly neighbor visits."

"That was my father." Keith rolled his shoulders back. "Eva and I are a bit more than neighbors, Captain."

The implication surprised me, but I covered any outward revelation. I wouldn't give him the satisfaction. He and Eva were around the same age, so it was possible.

"How do you know her?" he asked.

"I was stationed with Lieutenant Bryant in Germany."

Keith nodded and shrank back a tiny bit.

"Did you serve?" I sensed I already knew the answer from the new tension in his shoulders and how he avoided my gaze.

"I was needed to run the ranch—cattle, you know." He lifted his chin. "Food production and all."

The man I'd seen yesterday was fit and able enough to run a ranch. But Father had gotten William out of active duty through his connections, so I couldn't judge too harshly.

"Germany?" Keith eyed me testily. "I thought Eva was assigned to the Pacific Theatre."

Though they were more than friends, as he claimed, he didn't know much about her time in the war. If she had a deeper relationship with this man, wouldn't she have written to him about her time in Kötzting?

"She helped us with the horses we evacuated from Hostau and Janów Podlaski."

"Janów?" He blinked. "You were part of Operation Cowboy, then." He motioned toward Phantom's paddock. "Wait, is that Phantom?"

So, the man knew his horses.

"Indeed." I cleared my throat. "We're going to get him ready for show. I'm guessing we'll see you in the ring, then?"

His lips pressed into a firm line. I'd hit a nerve.

"I guess so." He gave a curt nod.

Eva strode out of the barn, her hair loose around her face in waves. Her funeral dress had been traded for some tan slacks, cowboy boots, and a light blue shirt that matched her eyes. She frowned at the two of us and ignored Keith, which sent tingles down my spine.

"Morning, Captain," she said. Once up close, I saw her hands were covered in dirt and rust. "Might I trouble you for a bit of repair advice?"

Keith's face flushed, and he stormed off to his vehicle.

"Are all your neighbors this sunny and cheery?" I crossed my arms.

She let out a long breath and shook her head. "It's a long, complicated story."

"It always is."

Her gaze caught mine as Keith's car peeled out of the driveway. "I take it you two had a nice chat?"

"I don't like him," I said.

"He's harmless."

"You sure about that? His father left quite a different impression yesterday."

She shifted and winced. "Victor is another matter."

I had more I wanted to say, but it wasn't my place. I hardly knew the woman, no matter how protective I felt especially now that she was my ticket to taming Phantom and perhaps finding Mira. Besides, we'd worked alongside each other while in uniform, both for a short time in Germany and figuratively across oceans and embattled lands. I would feel this protective over anyone I'd served with.

I rolled up my sleeves. "How can I help?"

Her body sagged with relief, and she motioned for me to follow her into the barn. "Thank you," she said over her shoulder. "I'm at an utter loss. I keep uncovering one issue after another. I replaced the main seal on this pump last week, since I'd seen Gramps do that before, but now it still won't pull water."

The hand pump was worn and rusted, thick red paint flaking off it. I knew very little about plumbing, but we'd had issues from time to time with the pumps at the airfield in Kötzting and the high demand with all the horses that needed water. I'd repaired a few with Eddie and had a sneaking suspicion the main culprit here was the valve. Considering the amount of rust and wear on the handle, I knew the pump had to be old.

"Did your grandfather have any spare pipes or wrenches laying around?"

"He never threw anything away, so there's probably a whole hardware store's worth of pipes around here." She showed me to his tool chest and then to a huge shed of wood, metal, pipes, and fence supplies behind the house.

I found the pipe that looked about right, and about as old as the pump. "Give me a few minutes, I'll have the valve replaced."

"Thank you," she said, looking toward the driveway. "Not everyone is so willing to get their hands dirty."

Was she alluding to Keith Merrick? If so, it explained the odd exchange before he'd left. I'd wager my inheritance that Keith didn't even know how to change a flat tire.

Twenty minutes later, after wrestling with the plumbing, I had the pump back together and the water flowed freely.

Eva sighed. "Thank you."

"Maybe you need some help catching up on these repairs."

She handed me a rag for the mud and rust now covering my hands and nudged a little brown goat away. "I certainly do, but as bad as the stables and equipment are"—she motioned around—"Gramps left the financial state even worse."

I nodded. She'd never accept my charity. "You know, I caught up with Eddie last night. His wife, Violet, is in New York with her sick mother, and he and his twins are looking for a summer distraction. I'm sure he'd help with all these things in exchange for room and board."

She put her hands on her hips, and I could see the wheels turning. "You think he'd want to do such menial tasks?"

"He's quite skilled and probably would enjoy the work. He oversaw the carpentry in Hostau to convert our trucks and Jeeps into horse transports for the pregnant mares."

"I'm not sure my cabins are even livable. I haven't checked them since I got back."

"Sounds like the perfect place for him to start."

"I don't know." She drew in a long breath. "The rattlesnakes might have taken them over."

"I'm sure he'll be just fine."

*You shouldn't be out here alone*, I wanted to add but held back. She was proud, and I sensed she'd do whatever she could to make it on her own. If Eddie were around, I'd worry less about her safety, considering the threat from her neighbors.

Besides, my timeline was short. I hadn't disclosed this fact—not until I knew if she'd be able to handle Phantom.

"I invited him and the kids out to see Phantom today, so we can chat more with him then." I put the rest of the tools away.

She shrugged. "I'm up for the arrangement if he is."

She filled a water bucket, and the little brown goat trotted behind her. I lingered, looking around the barn and taking an inventory of all the work that needed to be done. The barns and arena were massive and thoroughly weathered, but I could see the thoughtful varnishes and handcrafted work in the stall doors that alluded to a past era of splendor and pride. I'd wager the Birkstrom Ranch sign over the driveway was carved by the same hands too.

It reminded me a bit of the barns in Europe that we'd taken shelter in from time to time. Storied history, aged wood. I wondered if patching up this old ranch would breathe life back into Eddie's soul and alleviate some of the burden Eva carried.

Three months.

My clock was winding down with each passing second. I might not be able to see the finished project, but at least I could get things started.

# *Six*

## Eva

The air whooshed out of my lungs as I landed hard in the dirt, a puff of dust floating around me. Gramps had always made this look easy.

Again I'd tried to get Phantom to drink, and each time, he'd knocked me to the ground or spilled the bucket.

We'd regressed from yesterday.

Tiny rocks pelted me as Phantom bolted away, and the water bucket splashed all over me. My tan pants were caked with dirt, my blue blouse speckled with mud.

This was not going well.

Warren had kept his distance, though I could see from the lines in his brow and the tension in his jaw that he wasn't pleased. He'd left for town for some supplies a while ago, though I'd insisted on paying him back for any costs. I'd hoped for a miracle by the time he returned, but it didn't seem likely now.

In all the years I'd watched Gramps build trust with the water bucket technique, I'd never seen a horse so reluctant to give in.

I stood up, dusted off my pants, and winced at the tender spot on my thigh. I'd thought the horse had missed me with his hoof as I'd fallen, but he must have grazed me.

If Gramps had taught me anything, it was that you could endure beyond the point of thinking you could make it. He'd taken on all the lost causes and damaged souls that had come his way, including me. I wouldn't give up on Phantom until the last moment of my contract.

I left the paddock, refilled the bucket, and slid through the slats of the fence again. The heat of the day warmed up my damp clothes, and with each passing moment, I worried more about Phantom's health with his refusal to drink.

"Okay," I said calmly. "Let's try this again."

Phantom snorted as if challenging me back, and he sprinted toward me with teeth exposed. I stood firm and then stepped toward him as he neared, which broke his trajectory. He shied away, kicking out at me again, but more in casual anger than with any real intention of hitting me.

The narrow sides of his torso and his ribs popping through hurt me to see. I knew Warren had tried to keep him well-fed while searching for a barn to take him, but Phantom wasn't eating, wouldn't stop pacing, and, if I couldn't turn this around soon, could die of an ulcer or malnutrition.

I'd never forgive myself if he died on my watch.

If Gramps were here, he'd know just what to do. He was the eternal student who took every experience with horses as unique. Was I even approaching this the correct way? Was Phantom too dehydrated and manic to even build a bond with me?

I could hear Gramps's voice. *"Don't back down now, honey. If you give in and give the horse that bucket of water without him yielding to you, you'll never get your chance again."*

I had to persevere. For this method to work, I only had one chance. I needed him to know that I was not going to harm him, that he could trust me for water, food, safety.

Hours passed of Phantom inching close, then knocking the bucket out of my hands. My face dripped with sweat and my hair stuck to the back of my neck. My hands hurt from the metal handle that cut into my palm, but in addition to teaching me about the value of perseverance, Gramps had taught me that pain could be my friend.

My head swam and my stomach churned. I watched each flick of Phantom's ears, the way his eyes followed me, the flare of his nostrils. This was a dance, not a battle. We were still figuring out who was leading.

Phantom circled me again, and this time, I moved toward him. He shied away and tossed his head, the shift of dominance palpable.

When he inched back toward me, I pushed him away until his head dropped and his ears tipped forward ever so slightly.

The tiniest hint of submission.

I stepped firmly toward him, pushing him back as if to ostracize him from the herd. He stomped away, angry. The tables had turned—now I was leading the dance.

*"Attagirl."* I could hear Gramps's voice as if on the wind.

Finally, I stilled and let the horse venture toward me, timidly. His body twitched and tensed, but he snorted and sniffed the bucket, then plunged his lips in for a long drink.

I fought the urge to pet the light gray mane and forehead. We weren't there. Not yet. After a few gulps, Phantom walked away, head lowered and neck relaxed.

The tension had broken between us.

"Well done, Eva," a female voice from the fence called out.

I blinked and turned, dazed to see Cheryl Jenkins next to Warren. Both smiled and leaned against the fence, which told me they'd been there for a while.

I must have gone to that place again—the tunnel of focus where I lost all sense of time and place. Gramps always said a volcano could erupt nearby and I'd carry on, lost in my merry little mind.

"Cheryl, what are you doing here?" I walked toward them and handed Warren the bucket of water. He offered his other hand to help me off the fence after I scaled it. I accepted it, and as my boots hit the ground, I swayed ever so slightly and felt the edges of my vision blur.

Warren held up a canteen. "First things first."

"Thank you." I nodded and drank the cool water. "When did you get back from town?" I asked.

"An hour ago," he said, motioning to Cheryl. "We've been getting to know each other and enjoying the lesson."

Cheryl, only five or six inches shorter than Warren, smirked at me and wiggled her eyebrows. She had a long, narrow face and thin lips with round, hazel eyes. "Father always told me about Bill's tricks, and I confess I wasn't sure you'd pull this off."

"I don't think we're out of the woods yet," I said, glancing at Warren. His brow was still scrunched, but he was looking at me, not Phantom. I probably looked a little worse for wear after spending the afternoon in that paddock.

"What are you doing here?" I asked Cheryl. "This is a bit out of the way of Portland."

Cheryl reached for me and drew me in for a hug, which I returned stiffly. She'd always been so expressive, while I'd never really known what to do with my emotions.

"I came as soon as I heard about Bill," she said, squeezing me. Despite her skirt and stockings, the fact that she hugged me in my dirty, dusty clothes revealed her as a true horse person.

We were the only two women in the region who trained and showed, and we faced the handfuls of detractors who didn't believe we had a place in the show ring. Cheryl was a force to be reckoned with in the riding classes. At least Phantom was a few years away from that division. For now, he'd be shown in hand by halter and classified as a yearling horse.

"I invited Mr. Hayes to the association's banquet in June." Cheryl clasped her hands in front of her and rolled her shoulders back, as if transitioning from my friend to the local Arabian breed registry's board member.

"Excellent. He can go in my stead."

"Nonsense. I brought you a dress since you'll also give me the excuse that you have nothing to wear."

"You're ten feet taller than I am," I shot back. "It won't fit me."

Cheryl turned to Warren. "See, this is what I was telling you about. She's so difficult."

Warren held up his hands. "I don't want to get in the middle of this."

I took a final drink from the canteen and handed it back to Warren. He took it, held my gaze. The intensity of his concern reminded me that if I didn't make significant progress with Phantom, he'd haul him away, and this horse might never become the icon I knew he could be.

"I'll leave you two to catch up," Warren said, turning to Cheryl. "It was nice to meet you."

As he walked away, Cheryl drew in a long breath and grabbed my shoulders. "How are you, really?"

I pointed toward the house. "Let's sit inside."

Cheryl retrieved a small bag from her vehicle and then fell into step beside me.

Once we went inside the house, the cooler air soothed my aching body. The list of things to do rattled in my head. I hadn't expected the session with Phantom to take quite that long. I still needed to call all the farms in the area, see if there were any problem horses that needed training and if any of them were interested in some of the equipment I could spare around the ranch. Phantom's training fees would help toward the mortgage, but I still needed more to keep this operation afloat.

"I brought you this for the banquet," Cheryl said, pulling a long, satin, dark blue dress from her bag and hanging it on the coat rack.

"I don't want to go to the banquet."

"I didn't ask if you wanted to," Cheryl said with her hands

on her hips. "That's how you schmooze and get more clients. Bring the handsome captain with you and have a good time."

Pain throbbed through my head at the thought. I didn't have the energy in the moment to fight her.

"What's the latest gossip, Cheryl?" I asked as I slumped into a chair at the kitchen table. "How bad is it?"

She pressed her lips together and sat across from me, her expression neutral as if she knew I was going to ask this. Cheryl only visited when there was some sort of bad news from the association—like when Victor staged a board takeover, or when he tried to get Gramps kicked out of breed shows by alleging that he abused his horses. Cheryl and I knew that Victor had paid off a handful of board members and had a dozen of the judges in his pocket too.

Her tone was flat. "He's accused you of being improperly . . . entangled with your new client."

"He works fast." Anger swirled in me. "We've dealt with these sorts of attacks before."

Cheryl and I had always been the target of male trainers who thought our place was outside the show ring. And I had dealt with the waves of rumors and whispers in Baker once I joined the nurse corps. Some turned up their noses at the idea of a young woman in such an unseemly career, surrounded by men in such improperly unchaperoned environments. I'd never given those opinions any credence.

"I know the rumors themselves don't bother you." Cheryl hesitated. "But Victor is pushing for your membership to be pulled from the organization because of it. You remember the Martha Vanderhorn scandal back in 1938? This could be worse. You wouldn't be able to compete in any of the breed shows."

Disappointment and trepidation crept into my heart. Martha had been a farm owner in Southern California who had an affair with her married client—and she'd been run out of the industry in shame. This could derail every plan I'd put into motion and cripple my chances of getting Phantom onto the national stage.

I knew Victor would play dirty, but I hadn't expected this.

And I wasn't sure I'd be able to fight it.

## Warren

I'd unloaded my truck bed of supplies from the hardware store by the time Eva and Cheryl emerged from the house. Eva's body was tense, her arms crossed in front of her.

I finished stacking the last two-by-four and walked in their direction.

Cheryl put on a smile, though there was less energy behind her expression, which further confirmed my suspicions. "I'll see you in Seattle, then." She waved farewell and got into her sedan.

"What's wrong?" I asked Eva.

She drew in a breath but froze as another vehicle pulled into the driveway. Brilliant timing. Eddie and his kids.

"Let's talk later," she said.

Emotions collided through me as every potential raced through my mind. Watching Eva work with Phantom and speaking with Cheryl had been illuminating. I now had very little doubt that Eva was the sole person who could train Phantom—if he could be helped at all.

Cheryl had shared stories about competing with Eva in the show ring and growing up as the only two women competitors on the circuit. Cheryl's family ran a farm out of Portland and were heavily involved in the breed organization's leadership and operation. Bill and Eva had always been a bit outside the inner circle, she'd explained. They trained the broken and neglected horses, which didn't always include purebred Arabians. Thus, Victor and Keith Merrick were more renowned for their prized Arabian horses. The Merricks were a titan in this world.

As Eddie parked the car, I studied Eva's face. "How bad is it?"

Her jaw tightened, and she met my gaze with sadness. "You don't want to know."

My stomach rolled as it twisted into knots.

Eva plastered on a smile and approached Eddie with her arms open. "Eddie, so good to see you."

Two teenagers emerged from the car, one a sour-faced boy who I knew as Peter, and the other a blond girl who looked around at the ranch with a fascinated grin. Peter resembled his father with dark hair, thick eyelashes, and a gaze that didn't miss a detail. Annie was more sprite-like and reminiscent of the photo of Violet that Eddie had shown me years ago. Long blond hair, honey-colored eyes, and a pensive, quiet presence.

Eddie beamed and hugged Eva. "Good to see you, Eva." He grew somber and added softly, "I'm so sorry about Bill."

"Thank you." She angled her head. "Now, are these the famous Annie and Peter?"

Annie walked up beside her father, her hands tucked nervously in her pockets and her shoulders scrunched as if she could make herself smaller. Peter loitered by the car and didn't look our direction.

I recognized myself in the kid. I knew exactly how he'd react to being told to clean stalls or help around the farm. No, this would need to be a different type of negotiation.

Eva latched on to Annie immediately. "Want a tour of the barns? I'd love to show you the horses—and perhaps you'd like to ride?"

Annie's mouth fell open. "Really?" she squeaked.

Eva nodded and called over to Peter, "Want to join us?"

Peter didn't respond. Eva shrugged and smirked at Eddie. "Then I'll leave Mr. Sunshine with you."

She and Annie walked toward the barn, and Eddie stepped closer to me, motioning to Peter. "I don't know what to do with that kid."

I had a few ideas. For now, I had a different priority.

"Can I get your advice on some repairs in the barn?" I asked. "I have a proposal for you too."

Eddie lifted his bushy black eyebrows. "What kind of proposal?"

I motioned for him to follow and said to Peter, "I'd be careful around the gray horse. He bites."

Peter's gaze snapped to Phantom as if he was interested by the challenge. I knew it was what would have turned my head as a kid. The chance to prove someone wrong, the danger of physical harm. I'd always straddled the edge of chaos, and it hadn't served me well until I landed in the Second Cavalry. Mother and the endless tutors had tried to suppress that urge, doing anything they could to shape me into a respectable young man. What if we tried a different approach with Peter?

Peter might get a nip on the arm, which could humble him a bit, or he'd see the reflection of himself in the troubled young colt.

I led Eddie toward the barn, but he hesitated. "You sure he's okay?"

I slapped my friend on the back. "Trust me on this one."

We stepped from the blinding sunlight into the dark, dank barn. Eddie took a sweeping look around and whistled. Whether it was from admiration of the unique details or astonishment from the state of things now, I wasn't sure.

"Eva's got quite a lot on her hands here," Eddie said as he walked around slowly.

Eva and Annie were behind the barn at the two connected paddocks for the broodmares, out of earshot.

"She needs help," I said. "I want someone here I can trust."

Eddie picked up on the meaning beneath my words. We'd been in enough life-threatening situations that our communication was honed. "From what I hear, the Merricks down the road are quite the headache."

"I think they're dangerous."

He blinked. "Really?"

"I witnessed it." I still wanted to corner Victor Merrick the same way he'd pushed Eva around, but I smothered that urge.

Eddie's expression also went rigid. "Should we pay them a visit?"

"No, but would you consider moving here for the summer? Until school starts or Violet returns? I'm not sure how much I can convince Eva to do beyond that, but I will pay your salary and for whatever supplies she needs."

"Does she know about that?" Eddie put his hands on his hips.

I shook my head, glancing to make sure she and Annie were still far enough away. They sat on the top railing of a wooden fence with a chestnut mare nuzzling them. Annie squealed in delight.

"No, and she doesn't need to either," I said.

"She'll figure it out, Captain."

"In the meantime, I'll think of some other way to make sure she has someone here, but I just know something's off. With her grandfather gone, she's too isolated out here."

Eddie nodded, looking around the property with a sharp study—not as a handyman looking at needed repairs, but as a sergeant assessing threats and vulnerabilities.

I'd already done the same. This was a flat property with half-broken fences and no shortage of opportunities for a bad actor to access the barn, house, or horses.

Annie's laughter floated along the wind, and Eddie smiled. "Well, I know at least one person in support of this idea."

"Will you do this for me?" We both needed something out of this arrangement—he'd appreciate the singular purpose, and I'd feel a little more reassured that Eva wouldn't face Victor alone again.

Eddie glanced out the wide barn entrance, where we could see Peter walking up to Phantom's paddock slowly. The boy took in the horse, who stood at attention from the center of the paddock, ears up and eyes locked on the visitor.

"I don't know," Eddie said. "I need the work, but I don't know if I should move the kids across town. With Violet gone, they need stability."

Annie and Eva walked into the aisle, and Annie bounded over to her father, grabbing his hand. "Can I go for a ride, Daddy?"

Eddie looked at Eva. "Only if it's not an imposition."

Eva's hair curled around her face, windswept against her sun-kissed skin. For the first time since I'd arrived, her smile felt truly warm and genuine. "I have another hour before I need to work with Phantom, so it's no trouble."

Eddie nodded and pointed to his daughter. "You do what Miss Eva says."

Annie clapped excitedly and jumped on her toes.

Eva chuckled and pointed to a door down the aisle. "The saddles are there. See which fits you best."

Once Annie had disappeared, Eva grew more serious. "I'm guessing you two were talking business?"

"I'll think about it, Eva," Eddie said. "I'm not sure what's best for me and the kids right now."

"The apartment here in the barn is in decent repair," she said, pointing to a staircase in the far back corner of the aisle that led to the second level of the barn. "But it's rather small. Annie could stay in the extra bedroom of the house."

"I'd better check on Peter," Eddie said, taking a few steps out of the barn.

We followed him and then froze, our gazes locked on Phantom's pen.

Peter was calmly petting Phantom's neck.

Eddie looked at me. "Is he safe?"

Eva grabbed the man's arm soothingly and whispered, "Yes. I've seen this before. Sometimes horses treat people in different ways. Some are more trusting of children." She looked at me with a captivating smile. Her eyes sparkled, and her voice caught. "Maybe we've found Phantom's person."

# Seven

## Eva

The moment broke.

Peter must have felt our stares. He stepped back, shoved his hands in his pockets, and looked at the ground, kicking pebbles around and now ignoring the horse beside him. Phantom watched the kid as he meandered back toward the car and leaned against the trunk.

Warren hummed knowingly.

Eddie cleared his throat and turned to me. "You know, Eva, I think a summer here might be just what we need."

Relief flooded me, and I felt the same sense in Warren.

"I'd love that," I said. "I can show you around."

"I can look around on my own." He held up a hand. "I know Annie will be wanting that ride and don't want to keep you." He exchanged a look with Warren and then went back into the barn, looking all over the property as if with a new perspective.

Before I could escape, Warren turned and gave me the no-nonsense stare that only an officer could give. "Now, tell me what's going on. What did Cheryl tell you?"

Now wasn't the time. Annie was anxious to hit the trails, Eddie and Peter were close by. "It can wait. I overreacted in the moment."

"I don't think you're even capable of overreacting." His steely look indicated he wouldn't budge.

"Fine." My heart thumped against my rib cage. "Victor is spreading rumors and trying to make me ineligible to compete on the Arabian show circuit."

"What rumors?"

"About us."

"What about us?" His eyebrows bunched in confusion, and I wanted to wallop him on the side of the head to knock sense into him. Did I have to spell it all out?

The silence stretched.

I sighed. "That we're . . . involved."

Realization dawned on him, and he smothered a smile. "Oh, is that it?"

I felt a strange laugh build up inside me, and I slapped his arm with the back of my hand. "Stop that. This is serious."

"It's hard for me to picture Lieutenant Eva Bryant caring about propriety after all your years in the battlefield," he said. "Doesn't Cheryl ever work with other horse owners who are men?"

"Yes. Though she's married and works with her husband," I said. "And you're right. I don't really care. We've had these rumors flare up from time to time, mostly just from gossipy parties."

"So why is this one different?"

"Because Victor is trying to get my membership revoked and disqualify me from competitions and the championship running."

Realization spread across his expression, but then his joking smirk returned. "So, we have to get married." A slight dimple appeared with that cheeky grin, and he wiggled his eyebrows.

"Captain, be serious."

"You should call me Warren if we're now betrothed."

"Stop it," I said as seriously as I could manage, but his lightheartedness dredged laughter from deep inside. I couldn't even remember the last time I'd felt this levity—perhaps one of the quieter days in the field hospital, when the soldiers I tended were comfortable and safe and we joked about everything from a commander's bad breath to the men's failed relationships. I missed the comradery of those moments and felt the whisper of it return with Warren and Eddie nearby.

Or was the warmth in my chest whenever I was near Warren something different?

He shook his head and looked off in the distance. "Would it help if I went back to Philadelphia?"

"Victor will spin his lies no matter what," I said. "I don't want him to win by driving you off. You should return when your business demands it of you, not to protect me."

"I'll take care of this," he said firmly. "Cheryl told me a bit about the politics of the current board of directors."

"This isn't your burden."

"You never should have had this insinuated in the first place," Warren said, his voice now calm and icy. "You don't deserve that. I'll address this with the board, and I'll pay Victor a visit as well."

A blade of fear sliced through my chest. Dare we poke that hornet's nest? I hesitated to ask him not to. Warren was an imposing figure and had faced no shortage of risky situations. Would this make Victor think twice about wielding his power against me?

*"You don't deserve that."*

The words hit me. The little child inside me who had witnessed my parents' worst moments and greatest sins felt otherwise. I didn't deserve the kindness or loyalty of such good men as Warren and Eddie, nor did I deserve the support of a force like Cheryl. She'd vowed to stand up for me and fight against these unsubstantiated rumors, but she had to be careful to keep her board seat or she would lose all leverage entirely.

"Come on, Eva!" Annie called from the barn. "I found the perfect saddle, come see!"

My feet felt anchored to the ground. Warren seemed to recognize as much, and he stepped closer, lowering his voice reassuringly. "You're not alone in this. I've got your back."

Emotion choked me, and I could only nod, grateful beyond measure.

"You'd better get to Annie before she saddles up all by herself." He winked. "We'll talk more about our elopement later."

He walked back into the barn. The world spun around me, tipsy as if on a new axis.

There were still so many unknowns. I wasn't sure that I could deliver what I'd promised for Phantom. He deserved to be and should be a shining champion in the ring. Or should he be retired to pasture after such a tumultuous first year of life?

No, I knew better. Horses wanted a job, a purpose, a partnership. Same as any human. Sometimes they just needed help to discover it.

Perhaps I simply wanted to keep Warren close—his presence was soothing and captivating. But he had a home, a life, back in Philly. For all I knew, he had a girlfriend waiting for his return.

Despite our joking, there'd be no future for us beyond this working relationship. Whatever Gramps had claimed while on his deathbed, I knew I'd never be able to break free of the secret that had imprisoned me for twenty years. No future spouse, no children I could ever have, should share in the shame.

I'd never ask that of anyone.

Not even Keith.

Gramps had been right about a lot of things in his life. On this topic, he'd missed the mark.

## Warren

Eva's words bounced through my thoughts at rapid speed, rage boiling in my veins.

How dare Victor swoop so low. And if this Keith fellow was more than friends with Eva, why hadn't he stepped in?

I still hadn't confirmed Keith's claim. That went beyond my role as the owner of the horse she was training. Perhaps beyond being a fellow soldier and officer. But these rumors were a personal affront to her reputation. Mine, too, but I cared little about that. I wouldn't abide with her suffering because of my presence.

I wrestled with whether I should leave Baker, despite Eva's reassurance. If it meant things would be easier for her, I would fly out in a heartbeat. She was right, though, that my absence wouldn't deter Victor. I couldn't leave, not yet. I couldn't protect her from so far away.

"Everything okay, Captain?" Eddie asked, glancing past me at Peter leaning against the car.

"I'm going to pay a visit to the neighbors," I said.

"What happened?"

"More of the Merricks playing dirty."

Eddie started rolling up his sleeves. "I'll join you."

"You should stay here and keep an eye out." I held up a hand. "Get to work on the apartment so you can stay overnight as soon as possible."

"You know I don't like you charging in alone." Eddie crossed his arms and looked stern.

He was referencing the winter of '44 when I'd snuck into an SS camp and hadn't told the rest of my men. I had decided to play the odds without putting my men at risk. In that case, it had paid off, but nearly at the cost of my life. Eddie had been furious and watched me like a hawk afterward.

"This is different, Eddie."

"Is it?"

These moments had always been the times my mind was most clear. Everything else faded away, and I knew my purpose. I had a clear mission. The danger was all around, but I knew how to face it.

"I'll be back soon." I set out for my truck.

As I closed the truck door and fired up the engine, Eva ran up and knocked on the window. I rolled it down.

"He's got the entire county in his favor and the local sheriff in his pocket." Her ice-blue eyes were intense. "Be careful."

"I will." I shifted into reverse. As I left the driveway, I felt her gaze follow me.

I turned east, where the Merrick farm sat over sprawling green hills dotted with dozens of horses of every shade. Four long, narrow barns were painted white and gleaming in the sunshine. A lavish mansion sat beyond the row of barns. I recognized the feel of this place, antiseptic and cold. Not unlike the sprawling manors and high-society life I'd grown up around. I hadn't favored such opulence then, and especially now, I preferred the hand-carved, humble atmosphere of Birkstrom.

Keith approached me before I'd even parked the truck. He wore riding breeches and a black shirt, and his hair covered only half the look of contempt in his eyes. His boots and gloves were covered in dirt, confirming the fact that he at least seemed to ride and train his own horses.

"What do you want?" he asked.

I stepped out of the truck and closed the door. "I came to see your father."

"He's not here."

That took the wind out of my sails just a bit. "When will he be back?" I asked.

"You can discuss anything you need to with me." Keith darted a glance in the direction of Birkstrom. "Is Eva all right?"

My blood ran cold. Why would he ask that?

"You wouldn't put it past your father to hurt her."

The flinch in Keith's expression told me all I needed to know. My earlier assessment of Victor had been accurate. Eva was in danger. Not just her reputation or her membership in the horse association but physical danger.

Victor wanted her grandfather's ranch, and even Keith understood he'd sink to any depth to get it.

"Where is your father?" I asked.

Keith studied me for a long moment before he finally admitted, "He had a meeting in town. That's all I know."

I looked around the ranch, assessing. A handful of staff members, what seemed like hundreds of stalls, and an army of trucks and trailers parked along the rows of stalls. This was a large operation. What did they need Birkstrom Ranch for?

I reached for the door handle on my Ford. "If Eva matters to you in the slightest, you won't tell him that I came by."

Keith nodded hesitantly.

I reached the pavement of the main highway as my mind raced, and I turned toward the town of Baker.

I stopped at the most popular diners, the courthouse, and the barber. No sign or whisper of Victor Merrick. I didn't take him for the type who bought his own groceries or farm supplies, so I decided to head back to the Geiser Grand to ask Betty. She could be trusted not to spread the word that I'd been looking for Victor since she was firmly on the side of Birkstrom and Eva.

As I entered the lobby, I caught sight of Victor in the restaurant with two men in fine suits. His back was turned to me, his shoulders tense.

My father had done enough business with unscrupulous characters for me to know these were either mob enforcers or loan sharks. Instead of confronting Victor, I needed to know more.

They spoke in hushed tones, and I wasn't sure I'd be able to catch anything. I slipped past the restaurant and up the spiral staircase to the second floor, where there was an overhanging balcony. As I situated myself right above them, I stood as still as I could to overhear pieces.

". . . getting impatient. If we don't start construction soon, we'll lose the fair weather."

"You assured us you'd handle this . . ."

"There's an added complication." Victor's voice.

"We can arrange . . ."

"No, that's not necessary."

". . . no choice."

"I need more time."

"No promises."

My heart thumped and my fists clenched. Was this why he was pressuring Eva? Some sort of development planned for Birkstrom lands? I had every confidence that I was the added complication, which might have made matters worse.

I went back downstairs and hid my face from the view of the restaurant before slipping up to the front desk, where Betty looked up from reading a dime novel. I raised a hand to keep her from announcing my name and Victor hearing it.

"Who are those men meeting with Victor Merrick?" I asked.

"I'm afraid I don't know." She grew somber and shook her head. "They came in once before about three months ago."

"Anyone else ever join them?" Did Keith know anything about this? As much as I despised the man, that flash of fear in his face earlier had seemed genuine. He cared about Eva.

Betty nodded, removed her glasses, and leaned forward conspiratorially. "Mr. Yardley, the bank manager."

I slipped outside before the men paid their bill and left the restaurant, going to my truck a few yards down the street so I could follow them.

Victor came out alone and drove in the direction of his farm and Birkstrom Ranch. The other two didn't come out after him, which meant they were either staying at the hotel or had left through a back door.

I drove back to the ranch, a million thoughts rolling around in my head. This wasn't just Victor trying to beat Eva in the show ring or get her kicked out of the association. This was about stealing Eva's home—a thousand-acre ranch—and the potential payout of that land.

Money and power.

I'd need to change my tactics accordingly to protect her.

# *Eight*

## Eva

"I'll make that fellow wish he'd never messed with the likes of us," Eddie said with a few added curses under his breath.

I leaned back in the wicker chair on Gramps's porch as the light faded from the day. Annie and Peter were finishing up some beans and canned stew I'd rustled from the pantry while Warren had relayed everything he'd seen and overheard in town.

The stoic, unflappable captain ignored Eddie's tirade and stomping around, causing the occasional creaking of a loose porch board. He waited for my reaction.

What could I possibly say?

I inhaled a long, shaky breath. "The Merricks and the Birkstroms have bickered for five generations, back to when this land was first settled. Lawsuits, petty theft, practical jokes gone wrong, but I didn't think even Victor would go this far."

Warren's expression stayed neutral, except for a faint twitch at the corner of his jaw. He sat on the sun-worn wicker bench across from me, and though he spoke in a calm, measured tone, I saw the same fire broiling under his gaze that he'd had when he first arrived on the ranch and interrupted Victor cornering me.

"We can't infer too much from that conversation you heard," I said.

Eddie stopped beside me with his hands on his hips and a scowl across his weathered face. "Eva, you can't be serious."

My stomach roiled. I could believe it, but I didn't want to. As I spoke, I was trying to convince myself as much as them. "The Merricks want the farm, yes."

"Have they offered you cash directly?" Warren asked.

I nodded, tension tightening in my chest. I'd have to come clean about the situation, no matter how ashamed I felt. "When I returned home, I learned how far behind Gramps had let things fall. Including in payments to the bank."

Warren leaned forward, putting his elbows on his knees and folding his hands together. "How far behind was he?"

I looked out at the quiet, muted lands around the house. Phantom was a glowing white shadow in the evening hue as he grazed on hay. The barn lights were off, the broodmares tucked in for the night. The chickens had all nested in their coop, and only the humming of cicadas and chirping of frogs could be heard.

"It's dire," I whispered. "I've sold every spare piece of equipment, put the call out to every local rancher who might need a horse trained. With Phantom's training fees, I'll barely be able to keep the bank at bay."

Should any unexpected expense come along . . .

Warren nodded. "What about the farm loans through the VA?"

Defeat rushed in on me at the reminder. "I've appealed, but so far my paperwork keeps hitting a dead end. I'm unmarried, and they don't know what to do with me as a female farm owner."

I caught a small glimmer of humor in his eyes and sensed he was thinking about his earlier joke about us getting married. It did lighten my mood, slightly.

"The bank won't renegotiate terms?" Warren asked.

"Not with Victor—a guaranteed cash sale—waiting in the wings."

Eddie resumed his pacing.

I stood up. "I'll carry on as long as I can."

"I can help," Warren said, standing as well.

"You already are." I held his gaze. "You're doing more than I could ask of any client, and I can't accept anything further."

"Eva," Eddie said with a somber look, which felt out of place from the man who always smiled. "We can't just ignore the threat they've made against you."

"I can't let that rule my life either."

"Eva." Warren's look of defiance and determination morphed into a tender, apologetic pleading. I didn't want his sympathy. His patronage, yes, in exchange for the work I did with his horse. I wouldn't accept charity.

"I'll talk to Keith about it," I offered.

A shadow fell over Warren's face. "Are you sure he can be trusted?"

"Yes," I said without hesitation. "I consider him a friend."

Eddie and Warren passed a quick look between them.

"Keith implied . . ." Warren cleared his throat. "That you were more than friends."

Blast it all. Why would Keith have said such a thing? He knew it was over between us.

From inside the kitchen, the faint clinking of silverware turned into the sound of the running faucet and stacking of ceramic plates. I didn't want the children to overhear this.

"We'll finish this another time." I glanced at my wristwatch. "I'm due in town."

"For what at this hour?" Eddie asked, looking at his own watch. "It's nearly eight o'clock."

"I volunteer for a few night shifts a week at the hospital."

Warren frowned. "When do you sleep?"

"Volunteer?" Eddie asked. "Why don't you work there for some extra cash?"

"St. Elizabeth's doesn't have the budget," I said. "And I need the flexibility to not go in when I need to be here."

"If we do assume the worst of what Warren heard, then you shouldn't be going alone," Eddie said.

"I agree," Warren added quietly.

"You're both being paranoid," I said. "Besides, I'll be at a hospital surrounded by dozens of people. I'll be perfectly safe." I pulled out my key ring, unclipped a spare house key and the apartment key, and handed them to Eddie. "We don't normally lock doors around these parts, but I'll humor you that." I pointed to the house, where the two kids' voices floated up in irritated bickering. "Annie can help herself to whatever she needs in the house."

Warren crossed his arms. "Let me drive you to town at least so we can finish this conversation now."

In my mind, it was finished. Victor doing business with two questionable individuals had nothing to do with me. He wanted Birkstrom lands because we had the best water access and grazing lands within a twenty-mile radius.

"I'll be fine," I said to Warren. I needed a quiet drive into town to process everything. "I'll be home around two or three o'clock."

Warren stepped in front of me, and his eyes locked onto mine. "You don't have to face this alone, Eva."

"I know that." Gratitude, unease, and guilt all swirled in my mind. "I also need to know if I can run this ranch on my own merit. I'll fight the Merricks to the end, and if I don't have what it takes to save the ranch, so be it. But I need to know if I do."

"Victor has every card in the deck stacked against you."

A surge of confidence rose within me, warming my limbs and fighting back against the cool evening wind. I shrugged. "Well, I've been underestimated before."

## Warren

As Eva dressed for her shift at the hospital—I still hadn't quite worked out how she managed that on top of working from sunup to sundown on the ranch—Eddie tapped his toe impatiently on the rickety porch.

"We're not just going to sit by, right?" he asked, defaulting to me perhaps as a habit from our time in the Second Cavalry. The sergeant awaiting his captain's orders.

"No, we won't," I admitted. We'd have to do this carefully. Eva wanting to save the farm on her own was noble, and I would respect that.

When I'd returned from Baker earlier in the day, Annie had finished her ride in the arena and Eva again had been able to get Phantom to take a long drink from the water bucket in her hands. It was a marvel to witness.

With each passing hour, I was more confident that Phantom would be safe here, that I could leave for my senatorial run, and that Eva would watch over the horse I'd grown to care so deeply for.

But if she were in danger? Could Birkstrom Ranch be ripped away from her? Would she have anywhere else to go? I couldn't bear it if anything happened to a fellow soldier. Let alone the implications for Phantom, who was just finding firm footing here on this ranch with Eva guiding him.

She strode out of the house at that moment, wearing a nurse's apron, skirt, and light blue sweater. Her hair was carefully smoothed back and her face washed of the red desert dirt. This resembled the woman I'd known in Germany, though every version of Eva I'd seen had seemed to etch a new notch in my soul.

The woman fascinated me, but she wouldn't accept anything between us beyond that of trainer and horse owner. Her reputation and the future of the farm were on the line.

I'd respect that too.

I followed on her heels as she strode to her truck in the driveway. "We're not done discussing this," I said.

She smirked. "We are for tonight." She paused when she reached the driver's door. "I appreciate your concern. I really do." She drew a hesitant breath, and her gaze turned sorrowful as it swept over the farm. "I don't want to lose this. But there are still some lines I don't think Victor would ever cross. There's a code of honor among the families of Baker. I'll be careful, I promise."

Her words felt clinical and distant. As if she didn't consider herself a part of those families. It reminded me of Eddie's admission that Bill Birkstrom never had children. Eva was probably adopted. The rest of the blanks, I'd have to fill in another time, if ever.

Her naive assumption that Victor wouldn't betray the values of this land . . . perhaps she hadn't seen the same sort of death and evil that I'd seen in the war. I just didn't have that faith in humanity anymore.

"Drive safely, then." I opened the door of the truck for her. "And promise me that you'll manage to get some sort of sleep."

"I don't mind the work." Her eyes glittered in the dim evening glow. "The men need me."

"The men?"

"The soldiers." She tossed her purse onto the long seat and stepped inside. "I volunteer in the veterans' wing." Her voice dropped. "Though I wish I could do more. The town doesn't have many resources to help with what they've faced."

I knew what she meant. I wanted the same thing. If I hadn't already thought of her as a saint, I certainly did now.

She fired up the engine. "See you tomorrow."

I hadn't the words to answer, so I closed her door and watched her drive off.

Somehow, I found myself at Phantom's pen, leaning my elbows on the wooden fence. The sun had now set, and though the sky still had a deep-blue color, the rest of the horizon had turned haunting and dark. Phantom, with his light gray—almost white—coat, glowed in the low light. He watched me from the other side of the pen and paced slowly. Though he more calmly approached Eva to drink from the bucket, his body was still tense and ready to burst at the slightest trigger.

I knew how he felt. My soldiers knew it too. I saw it in their eyes, felt it sitting next to them.

Eddie came up beside me as if reading my thoughts. His shoulders were hunched and his eyes darted around the property. Eddie had seen too much, lost too many friends, to leave Europe without deep and abiding scars.

"You're not going to follow her anyway?" he asked.

I shook my head. "You ever hear much from Junior, Bennett, or Lucky?"

Eddie blinked as if surprised by the switch in our conversation. "No. Though Lucky was released from the hospital a few months back."

Lucky had lost his eye when we'd all thought we were safe. What was safety? What was it like beyond the war that had consumed our lives and souls for so long?

Eddie cleared his throat. "Boss, what do you want to do about Merrick?"

Awaiting his next orders, his mission clear again. Perhaps I was grasping for the same thing. Had I misheard the conversation in the Geiser? Had I assumed more than I should have?

Phantom nickered softly across the paddock and bobbed his head as if he smelled something on the wind.

I shook free the doubt in my mind. My instincts didn't fail me often, and everything within me knew that Victor was a threat.

"You know what I want to do, but for now we watch and wait," I said. "Tomorrow I'll drive to Pendleton to speak with the president of the horse organization and address those rumors." I knew face-to-face would be more effective for a circumstance like this.

Eddie nodded, the deflation in his chest evidence that he'd hoped for a different directive. "You know, I did hear from Colonel Roland recently," he said tentatively.

I hesitated. I should be telling the world of my intent to run for office, but the notion still hadn't taken root. I believed it was the right path for me, sure. Eva volunteered for night shifts at the hospital to care for our fellow soldiers, and I could do no less with the opportunities before me. We each had to play to our strengths.

Still, the thought of politicking didn't sit quite right. My officer promotions had been in the field—and a rare instance of moving from enlisted to officer ranks. After the casualties of D-Day and the immediate months following as we infiltrated enemy lines, there were vacancies to fill. My success in the field reflected the success of my men and our collective unit. It wasn't about me. It was about all of us. I only wanted the influence and power to keep my men safe and make sure they made it home.

"Going into politics?" Eddie studied me and must have seen my unease. "You sure that's a good idea?"

"Didn't we always talk about how we could do better than the jokers in DC?" I smiled, pushing back from the fence and putting my hands in my pockets.

He didn't return my levity. "Aren't we getting close to campaign season?"

"You want to be my campaign manager?"

"Have you told Eva about these plans?"

I shook my head. I needed to, but it still felt strange to proclaim that I thought I'd even have a shot to be elected to the Senate.

Eddie crossed his arms and clamped his jaw shut.

"I've never known you to hold your opinion, Sergeant Moore, even if it meant a formal reprimand."

He chuckled at that. "You do right by you, Captain, but I think you're needed here."

I'd only been in Baker for two days. And while I had to admit the town was charming, I wasn't sure I was built or cut out for country life. Philly and the Army were the only lives I'd ever known.

"August is still a few months off," Eddie said, shrugging. "I guess we'll see where things stand by then."

"I guess we will." I was hoping for a vote of confidence from my trusted friend.

"I'd better get Annie set up in the house." Eddie looked down, kicked at a stone. "Peter and I can sleep here on the porch tonight to keep watch over things. I'll call you at the hotel when Eva's back home."

I nodded my thanks, and we parted. Him to wrangle the twins, and me to my truck for the long, dark drive into town. As the miles of flat landscape passed, I ruminated on Eddie's words and the fact that as much as my gut had always been reliable, so was his. Perhaps even more so.

The last time I ignored his advice, I'd nearly gotten myself—and my whole unit—killed. Somehow, the stakes felt equally high right now.

# *Nine*

## Eva

**MAY 8**

The mornings after the hospital night shift were hard, but I couldn't waste any time in making progress with Phantom.

I slept for just a few hours and pulled myself out of bed at dawn. The house felt empty, even with the little roommate down the hall in the guest room and her handful of animals who had moved in with her.

Gramps's presence and fingerprints were all over the house, from the coffee-stained mugs to the jacket he'd left draped over the arm of his chair beside the radio. His worn-out canvas and denim coats still hung from the pegs in the hallway, smelling of him.

There'd hardly been a moment to think about the house or box up Gramps's things. I hadn't touched his room or bathroom. I'd moved back into my own room, which Gramps had left just as it was the day I'd left. One wall of ribbons and framed black-and-white portraits of the horses we'd trained. Another wall of halters, bridles, spare reins, cinches, and a few of my barn coats. The rest of the room was as utilitarian as the eternal bachelor

Gramps had been. I didn't care for wallpaper or decor that other women my age fancied.

Despite my minimal personal items, Gramps had kept stacks of mementos, old news clippings about the farm or his horses, and about a hundred wooden carving projects or small inventions. The spare room floor was piled with his carpentry patterns and plans. He'd made dozens of baby bassinets that had been gifted across Baker County, and some rocking horses with the signature Birkstrom Ranch brand carved at the base.

What would I even do with all his treasures and creations? Toss them out? Donate them to the hospital or shelter?

A stab of pain cut through my chest, and I slammed the thoughts aside.

I still expected him to walk around the corner, his footsteps to echo on the wooden floorboards.

I couldn't afford these distractions right now. The unfinished business inside the house meant little if I lost the property outside.

I stepped out into the sunlight nearly an hour past my normal start to the day. I spotted Eddie waving to Warren's car as it left the driveway.

"What's going on?" I asked as I stepped up to Eddie.

"Warren and Peter are going to Pendleton for the day," he said. "Got an early start."

"Pendleton?" I blinked. That was a good three-hour drive.

"Yeah, he didn't tell me much about why but offered to take Peter off my hands for the day. I caught him smoking in one of the stalls. I don't even know where he got the cigarettes." Eddie turned away and muttered to himself, "That kid just doesn't listen to me."

I stared after the vehicle that disappeared down the highway. I felt bad for Eddie, but my thoughts were locked on Warren. Strange that he hadn't mentioned anything the day before about going to Pendleton.

After feeding the horses, goats, and chickens, I grabbed the water bucket for Phantom and went about our new, calmer routine.

Phantom sniffed me and nudged my hand before he took a long drink from the bucket. I lifted my hand to stroke his broad forehead. His mane was tangled and his hair rough, but I hoped a few more weeks of grain, molasses, and nutrient-rich alfalfa would bring him back to full health.

Long after he finished drinking, Phantom stood next to me and swished his tail absently.

This was good. Tomorrow we could move to the next step.

I went to the tack room inside the barn, surrounded by the echo of Eddie fixing the last of the stalls. His efficiency was astounding. Now if I could only fill those stalls with new clients.

One thing at a time.

The tack room was full of dust, cobwebs, and brittle leather. It was only eight feet by eight feet, and each wall had rows of short wooden pegs full of halters, bridles, and harnesses. Below, saddles rested on wooden stands, surrounded by dozens of buckets of brushes, mane combs, and metal hoof picks.

I'd need my rope tomorrow to lasso Phantom and work on yielding him to pressure in a healthy way. A way that wasn't about fear, dominance, or power.

But where had Gramps put the rope? He'd kept a few of our prized saddles and show bridles full of aged silver in the living room, but the rest of my old saddles, bridles, and halters were in disrepair.

No sign of my rope.

I reached back behind a saddle rack, shivering at the cobwebs I brushed aside. I felt the twisted rope at my fingertips. Finally, a small victory.

As I lifted the coiled rope, my heart fell. The mice had gotten to it, a tattered section in the middle now down to just a few threads. This was one thing I couldn't wait to replace.

I found Eddie and told him I needed to go into town.

"Wait, wait." He stood up, nails between his teeth, a long

board under his arm, and several more boards at his feet. "I should go with you."

"Don't be silly." I let out a long breath. "You're in the middle of something and I'm just running to the farm store and back."

Eddie looked at the unfinished stall and then back at me. "Warren asked me to keep an eye on you."

The thought warmed me, though the precaution wasn't necessary.

Annie skipped by, chasing after my loose little goat that I never was able to keep fenced in.

"What if I take Annie with me?" I suggested. "Safety in numbers, right?"

He considered it and then nodded. "She'd probably love that too."

I gathered Annie from the chicken coop, where she was feeding and petting the hens. She excitedly jumped into the cab, and we set out for town.

The sun was nearing its high point for the day as I parked along Main Street in front of Delmore's tack store, and Annie and I walked inside. In the dim lighting, I blinked a few times.

The smiling older man behind the counter straightened and lifted his cowboy hat off. "Dear me, is that little Eva?"

"Hello, Delmore." I chuckled. "Good to see you."

He walked around the counter and enveloped me in a hug. "I'm so sorry to hear about Bill. He was a good man. The best of us." Delmore was the same age as Gramps, and they had been friends all their lives.

I motioned to Annie, introducing her as Eddie Moore's daughter. Annie nodded her head shyly, always more at ease around animals than people, it seemed.

"Do you have a lariat?" I asked. "The mice ate mine."

"Sure, I've got a few in the back." Delmore disappeared behind some shelves that looked like the cleaner, newer version of our tack room. Annie wandered through the aisles and studied the items with interest.

"Eva?"

My heart lurched at the voice behind me. I turned to see Keith dressed in his riding breeches and the plaid red shirt that he'd worn often as a teen.

"How are you?" he asked, holding several new halters and lead ropes in his hand.

"I'm fine."

He spoke quickly, as if worried I might walk away. "Look, would you be able to help me out with a new filly I need to start?"

The knot in my stomach loosened ever so slightly. "Are you sure you're asking the right person?"

"I've got too many and not enough hands." He flushed. "I'll pay for your services, of course."

How could I turn down a paying customer? But I knew Warren wouldn't like it—he didn't trust Keith.

Annie glanced my way a few times and paused at a rack of books near the front door. She picked up one with a cover I recognized, about an Arabian colt named Azam from the Kellogg Ranch in California. I had read that same book countless times, though my copy was broken and tattered at the spine.

I shifted my focus back to Keith. "You thought about what your father will say?"

"He doesn't pay attention to anything I do," he said somberly. Then he forced a smile. "I could bring her by tomorrow."

Delmore returned with my rope, and I turned to pay for the item. "The *Azam* book too," I said, winking at Annie.

"Thank you, Eva," she said, clutching the book to her chest. "I'll pay you back."

"How about you help me with feeding those goats and we'll call it even."

"Deal!" Annie opened the book and pored over the pages.

Delmore looked between me and Keith, tipping his head as

if asking if everything was all right. I nodded to reassure him. Delmore was one of the few in Baker County who had always been on the side of the Birkstroms.

"Let's go, Annie," I said softly. I turned back to Keith. "Bring the filly over, and I'll get her started under saddle."

His shoulders relaxed slightly. "Do you think Captain Hayes will take issue with it?"

"This is a business arrangement, Keith," I said firmly. "Nothing more. Are we clear on that?"

Annie and I stepped out of the store and into the sunlight. Keith hurried out after me, his hands now empty of the items he'd been shopping for.

"You didn't answer my question," he said.

I opened the door of my truck, tossed the rope inside the cab. Annie climbed in but watched Keith and me with wide, observant eyes. Heaviness pressed in on me. I wasn't getting through to Keith.

I crossed my arms. "Did you know that your father started some scandalous rumors about the captain and me? To get me expelled from the association?"

He flinched. "So that's what Hayes was talking about."

"What?" When had he talked to Warren?

"I'm sorry, Eva." He rubbed his forehead and shook his head. "You know if I thought I could find a way to be free of him, I would do it."

"You're not a prisoner, Keith." My voice dropped.

He huffed a laugh. "I was so jealous of you, you know. Leaving for the Army when you did. I would have done anything for five years of freedom."

My body tensed as a dozen of the worst memories flashed through my mind from the past several years. The catastrophic injuries, the piles of body bags, the rot and sickness festering in the jungle heat, and the battle in 1945 that nearly wiped us all out. My eyes stung.

Keith had fought his own war with a father who'd emotionally abandoned him after his mother died. But the men who had managed to make it home in one piece—they weren't always whole.

"Trust me, Keith," I said with a strained voice. "I'm glad you didn't have to see what we saw."

I muttered goodbye and got in the truck.

On the way home, Annie turned to me, her eyes wide over the spine of her book. "Eva? What is it that you saw in the war?"

I gripped the steering wheel until my knuckles turned white. "Has your dad talked to you about this before?"

"No."

My stomach churned. "I don't know if it's my place."

"Please, Eva? Mama says Daddy is different now that he's come home."

Weren't we all? "Well, we saw the worst of what mankind can do to one another."

She was quiet for a moment before whispering, "Is that what my dad saw too?"

"Yes, sweetie." My voice broke. I'd heard enough from the soldiers in my two weeks in Kötzting to answer without any doubt of the truth. "He was one of the good guys, though. He only did what he had to."

Annie lowered the book to her lap and stared out the window the rest of the drive back to Birkstrom.

## Warren

Even as Pendleton drew near after three hours of driving, the guilt stuck with me. I hadn't told Eva where we were going or why. She would have tried to talk me out of it.

The high desert and towering green Wallowa Mountains gave way to rolling hills of tall grass as we traveled north. Peter hadn't uttered a word, and I hadn't either. I recognized the crossed arms, clamped jaw. I had been that same kid more than a decade ago.

I wouldn't earn his trust with small talk. I also knew that I could outlast his stubbornness.

I'd called Cheryl the day before and gotten the business address of the association president, Stuart Davis, who was an accountant in the small rodeo town of Pendleton. The town looked a lot like Baker with stone and brick storefronts, tall windows, and expansive sidewalks. Small houses dotted the neighborhoods around the main strip of town, leading to the large railway and lumberyards.

I pulled into a parking space outside the office building that matched the address. "Let's go," I said as I shut off the engine.

Peter made no effort to move. "Why?"

I smiled. "We're going to set the record straight for Eva."

Peter's eyebrows knit together, and he followed wordlessly, seeming unsure of our exact intent but intrigued nonetheless.

Inside, I asked the secretary at the front desk for Stuart Davis, and the short-haired, bespeckled woman nodded and walked back into an office to fetch him.

A short, round man in a dapper suit emerged and put his reading glasses in the breast pocket of his shirt. "May I help you?"

I held out a hand. "I'm Warren Hayes, a former captain of the 42nd and the owner of the purebred Janów horse Phantom."

Stuart blinked. "Oh, Captain Hayes. I've heard your name, yes."

I smiled more broadly and motioned to the teen beside me. "This is my associate, Peter Moore."

Peter's shoulders straightened at the formal introduction, and he gave Stuart a cool, impassive nod.

"To what do I owe this visit?" Stuart asked, his voice hesitant as he led us back to his office.

"I'm confident that you know exactly why we're here," I said as Stuart closed the door behind us. His office was lined with mahogany shelves and leather-bound books, trophies and ornate Arabian horse statues.

Stuart cleared his throat. “Is this something we should discuss in front of your associate?” He looked at Peter, who had his hands shoved in his pants pockets and wandered around with the air of a menacing, defiant teenager.

I liked that Peter’s presence threw off Stuart. Not many people went against Victor Merrick, let alone a former soldier who brought a grumpy teenager along.

“There’s nothing sinister or secretive about our discussion,” I said, sitting in a chair and casually crossing my legs. “I’m concerned by the rumors I’ve heard, because they’re false.”

“Well, a member brought a concern to us.” Stuart sat at his desk, shifting his weight uneasily. “We feel it is our responsibility to hear out such concerns.”

“And did this member have any evidence or substantial reason for his concern?”

The man’s thick cheeks flushed. “Well, no.”

“I’d be concerned if the association took any action without due diligence.”

“Of course not,” Stuart hurried to say. He waved his hands reassuringly. “Rest assured, we don’t intend to take any action in this matter.”

“Excellent.” I sighed. “I’d hate to call on Colonel Kenneth Roland, who might have some opinion on how the association is running.”

His eyes went wide. Roland’s name was well-known among equestrians, and his reputation in the industry carried weight.

“That doesn’t feel necessary, Captain.”

“Great,” I said, clapping my hands and standing up. “In the future, if there are questions about my moral character or Miss Bryant’s, I expect you to speak with us both in person and immediately.”

Stuart stood, smiled, and let out a relieved breath. “Of course.”

"Wonderful. Shall we go, Peter?"

Peter was staring at a bronze statue on the bookshelf across the room and glared at Stuart with intensity. He was playing the role well. Skeptical. He followed me out of the office.

"Oh, and I'll see you in June at the banquet," I said to Stuart. "Though I'd hate to make the drive all the way out here before then."

I left the implication hanging, and I knew that Stuart would be careful going forward. Victor might be an intimidating force in the association, but Stuart now knew that I wasn't scared of him, not in the slightest.

"Wonderful," Stuart said with an awkward salute. "We look forward to that event and seeing Phantom in the arena."

I left the office without further comment.

Peter frowned at me as we got back into the truck. "What was all that about?"

"Fighting fire with fire," I said. "You hungry?"

He nodded.

As we ate at a diner on the edge of Pendleton ahead of the return drive to Baker, Peter watched me with a renewed spark of interest, and I felt the walls around him starting to lower.

"So, what were these rumors?" he asked.

Lying wouldn't get me anywhere with this kid. Not if he was a fraction like I had been at his age.

"Eva's neighbor knows that she's his greatest competition and is trying to get her barred from showing Phantom in the breed shows."

"What sort of rumors would get her barred?"

"Rumors of inappropriate relations. Crossing the line between trainer and client."

Peter chuckled. "Are the rumors true?"

"No." He was trying to get a strong reaction out of me. It wouldn't work.

The silence stretched a bit more as I sensed he was gearing up for another round of questions.

"You were in the war, with my dad?" he asked as he stared at his leftover french fries.

I took another swig of coffee and motioned to the waitress for the check. "Yes." I waited for Peter to ask more. We were testing each other, and I wasn't about to blink first.

He was silent until the truck was fueled and ready for the long drive back home. "So . . ." he said once we were on the main road, which stretched out to the southeast with the mountains far in the distance. "What was it like?"

"The war?" The question surprised me. My mouth went dry.

"Dad won't talk about it," Peter added.

"It isn't easy to talk about," I said.

"Why not?"

"I don't think anyone knew what it was going to be like—and things were hard." How could I put this in a way he could understand? I didn't even understand it. The brotherhood, the death, the soaring victories and crushing defeats.

"Did you ride in tanks?" Peter asked.

"Sometimes."

"Did you have friends who died?"

"Yeah." My stomach roiled, and my gaze swept over the barren horizon. "Too many."

Peter fell silent. Several miles stretched before he spoke again. "If Dad would just talk about things, I think Mom would come back."

"He's trying, Peter."

"Is he?" His voice went harsh.

I needed to be careful. This was a family matter, and Peter was already entrenched in his rebellious and distrustful place.

I figured I'd try a different angle. "He saved my life, you know."

Peter looked over at me. "My dad?"

I nodded, the memories rushing back from those first few

months in Europe, when we were learning the realities of the path before us. This wasn't training anymore.

"A few weeks after we arrived in France, we were clearing a small, abandoned town and I walked right into a nest of German soldiers."

Peter's focus was locked on me.

"A dozen Germans who were making breakfast—and I didn't have the rest of my group behind me like I should have." I could still feel the shock and remember the vacant, surprised stares of the soldiers.

"What happened?" Peter pressed.

"I fumbled with my rifle like an idiot, and I couldn't for the life of me remember the German words for 'hands up' or 'surrender.'" I chuckled. "Your dad had watched me go into that house and followed with a handful of our men. They broke in, held the soldiers at gunpoint, and we took them all prisoner. No one died that day, but I sure would have if he hadn't been right behind me."

The faintest of smiles broke at the corner of Peter's mouth.

"He always had my back. I know he loves you, your mom, and sister more than anything in the world. So cut him some slack, maybe?"

Peter's jaw twitched as if he was considering my words.

"Did your dad tell you how we rescued the horses?" I asked.

He shook his head.

For the rest of the drive, we talked about those final days of the war, the evacuation of six hundred horses from Hostau, the birth of Phantom.

By the time we reached Baker again, in the evening after the six hours of driving, Peter's questions were endless. Something had shifted within the kid. I hoped it would be enough to start rebuilding the relationship that had been broken by years of distance and war fighting.

Eddie deserved happiness. If he couldn't hold on to his happily ever after, what hope was there for the rest of us?

# *Ten*

## Eva

**MAY 9**

"Look, Miss Eva! Look what I found!"

I turned from the chicken coop door to see Annie walking up with a small bundle of white fur in her arms. My muscles tensed. Not another mouth to feed.

Annie held up a tiny, mewing kitten with dirty and matted fur. The girl's smile widened as she looked upon the helpless creature. "Can I keep her?"

I was grateful for the help on the ranch, but problems had still been multiplying across the one thousand acres faster than we could address them. At this rate, we'd never catch up.

I reached over, took the trembling kitten, and looked it over for injury. The little claws dug into my hand, and I scratched behind its ears gently. "She'll need a bottle of the goat's milk from the fridge and a warm bed in the house."

Annie nodded, bouncing on her toes. She took the kitten back and raced off just as Eddie strode up and shook his head.

"I'll never get her to leave this farm," he said. "You know that, right?"

"She might, as long as the goats and cats can come with her." Any animal not contained to a stall or coop had started following Annie around like the Pied Piper. Her flock grew daily.

"Violet hates cats," Eddie said, a shadow passing over his eyes. "I doubt it."

His voice changed at the mention of his wife, and a twitch in his jaw confirmed my suspicions. Eddie had shared few updates about Violet and how long she planned to be in New York. He had moved the contents of their small apartment in Baker to a shed behind the barn for the summer, to save on rent.

"I'm sure you'll work things out, Eddie," I said softly.

"I wish I had your confidence." He frowned and shook his head. "I'm grateful for all you've done for us."

He nodded at Peter, who stood at Phantom's pen again. The kid had been different today after his trip to Pendleton with Warren. Warren hadn't arrived yet, so I hadn't heard how it all went.

"I may never get through to his mother," Eddie said, "but I hope one day that boy will forgive me."

"Forgive you for what?"

"For leaving them all behind. I missed so much of their childhood, and he and his mother both blame me for our struggles now." He nudged the rocks at his feet with his boots, his eyes downcast.

"And Annie?"

"Annie doesn't say much, or she didn't until we came here."

My heart swelled at that but still ached for his family. The war had taken so much from us all.

Eddie looked over as a vehicle turned into the driveway. Warren. My pulse quickened, though I wasn't quite sure why.

Eddie returned to the barn and waved in greeting to Warren as he strode up, as handsome as a recruitment poster. I looked away, a bit surprised at that thought.

"Morning." He smiled warmly.

"Captain." I tipped my head.

He glanced past me and nodded at Eddie's son. "Peter still interested in the horse?"

"Hasn't left all morning." I crossed my arms. "How was your trip yesterday?"

"Illuminating."

"How so?"

"I had a conversation with Stuart Davis," he said. "That unseemly matter has been put to rest."

"What?" My heart thudded against my rib cage. "That's what you were doing?"

He chuckled. "I told you I'd take care of it."

He had said as much, but I hadn't expected him to talk with Stuart directly. Last I'd heard, Stuart lived in Washington State, not Pendleton.

"I don't know what to say."

"That's a first," he said with a teasing wink.

I crossed my arms, unable to feign indignance. Yet again, Warren had swooped in and defended me. "Well. Thank you."

He tipped his head in a slight bow.

I drew in a deep breath and started walking toward Phantom. "I was just about to try to take off that old ratty halter and see if he might let me handle him a bit more."

"Think he's ready for that? It's only been a few days."

"Well, if you'd give me more than a month . . ."

"You haven't seen what I've seen him do." Warren's humor disappeared. "Please don't rush things."

"I won't." We reached the wooden fence, and I rested a hand on the top railing. "We need to make some progress each day to keep his mind active and to help him move past being abandoned and neglected. We eclipse those instincts with new, better bonds."

"I think a lot of my men could use the same help," he said softly.

"I know." I glanced at Peter, thinking of Eddie. "I wish I could reach them all the same way that Gramps saved so many horses. The way he saved—" I bit my lip.

Peter, as if picking up on my study or the weight of our conversation, walked back toward the barn, head down and shoulders hunched.

Warren leaned on the railing beside me. "I've been thinking about that, you know. How to help the guys as they adjust to home. Some of them find the world a bit different than it was before the war."

"You can't save them all," I said, repeating the words that had been drilled into my head by every hospital administrator and commander I'd ever served under. Even Gramps had said as much.

"I'm still going to try," he whispered back, his words nearly stolen by the breeze.

The conviction in his voice plucked at a chord deep in my chest that pulled me toward him, churning emotions long forbidden. At the same time, I wanted to shake some sense into him, to convey the lessons I'd so painfully learned in the past five years.

I put my hand on his forearm instead, which drew his gaze to meet mine. "It starts with just one."

*Yourself.* Gramps had taught me that first and foremost. You couldn't take emotion in the arena with you. The horses picked up on it, acted out because of it. "Clear your mind, clear your heart," he'd say.

I'd never mastered this the way Gramps had. I wished he were here instead of me. The young colt deserved as much.

Still, I reached for the water bucket and climbed into the pen, where the light gray horse gleamed before me in the midday sun.

I couldn't pull myself from the brink of the abyss, the nightmares, and the ghosts that haunted me. But if I didn't find some way to set that all aside, I'd never be able to help this creature.

## Warren

*"You can't save them all."*

The wisdom of a combat nurse who'd faced death and impossible decisions.

Phantom trotted around the far side of the square paddock, his black eyes locked on Eva and his ears twitching. His silky gray mane danced against his neck with the smooth motions and high desert wind.

I fought down the rising fear, as I did each time, for Eva's safety against the animal nearly eight times her size.

Her focus tunneled in on the stallion. Her posture was confident and her energy calm. I saw the same competence and power she'd shown when delivering Phantom in Germany, and it set my nerves a little more at ease.

She picked up a coiled rope and walked into the center of the pen as Phantom trotted around the perimeter. With a few flicks of her wrist and a toss, she lassoed Phantom's neck.

"Nice shot," I said.

She smiled over at me. "We used to run cattle."

Was there no end to her surprising skills?

Phantom snorted and jumped with the rope around his neck, and Eva kept the line loose as he got used to the feel of it.

"Hey, boss," Eddie called from the barn. "Can I get your help holding these boards in place?"

I wanted to watch her work, but I could do more by helping Eddie with the repairs. I needed to trust her and her methods.

Her focus remained on Phantom as I walked away from the paddock. I had the sense she didn't truly know whether I was watching or not, so focused on the moment and the task at hand.

When I turned into the barn, Eddie stood in the shadows with his arms crossed and an expectant look. "What'd you find out this morning?"

Ah, so he knew, or suspected, why I had been so late to arrive at Birkstrom Ranch today. There wasn't any board he needed help holding.

"I made a few calls. Turns out Reid Erickson has a private investigation firm and is willing to dig into Victor Merrick and his associates."

"Thought he went to LA after he left Kötzting." Eddie frowned.

"He did." I shrugged. "He said he didn't mind taking a drive up to these parts."

Eddie chuckled. "We'll have the whole crew back together in no time."

It sounded tempting, but we'd been trained and honed as a group for one thing, and the world didn't require those skills any longer. Sometimes I wondered if it needed us at all or had forgotten us completely.

"In the meantime, we sit on our hands?" Eddie tapped his foot on the ground.

"We do what we promised Eva we'd do." I raised my voice, just slightly, out of habit. Eddie needed to rein it in or risk this whole arrangement going up in smoke. "Can I help with anything?" I started rolling up my sleeves.

He mumbled under his breath and pointed toward a stall at the end of the aisle. "Yeah, I was rebuilding that one down there."

We set about the task, and it felt like the days we'd spent after liberating Hostau, converting military trucks into trailers to evacuate the horses to Germany.

Peter walked to and from the barn apartment, listless and brooding. "Want to swing a hammer?" I asked him on one pass. He gave me a bored, patronizing look. Whatever progress we'd made on the drive from Pendleton, his teenage mood swings had returned in full force.

I'd never swung a hammer back then either. I hadn't learned any of this until Hostau, when Eddie taught me a thing or two. Now I found a certain joy in it.

"You got a cigarette?" Peter asked me back, and I shook my head.

He shuffled off, back toward Phantom's pen.

Eddie, who was finishing the last few nails at the end of the stall, hadn't seemed to hear the exchange. I guessed he didn't want his son bumming smokes off people. Perhaps when Phantom was better acclimated to the ranch and people, Peter might find purpose and solace there. Until then, I just hoped he'd keep out of trouble.

If it were me at that age, we'd be in trouble.

From the driveway, the sound of a truck pulling in drew our attention away from the repairs. I set down the tools and looked outside to see a truck and trailer circling the driveway and coming to a stop.

Eva was still in Phantom's pen, so I walked out to the new arrival, Eddie on my heels. Keith emerged from the truck wearing a short-brimmed hat and hesitated when he saw us drawing near.

"Where's Eva?" he asked.

"She's busy." I crossed my arms and looked at the trailer. "What are you doing here?"

Keith put his hands on his hips. "She didn't tell you about our arrangement?"

I felt the insinuation in my gut.

"We've been busy," Eva's voice cut in.

Eddie and I turned to her as she approached. Her strides were long, determined, her face smudged with dirt and her hair windswept in that heart-stopping way. Despite her small stature, her presence was a force that quieted us all.

She gave me a pointed look. "There wasn't time."

She was working with Keith now? There was a horse in the trailer. When had they even agreed to this?

It wasn't my business. Phantom was my business. That was all.

"I can take things from here," she said, turning to Keith. "This is the filly?"

Keith glanced at me and then nodded to her. "Her name is Naseem." He opened the trailer, and Eva walked in and led out a chestnut horse with tall white stockings and a thick white blaze on her face.

Eddie and I started to turn back when something caught my eye on Eva's arm—a hastily wrapped cloth around her bicep that was crusted with blood and dirt.

Peter walked up, casually looking at the trailer and the commotion.

"Are you all right, Eva?" Keith asked, as if seeing the wound at the same time.

Eva petted the filly and avoided all our eyes. "I'm fine."

Keith shot me a glare. "Was this your horse's doing?"

Defensiveness flared within me and fought back against my guilt. Was the injury from Phantom? When else could it have happened except this morning?

"Stop it," Eva snapped. "Keith, I'll call you when she's ready to be picked up in a few months."

I followed Eva and the filly, and Eddie instinctively held Keith at bay in the driveway.

"What happened?" I asked her as I fell into step beside her.

"It's nothing." She flushed slightly. "Phantom caught me off guard."

"I thought he was getting better."

She drew the horse to a stop and faced me. "Training a horse isn't always a linear process, and no two horses have the same path. I'm still making progress."

This sudden tension wasn't about the injury or my perceived lack of faith in her methods. "I'm sorry I didn't tell you about going to see Stuart," I said softly.

She blinked, and the lines in her forehead smoothed slightly. "You're free to do whatever you deem fit."

"It involved you and your reputation. I just wanted the matter put to rest, and I didn't want you to talk me out of it."

She looked toward the driveway, where Eddie and Peter spoke with Keith, all three squared off in rigid postures. "And I should have given you a warning that Keith was dropping off a horse today," she said. "I'm sorry about that."

"Does Victor know about this?"

"I don't think so." She drew in a breath. "But Keith's a paying customer, and Birkstrom needs every patron I can get."

"What if he's manipulating you or planning to say his horse was mistreated by you?" I crossed my arms.

"Keith wouldn't do such a thing."

"Victor would."

"Then I'll deal with that if it comes up."

Deep down, I knew Keith's reasons were more than just a business decision. He cared for her and wanted every reason to stay close, even if his father was a threat.

This was her farm, her life. I was only here a few more weeks or a few more months at the most.

I motioned to the wrap on her arm. "Are you sure you're all right?"

She nodded. "I've faced far worse bumps and bruises," she said while rotating her shoulder stiffly. "Even a bullet wound."

My whole body tensed. I hadn't expected to hear that. "What?"

She waved it away. "It doesn't matter."

"I thought the hospitals had been kept clear of the hot zones."

Something in my voice or my words seemed to rankle her, and she frowned. "In Europe, maybe. The islands were a different story."

I felt winded, as if Phantom had stepped square on my gut. I both wanted to know more and dreaded thinking of her in a situation like that. What my men and I had been through was horrible enough. The nurses and doctors were supposed to be safe from enemy fire.

"I'm sorry," I breathed. "I had no idea."

She hesitated. "That all seems so far ago."

"Really?"

She swallowed. "On a good day."

Good days. The days where the memories didn't bite at one's heels. Those were few and far between, I guessed.

In the driveway, Keith drove away, the dust lingering in the air for a moment.

Annie raced up to us, a little white kitten tucked in her arms. Her eyes were anguished, lips quivering.

Eva stroked the horse's neck, and the friendly filly quietly looked at her new surroundings. "What is it, Annie?"

Annie looked at me and grimaced. "It's Peter. I saw him steal something from the man in the driveway and run off."

Disappointment sank through my body. So much for thinking our conversations had meant Peter might have turned a corner.

Eva and I exchanged a look.

"I'll go look for him," I said. "Did you tell your father this?"

Annie shook her head. "He gets so mad at Peter . . . I just . . ." Her voice faded.

"It's okay," I said quickly. "I'll go find Peter and talk to him."

"He ran to the forest behind the barn," Annie said softly.

Eva started walking with the filly. "I'll let Eddie know."

I followed Annie's directions, weaving through the barn aisle that was littered with construction supplies from the task that Eddie and I had yet to complete. Behind the barn, I looked for any trace of the boy. I was surprised to see him sitting with his back against a tree not too far from the cluster of barns and pens before the sprawling valley opened beyond. He wore a black T-shirt and blue jeans and stood out among the tan brush and green grass.

"Peter, we need to talk," I said as I approached, but my words stopped short when his face came into focus.

Sweat covered his face, and his lips twisted in pain. He gasped and breathed quickly. A pack of cigarettes and a lighter engraved with the Merrick brand were discarded to the side as he gripped his leg and winced.

The rustle of the bushes and a distinctive slithering sound put my nerves on edge. I crouched down and lifted his pants leg to see two small punctures on his ankle.

Snakebite.

# *Eleven*

## Eva

My arm ached as I put Naseem into a stall and Annie followed close behind me. This morning had been a disaster, between Phantom biting me, Keith showing up at the most inopportune moment, and now Peter's truancy. I needed to tell Eddie. After our earlier conversation, I knew he would take this hard.

"Eva!" Warren's voice echoed from behind the barns. Something in his tone felt urgent, fearful.

I jogged out of the barn and toward his voice, my heart racing when I saw him carrying Peter.

Warren's expression was serious and deathly calm. "Rattlesnake."

That one word elevated my pulse but honed my mind to focus.

"Get him into the shade," I said firmly. "I'll get my kit."

I raced to the house and back without even slowing to tell Eddie. He'd follow me and find out soon enough. Nothing else mattered but immediately stopping the spread of the venom.

Warren had set Peter on a bale of hay in the aisle of the barn, and Peter withered in pain.

"Easy, Peter," I said calmly as I cut away the lower part of his pants leg and removed his shoe and sock. I pulled out a rubber tube and handed it to Warren. "Tie that gently at his knee. Don't cut off the blood flow, but it will slow the venom down."

Warren took it and followed my instructions. How long had it been since Peter was bitten? Fifteen or twenty minutes?

"Hold his leg steady." His ankle and foot were swollen, and the two small punctures oozed.

I'd known what to do for snakebites long before joining the nurse corps. Cut the wound, clean it, wrap it. Then, the hospital.

Behind us, Eddie paced and muttered to himself. Warren handed me items without even being asked. Annie cried and clutched the kitten as if it were a life preserver.

Once the ankle was wrapped, I met Warren's somber gaze. "We need to keep his foot below his heart and get him to the hospital. They have antivenom. Let's get him to my truck."

Warren and Eddie did as instructed. I took Annie by the arm and led her carefully behind them.

The men loaded Peter into the center of the bench seat. I turned to Eddie. "Follow us and reassure Annie, please. Everything will be okay," I said, squeezing his arm. Eddie nodded, but his eyes were still locked on his son.

Warren jumped into the driver's seat, and I kept Peter's shoulders steady as he bordered on passing out.

Warren looked across at me once we hit the wide, flat highway into town. The unspoken question: Were we too late?

In the open expanse of the road before us, the unknown and the terror crept in.

It felt as if every element fought against me, trying to pull me away from Birkstrom Ranch or destroy what chance we had to set things right. Were these all signs that my efforts were futile? I hadn't ever belonged in Baker anyway—I'd only been pulled in by Gramps's grace and convenient timing.

Would Eddie's family suffer from my folly? What other sacrifice might these cursed, captivating lands demand?

## Warren

An hour later, Eddie, Annie, and I paced the empty hospital lobby while Eva helped Dr. Harrison, Betty's son, evaluate and treat Peter.

Eddie and Annie were both silent, in shock.

I wrestled with the demons in my mind, old habits rearing up to cut my emotions away entirely so I could just focus on the threat at hand. This wasn't the battlefield, and I needed to stay present for Eddie and Annie. I couldn't just lock myself away to numb the pain as I'd learned on the battlefield.

Footsteps echoed down the hall, and we all turned.

Eva strode toward us, her face unreadable and her strides filled with purpose. The sight captured me, just as her competence had as she treated Peter.

Had her interventions been enough?

She came to a stop and looked at Eddie, taking in a deep breath.

In that moment, my heart stopped.

"He's okay." She smiled. "He'll have quite a bit of swelling for a few days, but we're confident we were able to save his foot."

The tension in the room broke like an overflowing dam, and Annie ran to her and hugged her around the waist. Eva laughed, but she looked exhausted, and her arm was still dirty and wrapped in a crusted strip of fabric.

"Can we go see him?" Eddie asked, his voice trembling.

She nodded, and he left with Annie at his heels.

When it was just the two of us, she pressed her hands to her forehead, smoothing the wavy hair around the side of her face behind her ears. I took her elbow and led her to a chair in the lobby, grateful when she sat without resisting.

She leaned forward, resting her elbows on her knees. I pulled a chair across from her and mirrored her stance, praying she didn't collapse.

I wanted to reach out and take her hands, but I held back. The image of her and Keith burned, though this wasn't the time or place to focus on that. I was her client. Nothing more. Even though being around her was so easy, so unique to anything else I'd ever known. I wanted to believe that I wasn't imagining it, but I sensed she felt the same way. She was relaxed, quick to joke, at ease in my presence. Or perhaps I was just searching for the signs I wanted to see.

What did it matter anyway? In a few months, I'd be chained to the campaign trail and then Washington, DC.

"Peter is in the same room that Gramps died in," she finally said, lifting her head to mine. "I hate that room. I hate that entire wing of the hospital."

"Why do you still work here, then?"

"Because they need the help." She looked around. "I thought if I forced myself to come back again and again, I might get over it."

Ah, her "form new bonds" approach. "I'm not sure grief works that way, Eva."

She flinched as if I'd physically landed a blow. I regretted the effect, but she probably needed to hear those words.

"How did Bill die?" I asked softly. I'd already rubbed the wound raw, so we might as well fully unearth it.

She looked at her hands, scrubbed clean but scarred and blemished from blisters and scrapes. "He didn't think it was anything other than a chest cold." Her voice was dry, detached. "A cold that lasted several years. Turned out to be lung cancer."

"I'm so sorry."

She shook her head. "He always took better care of the animals and the people around him, compared to himself."

"Sounds like you've followed in his footsteps." I pointed to the wrap around her wound.

Her jaw tensed, and she gave me a harsh look. "I'm doing the best I can."

"Maybe he was too."

The anger in her eyes broke and turned into sorrow.

I couldn't hold back any longer and reached for her hands, but a girl's voice cut in.

"Eva?"

We turned as Annie walked up to us. Eva's expression flipped to that of the ever-professional nurse. "What is it, Annie?"

"Peter's asking for you."

She nodded and stood, and this time, I followed her into the boy's hospital room but kept my distance. Peter sat up in bed, his hair still draped over his face but a grateful, tired smile peeking through. Eddie beamed to the side, his jovial nature shining through like a ray of sunlight in a stormy day.

How easily this all could have turned for the worse. Every day had been like that in the war, and hundreds of my men hadn't been so lucky to recover from the brink of death.

Eddie had a second chance with his son.

I had a second chance with Eva. I couldn't take a moment for granted, and I would do everything I could to see that her farm was safe, the legacy of Bill Birkstrom preserved.

At least, as much as she'd allow me.

If we didn't cast aside the weight of all we carried, it would crush us.

# Twelve

## Eva

MAY 13

"The wound looks good," I said as I wrapped clean gauze around Peter's ankle.

Eddie smiled down at his son as we sat at a small table in the barn's apartment and I checked the healing from the snakebite. Only a handful of days had passed, but Peter was a young and healthy kid, and the swelling was almost gone.

"Can I help you with Phantom today?" Peter asked, his eyebrows lifted in hope.

Eddie's face flashed with concern.

I smiled at Peter reassuringly. "I'd love your help, as always. I think Phantom finds your presence soothing."

"Dad, is that okay?"

Eddie pressed his lips together and then cleared his throat. "You still need to return those items to Keith Merrick, you know."

Peter's face flushed in embarrassment. "I know, Dad."

"If Eva says it's okay, you can help with the horse again."

Eddie helped Peter down the stairs of the apartment and then handed him his crutches. Another day or so and Peter could probably start putting more weight on the foot, and within a week, he'd be back to normal.

Thankfully. We were all grateful for the life that had been spared, and it seemed to fuel everyone on the ranch to spend each day to the fullest.

Something had truly changed within Peter, and we all felt it. He asked about Phantom constantly and pitched in with his father and Warren on some of the farm repairs. Though at first he had been so resistant to getting involved and lowering his wall, the boy now spent almost every moment with Phantom and helped me feed and water him.

But Peter's accident still replayed in my nightmares. If it wasn't the singe of bullet casings, it was the rattle of snakes.

Eddie still seemed a bit shaken by it all too, but I tried to give him his own space to process. He worked more than I felt like he should fixing up the cabins, especially in anticipation of another soldier coming to help.

Warren was picking up Lucky from the airport now. I looked forward to seeing the former private again—the one I'd treated my last day in Kötzting. I'd pulled Warren's stitches out before he left, grateful for one less medical concern on the grounds.

And at least Annie and Peter were both busy with the animals and never-ending chores. Dare I hope for a moment of calm in the chaos?

We'd put a water trough in Phantom's pen and had several days of successfully catching and haltering him. Today, I wanted to test him in a new environment.

"Can you open and close the gate for me, Peter?" I asked as we inched toward Phantom's pen.

"Yes, ma'am."

The brush with death had done wonders for his manners.

The wound on my arm was healing slowly, though it hampered my mobility. I gritted through the discomfort, put the halter over Phantom's big gray head, and stroked his neck gently.

He snorted at me, still a bit nervous with every interaction.

I walked him in a circle in his pen, testing that he'd stop when I pulled easily on the lead rope. Then I nodded to Peter, who hobbled on his crutches to open the gate fully.

I led Phantom through the posts, onto soil where he'd never ventured during his first week at Birkstrom. His black eyes looked around the expanse, as if the lack of a wooden fence around him meant this place was entirely scary and unpredictable.

"Let's go to the covered arena," I called to Peter so he could meet us there. Phantom and I moved through several fenced paddocks and the two towering barns toward the rectangular arena tucked behind the second barn.

The arena was the shining star of Birkstrom—one hundred feet wide by two hundred feet long and covered by a huge metal roof. It kept us working and training horses even when there was two feet of snow outside. It offered shade from the boiling sun and a soft bed of dirt for all the times I'd fallen out of the saddle.

Phantom trotted a bit in place and shifted sideways nervously.

I let him take this slowly. Given his history, no small task could be taken for granted. Rebuilding his trust and giving him the confidence to not fear every human or location would take time.

We walked into the big arena, where the shade was a welcome relief. I closed the gate behind us and then unclipped Phantom's lead rope from his halter. He flinched at the metallic noise and looked at me curiously.

I hoped my instincts were right, that he wouldn't just tear off and frighten himself by this new environment. Thankfully, he didn't. "Attaboy," I whispered, petting his mane.

Phantom watched me, stayed shoulder to shoulder beside me.

Peter walked up to the wooden half wall of the arena and leaned against it, watching us with a smile. "What are you doing now?"

I smiled back. Peter wasn't just brooding off to the side anymore. He wanted to know everything, be a part of every process.

"I want him to trust me, keep his focus on me."

"Why?"

Phantom huffed beside me, sniffing the new scents around him.

"So that when we go to the show arena, he doesn't get too distracted by anything other than my commands."

I circled to walk the other direction along the railing. Phantom followed.

"Why is showing the horse such a big deal?" Peter leaned his chin on his arms.

I walked over to Peter on the railing, and Phantom stuck his head over the wall and nudged the boy's cheek gently with his muzzle.

How could I explain it?

I closed my eyes and could see the arena before me—the dozens of horses all shined up, the riders and handlers dressed to the nines and proudly displaying their animals. I hadn't understood the allure either until I was there.

Gramps had explained things in his special way. He'd always had the right way with words, with horses.

I wished more than anything that he was here to explain such things to Peter, not me.

For better or worse, I was all Birkstrom had left.

## Warren

"It's more than just showing off your horse," Eva was saying as I walked with Lucky into the arena. She was speaking to Peter on the railing of the arena, and neither of them noticed our entrance.

I'd picked up Lucky from the local airport, and he was eager to get to work around the ranch. He remembered Eva fondly from her treating his eye after his convoy had been attacked in

Kötzting. I filled him in about the work to be done and the situation with the neighbors.

Lucky wore a triangular-shaped leather eye patch over his right eye despite multiple surgeries and attempts to restore his vision. He'd always been the most accident-prone of the Ghost Riders of the 42nd. His nickname evolved long before the stray piece of metal impaled his eye. The fact that he'd missed the sniper's bullet by mere inches . . . it was just another part of the lore that became Private Shawn "Lucky" Wright.

Now, in the doorway of the arena, we both went still to listen to Eva's voice. Peter had asked why showing the horse was important. I wanted to know too. I knew about the notoriety and the prestige of the industry. I knew how popular dog showing was among the country club elites, but I sensed it was something deeper for Eva. I saw it in her eyes and in the photos of Bill and her with their winning horses in the barn's office and the house.

"It's about the relationship," she said. "It's showcasing hours of unseen time bonding and fretting over every little detail about your horse. The feed, the trim of his mane, the care you take in cleaning your halter or saddle. Every bit of work you've invested over months and years all bundled into one moment, where a judge looks upon your complete picture and weighs it against the work that every other person has poured into their own horse, attire, and tack."

Her gaze drifted back into the arena, a dreamy grin creeping up her lips. I prayed that she wouldn't look my way and catch me staring. I couldn't take my eyes off her as she continued.

"It's about the hundreds of times you lose, when your efforts seem to go completely unseen. It's about the times your horse decides to disobey right in front of the judges after an otherwise perfect ride." She sighed. "None of that matters when you finally get the ribbon, finally feel like your efforts have shone through. You feel like you're on top of the world even if you just won the youth division class that had all of four or five participants."

Peter cocked his head. “So, all you get is a ribbon?”

“Yes, usually.” She chuckled. “Well, it’s a labor of love more than anything else.”

She seemed to come back to earth and looked over in our direction. Lucky saved me with a quick wave and a step forward, drawing her attention.

“Lucky!” she said cheerily.

Peter turned and smiled at me. “Hi, Warren.”

I snapped out of my reverie and followed Lucky to the edge of the arena. He looked over Phantom and spoke with Eva warmly.

Peter hobbled on his crutches, the sight still stinging ever so slightly.

If only I had gotten to him sooner. If only I could have saved him from even getting to this point. If only I’d seen him steal the lighter and cigarettes from Keith and stopped him then.

The world—and my past—was full of haunted “if onlys.”

“I need to put Phantom away,” Eva said with a glance at her wristwatch. “I have an auction to catch.” She looked at me and Lucky. “You guys want to join me? I wanted to bring two trailers.”

“Two trailers?” I said, crossing my arms.

She smiled. “Well, Eddie finished up all those stalls and they’re just too pretty not to fill.”

An hour later, the three of us stood at an auction yard on the other side of Baker, but this wasn’t like the US Army auction in Virginia. At this auction, most of the horses were bound for the slaughterhouse.

I leaned next to Eva along the broken and aged wooden fence, looking over hundreds of horses that were half starved, swaybacked, and dirty. “I hadn’t expected this,” I whispered to her.

She nodded somberly. “Gramps and I came here a few times a month. We’d buy any horse that looked like it could be saved, rehabilitate it, and sell it as a working cow horse to the local ranchers. It was steady income, and it was nice to save whichever horses we could."

The horses were of all different colors and sizes, but among the dust and muck of the pens, it was hard to really tell what lay beneath the jagged bones and drooping heads. I had to admire Eva's gumption and resourcefulness.

"How do you pick?" I asked.

She drew in a long breath. "It's a bit of a gamble, but I look for ones that don't limp, ones that look a little bit younger."

Lucky walked up with our bidding number, and the crowd quieted as the auctioneer stepped up on the block. The rest of the crowd were gray-haired, sour men with looks of disinterest. They were here to process the horses into dog food or glue.

"We can't save them all," Eva said as if to herself.

The auction began, the horses crossing the block in defeated, tired strides. Eva watched them with her eyebrows pinched together and her lips tight.

How did she handle this time and time again?

A dark brown horse plodded across the center pen. He was tall and lean with mud and manure caked to his tail. His left eye was missing, just a void of shadow as if it had been gone for some time.

The bidding started at twenty dollars. Eva lifted her number and won the horse uncontested.

Lucky turned to her with a teasing grin. "You trying to tell me something?"

She chuckled. "He has good bone structure and is at least ten years younger than every other horse so far. Maybe we'll call him Lucky."

"Well, I'm glad you see through the rough exteriors," Lucky said as he turned back to watch more of the bidding.

As I studied Eva the rest of the afternoon, it was true. She anchored onto the most harrowing cases and seemed to find something that no one else could see.

I grew only more impressed with this woman who stood so

confidently among a rough-and-tumble crowd and yet commanded such respect in the most subtle way. She interacted with those around her with a warm smile and remembered the auctioneer's name and even his wife's name.

A few of the men—those who were buying for the slaughterhouses—bowed out of the bidding anytime she lifted her number for a horse. It was as if they wanted her to save them.

Two hours and five purchased horses later, Eva led the quiet, bedraggled horses into the trailers. Their conditions were all similar to that of the one-eyed chestnut she'd first picked. One had half an ear missing from a trailering accident, and the others were starved and shaky on their feet.

As she shut the heavy metal door behind the last of them, she leaned against the trailer and let out a long breath. It was the only moment I'd seen her slow down all day. Where did she find such drive?

"You all right?" I asked. The buzz of the crowd had finally calmed as the auction grounds emptied. Lucky was checking the trailer hitch and doors on my truck and trailer, leaving Eva and me a rare moment alone. Evening set in around us, the dusky air and sky above glowing orange.

She nodded, but weariness in her eyes shone through for the first time. "These days are hard." She motioned to the auction building. A smile flashed across her face. "I always hated coming with Gramps and begged him to leave me at home. He told me I needed to face it and not hide from the truth of the world."

"I can't picture you hiding from anything."

She pressed her lips together and looked away as her cheeks flushed. "You might be surprised." She straightened and walked toward the cab of her truck. "We'd better get on the road. It's getting late."

As I drove my truck behind Eva and her trailer full of three horses ahead of us, Lucky studied me from the passenger seat. "So, what's the story with you and Eva, Captain?"

"There isn't a story."

"There should be."

"Give it a rest," I growled back. "This isn't high school. She's training my horse, that's all."

"That's not what the rest of us see."

"In the five seconds you've been in Baker?" I shot him a look of annoyance. "Keep your nose out of it."

He chuckled at my irritation. "I don't know how many of the guys wrote home about Eva Bryant when she showed up in Kötzting, but if I were you, I wouldn't let her slip away."

Lucky didn't know about my plans beyond Baker. At this point, I had no intention of moving Phantom from Birkstrom Ranch, but I couldn't get involved beyond that. Our futures were incompatible.

Each day, my own departure grew closer. I could rest easy knowing that Lucky and Eddie would protect Eva and the farm, but leaving this place would cut my own heart deeply.

I'd committed to Kenneth, and my conviction didn't waver from the bigger mission. Lucky was a prime example of the men we were trying to protect. He'd waited months for additional surgeries but never had his sight restored. It had left him without a job and without hope, until the opportunity at Birkstrom came along.

No matter how alluring Eva Bryant or how endearing Birkstrom Ranch, my fate rested three thousand miles to the east.

# *Thirteen*

## Eva

**MAY 18**

I poured everything into Phantom, working with him from sunup to sundown, especially since Annie had cheerfully taken over feeding the chickens, collecting eggs, tending to the goats, and growing her cat collection.

Eddie and Lucky seemed to find a never-ending well of projects that kept them occupied, and to my relief, they made use of the scrap piles that Gramps had amassed around the farm rather than needing to purchase new items. That man had never thrown anything away—supplies, horses, or people.

I'd sold the tractor to a nearby farm, which bought me another month to keep Victor and the bank away. The new auction rescues were settled in and steadily eating their way to full health. I couldn't train them until their bodies were stronger, which meant I was at least two months from being able to turn a profit. I had one more lead for a mare that needed a special hand from the Carson ranch, but even they were tight on funds, and we settled on a low rate.

Warren and Peter helped with Phantom, both keeping close to me after that horrible day where so many things had gone wrong.

Each day, Phantom made a bit more progress. We were able to halter him and lead him around calmly. We'd gone on long walks through the trees, and he didn't startle at every rustling leaf.

Now, however, he'd picked up a habit of kicking anytime he sensed someone or something behind him. He'd kicked at me twice now, thankfully missing. Two fence posts hadn't been so lucky. If I didn't cure this behavior, there'd be no chance of getting him into a trailer or taking him to local shows.

"What exactly are we doing?" Warren asked as I handed him a burlap sack and a rope.

We walked to the middle of the covered arena, and I pointed to a beam in the center of the overhead trellis. "You think you can loop the rope around that and hang the bag about three feet off the ground?"

"Probably." His tone was teasing.

I left and collected dozens of old horseshoes, a few hammers, and some metal brackets. Anything I could find to fill that bag. In the distance, Annie skipped around in the sunshine with her animal flock in tow.

I returned to the arena to find the rope and bag hanging in the center, the loose end of the rope in Warren's hand.

"Horseshoes?" he asked.

"Anything heavy or metal will do."

Warren's brow furrowed as I dumped the armful of horseshoes into the bag with a clatter. He held the rope taut.

I pointed to a metal ring at the side of the arena. "You can tie off the slack."

Warren crossed his arms and studied the bag. "Another Bill trick?"

"If it works."

He chuckled, the sound sending shivers of electricity down my spine, but I pushed the feeling aside. This happened more often each day.

"Do you want me to get Phantom for you?" he asked.

I nodded, enjoying that he felt more confident with his horse and that I'd been able to prove my methods to this point. We had just over two weeks left of our one-month arrangement, and Warren hadn't indicated yet whether Phantom would stay at Birkstrom Ranch or if he'd be finding another trainer. He hadn't talked about his plans much at all.

I'd need to ask him outright. The first local show was in three weeks, and I wanted to use that as a chance to prove that Phantom could be a star. The regional competition was another month beyond that. The national-level event was in Pomona, California, in late August. A tight deadline, but waiting until next year was out of the question. My farm, my home, could be lost by then.

It was this horse, or it was never going to happen.

Warren and Phantom walked through the open gate of the arena. The colt shone in the sun, eyes wide and neck arched as he took in his surroundings. In the past week, he'd put on some weight and his coat looked healthier, smoother. He'd need another month to truly look in prime condition, which meant the first few shows might be at risk if the judges were displeased. Every judge was different.

Peter and the brown-and-white goat, Patches, walked along the railing. The goats were always following one of the twins, begging for food scraps or chewing on the hems of their shirts. Buttercup was probably off with Annie and her motley herd.

Phantom snorted when he saw me and bobbed his head slightly. He nudged my arm as he and Warren came to a stop next to me.

I scratched his forehead and took the lead rope from Warren. "You'll want to step back," I said.

Warren ran his hand down Phantom's neck and then walked to the side of the arena, leaning on the wall next to where Peter and Patches watched.

I circled Phantom around the hanging sack. He spotted the strange object and jumped back, snorting violently at it. Still, he yielded to my firm pressure on his lead rope, keeping him from bolting away. Signs of our progress.

I let him circle, giving him some room with the lead rope so he could take his time to understand that the hanging bag wasn't going to attack him. After a few moments, he came to a rest and his panicked breathing grew slower, steadier.

"That's it," I said quietly.

The world around me disappeared as I watched every twitch of his skin, every flick of his tail. I waited until every sign indicated that he was ready for the next step. Never before. "A rushed lesson is a failed lesson," Gramps always said.

When Phantom lowered his head ever so slightly, relaxing and letting his guard down, it was time for the next step. I led him around in a larger circle as if the bag wasn't even there. Then I drew him to a stop and asked him to back up in a straight line, as we'd been practicing. He listened to my commands, following the sturdy and gentle pressure on his halter.

I kept my heart rate steady, my breathing calm, though I knew what would happen next. He couldn't sense any hesitation or nervousness from me. He needed to know I was looking after him and he could trust me.

After a few steps back, the bag tapped his rump and his back leg reacted as fast as a lightning bolt.

An earsplitting crash rang out.

## Warren

The sharp crack of hoof to metal sent the birds in the rafters to flight and Phantom nearly bolted, but Eva was ready. She pulled the lead gently, turning the horse's head, which redirected his forward momentum into a circle where she was the center point.

Phantom had kicked the bag, but with so much metal, it offered heavy resistance and didn't swing too far.

I smiled, appreciating Bill Birkstrom's tricks yet again.

The horse calmed after a few circles and looked at the hanging bag with wide eyes, his neck high and his head erect. He looked offended by the whole lot of it.

Eva chuckled, the sound drifting over to me and warming my soul. She spoke to the horse, and he seemed to take in every word.

She walked him in a circle around the arena, in turn stopping him, backing him up along the straight walls where there was no bag behind him, and rewarding him for his compliance. While I hardly pretended to understand her training methods, I knew right away she was ensuring that he didn't associate backing up with the frightening bag of metal.

When she again backed him up against the bag, Phantom flinched, raised his back leg as if to strike, and hesitated.

She immediately walked him forward and praised him.

Bill's methods, sure, but not every magician could perform the same illusions. Eva was a master all her own.

She repeated the exercise until Phantom flinched but no longer poised his leg to kick. She then draped the lead rope over his neck and, with one hand along his back, walked around behind him.

I held my breath, terrified the horse would strike as he'd done before. The power in his haunches could break her leg.

She walked without pause, without any visible sign of fear.

Phantom didn't kick, didn't tense. Didn't bolt ahead. He just watched her from the corner of his eye, waiting for her next command.

She pulled a sugar cube from her pocket and fed it to him, the signal for the end of the training for the day.

My breath released.

"That's neat," Peter said beside me. His gaze had been locked on Eva and Phantom too, but now he ran off with the goat trailing.

Eva took Phantom's lead and started to walk him out of the arena, then caught sight of me, seeming surprised that I was there. I loved how she would get so wrapped up in the horse that everything around her seemed to fade.

I walked alongside them into the sunlight.

"I'd like to start him on the trailer tomorrow," Eva said.

The relief of the past few moments gave way to an entirely new fear. I'd been nervous for this next step, after all the trouble and injuries Phantom and I had faced across the country each time I had to load him into the trailer.

Before I could voice my concern, we emerged from the shaded arena and the sight of three black vehicles in the driveway drew our conversation to a stop. Phantom snorted as if sensing trouble in the air.

"I'll see what this is about," I said. "You see to Phantom."

She nodded and watched me as I walked to the host of shiny black sedans. The first two drivers I recognized as the men who'd met with Victor. I hadn't seen them around in the past week despite my looking for them, listening for any news from Victor.

I glanced around for Eddie or Lucky, but they were nowhere in sight. Either way, I was ready for anything.

"Can I help you gentlemen?"

Four men approached, though why they were in three cars, I wasn't sure. A show of force, perhaps. The man in front had a barrel chest and suit buttons stretched to their breaking point. He was portly and short but had the air of authority, and he met my gaze without hesitation. The other three were looking around—for Eva, I suspected. Two were thin with black hair and sour expressions, and the third had thick glasses and a dark red beard.

"We're looking for Miss Bryant," the leader said, sizing me up with a quick glance.

"She's busy." I crossed my arms.

"We can come back tomorrow."

A threat.

"I'll take a message. What is this about?"

"I'd rather talk with Miss Bryant directly, Mr. Hayes."

Another threat. He knew who I was.

Reid Erickson had arrived in town a few days ago and was gathering what information he could on Victor and these visitors. I'd need him to work a bit faster.

"I'd prefer you deal with me."

"You have no standing here," the man growled, his hefty chin twitching in anger.

I stepped closer, my blood pressure elevated and my adrenaline surging. "Seems I'm standing exactly where I need to be."

The two slender men behind him moved toward me as if to engage, but their leader held up a hand. "We don't want any trouble. If you can give her my card, then," he said as he handed me a small white card with black text. "We have a very appealing offer, and she'd be a fool not to consider."

I prayed that Eva didn't walk up until they left—she probably would once she'd put Phantom in his pen. I didn't want to give them any sort of opening to pull her into this.

The three other men had started back toward their cars when the leader leaned in and muttered, "If you don't convey that message, Mr. Hayes, I'll do so myself." He looked around, his eyes famished and the farm beyond a feast. His gaze locked in the direction of Phantom's pen. Eva. "Next time."

"You'll try," I said.

Eva's warning about the sheriff being in Victor's pocket came to mind. Right now, Eddie, Lucky, and I were all that stood between these men and Eva. Between this farm being taken out from under her, or worse—physical harm.

"Give my regards to Victor," I called as they retreated into their vehicles.

They tore out of the driveway, kicking up rocks and dust that swirled around me. They'd be back, and they'd get more forceful each time, until they got what they wanted.

Next time, though, they wouldn't be the only ones with an army.

# *Fourteen*

## Eva

Though Warren urged me not to, I called Sheriff Lowe. I knew he wouldn't do anything, but there'd be a record of the visit, nonetheless. So at least if Victor made any sort of further threat, there might be a chance at justice.

Warren had faced off with those men, and for a heartbeat, I was terrified that he might even fight them. I couldn't bear it if Warren, Eddie, Peter, or Annie was hurt because of me. Because of my stubbornness.

Sheriff Lowe shuffled around the property, wrote a report, and told me to call him the next time those men showed up. Warren had been right. It had been a waste of time.

Warren and Eddie were planning and preparing to reinforce entry points and construct barriers. They drew up a map of the property and compiled a list of former Ghost Riders to call based on the perimeter and access points.

"I'm simply protecting my horse," Warren had said with a wry grin. "You can't fault me that. I'm entirely within my right to add in security at my expense."

There was no fighting him—and I was worried for Phantom's safety too.

"Do what you think is best," I said. "I'm going to focus on Phantom's training or none of it matters anyway."

The day was slipping away, and I'd agreed to pick up a new horse from the Carson ranch out in Joseph, three hours away. Once Sheriff Lowe left, I set about hooking up the trailer to my truck.

"Where are you going?" Annie appeared at my side as I removed the wooden pieces behind the tires of the trailer to keep it stationary. She held a small white chicken under her arm.

I brushed my hands on my pants and straightened. "New horse to train. I'm going to pick him up now."

"Could you look at Pepper's foot first?" she asked, lifting the chicken to me.

I hesitated. Each moment of delay was more work to pile on later. But even with the existential threat to Birkstrom, I knew the care of even the smallest and most helpless of creatures still mattered.

They especially mattered to Annie, who had become very dear to me.

I took the chicken, keeping a firm grip over her wings so she didn't flap free of my hold. One of her feet was swollen, with a large red circular sore in the middle.

"Bumblefoot," I said, handing the bird back to Annie.

"Will she be okay?" Annie's eyes were wide and horrified at this malady.

I bit back a patronizing smile, remembering how deeply I had cared for every chicken, puppy, kitten, goat, and calf at her age. Before life had accelerated and shifted in such a fundamental way that these matters felt trivial.

When had I lost that passion for these animals? I couldn't put my finger on it.

"She'll be totally fine," I said. "It's a small infection and most often heals on its own."

The girl let out a long breath.

"If you want to make her a bit more comfortable," I offered, "you can fill a small bucket full of warm water and put some of the soaking salts from under the sink in there. Then have her stand in that water for twenty minutes."

Annie brightened. She wanted some way to tangibly help—a feeling I knew all too well. Perhaps the youngest Moore would be a nurse one day. Though from what I had seen, I'd wager she would be a veterinarian.

The girl ran off, and I did the final preparations to the trailer to leave.

For the last hour or so, Eddie and Warren had been making a few phone calls to see if any other former soldiers were looking for work and could come to the ranch, as if preparing for battle. To Warren, this was war. I recognized the look in his eyes, the singular focus.

I couldn't let that happen. They'd just escaped Europe with their lives.

I had to get Phantom to the show arena, take on as many clients as possible. That was the only way I'd keep the bank at bay and any other sort of offer off the table.

I went to the house to get my handbag, and Warren knocked on the door and stepped into the kitchen. His gaze rested questioningly on the girl with a chicken in a bucket of water on the kitchen table.

A proper woman probably would have been horrified by the thought of the farm animal in the kitchen without having been fully plucked, but injured animals had always been a staple inside the Birkstrom Ranch house. I had cuddled many a sick goat in the living room next to the fireplace on cold winter nights.

My heart tripped over itself at Warren's insightful, curious gaze. He wore tan slacks and a dust-covered T-shirt that seemed out of place in lieu of an Army uniform.

I motioned to the chicken. "Bumblefoot." Then I patted Annie on the shoulder. "Make sure you dry the foot off well after her soak and try to keep it clean as long as she'll let you." I picked up my bag and walked past Warren into the sunshine.

He followed me.

"New client," I said over my shoulder. "I'm going to go pick up the horse out near Wallowa Lake." I reached for the driver's door, not waiting for him to protest or delay me further.

He slid into the passenger's seat and closed the door firmly behind him. "Can I join you?"

"You really don't need to," I said, putting the key in the ignition.

"You shouldn't go alone," he said, his voice gravelly and unyielding.

So be it.

As I turned onto the highway and drove south, I waited for him to mention the men who'd visited, the dangers on the horizon. The lack of any legal recourse we had.

He was quiet, looking out the window at the scenery beyond. He was good at this, waiting in the silence until I spoke first.

We had a lot to discuss. Phantom's progress, the shows I hoped to take him to over the next few months. Whether or not Warren felt comfortable with extending our training agreement. How much longer he planned to stay here in Oregon. Didn't he have a life waiting for him back in Philly?

I didn't really want to broach that question with him.

The miles rolled past and the warm breeze wafted through the open windows. The quiet was comfortable between us. A lot of things were easy with Warren. He didn't make me feel on edge like Keith. I looked forward to him being around. Just having him on the farm brought me a sense of calm, and I wasn't quite sure why.

"You were right about how special this land is," Warren said after a good fifteen miles had passed. "Back in Germany, you spoke so highly of Baker."

I shifted my gaze from the road to the trees, fields of wildflowers, and looming mountains in the distance. Warren had barely seen the surface of the splendor. I glanced at my watch—three o'clock. We had a few minutes for a quick stop on the way to the Carsons'.

"What was your life like in Pennsylvania?" I asked.

"Nothing like this." He shook his head as if in marvel. "Tall buildings, business suits, high-end parties."

"Sounds exciting." Though my tone didn't match my words.

He chuckled. "Some people seem to like it."

"Your family?"

"My parents and grandparents are part of the highbrow and high society of old." He waved a hand. "Though I did everything I could to reject those expectations."

"Siblings?"

"I have an older brother, William. He runs the family business now." His words were cold, detached. "I haven't even seen them since I got home. We've never been very close."

"Why not?"

"We never seemed to understand each other. He was the perfect rule follower," he said. "And I was skipping school more times than not."

"I can picture that." I'd always yearned for a sibling, though I was glad I didn't have one, given my family history.

I turned the truck and trailer down a sweeping road and pulled into a road hidden along a thick clutch of trees. He seemed surprised, checking behind us as if we'd been followed.

"Don't worry. We have the time, and I just wanted to show you the lake. It's a true gem of the area." I killed the engine and stepped out.

He followed and still checked our surroundings as if he expected Victor's associates to jump out.

I led us down a faint walking trail that Gramps and I had used to bank fish. The dancing of the leaves, the cool wind that skipped off the water beyond, the faint whiff of spring flowers

. . . Memories of my trips with Gramps came flooding back, and the grief of his loss rose faster than the ground when I fell out of the saddle.

My steps faltered and my chest tightened. I closed my eyes and struggled to breathe for a moment, until I pushed it all back down. Locking it deep inside where all the other sorrow, regret, pain, and despair swirled beneath the facade I'd perfected.

"Eva?"

Warren had noticed. I hadn't been quick enough to push it away. His voice was tender, patient in just the way he'd spoken my name. That gentleness threatened to rip my defenses loose.

"I'm fine." I blinked and cleared the cloudiness around my heart and vision. I had to be fine. There wasn't time for anything else.

I fell back into step, and we emerged through the tree line to overlook the wide, blue-green lake beyond. Dotted with trees and hills, the lake sparkled and winked at us as visitors.

"Wow," Warren breathed.

"Yeah," I whispered. "This was one of Gramps's favorite spots. He was a horrible fisherman. Hardly ever caught a thing. That didn't stop him from trying every chance he got."

Warren chuckled.

I sat on a fallen log off the trail, and he followed suit. "We'd camp out on that ridge there when the fishing was good," I said, pointing to an outcropping. "By good, I mean that Gramps managed to hook one or two over the course of three days."

"Father would charter a boat at the private country club sometimes, but never dared touch a worm," Warren said. "It was just a show of power and wealth."

"Maybe now that you've grown, you can explore the forests beyond Philly for something as special as this," I said softly.

He looked over and his jaw flexed. A mix of emotions clouded his face. It was the closest we'd come to talking about the future. Why did it feel strange? Like dangerous ground.

"That's a good idea," he said. "I see things through a very different perspective now."

My breath caught. Was he talking about the lake or something else?

We soaked in the splendor a few moments longer, the warmth of the sun on my skin, the healing of Warren's presence equally as tangible.

"Thank you for showing me this," he said softly. "I won't ever forget this sight."

But would he? Would he move back across the country and leave all this behind?

Bullets, snakes, and enemy soldiers alike—I'd rather face them any day than ask him that question. I didn't want to know the answer. From his earlier deflection, he didn't want to tell me.

It was one day, one moment at a time. Beyond that, the pain of loss, of failure. The potential of losing Birkstrom Ranch, of a world without Warren, Lucky, Eddie, and the kids. Things changed so fast, and I didn't want to let go.

"I bet the sunsets here are beautiful." Warren leaned forward and rested his elbows on his knees.

"I don't watch sunsets," I said. "Not if I can avoid it."

He turned to me, his eyebrows lifted in surprise. "Really?"

"Sunsets are too sad. I much prefer a sunrise. Sunrises are full of hope, promise, possibilities."

"You mentioned the sunrise over Beacon's Bluff."

Pain sliced through me. The girl who had the freedom and time for sunrise rides—she didn't exist anymore.

"Will you show me?" He straightened, turning to me, and his green eyes searched my face imploringly.

Everything in me wanted to show him the nearby ghost towns, the mountain trails, the desert plains, and especially the sunrise view from the bluff. The place I treasured and held so dearly in my heart. The place I'd die to protect.

My enthusiasm was a warning sign all its own. If I opened

that door, was I inviting something more? Something I couldn't give him?

I'd shown Keith that trail, that spot, just once. It had been a horrible mistake.

Warren? I knew he'd never treat me like Keith had. He was a gentleman through and through. He'd never betray me.

And that made it worse. I was a grenade, my secrets the shrapnel poised to tear through everyone and everything around me.

I couldn't open the door, not even a crack.

## Warren

Eva looked away and uttered a quiet "Maybe."

At least it wasn't a no. That felt like a ray of hope, like what she attributed to sunrises.

She stood and led the way back to the truck. My mind was consumed all the while with the confusing and captivating creature that was Eva. The woman who didn't enjoy sunsets. The woman who wasn't scared of a handful of thugs on her doorstep.

The lake, the view of the hills, and the mountains from the highway were all breathtaking. But nothing compared to this tenacious woman driving the truck and horse trailer.

Who didn't like sunsets?

That was something I wanted to more fully understand.

Yet I was keenly aware of how the clock was winding down. We were halfway into Phantom's contract, and the most dangerous lessons were still ahead for him. For Eva.

We drove another half hour to a sprawling cattle ranch that left Birkstrom's thousand acres feeling like a petting zoo.

Eva walked toward one of the barns, and I followed. She moved with a quiet assurance that drew people and animals toward her. Horses and humans watched her as she passed, and I couldn't blame them.

She introduced me to the ranch owner, and they chatted briefly next to a robust black mare that panicked and broke ropes whenever she was tied. The horse was muscular and impressive, so they didn't want to just retire her to pasture or sell her to another unsuspecting owner.

I was grateful for the additional horse to keep Eva busy and distracted. In the meantime, Eddie and I had made a few calls and would bring even more hands to Birkstrom. I wouldn't leave her alone in this fight, and I needed to know that the farm was secure for when I'd have to go back to the East Coast.

Eva took the mare by the lead rope, scratching the animal's neck and talking softly, before she loaded her and closed the trailer.

As we drove back toward Birkstrom, the sun slumped in the sky, dangerously close to one of those sad sunsets she avoided.

She seemed to sense that, looking over at me with lips pressed into a firm line. "Go ahead," she said with a light tone. "Ask."

"Ask what?"

She looked over with narrowed eyes.

"Well, I just thought sunsets were one of those things everyone liked." I twisted in the seat to face her as she drove. "Don't women find them romantic?"

She hummed a soft laugh. "I don't think I'm like most women."

That was clear.

"Do you like flowers, then?"

"No, it's one more thing to take care of." Her gaze kept steady on the road, but her grin widened.

"Going out to dinner?" I prompted.

"Only when you're on the road at a horse show and there aren't any other options."

"Jewelry?"

She slung a patronizing look to me at that one.

"Maybe you've just never had the right person give you these things."

She tensed. "Maybe."

I hadn't meant to strike a nerve. Her response at least confirmed my suspicions. "So, as a child, what did you wish for at Christmastime?"

She smiled and her shoulders relaxed a bit. "A new horse, of course. And there was always a new horse to train when Gramps was around."

"Not a new saddle?"

She shook her head. "I was happy to ride bareback, as long as I was riding."

My mind flashed back to the lavish, overflowing piles of gifts during my childhood. William had always wanted some sort of model train set, and as he got older, it evolved to a motorcycle or new car. Shine, luster.

Here, things were brilliant and gleaming in a different way. Earnest, natural, honest. I'd never latched on to any one thing or any hobby. Not until finding my place in the Army. I'd never known what to wish for.

The moment was right, the opportunity rare—I should tell her about the campaign and my plans in the coming fall. I wanted to know what she thought of the idea—going into a different kind of service.

We'd agreed to talk about the contract extension after the show in a few weeks. I wanted to know more about her. I didn't want to face the deadline ahead.

"So where is Beacon's Bluff?" I asked.

"It's a two-mile ride into the ranch."

"Have you ridden out for the sunrise lately?"

Her gaze locked on the road ahead, her voice dropping low. "I haven't been able to since I came home. Gramps was too sick, and then after he died, everything unraveled."

"You've hardly taken a moment's rest since I arrived."

"We don't have a lot of time." She shifted and glanced at the side mirror as if needing a distraction. “Birkstrom Ranch doesn’t have a lot of time.”

“If you never get the chance to see another one of the sunrises you love? Would it be worth it?”

She shook her head. “Now you sound like Gramps.”

I took that as a compliment. More than anything, I wished she’d let me help. What good was my gaudy trust fund if I couldn’t invest in what mattered?

My resolve faltered. I didn’t want to mention the campaign. Not now. I didn’t want to spoil the day.

We fell into silence as the miles drifted by and the sun crept lower.

I checked the mirror on the passenger side as we pulled into the ranch. A black sedan was there, barely at the edge of my vision. I could tell instantly that they weren’t an immediate danger—they were observing her movements. They’d probably been outside the ranch for days.

The bolder they got, the less time Eva would have to save her farm.

I’d do everything I could to make sure that she and the ranch were safe from this lingering threat.

# *Fifteen*

## Eva

**MAY 20**

It had been another hard-fought battle against Warren, Eddie, and now Lucky, but I was relieved to go back to St. Elizabeth's for another night shift.

Warren had been angry with me. He felt I was being too careless with my well-being, especially after Victor's associates had shown up only two days ago.

I didn't want to fight with them, but I found solace in my hospital shifts in a way I didn't out on the farm. The regional hospital, though the largest in the area, was understaffed, and the recovering veterans in the ward had become like family to me.

I went down the long hallway, tying my apron behind my back as I entered the narrow room with white curtains separating a half dozen beds. The lights were low and most of the men were asleep, except for former sergeant Eaton Price, or EP, as we called him. He sat up in his bed with cards strewn over his lap, playing solitaire as he always did. He was nearly recovered after an infection from an improperly treated bullet wound to his shoulder. He was in his late thirties and sported a scruffy beard and long hair.

"Evening," I said softly.

He looked up and smiled. "Eva."

I picked up his chart, checking the vitals notes from earlier that day. He was on track to go home soon.

My heart hammered in excitement at the prospect. "EP, has Dr. Harrison talked about your discharge yet? Your stats are looking great."

EP's expression fell, and he looked down at his lap, his brown hair falling over his eyes. "Yeah, he mentioned it."

I set the chart down. "What's with the long face?"

"I heard back from Justine," he said. His longtime girlfriend, a nurse he'd met during the war, lived in California, and they'd planned on her moving to Baker as soon as she could sell her house.

Something in his tone tempered my excitement. "And?" I pressed.

"She isn't moving," he said, his skin now pale. "At least not here. She's moving in with some new guy she met . . . her dentist or something."

My heart sank. Though I wouldn't have told him, this Justine hadn't felt like the right woman for him anyway. I didn't trust a woman who wouldn't be by her beau's side when he was sick and ailing for months in a hospital.

"I don't know what I'm going to do," he said. "I don't have anywhere to live—we were going to buy a house together."

I tapped my toe on the ground. "Come to Birkstrom for a while. Warren Hayes, Eddie Moore, Lucky Wright—we've been working on restoring the old cabins behind the ranch house and we have space. That is, if you don't mind working around horses and pitching in on the farm work."

His eyes lit up. "You mean it, Eva?"

I put my hand on his shoulder and squeezed. "Once you get

your potassium numbers down. Listen to Dr. Harrison and do what he recommends."

He nodded, and I went about the rest of my work for the next several hours.

Warren wouldn't mind the additional soldier. He wanted as many bodies as possible to defend against Victor and his threats.

The rest of my shift hurried by, and I returned to my car in the dark of the early morning. At two a.m., not a lot stirred outside the hospital doors.

I fired up the truck and drove through the quiet, dimly lit Main Street. Exhaustion swirled with the anticipation of EP joining the rest of the crew at Birkstrom. Warren had another soldier, John Bennett, also arriving soon.

The addition of so many people had filled something inside me that I hadn't quite realized was hollow. It soothed the ache of Gramps being gone, the stables feeling empty. Now Birkstrom felt like the buzzing hive of activity it had once been.

As I left the heart of Baker and the streetlamps faded away, the road was illuminated only by the headlights of my truck. Then a shimmer of something in the rearview mirror caught my eye.

The moon was faint and obscured by clouds, but as I watched the mirror, I saw it plainly now. My heart raced and my hands gripped the wheel. I paused at a stop sign before turning onto the highway.

A black sedan followed me from a distance with its headlights off.

This had to be Victor's thugs again.

They were keeping their distance, at least four car lengths behind me. But I didn't want them following me to Birkstrom if today was the day they planned some sort of action. There were too many people I cared about there.

I quickly turned left instead of right, returning to downtown Baker. The car followed.

Though there weren't many people awake at this hour, I knew one place to find the person I could always rely on.

The driver in the vehicle behind me seemed to recognize where I was headed. Their lights turned on, and they accelerated as I saw the gleaming white building and arched windows of the Geiser Grand ahead of me. Just a few hundred yards more and I would be safe.

But in an instant, the sedan smashed into my truck and sent me spinning.

## Warren

A rapid knock at my hotel door had me bounding out of bed and quickly checking the clock on the nightstand. A little after two in the morning.

I'd been on edge all night, ever since Eva had insisted on going in for her hospital shift. That worry left me tossing, turning, or pacing.

I pulled my pants on as I rushed to the door, wearing the plain white shirt I'd been sleeping in. I grabbed my handgun, held it at my side. Opening the door, I was surprised to see Betty in a thick robe and her hair wrapped in a net and curlers. I slipped my gun into my waistline.

"Captain," she said in a hushed tone. "Come with me."

I pulled on my boots and followed her down the spiral staircase and into the dining room that glowed with a few oil lamps.

My heart leapt into my throat. Eva paced in her hospital uniform, her hair ruffled.

I strode toward her, and she let out a breath when she saw me. As I neared, I saw a cut along her left temple that oozed blood. "What happened?"

"A black sedan followed me from the hospital. When I circled back to come here, it rammed into my truck." She looked in the direction of the front door. "I ran here on foot."

My blood boiled, and it took every ounce of strength not to take her into my arms and smooth the hair from her wound. "Are you okay?"

"It's just a scratch."

"That's not what I asked." I moved closer.

"I'll be okay," she whispered.

I hadn't ever seen an ounce of fear in Eva. Now she was shaken. She knew that Victor Merrick would stoop to any level.

His stooges were worse. Even I hadn't anticipated them being so bold.

Betty stepped up and rubbed Eva's shoulder in a motherly way. "Why don't you stay in one of our empty rooms for the rest of the night? We can discuss this all with the sheriff in the morning."

Eva met my gaze. We both knew involving the sheriff wouldn't do any good. But having her stay here for the night felt like the best option. Not that I'd be getting any sleep.

"Thank you," I said to Betty. "Can you see to her?"

"I'll put her in the room beside yours, Captain," she said.

I started toward the lobby door, but Eva grabbed my arm, her eyes wide. She'd seen the 1911 pistol tucked in my pants. "What are you doing?"

"Go with Betty," I said. "And stay here."

"Warren, please," she said. "I don't know how many were in the car or what they really wanted. They probably just wanted to scare me, not hurt me."

I cupped her elbow and held her gaze. "Well, I have every intention of scaring and hurting them."

"If they ambush you instead?"

I liked that she was concerned for my safety. Even if she'd been so frivolous with her own. "I'm familiar with these sorts of situations and risks, Eva."

"This isn't Germany," she hissed.

"No, but you're in the middle of a war, whether you admit it or not."

She shrank back and crossed her arms, looking ill.

"I'll be back soon," I said, brushing her cheek reassuringly, unable to resist the moment. I wanted more, but the brief feel of her silky skin beneath my fingertips would have to do.

I walked out into the cool evening air before she could protest further or slap my hand away for such a forward gesture.

I circled the block without making a sound. The streets were silent aside from the soft hum of the few electric streetlamps. Two blocks away, I spotted Eva's truck, facing the wrong direction and the door ajar.

Despite some broken glass on the street around the truck, there was no sign of any severe damage. Her taillight was broken, the bumper dented slightly. The key was still in the ignition and her purse was on the floorboard. Small mercies.

I scanned and walked several blocks further but didn't see any parked or loitering vehicles that looked suspicious.

I drove her truck back to the Geiser, parked it, and walked inside. She was still pacing the dining room, and Betty was nearly asleep in one of the chairs at a table.

"Perhaps you can convince her to get some rest." Betty sighed. "Roger is at the front desk if you need anything." Her youngest son worked the night shift. He must have been the one to alert Betty when Eva first came in.

Eva approached me, and I handed her the keys to her truck and her small handbag. "No sign of them."

"What do we do now?" she asked with a slight shiver.

"You get some sleep. They're getting bolder, and we'll need to plan accordingly at the ranch." I crossed my arms. "No more hospital shifts."

She nodded. "I'm sorry, Warren. You were right."

"I don't want to be right about these things." I softened my voice, the adrenaline that had raged in me now subsiding. "I just want you to be safe."

"I never would have expected Victor to do or endorse anything like this."

"Victor is mixed up with forces he doesn't understand," I whispered. "He might not know what he's unleashed on Baker."

"We can't let them win." She stepped closer, the nearness of her enveloping me. The steely resolve in her eyes showed no further trace of trepidation. The courage of this woman left me breathless.

"I don't intend to," I said. "The Ghost Riders haven't failed a mission yet."

# Sixteen

## Eva

**MAY 30**

Though we'd added a horse and one more soldier from the 42nd, and Annie had somehow brought home a mangy dog, there wasn't enough work or noise to distract me from Warren. Something had changed after our trip to pick up the Carsons' horse and that night when Victor's men crashed into my truck.

His words from our trip to Wallowa wouldn't stop echoing. "*Would it be worth it?*"

Well, I didn't have time for that either.

His commitment to not letting Victor or his associates win, the courage he'd shown in going out to track down the sedan, and the way he'd brushed my cheek . . . I couldn't tamp down the new longing deep in my soul.

After I'd agreed to stop my shifts at St. Elizabeth's, I sent word to EP that he was still welcome to join us on the farm when he was released. He'd shown up a few days later and slotted into the routines easily.

Eddie, Lucky, Bennett, EP, and Warren—they all watched over me like a hawk. I appreciated their care but also hated that we'd come to this point. The sooner I made my mark with Phantom and relieved the pressure of Victor trying to buy the farm, the better.

For days, I'd been slowly leading Phantom up to the trailer and had parked it in his pen so he was less threatened by the metal box on wheels. We were a little over a week away from the show in Redmond. It would be an eight-hour drive just to get to the fairgrounds. I needed to be confident that Phantom would be safe in the trailer, and that after the show he'd get back in. Otherwise we'd have to sit this competition out.

As Phantom relaxed and moved toward the trailer more willingly, I fed him his grain and hay inside it so he would associate it with positive feelings.

Warren seemed pleased by the progress, but he'd been busy with the soldiers and steady stream of repairs.

Today, I'd work with the black mare, Stormy.

She was calm and polite while being led around on the halter and even while being ridden. But whenever she was saddled, she couldn't be tied without pulling back. She'd snap a halter ring and run loose. Carson thought she could never be fixed of this—and it meant she couldn't be a working cow horse since such basic habits were essential on the trails.

I had a different theory and a trick that Gramps had used.

I grabbed the oldest, rattiest saddle I had and carried it over my shoulder as I led Stormy out of the barn.

Warren and Lucky stood near the barn entrance, looking out at the driveway and road beyond. Their faces were drawn, serious. EP was working on the cabins with Peter, but I had lost track of Eddie. He'd disappeared a few times in the last few days, now that there were more hands around.

I had some suspicions on Eddie's whereabouts that I wanted to ask Warren about when the time was right. For now, I had Stormy to see to.

As I passed by, Lucky smiled and nodded at me, though

Warren eyed the saddle over my shoulder. "You know, the horse usually carries that," he said.

"We're working up to that point." I walked past and didn't slow down.

Warren told Lucky, "Do your rounds, and we'll talk more later." Then he jogged to catch up to me, seeming intrigued.

"Have them doing rounds, Captain?" I cast him a teasing glance.

"Well, you might not take your safety seriously, but my men and I do." He seemed to realize how far into the woods behind the barn we'd walked. "Where are we going?"

I chuckled. "To the pond."

The cluster of trees split with a well-worn trail and dipped back into a lower, seasonal pond. Another few months and it would be all mud and bugs, but right now the water was four or five feet deep and teeming with plants and tadpoles.

"The perfect place for a soft landing," I said.

He snapped his gaze from the clearing to me with a tense expression. "For you?"

"No, not for me." I backed the mare to the edge of the pond. Her head faced away from the water, and she swished her tail, unperturbed and unsuspecting. There was a thick wooden pole and metal ring a few feet from the edge of the pond—purposefully installed by Gramps for this very type of behavior. It was a dangerous habit for the horses and handlers alike and one that Gramps had often treated.

Warren frowned. "I don't understand."

"You'll see."

I tied Stormy to the post, lifted the saddle, and placed it on her back. The horse's ears shot back, and her liquid black eyes showed white at the edges. She pulled back on the lead rope, and at the unyielding pressure from the sturdy post, her panic set in.

I pulled the cinch under her belly, tightened it, and then stepped toward her head.

She flung her head up, the lead rope straining. I pulled out my knife and cut the rope, and the soft sand of the bank gave way. The horse fell straight back, unable to recover her footing. She splashed into the water and thrashed for just a moment before finding her bearings, getting to her feet, and jumping toward us, unharmed.

I grabbed her sodden, muddy lead rope and pulled her to a stop.

The horse was covered in green algae, water, and mud. Her sides heaved from the shock of it, and her skin twitched as she tried to shake off the water and debris.

Warren's jaw dropped open, and he shook his head in wonder. "Another Bill trick?"

I nodded.

"Think she'll need another swim?" he asked.

Stormy lowered her head, resigned and no longer tense with the saddle firmly strapped to her back.

"I don't think so. Hopefully now she understands that the pressure of a lead rope is less scary than pulling back."

Warren patted the mare's neck, not seeming to care that his hand came away covered in pond muck. "What other tricks do you have?"

"I've got a few in my back pocket." I suppressed a smile. "If they're needed."

"I hope I get to see them."

I wanted that too. It warmed me at my core to see him impressed by my work, but that was a dangerous desire. He was my client, and that was all he could ever be. No matter how much I found the man endearing, charming, and kind, I had to keep my expectations—and my heart—at bay.

Once we'd agreed to a longer-term arrangement for Phantom, Captain Warren Hayes would disappear from my life once more, except for the occasional show and trip to see Phantom. He had alluded to commitments back in Philly, and he was a man of his word.

"Cheryl called to remind me about that fundraiser again." He shoved his hands in his pockets. "She's hoping you'll come too."

I grabbed a handful of mud from the seat of the saddle and flung it back into the pond with a splash. "I have no desire to rub elbows with the same group who accused us of an unprofessional relationship."

"Those people are usually cowards. Once you face them, they'll squirm." He smiled, those handsome dimples buried in a day's worth of stubble. "It'd be much more fun if you were there."

"Let's just get through the show next weekend," I said. "I'll think more about it after that."

Stormy perked her head up sharply, looking to the west where the cabins lay. A distant, faint whiff of . . .

"Smoke," Warren said, taking off in that direction at a run.

A stream of black cloud slithered up from the distance, and I ran behind him, dragging the frightened mare.

As we broke through the grove of trees, my heart lurched. An inferno wrapped around the first of the three cabins and roared. Lucky, Bennett, EP, and Peter all raced around it, two with buckets of water and the other two with shovels to toss dirt on the edges to keep it contained.

I locked Stormy in a large paddock where she'd be contained but out of the way, then raced up to Annie, who stood at the edge of the yard. "Where's your father?"

Annie just stared at the flames, wide-eyed.

Eddie's car wasn't in the driveway, so I had to assume and pray that he wasn't inside the cabin or hurt. I grabbed another water bucket and joined in to throw water at the edges of the monster that threatened to consume us all.

There wasn't a moment to spare. The tinder box that was Birkstrom Ranch could all be gone in the flash of a stray spark along the wind.

The heat of the sun and the flames seared my skin as we fought inch by inch to subdue the fire and keep it from igniting the rest of the buildings or brush.

After half an hour, the building was mostly a pile of rubble, but the fire was exhausted. We all were drenched in sweat, soot, and ash.

Warren approached me. "Are you all right?"

I nodded and just stared at the rubble. The remains of a small cabin that Gramps had built from scratch. "What happened?"

Warren's face was smudged and splattered with water. "Victor had his hand in this."

Fear and horror sliced through me. Could he possibly stoop so low?

"Actually, Captain." Lucky walked up, gripping Peter by the collar of his shirt. Peter's face was distraught and masked behind a layer of dirt and sweat. "We caught him smoking in the house. He dropped the lighter and it went up fast."

A different kind of fear and sadness washed over me.

The kid looked sick and ducked his head. He had returned the lighter and cigarettes to Keith days ago. So where had he dug these up?

"Didn't we talk to you about smoking?" Warren growled. He shook his head and paced. To Lucky, he asked, "Where in the world is Eddie?"

Lucky gave him a knowing look.

We all knew.

## Warren

After the dust settled, the smoke faded into the air, and the day had turned from one of hope to one of trepidation, I strode toward my truck.

I'd find Eddie. We'd get him back from the brink.

Eva jumped in as I turned the engine over. "Betty called," she said. "He's at Rocky's."

Her face was washed, her clothes changed, but the fear in her eyes was fresh. It had been a miracle no one was hurt, and another gift from above that the rest of the farm hadn't been damaged by the fire.

We drove in silence to town, though there were so many things I wanted to say. How much I admired and enjoyed watching her work with the horses. How I hoped she'd go with me to the banquet. How I dreaded ever leaving this place.

Right now, it was about Eddie.

We pulled down Main Street and drove past the Geiser and the courthouse to find a small, dark building at the very edge of downtown. This wasn't the pub for socializing or catching up with old buddies. This was one where people disappeared.

Eva strode in, unafraid and unintimidated by the hardened and rowdy men inside. The bar was simple and dirty, reeking of cigarette smoke, beer, and unwashed bodies. The heat of the day and the lack of ventilation made the atmosphere humid and sticky.

I kept close to her, sending a clear warning to each set of interested eyes. Several of them recognized her, waved in a friendly manner. Others were too far into the depths of their drinks to have good sense. A few looked at her hungrily, as if grasping for something good and pure.

She spotted him first as she weaved through the dirty and broken tables and chairs, heading for the back of the room and a stool at the bar. In the darkest corner, Eddie was slumped over the bar, holding an empty glass and hardly conscious.

I kept on her heels and reached for him at the same time.

"Oh, Eddie," she breathed, her voice full of sorrow and compassion.

My own anger dissipated in the same moment.

He clutched a photo of Violet from their wedding. He had

a black eye, a deep cut on his cheek, and blood on his lips, as if he'd been in a fight. He stared at the counter and mumbled incoherently.

Eva carefully pulled the glass from his hand and rubbed his back gently. "Eddie?"

He grunted. "She isn't coming back," he slurred. "She doesn't understand."

"Don't give up on us," Eva whispered. "Peter and Annie need you."

"They're better off without me." He put his head in his hands and rubbed his face. "I wish I'd never come home."

Eva took his elbow. "Let's get some rest, Eddie."

He jerked free of her touch and then looked like he had the spins. I grabbed his shoulders to keep him upright, and he slumped over me and muttered, "Was it worth it, Captain?"

His legs gave way. I braced myself and shook him awake enough to help him stumble his way to the truck. Eva paid his bill and followed.

Once he was in the cab of the truck, he fell across the entire bench seat and snored loudly.

"I'll bring one of the boys back tomorrow to pick up his car." I rubbed my face. "Let's let him sleep this off."

A thousand tasks waited for us back at the ranch, but it had been a long, hard day. She seemed to wrestle with the same conflict, her lips tight and her shoulders tense. She crossed her arms and nodded.

"Come on," I said. "When was the last time you consumed anything other than coffee?"

She shook her head. "I don't even remember."

"Thought so." I started walking across the street and she followed me.

We slipped into a booth at a small diner. Not exactly the way I'd hoped to take her out for a meal, but I'd seize the opportunity. Among the flurry of horses and repairs at the ranch, it wasn't often I had her company to myself. The rest of the diner was empty, overhead fans whirled, and noises from the kitchen filtered around us.

She ordered a sandwich and coffee. I knew she'd be up late into the night to make up for the lost hours this afternoon.

"What did he say to you?" she asked quietly.

I absently ran my finger over a small scratch in the surface of the wooden table. "He asked if it was worth it."

"The war?" Her voice cracked.

I nodded. I'd buried those thoughts, those questions. Eddie needed a beer or three to make that happen, and I wondered if that would be me someday. If the memories would break through my own efforts and haunt me all the same.

No, that couldn't be the answer. I had to help Eddie and others like Lucky, Bennett, and EP. We needed to help each other the way we'd been there for each other in the forests of Bavaria, the sands of Normandy. We had to live fully, or the lives of our fallen were all for naught.

The sunlight splashed upon Eva's face through the window beside us, casting a glowing light around her. Her expression darkened.

"I don't know how to help him," she said, staring at her hands folded on the table. "Gramps didn't have anything I can use for something like this."

I wanted to put my hands over hers, comfort her, but held back. Even with just the waitress and cook in the diner, I knew how quickly rumors spread in Baker.

"I don't know about that," I said. "I think Eddie could benefit from a dunk in the pond right now."

A smile broke across her face, sending my heart racing.

As quickly as it appeared, her smile disappeared. She glanced over my shoulder and frowned. Victor entered the diner and sat in a distant booth. He watched us with a flat expression.

It was time to leave. There was no telling where his associates might be.

I stood and reached for her to do the same, dropping a few bills on the table. She wordlessly followed, her stare locked on the man trying to run her out of her home.

I loved that she didn't cower, didn't duck her head even for a moment.

We went to the truck and leaned Eddie against the door, and Eva sat in the middle next to me. We both watched the mirrors until we were well out of town.

Eddie woke as we hit the open highway. "What happened?"

I ground my teeth to keep from cursing him.

Eva sighed. "Just another day in paradise."

# *Seventeen*

## Eva

"Put him in the chair there," I said to Warren as he hefted Eddie through the door and into the kitchen.

Warren's mood was dark and brooding. Victor's appearance at the diner was just another reminder of what we were fighting.

I put a cool washcloth on Eddie's swollen eye and turned to Warren. "Can you check on Peter and Annie and keep them away for at least a few more minutes? I'll get him cleaned up."

Warren nodded and hesitated as if he wanted to say something more, then left the house, his absence a gaping hole in the quiet room.

Eddie hung his head, his face pale. "I'm so, so sorry, Eva."

We'd told him about the fire on the drive back, after we'd stopped twice for him to throw up. At least that had woken him up a bit more.

"I don't care about the cabin," I said, pressing some iodine to the gash along his cheek—a cut from a broken beer bottle? "You can't be doing this anymore, Eddie. We need you here. Your children need you."

He turned away. "I didn't ask for this."

He wasn't talking about the iodine, or the work to do on the farm. It was something much deeper, something dark and inescapable.

"No one did," I whispered. "I see the shadows too. I hear their voices. I see the villages and lives destroyed."

"Violet doesn't understand." He shook his head. "I try to put it all behind me, but she thinks I just don't care."

"Don't lose hope." I put my hand on his arm. "Life can surprise you."

He gave me a sad stare. "It can also take everything that's ever mattered and smash it to bits."

Didn't I know. Platitudes weren't my strength. I quietly stitched up his cheek, put a bandage over the wound, and cleaned his hands and face of stray blood.

"He cares about you, you know," Eddie said, his words still slurred.

"Who?" I put my supplies back into my bag.

"The captain."

My cheeks flushed, but I kept tidying up the bloodied gauze and towels. Eddie was drunk, didn't know what he was saying.

"I think he's making a mistake, going to Washington." He continued to mumble.

Washington? Did he mean the fundraiser in a few weeks in Seattle?

"You need a good night's rest, Eddie." I took his arm and led him out of the house and toward the barn so he could get some sleep. The evening air was cooler, and the smell of singed wood still lingered.

"Maybe if you talk to him, he'll stay," Eddie droned as he shuffled his feet beside me. "He cares for you, you know."

I stumbled as he put more weight on me but pushed him forward. Just a few more steps to the barn and one small set of stairs. Hopefully tomorrow he'd be back to his old, jovial self.

"Washington would be a mistake," he said. "I've made mistakes too."

"We all have," I said.

His mumbling went further into the unintelligible as I pulled him up the staircase and into the apartment. He collapsed onto the bed, and I closed the door quietly behind me and went back into the barn.

Annie raced by with her parade of animals. Goats, a cat, a dog, and one particularly friendly chicken followed her in search of scraps.

The sight eased the weight and ache in my chest ever so slightly.

"Is Dad back?" Annie asked, hesitating for a moment. The new goat started chewing on her shirt hem.

"Yes, just sleeping." I glanced around. "Where's Peter and Warren?"

"At the cabins," she said and bounced off. Her shirt was torn at the hem, but she was unfazed.

Good, at least I could trust that Warren was talking to Peter, making sure he was okay. The boy was troubled, but he wasn't a bad kid. He'd worked hard, especially since recovering from the snakebite, and seemed to appreciate his second chance at life.

Eddie had seemed only more troubled by the experience. That was when his drinking had grown more intense.

I fell onto a spare straw bale and covered my face with my hands, exhaustion washing over me. Work had always been my constant distraction, my solution to the emotions and memories I could never make sense of. Yet even with the never-ending well of tasks, I suddenly felt I was grasping at the air and had nothing to anchor me.

I closed my eyes, voices and memories rising and threatening to choke me.

*"Was it worth it?"*

I tried to picture the last sunrise I'd seen—and I couldn't.

A deep voice pulled me out of my fruitless struggle. "Eva?"

Warren stood beside me, removing leather gloves tinted black from moving charred lumber and debris.

All the questions and unknowns raced through my mind—along with Eddie's drunken mumblings about how Warren cared for me.

"Would you meet me here in the barn around four a.m. tomorrow?" I asked.

I knew I shouldn't open the door, shouldn't even extend the invitation. I'd been vague before when he asked about seeing the sunrise over Beacon's Bluff.

He blinked. Probably wondering why now, with everything else that had happened in the past twenty-four hours.

"Of course," he said.

I nodded and headed toward the house. "I'll see you then."

I was playing with fire, and no amount of leather gloves or water in a bucket would protect me.

## Warren

By the time I left Birkstrom that night, after making sure Eddie was sober enough to be useful if something happened on the grounds, it was nearly ten p.m. If I raced back to the hotel, I might get a handful of hours of sleep. Not that I cared.

I woke ahead of the three a.m. alarm I'd set and drove back out to Birkstrom in darkness. I'd need to tell Eva about my plans to run for the Senate. This morning. It would be the best chance at speaking to her one-on-one. The thought still churned my stomach.

The soft orange glow of a lonely light bulb lit my way to the barn, where another light inside was on. When I stepped into the quiet aisle, my heart stopped. She wore a light blue plaid blouse, tan pants, and her hair loose over her shoulders, different from her normal ponytail.

I hadn't even realized I'd come to a stop until she turned, caught my eye, and gave a jerk of her head to motion me over. "Gotta hurry if we want the best seat in the house," she said.

Her two mares, both tied to the stalls and saddled, were quiet, their ears drooping as if they weren't quite awake yet. The tan mare, Acorn, turned as I approached and nuzzled my hand. The other, Autumn, sighed as Eva tightened the cinch and gave the saddle seat a pat.

Eva handed me the reins. "When was the last time you rode?"

"Evacuating Hostau." A bolt of dread shot through me as I realized how sore I might be for the next few days. "It was the first and only time I've ridden."

She chuckled. "Autumn is a cream puff." She scratched the horse's neck. "She'll look after you."

We walked out of the barn, the clomp of the horses' shod feet against the hard-packed dirt floor echoing around us. There wasn't another sound aside from the rustle of leaves and the gentle huff of the horses' breathing. That, and I'm sure my heartbeat was loud enough for the whole county to hear.

Phantom nickered from his pen, a ghostly figure in the dim light but glowing with his brilliant light gray coat. It was good to see him settled, happy, and safe. I'd come around to Eva's belief that he was destined for more. For the show arena and renown.

At the edge of the paddocks, Eva turned and motioned to the saddle. "Let's go, Ghost Rider."

We mounted up, and she led the way. Autumn followed Acorn without any direction from me. From the way Eva's shoulders relaxed, I felt even further at ease.

Whatever had prompted her to ride today and invite me along, I wasn't quite sure. But I thanked God for the opportunity.

The valley was flat before us, lined with trees at the edges and sloping up into a tall hill that disappeared into a blanket of foliage. I'd bet that was Beacon's Bluff, as it pointed directly to the east.

The morning air was crisp and fresh. Rabbits darted from tree to bush in the distance.

After an hour, the ground rose upward and we trekked toward the sky with no end in sight.

Eva checked over her shoulder to see I was still following, and her hesitant, timid smile captured me with a power I didn't expect. The glow of light on her skin, the dark locks of hair loose down her back—she was stunning.

The rest of the trees, flowers, and splendor passed by me without cutting through that vision. My thoughts drifted to yearning for more moments like this. What would life be like with Eva at my side?

The incline leveled out, and a clearing loomed ahead in the trees. As the trail widened, Eva reined her horse beside mine. I didn't want this to ever end. Once the sun came up, we'd need to get back to all the demands of the day.

"We can leave the horses here." She pulled Acorn to a stop, and Autumn stopped automatically. Eva dismounted and tied her horse to a wooden post.

I slowly swung my leg over the back of Autumn, already feeling the ache throughout my lower body. The rest of today helping Eddie redo the cabin roofing might be painful.

Eva tied Autumn's reins for me and then walked into the clearing. The sky had lightened to a bluish hue, the sunrise mere moments away.

Beyond, another valley slept peacefully in the shadows of the dawn, circled by mountains in large waves of earth and soil frozen forever in mid-crest. The landscape was scattered with small trees and sagebrush below and towering evergreens on the higher elevations. A blanket of flowers wove a tapestry of yellow, pink, and purple. It felt like the quintessential Western setting for any cowboy dime novel.

Ahead, in a gap between the trees, stood a tall, handmade

wooden platform. She climbed up the ladder and I followed, surprised by the sturdiness despite the cracked, aged lumber.

"Did Bill build this for you?"

"His father built it for him. We had to replace a few boards over the years, but it's a Birkstrom family creation." She winked. "Keeps you from sitting on the ground with the snakes."

On the top, she sat on the edge and hung her legs over the side. The wind blew her dark waves as if caressing the smooth strands.

I sat next to her at an appropriate distance. "Why now?" I didn't want to shatter the fragility of the moment, but I needed to know.

Her gaze pored over the horizon, and she pressed her lips together, pensive. "You were right at the lake." She turned her head to me and touched her chin to her lifted shoulder. "Is it really worth it all if I don't take these moments?"

Her words spread warmth through me. "So, why'd you invite me?" More treading onto thin ice.

"I wanted you to see what it is you're helping to protect."

The sky began to turn pink, orange, red. The light spilled over the tan dirt and green trees and turned into a kaleidoscope of colors. The sun's rays grew stronger with each passing second, turning the hues from dark to brilliantly bright.

It was breathtaking.

My gaze locked onto Eva, her pale blue eyes watching the sunrise and a hint of pain evident in her creased brow.

I cared about this land and the farm as a sanctuary for Phantom when no other barn would take him. But that wasn't the only reason, or even the main reason, for bringing in Eddie and the rest.

I cared about her.

What was I to make of these feelings? What could I do when her life was here and mine would be three thousand miles away? If I failed to be elected, Kenneth had urged me to strive for a mayorship or governorship and then run in the next cycle. He also had felt very confident that my chances were more than certain. If I was elected, I'd serve for six years in Washington, DC. Anytime the Senate wasn't in session, I'd need to be back in Philadelphia.

How could I ask her to move her life or pause it if we were to strive for something more?

I couldn't. Her life and dreams were here in the soil, trees, and sky.

There simply wasn't a future for us.

The sunrise splashed over her soft skin and painted her hair in warm shades of amber and pink.

She turned and seemed surprised by my study. "Something wrong?"

I opened my mouth to confess my future plans, but a distant crash and rumbling sliced through the silent morning. We turned toward the sound, my heart racing and my hand going to her arm protectively.

"Is that typical?"

She shook her head. "Not this far into the property."

So much for the perfect moment to talk with her. So much for a peaceful sunrise for Eva to feel more grounded and connected to her home. There was no peace for her until the threat of the Merricks stealing her land by finances or force was neutralized.

I wouldn't leave her alone until I knew she was truly safe, which meant I had little time to get to the bottom of this.

# *Eighteen*

## Eva

"Let's get to the horses," I whispered.

Warren helped me to my feet, and we climbed down the ladder and retrieved the horses. His grip was firm and reassuring.

My mind whirled at the immediate shift from this moment watching the sun crest the hills beyond, sensing Warren was about to share something important, to the suspicious noise that shattered it all.

I untied both horses and jumped into Acorn's saddle. "Let's go check it out." Once Warren was also mounted, I swung my horse toward the noise. "Hold on tight. Autumn will just follow me."

"Eva, you should go back to the house," he said.

I kicked Acorn's sides, and we bolted into the woods, Autumn's hooves thundering behind us. Another loud bang rang out along with the rumbling of vehicles. Neither Eddie nor the other men had reason to be this far into the eastern edge of the property. This was the best view of the sunrise, sure. But it was also the border of the Merricks' property.

I glanced behind and saw that Warren leaned forward against the horse's neck and moved naturally with her fast gait.

I wouldn't go back and cower at the house, letting him fight my battles alone.

Branches whipped my face and I ducked, trusting Acorn to lead the way through the trees. When we burst out of the thicket, I drew her to a stop. Warren and Autumn stopped beside us, both horse and rider breathing fast.

Before us, several black vehicles sped away in a huff of dust, leaving behind skid marks and a gate in pieces.

My heart hammered and my mind raced at the possibilities. What had they been doing? I looked down the roadway, which led to the farm.

Eddie. The kids. Phantom.

"Let's get back to the barns," Warren said as if his thoughts mirrored mine.

We raced back, the horses drenched in sweat, my own face covered in dust and scratches from the branches.

"Eddie!" I shouted, jumping off the horse and leading her behind me. "Bennett!"

Eddie came bursting out from the barn with a shotgun in hand, wearing his pants and a dirty T-shirt, the suspenders loose over his waist. "Eva? Warren? What is it?"

EP ran out too, looking to Warren. Warren handed me Autumn and strode toward the house, pulling a sidearm from the back of his waist.

"Everyone okay?" I asked.

"As far as I know. Why?" Eddie spun around, looking for a threat.

"Warren?" I called after him, running with him to the house.

He held up a hand, came to a stop. "Let me clear the house. You stay with Eddie."

Fear jumped into my throat at the thought of him facing some unknown danger alone. I grabbed his arms and shook my head. "No, wait for the others."

"Don't worry." He stepped closer and brushed my cheek with

his thumb. His voice was confident and instantly calmed me down. "Stay here and check in on Phantom."

I knew deep down he'd faced more dire odds and larger threats than this—but he wouldn't be here, wouldn't be the target of Victor and his allies, if it weren't for me. If it weren't for my potentially futile attempt to save this ranch.

I loosened my grip, and he slipped away, disappearing into the house. Lucky and Bennett checked all the other barns while I waited beside Phantom's paddock. A few long, tense moments later, Annie and Warren walked out.

Another hour passed as we searched every inch of the property and came up with nothing out of place, no sign of damage or sabotage.

By the time the others returned to their regular tasks, I'd put Acorn and Autumn away but paced the barn aisle with my arms wrapped around my middle. I couldn't fight down the nervousness and rising dread.

Who was in those cars? Why were they on my property? Were they the same ones who'd hit me on Main Street? What was I doing thinking I could fight Victor Merrick once he'd set his mind to something?

"Eva?"

I jumped at Warren's voice behind me.

"I'm having second thoughts about all of this." I motioned to the apartment and cabins beyond. "What if someone gets hurt?"

"Calm down." He frowned, and his eyes searched my face. "Each of them knew what they were signing up for."

"Peter and Annie didn't." I looked at Phantom's paddock. "Phantom has probably improved enough to find another barn, a different trainer."

"You're giving up already?" he fired back, taking two steps closer to me and trapping me with his gaze. His tone shifted from consoling to challenging.

"Of course not." I ground my teeth together. "I just want

you, Annie, Peter, Phantom, and the rest of the Ghost Soldiers out of the crosshairs."

"Too late for that." He tipped a grin. "You think there's any chance we'd leave you here to just fend for yourself? We're too invested. Once these men get on a mission, they finish it."

I knew it might be the same for Victor.

I rubbed my face, turning away from him and walking into the office. I sank into one of the wooden chairs. Warren followed me, pulling a chair across from me and sitting.

"I know this fear," he said, his eyes clouding with intensity. "The burden and responsibility when lives are in your hands. We're not following orders blindly here."

They also didn't have all the information. They didn't know the sordid history of my family. I didn't deserve their support and kindness.

"We've called in a few more Ghost Soldiers who need some work—Mason and Junior."

Relief etched through the stone wall in my heart. More men might help to even the odds. It also meant more lives I was putting in harm's way.

"It'll be okay," he said. "None of this diminishes the power of that sunrise. Or the need for you to keep up those morning rides."

I closed my eyes and pictured the tapestry of orange, red, and yellow. It had been as beautiful as I'd remembered, in a world where so little lived up to the memory.

"What were the men in those cars doing at that gate?" I asked.

"I'm guessing they were scouting. We'll set up better watch posts and reinforce all the gates with metal instead of wood."

"Birkstrom isn't set up to be a fortress." Too much flat land, too many trees, too many exits and trails.

"We'll do what we can."

I laughed, unable to put up any more of a fight. "I guess there's no way I'm getting rid of you, huh?"

Something flashed across his face, and he leaned back.

Suspicion flared inside me. There was something he wasn't telling me. Something big. I'd felt as much during our conversation at Beacon's Bluff, and now I knew it.

But who was I to judge? I had my own secrets. It was just another reminder of the unbreakable barriers between us.

## Warren

JUNE 7

"What have you found out?" I asked Reid.

We'd met at a small diner in La Grande, almost two hours north of Baker, to avoid Victor's men getting any possible whiff of my angle. Reid Erickson had always had a knack for intelligence gathering and interrogation. He looked the part now, with a tipped fedora and suit as if he were Humphrey Bogart in *The Maltese Falcon*. He even had the same tall forehead as Bogart.

Reid had been digging into Merrick for over three weeks. Birkstrom now had an army of seven crammed into the two tiny cabins and barn apartment while we rebuilt the third and fourth. We hadn't had an incident since that morning ride I took with Eva.

"Victor Merrick is working with a group of investment moguls originally from New York," Reid said, reading from his notepad full of scribbles. "They're hoping to make Baker a destination once more like it was in the gold rush days."

"Any ties to the Mafia?"

"There are always ties to the Mafia."

"How did Victor get involved?" I swirled my now-cold coffee.

"Debt. He's leveraged or sold everything of value just to stay afloat. They want Birkstrom Ranch to put in a housing development. It's a prime location. Beautiful views, from what I hear."

I nodded. The scenery from Beacon's Bluff was still seared

into my mind. If a house or two were placed on that bluff, it would fetch top dollar.

"Is Keith involved?"

"Not that I've seen." Reid drew in a long breath. "He keeps to himself, and I couldn't dig up much about him. The horses are his life."

I wanted something definitive on Keith so I knew whether he was trustworthy or not. Eva's loyalty to him still bothered me, though I wasn't sure if it was my gut or jealousy.

"There's something else you should know," Reid said, lowering his tone even though we were the only souls in the diner aside from the waitress and cook. "They're watching you too. I've seen several different cars and a few different faces, but you've got a tail."

I nodded. I'd suspected this for some time, ever since our drive to pick up Stormy. Was it in relation to Eva? Or was it something tied to my political ambitions? Kenneth had warned me that my life would soon be under scrutiny.

"Want me to stay on that and see if I can catch them and learn their identity?" Reid asked.

I looked out the window at the flat, barren desert beyond. "I only care if it's a threat to Eva."

Reid winced and flipped his notepad to a different page. "I wanted to ask you about the girl too. You know she's not a Birkstrom by blood, right?"

"I didn't hire you to investigate her."

"Some of what I found might be relevant, Captain."

"I don't want to hear it," I said. My heart pounded and my thoughts were spinning at the possibilities. What had he uncovered? Would it change my perspective on her?

No—nothing could. Besides, Reid was only here to give me the information I needed to protect her.

"Okay. I'll keep looking into Victor and report back in another week." He stood and dropped a bill on the table to cover his coffee, which he hadn't touched either. "Just be careful, Captain. I wouldn't get too attached to the lass."

I wouldn't take the bait, wouldn't flirt with that temptation to invade her privacy. "Keep to your assignment, Reid." I paused. "Please."

"Got it."

Reid's comments consumed me as I drove back to Baker, the hot air swirling about the cab and doing little to ease my rising anger at Victor. Though the past week had been quiet, there was a palpable tension in the air. Eva kept busy with Stormy and Phantom and all of Annie's rescued creatures, but it was only a matter of time before Victor made another move.

A land development had the potential for a big payout. Desperate men could do terrible things.

I'd dug into more of the loan details and the local bank to ensure they were free of external influences. A lifetime watching my father's business dealings had left me with enough of a sense to know whether Eva was dealing with an honest broker or not. From what I'd found out, at least the terms and bank were clean. Bill had taken a second mortgage, which meant the farm was truly underwater, but Merrick's associates didn't seem to influence the bank in any further way.

As for whether Eva could get some of her veterans' benefits to get better terms, she was right about the paperwork only running into brick walls. There weren't enough former nurses trying to save their family's horse ranch to provide any precedence.

I arrived back at the ranch to see Eva and Phantom walking around the driveway, the trailer connected to her truck and the back door open. Phantom's neck was arched but his focus was on Eva. He listened to her, watched her for cues.

Over the past week, despite his eating in the trailer and living with it in his pen, Phantom had yet to willingly walk into the trailer whenever it was attached to a vehicle. He seemed to know the difference.

Eva's shoulders slumped as I approached. She greeted me with a tired, defeated smile.

"Going that well, huh?" I said.

"I've never met such a stubborn horse." She huffed. "We're running out of time."

The show in Redmond was tomorrow. We needed to leave in the morning.

Annie, who was always skipping from one side of the property to the other with her long stream of animals at her side, wandered up and waved to me. "Morning, Mr. Hayes."

Patches walked up to Eva and started nibbling on the lead rope in her hands. Eva sighed and shook her head at the goat. "You have any bright ideas, Patches?"

Annie giggled.

I held back from reassuring her that it would be fine if we skipped the show—that all I really cared about was Phantom's well-being and her safety. I knew it would only drive Eva harder to prove me wrong.

Then something seemed to click in Eva's expression. She stared at the goat and looked at the trailer as if seeing it anew.

"Annie, would you fetch a halter and lead for Patches? There are a few goat-sized ones in the tack room."

Annie nodded and jogged off, always happy to be assigned a task.

"What are you thinking?" I asked.

"I'm not sure if it will work." She stared at the trailer as Patches moved from chewing on the lead rope to biting at the hem of her shirt.

Annie reappeared with a halter and Eva placed it over the goat's face, careful of his floppy ears. She wordlessly handed Phantom's lead rope to me and then took Patches toward the trailer. She loaded the baying animal and then came back for Phantom.

She gave me a hesitant smile. "Some horses like to travel with a buddy."

I took Annie's shoulders and guided her to the edge of the driveway to give the horse and trainer some space.

Phantom stared at the trailer, hearing the continual calling from the goat.

I held my breath as Eva walked him straight toward the open door. His ears pointed forward. He seemed intrigued to see Patches in the trailer.

Eva walked with long, confident strides and no hesitation. Unlike every other attempt where Phantom had skidded to a stop, he clomped straight into the metal box and nickered a greeting to the goat.

Eva tied off his lead rope inside the trailer, walked out, and closed the door behind the horse. She locked the door and beamed with her eyebrows lifted in surprise.

Annie and I clapped, which startled a few of the animals at the girl's side. The chicken darted away, squawking.

Eva walked over to us and crossed her arms. "We'll give him a few minutes in there and unload, then try again this evening."

"Bill would be proud," I said, enjoying the flush that crept up her cheeks at my compliment.

After she opened the door and pulled Phantom out of the trailer, calmly and without incident, she turned Patches loose, and Annie raced off again with her pack intact. Phantom went back to graze in his new, larger pasture.

I followed Eva into the barn, the shade easing the heat of the day just a tad.

Now the countdown truly began—only twenty-four hours before the show. Eva paced the office, putting a thin leather show halter in a bag along with a few papers and brushes. A blue suit jacket, pants, and a pressed blouse hung next to the door and all the framed photos of Bill and the horses he'd trained over the years.

I leaned against the desk and tried to suppress a smile at her obvious nerves.

She caught my study and shot me a glare. "Stop that. I'm trying to exude professionalism and proficiency here."

"You don't have anything to prove to me, Eva."

"Maybe," she said and grew quiet. The office seemed to fold in around us. "But I have everything to lose."

I ached for her and the dire reality that she faced. Still, I had all the confidence that she would be able to make a name for herself and resurrect the prestige of Birkstrom Ranch. If Victor didn't sabotage and steal it from her.

She'd fight until the very end, even if it killed her.

# *Nineteen*

## Eva

**JUNE 8**

We pulled into the fairgrounds just as the evening light began to fade. Annie had long since fallen asleep on Warren's shoulder during our eight-hour drive from Baker.

Phantom hadn't thrashed or shaken the trailer through the long winding roads of eastern and central Oregon. But it was still warm out and we were all tired from the long drive. I could only hope that he'd lean on our training from the past four weeks and remain calm in this new environment.

Dozens of people and other horses milled about the grounds, all preparing for the next day of showing. Warren and I got out of the truck's cab while Annie woke and stretched sleepily.

In my truck, an hour or so behind us, newly arrived Ghost Rider Mason Phillips would come to stand watch at the stalls overnight. Eddie, Peter, and the rest had all stayed behind at the farm.

Warren looked around at the grounds, presumably searching for any sign of the Merricks. Keith would certainly be here, but from what Cheryl had told me, Victor hardly appeared on the circuit anymore now that Keith managed the farm.

I looked through the metal slats of the trailer, relieved to see Phantom standing, alert but not frantic, and Patches bleating softly at his feet. Annie had made me promise her a hundred times that Phantom wouldn't squish the goat. I had been confident he wouldn't, but the confirmation set me further at ease.

"I'll register at the show office and see where our stall assignment is," I said to Warren. "Will you stay with Annie and the horse?"

He hesitated as if not wanting to leave me alone.

"Don't worry," I said, backing away and holding his gaze. "Victor won't try to take me out in front of a hundred other competitors."

"You give him too much credit." He crossed his arms, his frown deepening.

I walked across the sprawling gravel and pavement between two large arenas, to where a small office was tucked into the side of an oval dirt arena lined with raised benches for the onlookers. A bolt of excitement shot through me. Victor himself couldn't bring my mood down. It had been so long since I'd stepped foot in the show ring. Now I was here with none other than Janów Podlaski–bred war survivor Phantom.

A line of a half dozen other trainers and riders streamed out from the square office, and I fell into place behind a few faces that were familiar. But no one seemed to recognize the Birkstrom girl after five years of war had aged her.

That was fine. I wanted to focus on my thoughts, my step-by-step plan for the next day, when Phantom would make his mark. Hopefully in the best way possible.

"It's nice to see you smile again," a voice said over my shoulder.

My body tensed and I turned around, thoroughly unsurprised to see Keith behind me, his blond hair brushed aside and his perfectly white teeth gleaming at me.

"Hard to find a reason to smile when your father is trying to take my land," I said, turning back toward the office and avoiding the heat of his gaze on my neck.

"He wants to buy it." Keith shifted behind me, lowering his voice. "It's just business."

"Not for me."

"I told him that you wouldn't agree, that he should give up. He's stubborn."

"He's more than that," I whispered. Malicious. Manipulative. Evil.

I reached the front of the line, paid the entry fees, and received Phantom's stall number for the night and the numbered paper armband for our class in the morning. I whirled away from the desk, striding long to avoid Keith, but he jogged alongside me.

"Can't we just talk, Eva? We used to talk all the time."

I turned around, stepping out of the wide doorway that was visible to the parking lot and Warren. I didn't want to create a scene.

"Do you want to explain why your father's associates came and threatened me and my client? Why they broke through the east gate and trespassed? They chased me and hit my car in the middle of the night."

His jaw fell open. "I had no idea."

"I know you're not your father," I said, my voice cracking. I wanted to believe such things were true. That I wouldn't and couldn't be held to the sins of my own parents. While I had been a child when my parents committed their crimes, Keith was now a grown man. He couldn't be so oblivious. "If this doesn't stop, there's going to be blood on his hands."

"He'd never hurt—"

"Really?" I moved in closer. "How many times has he hit you, Keith? You don't think he's capable of violence?"

Keith shook his head and turned away. He might have known my darkest secret, but I also knew his. I doubted that Victor still beat him like he had when Keith was a child, but I saw the depth of fear in Keith's eyes.

"I'll do what I can," he said. "Things are tight around the farm, and he keeps talking about his legacy in life. He feels desperate."

"I know the feeling." I released a laugh and started to walk away. "I need to go unload Phantom."

"Hey, Eva," he called out.

I froze in the towering doorway of the arena and turned to look at him.

He smiled that boyish grin I'd known most of my life. "Good luck tomorrow. I'm glad you'll be in the arena again."

"Me too." I smiled, my heart softening ever so slightly. "See you there."

## Warren

I sensed the shift in Eva's mood right away, but she quickly set about unloading Phantom and getting him to his stall for the night. After she closed the stall door, she darted a look at Annie, who wandered the long row of stalls in the barn adjacent to the larger covered arena and looked at all the horses.

"Keith's here," she said. "I don't think Victor is."

"No doubt his men are watching you and waiting for their opportunity."

"I know." She looked at Phantom nervously.

"Mason will be here soon, and we can trust him to keep a sharp eye." I knew so from our times on the front lines. Mason Phillips had arrived a few days ago and brought his Bible and cowboy church services out to the pasture. He was the one who'd guided my faith back during the war after a childhood of rebellion and an adulthood in a fog.

She rubbed her forehead. "I'm just so tired of looking around every corner."

I sensed she meant more than just the past month of Victor's threats.

I fought back the urge to take her in my arms and reassure her. I couldn't cross that line, especially not while so many others wandered nearby.

Annie skipped up and smiled into the stall. "They look happy," she said about Phantom and Patches.

And they did. Phantom's head was low, relaxed, and his ears twitched from side to side. This was a far cry from the horse I'd brought to Birkstrom only a month ago.

"Well," I said, "no matter what happens tomorrow, we should discuss that longer-term training contract. You've worked some magic."

Eva's eyes lit up. "Really?"

"Absolutely."

Once Mason arrived and we'd departed the fairgrounds, we grabbed a meal at a nearby diner before reaching the hotel for the night. We checked in, Eva and Annie sharing a room and me next door to them. Annie ran into the room, but Eva lingered at the door.

"I'm too nervous to sleep," she said. Her chin tipped up and her eyes sparkled in the dim hallway. "Would you want to go for a walk around town?"

I tried not to sound too eager. "Of course."

She told Annie to lock the door and stay in the room no matter what, and then we left the hotel to walk down the long stretch of the main street, which felt a bit reminiscent of Baker with brick buildings and a variety of shops and diners. Coca-Cola signs flashed above the tavern across from the Cent-Wise Drugstore. Lights glimmered now that the sun had set, though most businesses had closed for the night and few cars puttered down the street.

She put her hands in her pockets, and her gaze seemed to absorb everything as we strolled by.

"You don't sleep much, do you?" I asked. Whenever I left the ranch in the evenings, she would still be working or doing chores, and she was always there when I showed up right at dawn.

"I hate sleeping."

Hated sunsets, hated sleeping.

"You have nightmares."

She nodded, keeping her gaze straight ahead.

"The war?"

"It's been most of my life—some things from my childhood that I'd rather not discuss." She flashed a sad smile. "Tragedies are tiresome."

There was nothing tiresome about this woman. I wanted to learn more, dig deeper.

"Gramps hated it," she said. "I would sneak out of the house at night and play in the barn."

"I snuck out at night, but for different reasons," I said, wiggling my eyebrows.

"That doesn't surprise me. I'm guessing you like to break the rules."

"Only the dumb ones."

We swerved around a small bench on the sidewalk, each taking a different side and then coming back together, her hand brushing mine ever so slightly. We ended up a bit closer than when we'd started.

"When did you join the Army?" she asked.

"After Pearl Harbor," I responded.

"Same." She smiled. "And how did you adapt to military life? You, the rule breaker?"

"It seemed to just click somehow. I hadn't been close to my brother growing up, but I found a connection with my fellow soldiers right away."

"I heard you broke a few regulations once you were in Europe."

The bemused smile she flashed in my direction made my heart stumble all over itself.

"You heard about that, huh?"

The streetlights buzzed on around us, and the amber glow caressed her face.

"The boys couldn't stop talking about the 42nd's antics in Kötzting."

"Well, they're a gossipy bunch," I said.

"Is it true that you charged a sniper nest all by yourself?"

"That wouldn't have been proper protocol."

"Eddie's still mad at you for that."

"Well, to be honest," I said, rubbing the back of my neck, still able to feel the scar from the stray bullet that almost took my life, "I should have listened to him."

She fell silent, kicking at a small pebble on the sidewalk.

"What was the Pacific like?" I asked. "Compared to what you saw in Kötzting?"

"Humid." Her head lolled to the side as she seemed to drift back to those islands. "So many bugs. So many injured. I wasn't sure any of us would ever make it out of there."

"I'm so sorry," I said. I'd spent enough time at field hospitals with my injured soldiers that I knew well what the nurses faced and the horrible burden they bore.

"I thought things would be different." She stopped walking and faced me. "Coming home. I'm not sure I really left those islands behind."

My throat was thick with emotion. "I know what you mean."

"At least you and your men were able to make such a difference at the end." Her eyes lit up. "Saving those horses. Phantom. Mira."

"I've still got some of my contacts looking for her." I held up a finger. "We'll find her."

Her gaze shifted from my face to a spot in the distance behind me, and she moved slightly closer, her smile suddenly wooden.

"Don't react," she whispered, meeting my eyes once more. The light humor had gone serious, though she feigned the same playful smile. "We're being followed."

I nodded. "Since 5th Street."

She blinked. "You knew this whole time?"

"Don't worry." I slipped my arm through hers to continue our stroll as if nothing were amiss. The closeness was even more tantalizing and befuddling to my brain. "You're safe with me."

She put her hand over my arm, relaxed and natural. Was she going along with the act? Or did we just happen to fit together this perfectly? "I do trust you," she said, her voice shifting back to that teasing tone. "Despite the other stories Eddie has told me about you."

"Now, if he's told you about that time in Italy, I'll kill him."

"Not yet, but I'll ask." She hummed. "That leave you took in Cairo, though?"

"Lies. Utter lies."

Her laughter floated over me and tangled around my heart. Despite the lingering threat in the shadows behind us, I didn't want this night to end.

# *Twenty*

## Eva

**JUNE 9**

The crowd around the arena wall drew a collective breath as Phantom entered the smaller warm-up area, only a few moments from his debut in the in-hand yearling class. He was years away from the more prestigious stallion age bracket, but the colt yearlings were watched carefully for that next breakout champion. I'd also be showing him on the ground rather than riding. He was still two years from being old enough to break into the saddle.

I was at ease in my pressed, sky-blue blazer and matching slacks. My boots were painted to match, and my hair was swept into large curls and pinned back. I had adorned my face in blush, liner, and lipstick—part of the pageantry and drama that was the stage of the show arena. I had tan gloves and a short crop in hand to use as a guide for Phantom.

We'd practiced for days, and I hoped he'd remember his training in this new environment. The halter, or in-hand, competitions were all about the stature and physical features of the horse. It was breeding, fitness, and presentation.

Phantom, today, was in top form. All eyes were locked on him. All eyes except Warren's.

When Annie and I had emerged from the hotel room that morning, he'd taken in my appearance with an appreciative look. I knew that blue drew out my eyes. Cheryl had advised me so years ago, and it often complemented the striking black or dark brown horses or shining gray horses like Phantom. Though I never wore makeup outside of the arena, Cheryl had taught me how to expertly apply it. Even after five years out of the ring, I remembered a thing or two.

"Isn't she beautiful?" Annie had said with a giggle. I'd let her use a bit of my blush and lipstick.

My heart thudded, nervous of Warren's response. "Oh, come on," I said, waving a hand. "Let's get to the fairgrounds."

Warren reached to take my small bag to load into the truck, and he whispered in my ear, "You look stunning."

My neck went hot.

Even now, holding Phantom's lead rope among two dozen other horses and handlers swirling around us, I felt dizzy at the memory of his words, his breath on my ear.

Now wasn't the time for such distractions. Or ever.

Phantom's eyes took in everything, his nostrils flaring. Our hundreds of hours working together shone through as he watched me, listened to me. Though I was prepared for him to jump or lash out, I kept calm.

No matter how we placed in the class, I'd be able to keep Phantom at Birkstrom. At least that matter was put to rest. I'd need a strong placing to truly capture the attention of potential clients. I couldn't keep my farm afloat with just one or two horses to train.

I had to rebuild the empire.

Warren sat in the stands with Annie. The young girl took in the sights with saucer-wide eyes. He looked nonchalant, but I caught his frequent glances my way. It wasn't because he was nervous about the horse. At least, I guessed as much. Good. If I turned his head, perhaps the judges would remember us too.

A few hushed voices brushed my ears. "That's Birkstrom's granddaughter."

"Oh, I remember her."

Just before our class began, Cheryl walked into the practice arena and beamed at me. She also wore a fine coat and slacks in a dark red hue that brought out the auburn in her hair.

"I never would have recognized him." She motioned to Phantom. "Or you, for that matter." Then she frowned at Keith, who walked in a wide circle on the outside of the warm-up arena. "Is Merrick giving you any trouble?"

"Not yet." I scratched Phantom's neck in his favorite spot, right at the edge of his shoulder. "That yearling of his is going to be stiff competition."

Nearly identical to the filly he'd brought to Birkstrom, Halima was solid chestnut with a white streak down his forehead and four tall white stockings on his legs. He moved like he floated on a cloud, and his neck arched with perfect precision. It was what the breed books would have labeled the ideal Arabian horse, in every way. Halima was of Egyptian breeding, which had been a popular preference of the judges, per Cheryl's gossip.

Would the war orphan from Poland get any notice?

"Colt yearlings!" the show steward announced.

That was our cue to line up and enter the main show ring, which spanned a hundred yards in length. The center boasted a small dais where the panel of three judges watched and evaluated each horse and handler. Each competitor would guide their horse in a loop along the rectangular arena, walking, trotting, or halting as directed by the steward.

"Good luck," Cheryl sang as she skipped out of the arena and toward the stands.

I inhaled deeply, remembering Gramps's deep, comforting

voice. He'd always stood right by the entrance gate, in the same spot.

*"If you've done the work, there's nothing you can do except put on a good show for the judges."*

It was time for the judges and other trainers to see what made Phantom so special—what I'd found in Europe. His distinct bloody shoulder mark was a showstopper.

As the other horses moved into place to enter the show ring, I fell into line behind Keith and his colt.

Keith looked over his shoulder, his blond hair oiled back and his shoulders rigid in his black suit. "Good luck, Eva." He smiled kindly, and I saw the boy I'd once loved.

"Yeah." Victor appeared on the railing. In Gramps's spot. "Good luck, girlie."

"Let me guess," I shot back at Victor. "You're here to pay off the judges so Halima and Keith have a fighting chance."

"Not only that," Victor said after Keith moved forward into the arena. "I'm here to remind you that my offer has a time limit. If we don't make a deal before the summer ends, I can't guarantee my business partners will remain as docile as they've been thus far."

Docile? The line moved forward, and my head wasn't in the right place. Phantom tensed beside me, snorting forcefully.

All the attacks we'd faced at Birkstrom, and it would only get worse.

I had to get myself together, but my thoughts reeled as we ran into the arena.

Ready or not, the show must go on.

## Warren

Eva led Phantom into the arena with her head held high, the horse trotting alongside her in a drifting, flowing motion. The onlookers around me froze in their seats, all eyes on that captivating duo. Keith and his horse also drew a lot of attention.

But something wasn't right. Even though Eva wore a dazzling, performative smile, I recognized something strained in her expression. Surely she was nervous, but everything about her ability to act under high pressure belied that as the cause.

As Eva and Phantom walked by us along the railing of the arena, Annie clapped and wiggled in her seat.

All three judges watched the gray stallion with the bloodred mark on his shoulder. I only had a vague idea of what they were looking for in terms of the animal's physique, but if the attention they gave was any indication, Eva could be at the top of the placings.

The contestants cycled through walking and trotting, then lined up in the center of the arena, facing the stage of judges. The judges wandered around each horse as the trainers and owners stood next to them. All the horses stood in a similar stance as if they were a row of children's toys.

Moments stretched in anticipation of the announcement of the winners. The top five horses would be awarded ribbons, and the top two spots were the most coveted places. Reserve champion and grand champion.

In another month, the regional championship show would be essential to qualify Phantom for the national-level competition. A reserve or grand champion placing at the regional show was required. How Phantom did in this class would indicate our chances there.

An announcer spoke into a microphone and listed off the fifth, fourth, and third place entrants, none of which were Phantom. That meant . . .

"Our reserve champion, Eva Bryant and Phantom."

Annie jumped excitedly, though I spotted the slight drop of Eva's shoulders. She still nodded graciously to the judges and took the ribbon from the steward in the ring.

Keith was named the grand champion. The winning horse had a garland of flowers and a ribbon draped around his neck, and they took a victory lap around the arena before the rest of the competitors were dismissed.

The crowd applauded, and Annie and I made our way down the stands to meet Eva back at the stall. I watched Keith and his smug smile as he left the arena. He walked directly across my path toward the stables.

"A notable start for your colt." He glanced behind him as Eva walked with Phantom. Her gaze was down and thoughtful as she headed toward the stables, not seeing us as she left. Annie ran off after her, but I blocked Keith from continuing on his way.

"I agree," I said. "Especially considering all of the extra hurdles Eva faces around Birkstrom from your father's illicit activity."

"You have no proof of such things." Keith's jaw tensed.

"You sure about that?" I smiled slightly.

The anger that flared in his expression confirmed my suspicions. Keith knew enough, but he wasn't certain of any of it. He didn't know for sure that something could point back to his family. Would that make him more cautious? Or less?

"Safe travels." I tipped my head and walked away before he could respond. He might have won the class, but he coveted a different prize far more.

When I reached Phantom's stall, Eva had put the horse away and was hanging up her coat jacket, the flowy white blouse below a striking contrast to her dark hair and deep red lipstick. Annie stood on a stool in the stall, brushing Phantom's mane, with the goat at her feet.

"Phantom looked amazing out there," I said. *So did you.*

She smiled at me sadly. "I wished for a bit more."

"The Merricks are the favorite, but Phantom had the crowd hypnotized."

Her cheeks flushed. "I hope we'll get a better chance at regionals."

"Better chance?"

"Victor is here." Her smile vanished. "He admitted that the judges were paid off."

That was what had thrown her off at the start of the class. Perhaps I could put Reid on that angle, and if I had enough of a smoking gun, I could present this to Cheryl to take to the association's board.

"I'll work on that."

She shook her head. "You can't solve every problem in the world, Warren."

"I can try."

Something swirled in her gaze. Gratitude? Admiration? That same magnetic pull that had drawn me to her last night while we walked down Main Street captured me again.

"Well, while you do that, I'm going to pack up so we can head back home," she said.

Mason walked down the aisle, his steps thundering on the compacted dirt floor. "Boss, we've got a problem."

My heart jumped into my throat. Eva turned to look at him.

Mason motioned a thumb over his shoulder. "Better come see."

I took Eva's shoulders. "Wait here with Annie."

She hesitated but then nodded. I felt better with her here, watching Phantom. There were enough public and other trainers nearby that she'd be safe.

Mason led me to the parking lot, where my truck sat beside Eva's with the trailer. Several tires were cut, now flat against the gravel below.

Bold of Keith and Victor—and what was the intention with this? It felt childish and retaliatory. Was there a benefit in delaying us further?

"Call Eddie and let him know. Something might be in the works in Baker." I handed a stack of bills to Mason. "Do what you can to secure the tires we need, as fast as you can."

He raced off to find a telephone, and I hurried back to the stalls.

Eva paced with her hands on her waist, her hair now loose of the pins and framing her face in waves.

"Tires were cut," I said. "Does Cheryl have a truck or trailer we can borrow? I don't want to delay our return any further."

She stepped closer, lowering her voice. "Why on earth would they do that here?"

My mind raced. It had to be a distraction. It was something my men and I would have done to an unsuspecting SS troop, cutting their tires in the night or stealing all their vehicle keys.

"We need to be ready for anything. Mason will call and warn Eddie and the rest at the ranch."

She breathed a soft laugh. "Not even a moment to celebrate second place."

"When this is all over, we'll be celebrating the grand championship at nationals."

"Indeed." She pressed her lips together in a coy smile, the dark makeup around her blue eyes making them stand out more than ever. "Grand champion at nationals is only the start."

I hoped so.

It was also the same month that I was supposed to start my campaign for Senate. I'd have to choose.

Looking at her with the red-and-gold ribbon tied to the stall behind her, I wasn't certain what I'd do. My soul was split in half.

Mason ran back down the aisle. "I can't get Eddie or anyone from the ranch on the phone."

I exchanged a look with Eva. We had to get back to Birkstrom as fast as we could.

If it wasn't already too late.

# *Twenty-One*

## Eva

JUNE 10

"We did the best we could," Eddie said as we walked through the tattered, charred remains of the other two cabins. "The fires were too strong."

Peter stood at my side with downcast eyes. "I promise, Miss Eva, I didn't do it."

"I know." I put my hand on his shoulder and squeezed reassuringly. "We know who did this."

My mind was numb, my body exhausted. We'd driven straight through the evening and arrived at a pile of embers that had burned through the night. I hadn't slept, and Warren hadn't left my side.

Eddie's head hung in defeat.

Warren kicked over a board and stomped out a hot spot. "This isn't your fault, Eddie."

"Should we call the sheriff?" Eddie asked.

"No," Warren and I said in unison.

He met my gaze, a thousand different emotions cascading

through his green eyes. One clear message shone through: resolve. He was ready for war.

"Was anyone hurt?" I broke his gaze, terrified of what might lie ahead.

"No," Eddie said.

Not this time, at least.

I walked to the driveway, where the wooden sign Gramps had whittled for years hung charred and broken from the chains of the overhead post. My hands trembled—in rage, in disbelief. I ran my fingers over the black edges of the four-foot-long sign. One of the ends, thinned by the flames, broke off and fell at my feet.

I grabbed the rest of it and tore the whole thing down, the rough edges scratching and cutting into my palms. It hit the ground with a resounding thud.

The Birkstroms had built a legacy here, and in a matter of weeks in my hands, it had turned to ashes.

Three vehicles pulled into the driveway. My truck, Warren's truck, and Cheryl's car driven by an employee of hers. We'd borrowed her truck and trailer to get home while Mason remained in Redmond to get the tires fixed.

I strode alongside Warren to talk with Cheryl. Smoke hung in the hot, humid air, and it smelled as if a lightning storm was on the way.

"Are you all right?" Warren asked quietly before we reached the new arrivals.

"Where does it go from here?" I came to a stop, out of earshot of everyone. The horses snorted and ate contentedly in their paddocks behind us, but Phantom paced nervously with all the strange commotion. "Someone is going to get hurt."

"We'll make sure it's them and not us," he said. "We'll fight back."

"This isn't Germany, Warren." My breath caught in my throat.

"What's the alternative?" He rubbed his face, exhaustion

creeping in on his angered and determined expression. "Hand over the farm?"

The weight of it all pressed down on my shoulders. "I don't know."

His expression softened, and he motioned to Eddie and the rest who were already cleaning up debris. "We're not scared of a little fire. These guys have faced far worse."

"They're supposed to be safe here." My voice rose and my heart raced. "No one should have to die because I'm sentimental about a farm and stupid sunrise."

Terror gripped me and stole the air from my lungs. My skin felt cold, clammy, and my fingers trembled. Darkness closed in around me, and I felt myself swaying on my feet. Something steadied me, but voices and conversations grew muffled and distant.

How could I have let this happen?

"Eva?"

*Killers. Robbers. Con artists.*

The headlines flashed. The words I'd seen Mama and Daddy fawn over.

I'd done all I could to preserve life and make up for the death and destruction my parents had brought upon the world. I'd failed. Would I have blood on my hands, just like them?

"Eva!"

Someone held my shoulders, gave me a little shake.

I blinked and my vision cleared. Warren gripped my arms and studied my face with concern. Cheryl was over his shoulder on one side, Eddie on the other.

"Eva?"

"I'm fine." I shook him off and pushed away.

I wasn't. I wanted to thank Cheryl for all she'd done. But I was drowning. Victor's words right before the class started swirled and grew louder in my ears.

"I need some space," I said. "I'll be back later."

I fled the small crowd as fast as I could, hoping no one followed me. I needed to breathe.

I jumped on Acorn bareback, and as I held on to her mane, I nudged her with my heels through the paddock gate, then closed it behind us. I leaned forward, held tightly to her silky hair, and kicked her sides.

She bolted forward, and Birkstrom disappeared behind us.

## Warren

"That's not the first time she's run away from me." Cheryl handed me the truck keys and winked. "I guess I have that effect on people."

I couldn't find the energy to smile at her joke, and she deflated a bit. Eddie wandered back to help the guys clean more of the damaged cabins.

Cheryl put a hand on my arm. "Don't worry about her. She's tough."

I wasn't sure Cheryl knew all of what Eva was facing. The nightmares on top of nightmares, and the looming threat that piled on even more of her greatest fears. The burden she'd brought home from years of combat.

Eva wanted to save people and animals. With the Merricks burning down pieces of her ranch bit by bit, she didn't even have a hospital or headquarters to fall back to.

I started to follow Eva's path, but Cheryl pulled my arm to stop me. Her humor was gone and her gaze was heavy with meaning. "Perhaps she should work this out on her own."

I straightened and faced her. "What do you mean?"

"I've heard a rumor that you might be moving to DC." Cheryl crossed her arms. "So maybe she needs to sort through all of this without you."

Cheryl, the queen of gossip.

"I would never hurt her." Not intentionally. Wasn't the plan in August to leave? I wouldn't have anything other than a few spare weekends to visit Phantom—to see her—once I started my term as senator. "Have you told Eva?" I asked.

"No. This one's on you, soldier." Cheryl stepped closer and lifted her eyebrows at me. "A client would wait here while their trainer took some time alone."

I knew that was true. I shouldn't go after her.

"See you at the banquet on Saturday," Cheryl said.

"I'm not sure that makes sense to attend right now."

"After the splash she made yesterday?" Cheryl pointed at me. "If you want her to line up new clients to get this place back up and running, you'll get her to Seattle."

Moments later, she departed, along with the groom she'd brought, driving the borrowed truck and trailer.

Eva hadn't bothered with a halter or saddle. Acorn was well trained, but what if she fell, hit her head?

Cheryl's advice rang through my mind. Would I send the wrong message if I went to find her? If it had been Eddie who ran off, would I be as concerned?

Eva had been clear about our relationship. Client and trainer.

I knew where she was going—her sanctuary at Beacon's Bluff. I remembered the route, and Autumn did too.

Eddie walked up and handed me a canteen. "She might need this."

I took it, and the clear signal of what he thought I should do.

I saddled Autumn rather clumsily, had Bennett check my work since he'd ridden his whole life, and then followed Eva's path.

I found her where I expected, on the wooden structure built two generations prior. I tied Autumn to the tree, though Acorn grazed nearby, unrestrained. Eva sat with ankles crossed and knees to her chest, looking at the horizon.

There wasn't any sign of tears. No red-rimmed eyes or tear

streaks down her dusty cheeks. I hadn't ever seen her cry, even after all the setbacks we'd faced.

I sat beside her. The humid air whirled around us, the trees swaying in the increasing wind.

A storm was coming.

She closed her eyes, the soft tendrils of her hair sweeping over her face. "Did Cheryl bring up the banquet again?" she asked calmly.

"Said you have to go."

She nodded and opened her eyes, brushing the hair behind her ears. "I know I should. But it's another two days of training lost."

"You should capitalize on the momentum from the show." I handed her the canteen.

She looked over at me sheepishly. "Will you come with me?"

"Of course."

"I thought about what you said." She drew in a deep breath, took a swig of water. "That we need to fight back. I know a guy in the FBI. I think he might be able to help since Sheriff Lowe is compromised."

"FBI?"

"A patient I treated in Guam works for the Bureau now. He owes me a favor."

"What for?"

"He was laid up for weeks and nearly lost both legs. I helped him write some thoughtful letters to this girl he liked back in his hometown." She smiled. "He made a full recovery and married that girl."

"He definitely owes you."

She rolled her shoulders back. "I'm guessing Victor is monitoring our phone conversations, since the line is shared. We can make some calls in Seattle."

I wanted to ask about the fear in her eyes and what dark place she'd gone to back at the ranch. I wanted to protect her from ever going to that place again. But now it was business as usual.

She was strong, resilient. Cheryl was right. Eva hadn't needed me to come rescue her after all.

Yet, as the silence stretched between us, I could feel her pain and fear still radiating.

"I do like having so many people on the ranch." She pressed her lips together. "It feels like it was when I first came to the ranch, when Gramps had five or six wranglers working for him and we ran hundreds of cattle each year."

"How old were you?"

"Six." Her voice was barely audible.

"What happened to your parents?"

She looked down at her lap and breathed, "They died."

So alone at such a young age. No wonder she was so tough and self-sufficient.

"How did you find Bill?" I knew I was venturing into uncharted territory, implying she was adopted.

She met my gaze with her eyebrows raised in surprise. "How did you find out?"

"There's a rumor . . ."

"That Bill Birkstrom never had any children." She lowered her knees and hung her legs over the edge of the platform. She lifted an eyebrow as if considering whether to tell me or not. "It's one of the town's most favorite stories to gossip and theorize about."

I held my breath, praying she would tell me more. The wind whooshed, making the platform creak ever so slightly.

"I ran away from an orphanage in Philadelphia, hopped the train, and ended up in Baker before I nearly got caught and ran from the train stewards."

My pulse quickened. She'd grown up in Philly too? Though our circles might not have overlapped, something stirred deep inside me knowing we'd been that close, even as children.

She handed back the canteen. "Bill found me under a bench on Main Street that night and took me in. And though I did sneak out every night, there wasn't anywhere for me to go from here. I was too short to steal the car and couldn't walk the forty miles back to town in the dark."

"The horses saved you," I said, repeating what she'd told me in Germany.

She nodded. "They did."

I thought of Eddie, Lucky, EP, Bennett, Mason, and the changes I'd seen in them over the past few weeks. No matter how much work they had in a day, they'd always stop to give one of the mares a scratch on the neck or sneak a carrot to Phantom. The horses had a way of reaching them.

Eva fell back into her thoughtful silence as clouds rumbled in the distance, lightning streaking at the very edge of the horizon. "It won't crest the mountains to the east of us," she said faintly. "The storm. Those clouds never seem to make it into this valley. Perhaps that's why I never thought I'd lose Birkstrom. The storms had always passed us by."

"You've faced the storms now," I said. "Head-on."

Her eyes locked onto the distant clouds. "I think the worst storm is yet to come."

# *Twenty-Two*

## Eva

**JUNE 15**
**SEATTLE, WASHINGTON**

"Thanks, Harold," I said into the receiver. "Tell Lorraine I send my love."

I hung up the phone and turned to Warren, who leaned against the wall and looked like a detective in a fedora and suit, perusing a newspaper but mostly listening to my conversation. We'd arrived in Seattle only a few hours ago after a long day of driving and had just enough time to call Harold Jefferson at the FBI office in Langley before we needed to dress for the banquet.

"He couldn't guarantee they'd find anything," I said with a shrug. "But at least they've heard our side of things first."

Warren folded his newspaper and glanced around the hotel lobby. We'd been careful to lose the two men following us from Baker in a black sedan, but it was no secret to Keith that we'd be attending the fundraiser tonight.

The past week had been a flurry of activity, working with Phantom, rebuilding the cabins, setting up temporary lodging for the now seven men who lived on the ranch. I adored them all and had met several of them in my two weeks in Kötzting. EP had also been settling in well, getting to know the closely knit men of the 42nd.

Now all roads in and out of the property were carefully watched, gates were reinforced, and a lookout tower had been hidden in one of the tallest pines behind the cabins.

Birkstrom was a fortress.

That meant leaving for Seattle hadn't been as hard as I'd expected. Annie hated being left behind, but she took her duties seriously—she was to look after the chickens and other assorted animals. Bennett was able to exercise all the horses in my absence, and even Phantom tolerated him.

With returning Stormy to the Carsons' ranch after successfully curing her habit of breaking halters, I had enough for another mortgage payment and breathing room for another month. I was also able to work with the half-blind auction rescue, as that gelding was now looking more robust. Hopefully I could get him solid under saddle and then sell him.

Keith's filly was also progressing well. A few months more and I could close out my business with him.

An hour after Warren and I parted ways to get ready for dinner, he knocked lightly on my hotel door. I took one last look at myself in the mirror and froze. In the deep royal-blue dress with my hair spilling in curls over my face, I was the spitting image of my mother.

My makeup accentuated the similarities. Oval eyes, high cheekbones, heart-shaped lips. I looked nearly the same as her photos in the newspaper from when she'd been arrested at age twenty-five. Younger than I was now.

"Eva?" Warren's voice was deep on the other side of the door. I'd taken too long to answer.

I grabbed my small black handbag and hurried to the door, the satin dress as foreign to my skin as the heels were to my feet.

When I drew the door open, my heart went still.

He wore a jet-black suit and had his brown hair styled to the side. His mouth fell open as his eyes pored over my appearance. "You look . . ." he said, his voice fading.

"Horribly impractical," I said, closing the door behind me. "Cheryl insisted I wear it."

He closed his gaping lips and cleared his throat. "Well, practicality aside, you look beautiful." He offered me an arm.

I took it, surprised by how right it felt.

No, I couldn't think such things. I needed to keep my distance—though the fight might be futile. Warren had become an integral part of my world, and I couldn't even picture the ranch without him there. Peter followed him and idolized him. Eddie hadn't consumed alcohol since that day we'd found him at the bar.

Warren was our rock.

He still hadn't been clear on his plans or how long he planned to live out of the Geiser Grand. The weekly bill had to be horrendous. We'd discussed him moving into the apartment of the barn or one of the cabins, but he worried about the perception after Victor's earlier attempt to cast a shadow of impropriety on our working relationship. He'd also been vague but firm that he'd one day need to return to Philadelphia and wanted the on-site accommodations to go to the soldiers who might stay more long-term.

He led me to his truck, and we drove to the large banquet hall. He glanced at me often during the drive. I suppose it was like seeing a duck wearing a skirt. I'd never paid any attention to my appearance aside from the hair and dress regulations in the nurse corps or the theatrical makeup of show days. The only other dress I'd ever worn had been at a school dance that I'd snuck out to with Keith.

My stomach sank at the thought of seeing him tonight.

That distracted me until we reached the banquet hall. Small lights and gold foil decor filled the room, and tall windows overlooked the city. Seattle was a mix of brick buildings and neon signs all packed into the narrow streets along the dark waters of the Puget Sound. The shipyards and airplane manufacturers had left the area in a haze of post-war resettling and half-abandoned industrial lots.

Warren leaned in. “I prefer Beacon’s Bluff.”

“Me too.”

“You made it!” Cheryl rushed over in a flurry of black velvet, and she kissed me on both cheeks and then Warren as well.

Her husband, Lewis, walked up and I introduced him. Cheryl looked between us, and her gaze lingered on my arm looped through Warren’s. I dropped my arm and stepped away.

“I’m glad I caught you both,” she said. “From what I hear, you’re still looking for that little gray mare from Poland. Mira?”

My heart leapt.

“Rumor is that she and a few other Janów horses will be sold at auction in Scottsdale on the 24th.”

Just over a week from now. I looked at Warren and saw the same spark in his eyes.

“Sounds like we’ll need to check that out,” he said.

The 24th was a bit close to regionals, but this was Mira. We couldn’t pass up the opportunity to find her.

Someone waved to Cheryl from across the room, and she floated away.

I smiled at Warren. “Wouldn’t it be wonderful if we found her?”

“Will we be bidding against each other this time?”

“I hope not.” I sighed. “I can’t afford that game.”

He led me to a table set with ornate cutlery and dishware. “Perhaps we each go in halfway? She stays at Birkstrom, but I have shared ownership in her future progeny?”

A long-term business arrangement? I liked that idea a lot. I knew he was trying to preserve my pride by offering to split the cost of Mira, since I hadn’t any funds to spare. My limbs went numb and my heart raced at the thought of such an arrangement.

That meant no matter what he did at home in Philly, he'd have a reason to come back.

We sat at the table, and an elder couple took seats across from us a few moments later.

"Mrs. Hartford, Mr. Hartford," I said, recognizing the owners of a stables near the Canadian border.

Elaine Hartford squinted at me through her thick glasses and then blinked in amazement. "My heavens, is that Bill Birkstrom's girl?"

"It's nice to see you again." I motioned to Warren. "May I introduce Warren Hayes, who owns the Janów-bred stallion Phantom."

"We heard about that horse." George Hartford stood to shake Warren's hand. He looked at me. "Bill said you'd gone into the nurse corps?"

I nodded. "Warren here served as well, as a captain in Patton's Second Cavalry."

George slapped his knee. "By Jove, really?"

Warren gave me a patronizing look. I think he hated the spotlight as much as I did.

"Part of Operation Cowboy, in fact," I added.

George leaned on the table and questioned Warren further, but Elaine just stared at me, and it started to make me uneasy.

After a few more moments, her husband noticed it too, nudging her with his elbow. "Stop staring, Elaine. You're being rude."

"I'm sorry." Elaine waved a hand and picked up the water glass in front of her. "You just look so much like—" She shook her head and laughed. "I know this is silly, but Irene Chalmers."

I froze, careful not to let my surprise or terror show through my mask. I schooled my breathing so as not to indicate just how fast my heart was racing. "Oh, I get that all the time," I said, waving a hand breezily.

That was partially true. Irene and Raymond were still celebrities, even posthumously. But no one thought of Evelyn Chalmers, the child who had survived her parents' crime spree and graced the headlines for weeks after their bloody end.

Elaine looked at her husband. "Do you remember that, about twenty years ago?"

George nodded. "Everyone remembers that, except these youngsters, probably."

"Oh, I remember," Warren said, his voice deep and thick. "I grew up in Philadelphia." He took in a long breath. "My father owned the bank where they were killed."

Something shattered inside me. "Your family owns the Continental Savings and Loan banks?"

How had I missed this? It was clear he'd come from a wealthy family, but there were dozens of Continental Savings and Loan branches across the East Coast. And my parents had robbed most of them.

Warren looked at me with a deep notch in his forehead, as if confused by my question.

Elaine cut in before he could answer. "What was that like?"

"I just remember a lot of police around." Warren's attention went back to the Hartfords. "Several of our employees were injured that day and in other branches during their crime spree."

"How exciting," Elaine said with a sickening smile.

"People died." Warren frowned. "I don't find that exciting."

"Oh, of course," Elaine said somberly.

My chest tightened, the dress constricting around me like a python. "Excuse me," I said as I stood. "I'm going to the powder room."

Warren stood and put a hand on my back. "Everything all right?"

"Of course," I squeaked. "I'll be right back."

I fled the room that was now thick with people. I caught a glimpse of Keith's distinctive blond hair out of the corner of my eye but didn't slow my flight.

I reached the outside door and burst into the cool air. The

breeze over the Puget Sound wafted over me, carrying the scent of salt and fish. It roiled my stomach further. I leaned forward, one hand on the wall, gasping for breath.

I had to pull it together. If I didn't, Warren might suspect something, and I couldn't risk that. No one could know that I had any connection to the Chalmerses. I just looked a lot like that notorious woman who'd met a tragic end.

Gramps had always insisted I embrace my true name and past. He was always so focused on his horses that the events of the rest of the world never distracted him. He didn't understand the fury of the public and their obsession with the macabre.

I pulled air deep into my lungs, desperate to bury these memories back where they belonged.

As for Warren, there couldn't be a future business arrangement with Mira. If he learned the truth of what I was hiding from him . . . I couldn't bear the thought of how deeply it might hurt him.

That was just the way of the world. I'd honor my commitment to Phantom and bring him to the national championship show. Beyond that, I'd arrange another trainer to take over. That meant I'd need to bring in enough clients to survive without Captain Warren Hayes in my life.

I'd do what I could to protect Warren. Any association with me could be devastating to him and his family name.

I straightened, smoothed my hair, and brushed my hands over the fabric of my dress. I'd practiced this routine my entire life.

I would never allow my parents to claim more victims than they already had.

## Warren

Watching Eva float through the crowd, smiling and conversing with everyone who crossed her path, I was torn between admiration and suspicion.

She was polite and practiced, introducing me to dozens of people I'd never remember. I was terrible at recalling names, which Kenneth once admitted would not help in any career beyond the military, where I had the crutch of names printed on patches or dog tags.

Eva's earlier departure from the table still troubled me. There had been something in her eyes—something she'd been quick to hide. I couldn't make sense of it. Now it seemed as if nothing was amiss.

She enchanted people the way she captivated me, and she remembered the smallest details of every family, farm, couple, or horse. A gentleman with a thick black mustache and top hat laughed with her as they recalled the time his horse had gotten loose on the grounds and Bill had been the only one able to catch it.

In the amber glow of the ballroom lighting, a few faint marks on her arms caught my eye—scars I hadn't seen before. But then, she often wore long-sleeve shirts to keep from getting burned under the harsh summer sun. They were small, rectangular marks where the skin was just a bit smoother, a bit lighter, than the area surrounding it.

"Mind if I steal her for a moment?" Keith's voice cut in and chilled the mood.

My fists clenched instantly, but I knew there were appearances to maintain. I was just her client.

Eva's smile faded a fraction, but she nodded politely to the man she'd been speaking to and gave me a quick glance. I took her meaning—she would talk to him alone. I'd stay close.

Keith looked dapper, exuded bravado and confidence. Eva brushed past him and walked a few yards away, out of earshot. Keith looked at me with a hard, notched brow. I stared back without wavering.

"Five minutes," I whispered to him as he turned to follow Eva.

As the small crowd around me discussed the weather, I watched

Eva and Keith from the corner of my eye. Eva's back was rigid, her arms crossed and a deep frown etched in her face. Keith motioned with his hands and was obviously trying to apologize.

Two of his five minutes remained.

Cheryl's news about Mira changed the outlook for the next few weeks. We'd need to fly to Scottsdale and arrange a paid transport for the horse back to Oregon. Anything else would consume too much time to get Phantom ready for the regional competition.

Keith reached for Eva's arm, and she pulled back from his touch. I strode over, cut right in front of Keith, and put a hand protectively on Eva's back.

"Shall we call it a night?" I asked. We'd already endured the dinner, dessert, and droning speeches.

"Yes, please." She sank into my touch and nestled in close to me as I led her through the dining area and into the lobby of the sparkling building.

Keith's footsteps echoed behind us, and I smiled at the opportunity as we emerged into a quiet, empty hallway. No one was around now.

"Warren, don't," Eva muttered in warning.

But I had already swung around, and I grabbed the man by his collar and tie and slammed him up against the wall. The framed artwork shuddered beside us.

Keith sputtered and cursed.

"Shut up," I growled. "You'll leave Eva alone, and you'll also do well to tell your father that we're not scared of him."

"I'm not responsible for my father's actions."

"You're responsible for your own inactions." I let him go, and he straightened his suit with a jerky motion.

He looked at Eva. "Is this how you feel?"

"Yes," she said without hesitation. "Whether you admit it to yourself or not, you're involved, Keith."

He staggered back as if she'd struck him. Then his focus

snapped back to me as his face and neck flushed. "This is all because of you," he hissed.

"No, it's not." Eva stepped in, firm. She looked sad, exhausted, and small. The blue dress was dull in the dim lighting, and her skin prickled with gooseflesh. "Good night, Keith."

I took off my coat and draped it over her shoulders, setting us back on the path to the parking lot once more. Keith didn't follow.

When we reached the truck, she paused outside the door and closed her eyes.

"Want to go for a walk? Or a drive?" I offered quietly, seeing that common hesitation I'd come to recognize when she searched for something to do aside from sleep.

Her gaze lifted gratefully to mine. She pulled my coat tighter around her and nodded.

We drove the streets for a long time in silence as she looked at all the passing buildings and lights. I was careful not to lose direction, but she consumed my thoughts.

We crested a tall hill, and I pulled off at an overlook that had several picnic benches and a view of the city lights below.

"This is beautiful," she said, stepping out of the truck.

We sat on the top of a picnic table, as if for an even higher vantage point. Her body was close to mine, enveloped in my coat.

"Gramps had a knack for finding viewpoints. Whenever we drove to a show, we'd stop and eat our lunches in places just like this."

I chuckled but had to put most of my focus on not reaching around her and holding her.

"What's your family like?" she asked.

Not exactly a warm tale for a beautiful night like this. "William runs the day-to-day operations of the banks, but Father still sits on the board. Mother runs a few charities to keep herself busy."

"Is William married?"

"Yes."

"Any nieces or nephews?"

"I'm not even sure. Their wedding was a huge splash, but all I know is that they don't typically live in the same estate. If their marriage is anything like my parents', it's probably a dreary affair."

Mother and Father were hardly ever in the same room. I'd only ever felt that their marriage was a contractual obligation. It was cold, distant, and vitriolic.

"I'm sorry to hear that."

"Me too." I leaned my elbows on my knees. "It's not what I want for my life."

She was quiet for a moment. "Do you want kids someday?"

"With the right woman, yes." My pulse picked up at that thought. Eva Bryant undoubtedly was the right sort of woman. If only our lives would fit together. "What about you?"

"No." She shook her head, her gaze avoiding mine. "That's not in the cards for me."

"You're so good with Annie," I said. "You'd be a great mother."

She bit her lip, and for the slightest second I thought I caught the gleam of a tear at the corner of her eye, but she blinked it away.

"It's a long story." Her voice went more firm, unquestioning. "I have no intention of ever getting married."

A dart of pain cut into my chest, the words surprising. This woman wasn't like anyone else I'd ever known. The tragic story I didn't yet know, the nightmares, the distaste for sunsets, hating flowers and jewelry.

Someone had hurt her, deeply.

"Never?"

She reluctantly met my gaze, her light blue eyes almost haunting in the dark. "Never."

I shook myself from my stupor and swallowed back the surge of disappointment. It didn't matter. Our futures were on two completely different paths.

“Why do you think Bill never got married?” I asked.

She sniffed and scrunched her shoulders upward. “He almost did. Marianna Clairmont. They dated throughout high school, but she died of influenza before graduation, and he never got over her.”

“He must have really loved her.”

“Yeah, I think he did. They planned a life together, and he proposed a few months before she passed.”

I couldn’t imagine the pain. The only version of marriage I had known had been quite the opposite. Marriages of convenience, of power. Of finding a proper match in status and industry. I’d rebelled against every attempt Mother threw at me to set me up with some heiress in high school, and signing up for the Army had been my path to freedom.

I hated that Eva now knew my family’s business by name. I only ever wanted to be Warren. Not even Captain Hayes. Senator Hayes would be a whole other title I didn’t want but knew was necessary.

She swayed ever so slightly, and I wrapped my arm around her. “We should get back. You need some rest.”

She closed her eyes and leaned her head against my shoulder. “This is the one time I won’t argue about that,” she mumbled.

“I’ve seen you stack two tons of hay bales in ninety-degree weather and never slow down,” I said. “And a banquet wears you out?”

“People are exhausting.”

I chuckled, stepped off the table, and reached for her hand to help her down. The distant sounds of vehicles in the streets beyond, the buzzing of bugs and rustling of trees—everything faded as she held my hand, stepped from the bench seat, and landed right against me, looking up at me.

Her eyes searched my face, her throat bobbed, and her lips opened as if to speak. Her red lipstick had faded away, leaving just the pink hue I adored. I couldn't—shouldn't—overstep when I knew all that lay in jeopardy.

If I kissed her, if I asked for us to be more than just business partners, would I risk it all? Was it better to be in her life as just her client than not be a part of her world in any way? She'd stated the terms so clearly. We were just trainer and owner.

Still. There was a longing in her eyes that I wasn't imagining. It was laced with regret and such a deep, endless sadness.

"Eva," I whispered, wanting so badly to know what had hurt her so—*who* had hurt her. I cupped her face, her skin cool against my warm hands. She closed her eyes and leaned into my touch, which nearly uncoiled all my resolve.

She put her hands over mine and trembled. I pulled her closer, one inch at a time, lowering my face to hers until our lips were nearly touching. Though I ached to erase those fractions of an inch that felt like a mile between us, I waited for her. For her to choose what she wanted, both in this moment and down the road for us.

I didn't know how it could all work out, but as I looked upon her in the starlight, I couldn't ignore the gravitational pull I felt for her.

"Warren," she breathed. "I can't."

Disappointment jolted through me, though I treasured the momentary feel of her in my arms, tucked into my body. I stepped back, the separation as painful as any wound I'd ever experienced.

She crossed her arms and held my gaze with notched brows. "I'm sorry."

"Don't apologize." My chest wanted to split in half. "Let's get back to the hotel." I worried that if we spoke any further, she'd say something I didn't want to hear.

I wished I could unwind the damage I'd just done and restart the day, never treading so close to that boundary that couldn't be uncrossed.

She was silent all the way back to the hotel until I bid her good night at her room door, just next to mine. She handed me back my coat, which smelled blissfully of her lavender soap.

"Thank you," she said softly.

"For the coat?"

"For sticking up for me with Keith." Her voice went raspy, strained. "No one other than Gramps has ever done that for me."

My heart broke for her in that moment, to think of how alone she was in the world. Or used to be. Now Eddie and the guys—we were here for her. I wanted to say something reassuring, but words failed me.

"Good night, Warren."

She closed the door, and I stared at it.

I didn't want her to ever be alone. I'd have to tread far more carefully to get her to trust me and open her heart to me.

Beyond that, I'd need to figure out where my own heart and future truly lay.

# *Twenty-Three*

## Eva

**JUNE 17**
**BAKER, OREGON**

The day after we returned from Seattle, I rose before the sun and jumped on Acorn for a ride to Beacon's Bluff.

The sun's rays warming my skin, the rough boards beneath my hands—it all tied me back to what it was I was trying to do. After that night in Seattle, I was unmoored.

Warren. Keith. The Hartfords' comments about my parents.

And now a trip to Arizona in search of Mira. With Warren.

I wasn't sure I could trust myself around him. He had a way of making me share more than I wanted to. Of making me want to commit to things I'd sworn off for eternity.

The truth was, he needed to go back to Philadelphia, or I might give in to his charm. I could so easily fall in love with him.

I'd been here before. I thought Keith had been the one for me. Then I told him about my past, and he'd cast me aside.

Now I was older and knew better. I knew what that secret would do to Warren and his reputation. He'd put on a brave face and tell me that my secret didn't matter to him. I was certain of that much, which meant it was even more important that I shielded him from this. I had to protect him and his family's name.

When I returned to the barns, Warren was filling up the grain bins for the morning breakfast for the mares and Phantom. My heart warmed in admiration of how this man—the son of a banking dynasty—was here in my ramshackle barn in Oregon, serving grain to a handful of auction-rescued horses.

He looked up as I rode Acorn to the barn entrance and slipped off. I'd gone back to my old habit of riding without bit or saddle.

"I mentioned our trip to Scottsdale to Eddie," Warren said. "He asked if Peter and Annie might go with us."

"That's a great idea." It would be more proper than Warren and me being alone, so far away. In Seattle, we were around industry acquaintances. Warren had also proven that he cared little for others' opinions. It was nice, a bit like how Gramps had faced the world.

It was a trait I didn't seem to possess.

"Annie might be disappointed when they don't allow Patches on the airplane," Warren said.

"I won't be surprised if she smuggles the kitten and chicken in her suitcase," I replied with a laugh, leading Acorn toward her paddock.

I had calls to make and three horses to take delivery of in the next few days, after all the conversations at the banquet. The aisles of Birkstrom were filling, if slowly.

Would it be enough?

Near the site of the old cabins, construction of new houses had begun. The piles of supplies Gramps had collected were running low, and I'd noticed Eddie making more frequent runs into town.

I couldn't fight it, though. These men needed safe places to sleep, especially once winter came around. If they were still here, that is. I'd sort that all out after the national competition.

I'd make sure one day that Warren was repaid for all he'd invested.

Lucky and Mason walked toward the barn, waved cheerily, and set to work on repairing the final few stalls. It was a marvel to see that after more than a month of dedicated hands, the stalls had secured boards, doors with smooth hinges, and proper lighting and plumbing.

Gramps would have been tickled.

A pang of longing hit me in that moment, and the itch of tears clawed at my eyelids.

I hadn't cried since my parents died. I buried it all down as I always did.

I put Acorn back in her pasture. Warren picked up the grain buckets, and I caught him glancing my way, studying me in a thoughtful, concerned manner.

Our drive back from Seattle had been pleasant. Light conversation and talking about all the different trainers and horse owners we'd met the night before.

It was almost as if we hadn't nearly kissed and ruined everything.

I retreated to the house and found Annie in the kitchen with two kittens on the table drinking out of a bowl of milk. "Cats off the table," I said, for at least the hundredth time.

Annie smiled and moved the kittens. "I think Speckles will have her kittens soon, Eva."

A dull pain throbbed in the base of my skull.

Annie disappeared and came back with a rusted, black metal box the size of a shoebox. "I was looking for a box for her and her babies and found this."

My heart stumbled to a stop, and I sank to a chair at the table. I hadn't seen that container in some time.

She put it on the table and pushed it toward me. "What are these?"

I touched the top of the lid, the cold, pitted metal, and a wave of memories washed over me. I knew every item inside without even opening the box. Gramps had kept it for the past nineteen years of my life.

War medals.

The regional champion ribbon I'd won at age eight.

Gramps's dog tags from the Great War.

A casing from a .45-caliber bullet, one of the many that had buried and burned me as I huddled on the floor of the Chevy during the shootout. My hand instinctively went to my forearm, where the burns still showed on my skin.

That casing was the only item I'd kept from my life before Birkstrom.

I picked up the box and tossed it onto the kitchen counter with a clatter. Annie yelped in surprise.

"Sorry, Annie. Not that box. Can you see if your father might need your help right now? I need to make phone calls and could use some quiet."

Annie nodded, scooped the two kittens up, and raced out the front door.

Guilt filled me for being so cross with her. I pressed my palm to my forehead, circling the kitchen and eyeing the metal box. The clasp in front looked seized shut. Good riddance.

Mrs. Hartford's comments in Seattle. Warren's connection to that fateful bank. Annie unearthing this time capsule.

No matter how much I ran from it, my parents' shadow was always there to blot out the sun.

## Warren

JUNE 19

I finished the morning feedings and lifted my head to look in the direction of Beacon's Bluff. There wasn't any reason to worry. It was a good thing that Eva was taking her morning rides again. There'd been a new light in her eyes and a fire in her step ever since.

The last few mornings, we'd fallen into a routine. Just as I arrived at dawn and began to feed, she and Acorn would ride up, a vision of an angel on horseback without bridle or saddle, hair flowing in the wind, cheeks pink from the sun.

Today, she was late.

Eddie walked by with a bale of straw.

"Who's patrolling the east gate?" I asked, motioning to the rising sun.

Eddie set the bale down and clapped his hands together. "Junior, I believe."

My heart froze. "Junior was just walking past the house on his way to the west gate."

Eddie looked at his wristwatch and then checked for Acorn. "She's not back yet?"

"I'm taking the truck," I said, dropping the grain bucket and racing to the driveway.

"I'm coming with you." Eddie kept pace with me.

There was a thick enough dirt road now, given our patrols and monitoring across the one thousand acres, for me to reach the bluff in less time than if I saddled and rode Autumn.

"Lucky!" Eddie called out. "Take point, we're going east."

"Roger," Lucky yelled.

"Dad?" Annie ran up from the chicken coop. "What's going on?"

"It's probably nothing, sweetie, but stay in the house, lock the door."

Annie looked around, mouth agape and eyes wide.

We'd talked these drills through dozens of times. Everyone knew what they were supposed to do, but Annie hadn't ever experienced this for real. Regardless, I needed to focus on Eva right now.

I pointed to Lucky and then to Annie. "Make sure she gets inside."

A gunshot rang out over the valley, and everyone on the ranch jumped into action.

I drove down the road to the bluff, careful not to drive fast and spook Acorn if she was on her way back. The road wove toward the east gate that we'd reinforced. It was wide open.

Fear drove me forward, and I pushed the accelerator down. We parked at the base of the hill, and I took off running toward the platform. Eddie followed, pulling his pistol out of his boot and covering every angle.

I reached the top, but Eva was nowhere in sight. There were fresh hoofprints—she'd been there this morning. Why hadn't we seen her along the road?

The sound of horse hooves on the hard-packed dirt echoed, and I turned to see Acorn running at us, riderless. The horse circled us, and I took off running in the direction she'd come from. She bolted back toward the barns.

EP and Bennett came up in a truck behind us, rifles in hand, and Eddie told them to go to the gate to stand watch.

My mouth was dry, my heart racing. My vision focused in on the path before me, and everything else blurred. I had to find her.

In the tracks below, I could see distinct horse hooves change into longer sweeps of a body—arms and legs crawling away.

She'd fallen off.

Where was she?

Then I saw her, leaning against a thick pine tree ahead.

"Eva!" I ran to her.

She stood upright, though hunched and covered in dirt and patches of blood. "I'm glad it's you." She winced. "Thought that stupid horse was going to lead them straight to me."

"Them?"

"Victor's men. They fired into the air while I was mounting Acorn. They must've wanted to spook the horse and make it look like an accident." She shook her head. "I jumped down the hill and tried to hide."

"Eddie's searching the area." I scanned her for injury. There was a cut above her eyebrow that bled down her face, and she was covering her side with both hands. "Where are you hurt?"

"I'm fine." She leaned against the tree, and sweat beaded her forehead. "I hit about a dozen rocks on the way down. That's all."

There were other scrapes and cuts along her neck and collarbone. If she fell down the bluff, she could easily have broken a rib.

"Can you walk to the truck?"

She took a step, then winced. "My ankle is twisted."

I swept her into my arms and carried her back up the hill. She tucked her head against my neck, pain creasing every corner of her face. Her hair was damp with sweat and caked with dirt.

Terror still gripped me, even though I held her in my arms and I could trust the men to make sure the ranch was secured once more. We'd messed up. And it nearly got her killed.

No one else had known of her place along the bluff. If I hadn't been here, what might have happened?

Eddie rushed up to us, and he looked her over with rage and relief. "I'm going to kill Merrick."

"Get the truck," I instructed. "Start with that."

"No one's killing anyone," Eva muttered, her skin hot against mine and her eyes fluttering closed.

"Stay awake, Eva."

We drove back to the house, and EP saw to checking Acorn for injury and putting her back in her stall.

Annie ran outside, and Eddie grabbed her shoulders to keep her back from Eva as I carried her in and set her down on a long couch in the living room.

"Dad? Is she okay?" Annie cried into her fists.

"Let's get Warren the medical kit and then give them some space."

"I'm fine, really." Eva groaned. "Nothing's broken."

"You scared us," I said, my voice thick. I couldn't admit just how scared I was.

"Could you get me a cold washcloth?"

I went to the kitchen, pulled a clean cloth from a drawer, and ran it under the faucet. I spotted a metal box to the side of the sink and wondered if it was a first aid kit—we'd need some iodine to clean her cuts.

The latch was stuck at first and the hinges creaked. It wasn't medical supplies.

A Purple Heart.

A Silver Star.

A Distinguished Service Medal.

I closed the box, realizing I shouldn't have seen this, not without her permission.

In that moment, my entire perspective on Lieutenant Eva Bryant changed. Those weren't common accolades. They indicated that she had seen the worst of the war and she'd been seriously wounded in combat. That she'd saved a lot of lives.

I took the washcloth and a glass of water to her. She pressed the cloth to the cut on her forehead and sank back to the couch.

"Should we take you to the hospital?" I asked.

She shook her head. "Just stay with me?"

"Of course." I put my hand over hers. Now that my adrenaline had subsided and the intensity had eased, exhaustion pressed in on me.

She opened her eyes and focused on me. "Warren, I'm okay, I promise."

"I'm so sorry, Eva."

"This isn't your fault."

But it was. Victor's men had been waiting for us to make a mistake.

"Keith must not know about this." She shifted uneasily. "He wouldn't risk my safety."

"He loves you."

She nodded.

"Were you more than friends?" It was the question I couldn't ask when we first met, and the question I didn't really want to know the answer to.

She sat up so our faces were level. "For a time, yes." She studied my reaction, but I guarded it.

"Why did it end?" I hoped that it had ended. Though I had no evidence to suggest she was still in love with him. I cared more about who had ended it.

She lowered the washcloth and looked at it in her lap, folding it to a fresh side. "We were young, probably drawn together by the thrill of rebelling against our families." She pressed the cloth back to her forehead, giving me a measured look. "In 1941, I went into the nurse corps while he stayed in Baker and started seeing other people."

The fool.

"Is he the reason you'll never marry?" I had to ask. I needed to know.

She hesitated, confirming my suspicions without words.

"I'll have a talk with him about Victor's men," I said.

"Perhaps I should."

"I'm perfectly capable of having a rational conversation with him."

"Your clenched fists suggest otherwise." She looked at them pointedly.

I reached over for her nurse bag and pulled out the cleaning supplies for her wounds.

She took the iodine from my hands and gave me a teasing smile. "This is probably a job for a nurse, not an officer."

"I'll never live that down, will I?"

"Not anytime soon."

My heart lifted at her light mood and our shared joke.

I wanted so much more than that, though every obstacle that stood in our way made it entirely impossible.

# *Twenty-Four*

**Eva**

JUNE 22

This had to stop.

The attacks from Victor.

My propensity to end up in Warren's arms.

All of it.

It had taken days of convincing Warren to let me, but I called Keith and he and his father agreed to meet me at the Geiser's restaurant. Warren insisted that he was at least nearby and that we met in a building where he knew the layout. I was certain, too, that Eddie and Lucky were in the truck around the street corner.

The bruise on my forehead was deep brown and purple, which I tried to cover with some makeup. I knew it would affect Keith, revealing the truth of his father's actions. He wouldn't be able to see the bruised ribs or discoloration along my hip, shoulder, and back.

I walked in to find them already seated at a table, and Keith rose as I approached. He looked at my face and his expression fell into one of horror. Victor only sipped the whiskey in his glass and watched me from the corner of his eye as I sat across from them. It was a large, circular table meant for eight, which meant a vast chasm spread between us, so fitting of our situation.

"Finally ready to make a deal?" Victor asked.

"It's time for this all to stop." I looked at Keith. "Someone is going to die if you keep doing this."

"We aren't doing anything." Victor shrugged. "You certainly have no proof if we were."

"You might have the sheriff on your side," I said, "but there are other law enforcement agencies in this country."

"Oh, is your captain pulling strings now?"

I bristled. "I'm pulling strings."

"You're nothing without this army that you're paying through the nose for, I'm sure." Victor pointed upstairs to the hotel rooms. "I bet that captain of yours is here right now."

"Of course he is," I said.

Keith glanced around as if looking for signs of Warren.

Victor growled. "You've scraped together enough to keep from foreclosure. For how long?"

"For as long as I have to."

"I can only speculate how you manage to keep so many men so loyal to you."

"Must be my feminine wiles," I said flatly.

"Or something more unseemly."

"Father," Keith hissed, but instantly recoiled. I knew the look he had—the same one he as a young boy had whenever he showed up with a different kind of bruise, the kind he got when his father struck him.

Victor gave Keith a look that silenced him and made him shrink back in his chair. Did Victor hold such sway over his son, though Keith was a grown man?

"What if I pay you double the value of your land?" Victor said, eyes flashing.

Birkstrom was worth quite a lot. Would these development plans of his really be so fruitful?

"Eva." Keith sighed. "The land is too big for you to manage. Take the money and buy a smaller plot with an arena and barn. It just makes more sense."

"Not to me." I shot him a glare.

"I can bide my time," Victor said. "You and that gray colt won't qualify for the national show and all your contracts will dry up. It happened year after year for Bill too. Why would you be any different?"

The words drove a knife into my chest, even though I had braced myself for all insults from this vile man.

"At least I win or lose with my integrity intact," I said. "I'll never stoop to your level."

Victor rose, the chair clattering to the side. "Then we don't have a deal?"

"I guess not," I said.

The elder Merrick stormed out.

Keith gave me an apologetic look and stood to follow him. "I'm sorry, Eva."

"How can you let him treat you like this?"

"You think you would be able to stand up to your parents if they were still alive?"

"We're not kids anymore, Keith."

He looked in the direction his father had left. "Look, you have your connection to your land, and I am tied to mine, to my family. I must honor that."

"Not when it leads you down such a dark path." I stood too, praying he would hear my words. "Don't let him take this piece of your soul."

"You're right." Keith rolled his shoulders back, straightening his jacket. "We're not kids anymore. Our choices aren't so simple."

He walked out of the restaurant, the chill in his voice leaving me frozen in his wake.

I was glued to my spot until Warren emerged from the spiral staircase to my left. He looked toward the lobby and then studied me as he sat in a chair beside me.

"I'm guessing you heard all of that?" I asked.

He lifted his eyebrows and pressed his lips together. "If you sit at one particular table on the second-floor balcony, you just so happen to hear everything said in the restaurant below."

At least that saved me the effort of summarizing how the conversation went. I wondered what he thought of Keith's comments about my parents.

"What now?" I asked. We were going to Arizona the next day. Was it safe to leave Birkstrom at all?

"Now we know where Keith stands, but we keep to our plans."

Ever the unwavering leader.

Was Keith right, though? Should I take the money and set up a new farm where the Merricks' shadow wouldn't hang over my head?

Warren must have seen the doubt in my eyes. "Don't worry. I have a few more ideas."

"What if my feminine wiles run out before we figure this all out?" I tried for a light, teasing tone, but it fell flat.

"We're Ghost Soldiers, Eva." He brushed my hair gently from my face. "We're not about to leave until the mission is over."

I both wanted the mission to be over and wanted to find some way to keep them around forever. After my five years in the Army, this new version of Birkstrom full of soldiers and two teenagers felt more like home than I'd ever known.

*He* felt like home. Imagining a future without him hurt worse than that tumble down the bluff.

But this was my mission now: to prepare for a life one day without Warren.

## Warren

JUNE 23

“Let’s go over this one more time,” I said to Eddie as we sat around the dining table of his tiny apartment.

Peter and Annie were packed for our flight that evening and listening to the radio in the ranch house. Eva was supposed to be packing, but I guessed that she was flitting about the barn with last-minute butterflies. She had traveled the world twice over, but leaving while Victor’s threat still loomed and the regional show was only three weeks away . . .

She’d tried twice to back out and send me to Scottsdale alone. I didn’t want to leave her behind. She was safest next to me, and my time with her was short. I’d need to tell her as much on this trip. Until this point, I hadn’t been clear about the duration of my stay. Was there any hope for us in the future?

Eddie stretched his neck and groaned. “We’ve been over this a hundred times, boss.” He looked at the refrigerator, and I wondered if he was hankering for a drink.

“I need you in command here,” I said firmly.

“I know. I am.”

“No drinking.”

“No, not a drop, boss. I promise.”

My bravado softened. “Did Violet return your calls?”

“Actually, yeah.” Eddie flushed a bit and smiled tentatively. “She said she’d fly back soon so we can talk about things.”

Hope filled me for the Moore family. I wanted nothing other than the happily ever after Eddie deserved.

“Reid is tailing the Merricks,” I said. “He’ll notify you if they’re acting suspicious.”

“Take care of my kids,” Eddie said softly. “Thank you for bringing them.”

“We’ll be back before you know it.”

“I hope so.”

That afternoon, we piled into a four-door sedan that we'd borrowed from Lucky to drive to the tiny Baker Municipal Airport, where Eva had called in a favor from an airman she'd saved in the Pacific. He'd take us to Scottsdale and back with minimal refueling stops so we didn't have to waste any time with commercial flights.

Captain Tarron Johnson was a broad-chested man with a severe limp and a wide smile. His red hair was curly under his pilot's cap. He lit up and hugged Eva, introduced himself to the kids and me, and then ushered us onto the plane. We had a few hours of travel, and the auction would begin right after we landed.

We loaded quickly into the empty Douglas DC-3, where the kids spread out along the empty seats that normally fit two dozen. Eva sat next to me, her gaze locked on the window and world beyond, but her body tilted toward me so our shoulders brushed together.

Peter and Annie giggled from the back of the plane, and once we were in the air, they stared at the landscape below.

"What was Tarron's story?" I asked Eva.

"He ended up with a terrible infection, and the doctors had given up all hope." She leaned her head back on the seat and smiled faintly. "I stayed with him night and day for weeks and he eventually pulled through."

"You have a gift, saving so many."

A cloud of sadness filled her eyes. It never seemed to be enough—the people she'd saved, the horses she'd rescued. Perhaps this sentiment was tied to the tragic tale from her childhood that she hadn't yet told me.

How could she not see how much good she had done in the world? But telling her as much felt futile.

The drone of the airplane and the chatter of the kids in the rows behind us became the background to a comfortable silence as the hours passed. I knew the quiet wouldn't last, not once we landed in Scottsdale nor once we returned to Birkstrom.

I hoped that Victor and Keith might give up, but I had seen their type before. It would get a lot worse before the dam finally broke.

# *Twenty-Five*

## Eva

JUNE 24

A thrill raced through me as we strode across the grounds that hosted the grand Scottsdale Arabian Horse Show, where I'd had some of my most notable wins.

I missed Gramps even more in this moment.

Now the grounds served as the location for another Army surplus sale of horses from the remount program as well as the Thoroughbreds, Lipizzaners, and Arabians that had been deemed spoils of war after Operation Cowboy.

Annie bounced on her toes beside me, taking in the bustling crowd and horses in distant pens. Warren and Peter walked behind us.

We had flown in the night before, stayed at a small motel near the show grounds, and arrived at the auction early this morning to get registered and find a spot in the crowd. Despite our early arrival, there was still no time to look through the hundreds of horse pens to confirm if Mira was even here.

"Captain Hayes?" a woman's voice rang out beside us, and all four of us turned. I recognized the slender brunette with piercing brown eyes waving at us.

"Adia?" Warren broke out into a smile. He reached her first and hugged her in greeting.

Adia Kensington pulled me into an embrace and then looked between the two of us. "What on earth are you both doing here? Together?" She glanced at the twins in confusion.

"Do you remember Eddie Moore from Hostau and Kötzting? These are his children, Annie and Peter." I motioned at Warren. "The captain and I are . . . well, I'm training Phantom. You might remember him."

"Oh, Phantom. Beautiful colt, bloody shoulder."

"What are you doing here?" I glanced around. "Where is Bret?"

I had met Adia and her fiancé, Bret Conway, in Kötzting. After VJ Day, when I'd returned to Europe to find Mira, they'd still been stationed in Germany, awaiting further negotiations on the prized stallion Lubor, who they had planned to import to Adia's farm here in the States.

"He's still in Germany with Ewan and Lubor until the paperwork finally clears for the horse and Bret's discharge from MI6." Ewan was her adopted Polish son. "I came back to chase down as many Janów horses as we can find. The lineage is all but extinct. We're hoping to get Lubor home by the end of the year. You must be here for Janów horses too?"

"Just one."

"Which one? I only saw a few." She opened her program with the list of horse names that were up for sale.

"Mira."

Adia blinked and looked confused. "Mira's here?"

Dread filled my stomach. Mira was worth a fortune based on her lineage. Adia knew that—she'd been with the Janów Podlaski horses in Poland since 1937 and had even traveled with them to Hostau during the Nazi occupation.

Warren passed me a hesitant glance. "I confirmed with my source that she was on the list for sale."

"I didn't see her in the pens yesterday during the auction preview." Adia looked through the printed list of horses. "Oh, I do see a Mira listed. Perhaps I missed her when I looked through the lot."

I hoped with everything inside me that she was wrong and that the Mira listed on her sheet of paper was the Mira we sought. We didn't have time to see if she was there, not without losing our seating among the thick crowd. We'd have to see whether the right horse walked across the auction block.

Adia turned and talked with Annie and Peter.

I stepped closer to Warren. "If we wasted three days for nothing . . ."

"We don't know that yet," he said.

The first horse walked into the small arena at the center of the large crowd and below the elevated platform where the auctioneer and several assistants stood by. From here, everything would happen at lightning speed.

Warren and I had agreed to a price we'd be willing to split. I'd need to discuss with him later that I'd trade that amount for a future foal when I moved Mira and Phantom to another trainer. I wasn't ready to have that argument with him now. When it came to that point, I'd probably have to tell him the full truth, and only then would he understand why.

Horse after horse cycled through the stands. Mixed-breed horses, former track horses, draft horses, Thoroughbreds, Arabians, mustangs—everything that the US Army had once acquired was for sale. All Army property being sold like the excess Jeeps and trucks. No longer needed now that the world had laid down their arms.

Adia bought a few horses—some of the Janów horses I otherwise would have snagged if I wasn't leveraging every cent I had to bring Mira home.

"She should be next," Adia said. We both stood on our toes to look for any sight of the gray mare.

Warren muttered a curse under his breath, and Adia echoed it. My heart sank, and I hadn't the breath to spare for words.

It wasn't Mira. It was a chestnut-colored mare who probably was named Mira, but she wasn't Janów bred. She wasn't the mother of the bloody shoulder colt.

"I'm going to walk the barns," I said. I held my hand up to stop Warren from speaking. "I just need a moment."

I wandered through the barn aisles, turning without thought or destination. Finding Mira felt like another pointless chase that would forever be out of my reach. The same as any dream I'd once had—of a future with a family, of finding some way to make up for all the damage I'd caused.

I'd hoped Warren might have been the good luck charm I needed. He'd find Mira one day. He'd change the world in a way I never could. He wanted to save thousands, not just the handfuls of men and horses that fit in our makeshift tents and bunks at Birkstrom.

A heart of gold and the son of a banking dynasty. He had the resources to do what I never could.

I'd known his time was limited in Oregon. A few short months and then it would all be over.

Whether Phantom won or lost in the national competition, the prestige from that show would see to it that he'd never be cast out from a stables or trainer again. I'd be able to rest easy knowing Warren would keep him safe.

"We'll find Mira, I promise."

I turned at his words, not surprised to see him behind me in a quiet row of stalls along the back portion of the grounds. The auction crowd still congregated near the block as more horses filtered through. Adia was probably still bidding on the few Polish Arabians left.

Several thumps from a nearby stall drew our attention, and we exchanged a glance. Warren walked toward the sound and peered into the stall, his body relaxing at the same time I recognized the sound as a hoof against wooden boards. He waved me over and gave me a smile.

"This feels familiar." His eyes sparkled.

Indeed, a gray-colored mare, a Thoroughbred, with a massively large belly circled her stall of fresh straw.

"Should we notify the auction staff?"

In that moment, I spotted all the warning signs I knew to look for. The mare turned, revealing discharge that I recognized as infected, abnormal. We had to get the foal out, quickly.

"There's no time." I rolled up my sleeves, stepped into the stall, and put my hair back into a ponytail.

The mare groaning and lying down with a long sigh brought our attention back to her. Warren followed me into the stall.

The foal needed to be pulled right away. The placenta must have ruptured, which meant the foal would be drowning.

Warren moved with confidence and strength, and together we pulled the new life free of his mother.

Moments later, the little foal sat in a puddle of fluid and blood on my lap. Sweat covered my face.

"We should probably fetch someone now," I said. Something tugged inside my chest as I watched Warren stroke the mare's neck gently and look upon the foal with such care and tenderness.

He seemed hesitant for the moment to end too. "I'd forgotten just how amazing this is."

The rush of adrenaline, the joy of new life. The marvel of God's craftsmanship.

"I never tire of this," I whispered.

"I hope not," he said as if catching the somber undertone of my words. "Soon Birkstrom will be bursting with foals."

I looked down at the foal as its tiny nostrils flared and took in the new world around him. Helpless and frail, this young life was an echo of a world torn apart by war and cultivated anew on a different continent. It wouldn't have made it even this far without Warren, Kenneth, Bret, Lucky, and the Second Cavalry soldiers who had liberated six hundred horses from capture.

"You should know this is part of your legacy—what you and your men made possible," I said.

"It's easy to forget." He dipped his chin. "It's easy just to focus on the baggage we've carried home."

"I know."

"You've probably seen more than most," he said quietly. "I saw the box of medals on the counter."

The words cut me in half. Air escaped my lungs in a gasp. "Annie found the box." I cursed myself for not hiding it back in the bottom of the closet.

His voice was low and full of emotion. "Those medals are not handed out lightly."

"I'm aware."

He didn't back down from my terse words. "Do you want to talk about it?"

"No." I focused on the foal, wiping more of the fluid from his coat with my handkerchief.

The mare stood and turned, sniffing her foal and taking over the work for me in licking it clean. I stood and looked at the mess all over my shirt and slacks.

I went to leave the stall, but Warren stepped in front of me. "You've given everything to the soldiers and horses around you, Eva. Have you taken time to care for yourself in all of this?"

My defenses rose. "Have you, Warren?"

He flinched. "I've dealt with it enough."

"Maybe I have too."

He moved in closer. "You're the most frustrating, stubborn woman I've ever met."

"I'll consider that a compliment."

He eased back a small step and shook his head. "I just don't want you to be alone with all of this."

His words washed over me, and warmth spread through my limbs. How did he know that I was alone? That I was swirling in a sea of uncertainty and doubt without Gramps here to anchor me. But I loved having Eddie, Annie, Peter, and the rest here. It was so easy to be next to Warren, and I felt the absence of his presence so painfully whenever he wasn't nearby.

Fire scratched at my eyelids, the feeling abnormal and terrifying. I drew in a deep breath, my body shaking in protest. My vision blurred. I hadn't cried a single tear in the past twenty years. After what my parents had done, and what the press had done to me when I had no way of escape, I'd vowed to keep it all locked inside.

It had worked year after year, battle after bloody battle. I wasn't the one who broke down—I was the one who comforted those around me. I was the rock, the shoulder among the tempests.

Now my feet wavered, my foundation crumbled. Around him. Only ever around him.

I didn't even notice how it happened, but I was pressed against his chest, my face buried in his shirt that smelled of straw, sweat, and his soap. He wrapped his arms around me, with no care to the mess of fluids and afterbirth all over my shirt and pants. He just held me, pressed his cheek to the top of my head.

After a few moments, the rapid beating of my heart slowed and my breathing steadied. I willed the tears back, though I knew I was safe with him. Safe to cry, safe to laugh. Was it even safe to tell my secrets?

I yearned for it. The past month of him working alongside me had been a happiness I'd never hoped for.

I put my hands against his chest and pushed away slowly. Painfully.

"You don't have to talk about the war." He looked down at me. "But I'm here if you need me."

*I do need you*, I thought, biting my tongue. *More than you'll ever know.*

Footsteps rang out from down the hall, and a groom walked up. I stepped away from Warren and put a smile on my face. "Just in time. It's a boy."

The groom brought over other auction staff and a veterinarian to assess the colt, so we took our leave and found Adia, Annie, and Peter near the front gates, the auction now ended.

I couldn't get the conversation out of my mind, nor the way Warren's arms felt wrapped around me.

What in the world was I going to do now? How would I be able to push him away to protect him and his reputation if I yearned to be next to him?

Bret and Adia had fought through a war to be together. Warren and I had found each other again despite massive odds. Even though I was the wrong woman for him.

A future with me was a field littered with land mines.

No one would walk away unscathed.

## Warren

As the sun sank behind the show grounds, Eva and I finished helping Adia load up the last of her horses bound for a nearby stables, where she'd board them until their home purchase finalized and Bret, Lubor, and Ewan were able to return from Europe.

"I'm heading back in a few weeks," Adia told me, brushing some horse hair from her hands. Eva, Annie, and Peter stood several yards away, looking over a group of white Lipizzaner horses. Adia crossed her arms and looked at me, a knowing smile spreading across her face. "I heard from Kenneth recently. He mentioned you've been looking after Bennett, Lucky, and some of the others from the 42nd."

"If you hear of any other fellow soldiers who might need a job and a home, let me know."

"I will." She frowned. "Kenneth mentioned you were running for office, though."

I winced. "I return to Philly in August."

"Are you sure about that?" Her tone went brittle.

"I made a commitment to Kenneth," I said.

Adia jerked her chin toward Eva and the children. "What about them? They need you—or at least Eva does. Kenneth can find another person to shepherd into office."

"It's complicated."

She shook her head. "If I learned anything from six years of war, four of them separated from the man I love . . . it's simpler than you think."

She walked away and left me alone and bewildered. I respected and trusted Adia. She and Bret had endured a lot under the German occupation of Poland. But she didn't know me, my heart, or my loyalties.

We said our farewells, and the next morning, we took a taxi to the airfield and loaded onto the Douglas. We greeted Tarron and settled into our seats. Eva and I sat near the front again, next to each other, and Annie and Peter bounced around the back of the rows. The night before had been quiet, all of us filled with the disappointment of defeat. A simple meal, an early retirement to the hotel.

The jostle of the plane as we settled into cruising altitude pushed Eva and me closer together, her shoulder brushing mine. Adia's words burned into my mind, along with Eva's accusations after we'd delivered the foal.

I was quick to help men like Mason, Bennett, Lucky, and EP and call out her medals being hidden in a rusted box. I wanted to pretend that I also wasn't afraid of going to sleep. That my nights weren't restless and plagued by shadows.

"We'd been pushing into Germany for a few weeks by late

1944," I said somberly. "We'd take two steps forward and one giant step back. Lost two or three guys almost every day."

She turned in her seat, her blue eyes tender under her thick black lashes.

"I tried to get permission to pull back and wait for more reinforcements." My throat constricted. "I didn't want to go into a situation I knew we couldn't win."

"They told you to press on," she whispered.

I nodded. The words froze in my chest, the shame and guilt I'd wrestled with rising in me and threatening to take me under.

She put her hand on my arm reassuringly. It soothed away the tide of emotion.

"I wanted to defy the orders, but I knew it would mean I'd be dishonorably discharged. That my men would be sent in under someone else. So I took a few of my most trusted men to get me to the edge of the SS camp, and then I went in alone and set timed C-4 explosives throughout most of the camp while they slept." I rubbed my neck, the pain still echoing through every limb. "I got shot in the shoulder and was caught in the blast of the last explosion, but my guys—Eddie and Lucky—they all pulled me out and got me back to the unit."

Her mouth dropped open. "Oh, Warren."

I shrugged. "Eddie had warned me not to do it, and I should have listened. I nearly got sent home, but I begged the medics to clear me for combat. I sent us into a hot zone too quickly, and we lost more men. After that, I didn't play around. Going into Hostau was the only time I deviated from the methods that we'd honed to perfection. By 1945, we were catching the Germans by surprise."

She squeezed my arm.

"I still regret those early days and how many men never made it home."

She leaned her head against my shoulder as if she knew that words wouldn't undo the pain or lives lost. Her touch was more soothing than any word. I leaned my cheek on top of her head, breathing in the lavender scent of her shampoo that always took me back to Kötzting.

"My hospital was overrun by enemy forces in August 1945, just a few days before the ceasefire," she whispered.

My heart lurched. That had been only two months after I'd met her in Kötzting.

"We were unprepared." Her breath caught. "So many men died."

My stomach tightened, and I fought the urge to sweep her into my arms as if I could protect her from what had happened almost a year ago.

"I tried to hide as many patients as I could, and a few of the nurses. Some of the doctors took up arms and tried to fight them off." She trembled. "One of them fell beside me, so I picked up the M1 and fired back." She hesitated.

I searched her face. Her eyes and cheeks were dry, but she stared at a distant point. Anger, revulsion, horror all passed over her expression. A nurse, sworn to preserve life, called upon to face a violent enemy—to take their lives to save hers and those around her.

"The injured soldiers, a few doctors, nurses, and orderlies—we fought them off for almost twelve hours before reinforcements arrived."

I could only imagine how terrible that had been—no proper cover, no means to retreat without abandoning the injured to capture and torture.

Eva had certainly known the horrors of what capture would mean for her and her fellow nurses. No one was spared even in those last days of the war.

"I just want to forget it all," she said.

"Me too," I admitted.

Silence mixed with sorrow, and yet a thread of healing spanned the air between us as the plane began to descend into Oregon and real life wrapped in around us.

As the plane touched down, our fingers were intertwined, laced together in comfort and consolation.

I didn't want to ever let go.

In six weeks, I'd have to.

# *Twenty-Six*

**Eva**

JULY 13

The weeks after we returned from Arizona passed in a flurry of training, packing, and further barricading the property.

Warren had kept busy in the past week. We'd hardly exchanged two words. Even still, I'd never felt so close to someone.

What we'd discussed on the plane might have reopened the deepest pain in my soul, but it also washed the wound clean. Every time I brushed past him, without a word said, I felt the reassurance and ease of sitting next to him on the plane. How his hands had captured mine and didn't let go.

Now, after two days of driving, we'd arrived at the fairgrounds near Salem.

Three trucks, one horse trailer. Two teenagers. One horse. One goat.

One desperate prayer in my heart.

Annie, Eddie, and I had driven the horse trailer, Peter and Warren another truck, Lucky and Bennett the third.

We all knew the plan. Warren would stick close to me, Eddie

would guard the horse and camp out in the stables with Peter, and Lucky would watch over the trailer and truck to avoid us being stranded once more. Bennett would watch for signs of any bad actors.

I slept very little, my nerves taut and my mind consumed by the tasks ahead.

The morning dew still clung to the ground and hung in the air. Peter and Eddie snored loudly on their cots next to Phantom's stall, and Annie giggled at them. We were at the end of the row of stalls, and slowly more competitors arrived on the grounds.

I stroked Phantom's nose, the dark gray muzzle as smooth as silk.

Warren approached and leaned on the stall, studying me with his gaze that never missed a detail. "Are you okay?"

"Just the normal nerves." I smiled.

He gave me a suspicious look. "The normal nerves of competing against your neighbor who has threatened and attacked you?"

"A Birkstrom legacy, unfortunately."

He rolled his shoulders back. "Well, I've had Reid Erickson investigating these judges in the past few days, and he reports that they're all clean. Cheryl confirmed that she'd heard the same thing. Phantom has a fair shot."

"That feels even more intimidating somehow."

"You've spent nearly every hour of daylight working with him for the past two months." His smile and gaze sparkled in pride. "Phantom just has to dance, and he'll enchant them all."

He left to go check in with Bennett and Lucky. I closed my eyes, drawing in a long breath. He was right. Phantom was in top condition, and his bloody mark shone out of his fading gray coat, which had become whiter with chestnut speckles throughout.

"Lieutenant Bryant?"

A deep voice behind me and the use of my former rank caught me off guard. I whirled and blinked. "Colonel Roland?"

The man with dark hair and patient eyes drew me in for a hug.

I laughed and shook my head. "What on earth are you doing here?"

He shrugged and looked around. "Looking for your client. Warren has been dodging my calls for weeks, and I figured I'd have to come out. Adia let me know you both planned to be here."

Something foreboding tugged in my gut. "Warren?" Dodging his calls?

Kenneth's smile never waned. He shoved his hands in his pockets and let out a long breath. "I'm sure you know the man is irksome." Then he seemed to catch on to my confusion. "Surely he's told you?"

My mouth went dry, my ears starting to ring. "Told me what?"

"Unbelievable." Kenneth laughed. "I tell you, he's going to be the worst politician. We're lucky that he also happens to be a shoo-in."

Shock crept up from my toes, weighing my feet down like I was sinking in cement. "Politician?"

"The next United States Senator of Pennsylvania." Kenneth's eyes sparkled. "We have some big plans to better support our soldiers. I'd love to hear what you think of some of these bills we plan to introduce."

He continued to speak, but the words were muffled as my head spun.

It made perfect sense. Warren had hinted at returning to the East Coast. That he wanted to save them all. What better way than through federal legislation?

Kenneth was right. Warren would be an easy win for the office. He was a war hero, made famous by Operation Cowboy publicity, and his family ran the largest banking system on the East Coast.

The only thing that would cripple his chance? The press and public finding out that he was working with me, the daughter of the most notorious criminals that his state had ever seen.

If I had thought for even a moment that we had a chance beyond our business arrangement, those hopes now shattered to the ground.

Forget the personal pledge I'd made never to burden another with my family's shame. It wasn't just his family's business that might suffer from my association if the truth came out.

My name, my history, would be a nuclear bomb to his political ambitions.

## Warren

Lucky and I left Bennett to make the rounds of the parking lot and fairgrounds perimeter for any sign of Victor's goons. Lucky droned on about why I needed to take a chance and ask Eva out to dinner. I think the boys had a wager between them.

My blood went cold as I turned down the row of stalls and saw a familiar figure beside her. "Kenneth?" I asked. "What are you doing here?"

Lucky greeted his old commanding officer with a loud exclamation and a slap on the shoulder, rousing Eddie from his sleep and prompting him to do the same. My pulse raced and my mind swirled with dread.

Eva caught my gaze and offered a sad smile. Kenneth had told her. I moved toward her. I needed to explain, needed to apologize for not being the one to tell her myself.

What a fool I'd been. I had squandered every chance I'd had.

She held up a hand to stop me. Now wasn't the time.

While Eddie, Lucky, and Kenneth exchanged pleasantries and then looped me into their fervor, Eva put her jacket on, put the thin leather show halter on Phantom, and led him from the stall. Annie ran alongside her as they walked toward the warm-up arena. There wasn't much else I could do.

The damage had been done.

Kenneth stepped up next to me and elbowed me sharply in the ribs. "You didn't tell me the trainer you were working with was Eva Bryant," he said. "I didn't know she was Bill's granddaughter. No wonder you ignored my calls."

My face went hot, and I ground my jaw together. "Why are you here?" I asked.

Kenneth's mood shifted in response, and he crossed his arms. "Don't get mad at me. I thought you'd told her—or anyone here—about your Senate run. Maybe you're not serious about the race."

"Things are complicated," I said. "Her life and ranch are on the line."

"Her life?" He blinked. "This isn't the Wild West, Warren. Bring in the authorities. I need you back in Philly soon if you want to give this a shot."

"It's not that simple." I started toward the arena so I could at least watch over Phantom and Eva.

"Look, if you want to withdraw, you're giving up the best chance you've got," Kenneth said, following me. "Senator Smith is highly unpopular right now, and if you yield to some other candidate, you might not be able to beat the incumbent again in the future."

"I know, I know."

"Be honest with me." Kenneth stepped in front of my path.

"I told you I'm still in the race," I said. "What more do you want?"

"I want what's best for you." He crossed his arms. "Are you in love with her?"

Love? I treasured each moment by her side, felt her absence so acutely. I looked forward to seeing her each morning and dreaded the end of the day when I left the ranch.

But our paths were on different axes. Her life was anchored here in Oregon. Mine was in Pennsylvania. How could we ever bridge the chasm between us? I could never ask her to give her life up, and if I abdicated the senatorial run, I might never have the chance again. What if we grew to resent each other?

"Look, we agreed I'd return in August." I stepped around him. "I need at least that much time."

He didn't follow me. This complicated an already high-stakes day.

What did Eva think of this news? It killed me not to know, but I'd have to respect the space she wanted. She needed to focus on Phantom.

"Do I sense some conflict between you and your esteemed trainer?" Keith appeared beside me, leading his prized yearling. The horse's chestnut coat gleamed in the sunlight.

"Worry about your own performance," I said without pausing to humor him. "You don't have the judges in your pocket today."

"I will be there for Eva when you break her heart."

That drew me to a stop. It wasn't true—I wouldn't break her heart.

Or would I?

Keith drew closer and lowered his voice. "We have a history that you can't ignore, *Captain*. She'll turn back to me once you're gone."

"You may have known her longer," I said, turning and staring him down. He shrank back, something he'd probably learned from his domineering father. "But you overvalue your own worth if you think she holds you in such esteem."

Anger flickered over his face.

The horse stomped the ground and snorted, and I took my leave.

If Keith suspected disharmony, things might be more dire than I thought. We had to get through the rest of this day, and perhaps I could smooth things over with Eva later.

I prayed she would hear me out.

Even if she did, my time was limited. This life would be another ghost of my past. My future was set on the halls of the

Senate building in Washington, DC. That was where I'd make a difference. I'd already given my word. I couldn't back down now.

Even if everything in my heart and soul pulled me in the opposite direction.

# Twenty-Seven

## Eva

Phantom sensed my unease as we walked around the warm-up arena. He pawed the ground, pushed me with his nose, and pulled against my hold. If I didn't get my emotions in check, I'd squander this chance to elevate Phantom's reputation and Birkstrom's shot at new contracts.

Gramps had taught me countless times that I needed to put the chains of my past aside or they'd drag me down. Phantom, so burdened by his own history, was even more sensitive to my energy.

I closed my eyes and drew in a deep breath. The world disappeared around me, and I felt the movements, anticipated Phantom's behavior.

When I opened my eyes, I gave the young stallion a firm pull on the lead rope and backed him away to reestablish my control and assertiveness. He responded with a dip of his head, as we'd practiced. His ears twitched, his gaze focused back on me.

"That's it," I whispered to him. "Nothing else matters right now."

This was why I found such refuge in horses. They didn't care about my family, my mistakes, my flaws. They only cared about the moment, the attention you gave them, the next ride.

I ignored Keith entirely, brushing past him to line up for our class. My shoulders back, arms lifted, and chin raised. Every move practiced and polished to showcase the horse beside me.

The class was large, the arena almost twice the size of that in Redmond. We'd have more space to fly. And I had an extra trick up my sleeve that I knew would truly dazzle the crowd.

The announcer called out the start of my class. Gramps's voice drifted through my mind. He was always there on the railing right at the entry gate, offering a wink and a final word of comfort and advice. *"Show 'em what you're made of."*

The line of horses and competitors moved forward, and I swallowed back the nerves.

My heart tripped over itself. There he was. In Gramps's spot.

Warren.

He leaned against the wooden railing, and he tipped his head in a reassuring nod. He exuded confidence—in me.

I put on the smile I'd practiced hundreds of times, but for Warren, it was real.

I led Phantom on that wave of energy into the arena, and he followed each command. The judges' attention never waned from my gray, bloody shoulder colt. He stood out from the other horses with his unique markings, the flow of his gait, and his pristine build.

Despite his dark past, he looked upon the crowd and reveled in the attention. He arched his neck further, his tail curved even higher, and his flowing mane and tail were like a silk sail on the wind.

If there were such a thing as a unicorn or Pegasus, it would pale in comparison to Phantom's display in that arena.

As we lined up in the middle after the judges had evaluated the horses at a walk and a trot, I couldn't contain the utter joy that flowed from within.

Then the judges' placings came over the speakers.

## Warren

Every soul in the arena saw what Eva and I had seen in Phantom when he'd arrived in Kötzting.

And yet, I only had eyes for the horse's handler. She shone. Phantom was a unique figure, yes, but she was the magician who had the world transfixed. With her pale blue suit, matching eyes, and the smile that drew everyone's attention, she had honed this diamond with her careful hands.

It was no surprise to anyone, except perhaps Eva, when the announcer named her and Phantom the grand champion of the class. She accepted the rose garland and a long, flowing blue ribbon and nodded her thanks to the judges—three men in tan suits and fedoras, still staring in wonder at the horse.

As was custom, she was to lead Phantom in a victory lap around the arena. She moved him clear of the line of other competitors and then lifted her arms. Phantom reared, pawing the air in a breathtaking display. There was no element of fear or lack of control.

The crowd broke out into applause and cheers, which only excited Phantom more. He stomped and snorted, and as they trotted the final lap, his hooves seemed to hardly even touch the ground.

The stands continued to shake with excitement long after they'd left the arena.

I followed her out, but my attention shifted to Keith. His expression was twisted, his shoulders hunched as he stalked out of the arena, jerking needlessly on his horse's lead rope in frustration. He'd only placed fourth. A far cry from what he was used to.

We'd kicked the coiled snake.

I followed him at a distance from the arena, where he went straight to his trailer and truck, barking orders at his grooms and demanding they pack up the other two horses they'd brought to show.

I doubted this was a reprieve of any kind. When he returned home and notified Victor of Eva's success, Birkstrom Ranch would be directly in their sights. After the last show, they'd tried to burn the ranch down. What might happen now?

I made a call from the arena's office to warn Mason, and he assured me the men at the stables were on alert.

I couldn't avoid Eva any longer. I needed to face her understandable wrath with Kenneth's news and my lapse in judgment.

Had I kept the information because I wasn't sure I'd even go through with it? No, I'd never wanted to back out. I owed it to Kenneth. He'd always looked after me and my men in the 42nd. If I withdrew, I'd leave him without the additional support he needed in the Senate to pass the legislation he was working on.

I defied the rules that I felt were unnecessary, pointless. I pushed back against the pressures when it put my men in danger. I wouldn't back out of something I'd promised a brother in arms. Especially when I had no future here, not when Eva had made it clear our relationship was strictly business.

Despite our moments of connection in Arizona and on the plane, she'd avoided me since then. Perhaps I'd hoped for something that was never meant to be.

Cheryl fell into step next to me as I walked back to the stalls to find Eva and the rest of the crew. "Congratulations." She elbowed my arm excitedly. "People will talk about that performance for years."

"They should. It was all Eva."

"Don't discount the value of your patronage," Cheryl said. "She was in a rough spot before you arrived."

"So was I."

Cheryl studied me with narrowed lashes. "Have you told her that?"

I didn't respond. Of course I hadn't.

We reached the stalls before she could say anything further, but her skeptical stare left me without a doubt to her feelings on the subject. Perhaps she saw something I didn't. Did I have a chance to be so honest with Eva?

After my failure to tell her about my Senate run, probably not.

Eva's hair had fallen from her pins in dark, chocolate waves. Phantom was in his stall with a fresh bucket of grain and Patches at his side. Annie clutched Eva's waist while Eddie, Peter, and Lucky were all speaking over one another about their wonder and marvel of the performance.

Cheryl snuck in through the group and gave her friend a hug. "California and the national stage await, dear one," she said.

Eva drew in a long breath. "Phantom is ready."

Was she? Was I? I planned to fly into the national show, but I wouldn't be living in Oregon anymore. My world, my reality, would be entirely different.

It would no longer involve Eva every day.

The thought hurt as bad as any bullet, blast, or broken bone.

The excitement eventually simmered down, until Eva and I were the only ones left at Phantom's stall. Annie, Peter, and Eddie went to get some lunch, Lucky went to nap, and Cheryl had her own horses to show.

Eva removed her jacket, rolled the sleeves of her white blouse up to her elbows, and tucked her hair into a ponytail. Back to the woman I knew.

The stall next to Phantom's was full of tack, supplies, and two bales of hay. Eva sat on one of the bales and nodded for me to sit on the other.

"I'm sorry, Eva. I should have told you sooner."

She held up a hand and shook her head. "I think it's great that you're running for the Senate."

"You do?"

She looked away as if to mask a measure of disappointment. "The country needs good leaders." Her voice caught. "You're one of the best."

The compliment felt more like a death sentence.

I couldn't explain it, but I had wanted her to say the opposite. To be angry, to rage against my insensitivity. This, I hadn't expected.

I swallowed a lump of emotions. "You should have heard the news from me, not Roland."

She shrugged. "It doesn't change anything."

Another knife to my gut. It didn't? Well, I guess that was where we stood.

I didn't miss the flash of pain in her eyes. Was she trying to spare my feelings?

"When does your campaign start?" She picked up one of her gloves, brushing the dust from it, and then stared at it absently.

"August."

Her gaze shot to mine. "That soon?"

Perhaps it was a stretch, but I had the feeling she would miss me. Miss this. Whatever this was.

"I'll fly into California for the national show. I won't miss it," I said. "I promise."

"Perhaps it's better if we find a trainer closer to Washington, DC, for Phantom."

"No," I said too quickly. "He's comfortable here, with you and Patches."

"You can take the blasted goat with you." Her tone was terse.

"I don't want the goat."

I wanted her. I wanted Phantom to stay at Birkstrom.

She pressed her lips together.

I needed to divert the conversation. I didn't like this direction.

"When did you teach him that little trick?" I asked.

"To rear?" Her cheeks flushed. "You've seen him do that plenty of times."

"Not on command, not under control," I said. "It was beautiful."

"Just wait until you see what I have planned for nationals." Her eyes sparkled again, and I hoped we were back to where things had once been. The timeline counting down in the background, yes, but that easy comfort and banter between us back.

Phantom was an unstoppable force. This meant new clients for Eva. Birkstrom was safe, at least from foreclosure. Whether that would dissuade Victor or his associates was yet to be seen.

Now that Phantom had superseded the Merricks' best horse, he'd also be a target.

Eva was on top of the world, but we were more vulnerable than ever.

# Twenty-Eight

## Eva

JULY 15

The heat of the day wrapped around us by the time we returned to Birkstrom, unloaded the trailer, and shared the stories with the rest of the men about all that had happened.

Everything was different now.

I pulled the champion ribbon from the stack of my clothes in the trailer's tack room and walked to the barn office. This wasn't my first champion ribbon, but it was the first without Gramps by my side. Without Gramps training the horse from scratch.

This win was all my own.

I placed the ribbon on the wall next to the photos of Gramps and myself over the years. Black-and-white prints of champion horses. Dusty ribbons and bronze trophies rested along the wooden shelves. Each one was such a vivid memory, each one a true emblem of the blood, sweat, and tears it took to reach the top of the class. To beat out the better-funded, better-staffed barns. Gramps and I were just two misfits from eastern Oregon.

Phantom deserved his place in history, and then some.

Eddie walked up to the door and paused, a big grin on his face and his hand clutching someone else's, but I couldn't see who it was.

"Hey there, Eddie." I turned from the shelves.

"I wanted you to meet someone." He stepped forward, leading a blond woman into the room. A taller but identical copy of Annie.

My breath caught. "Violet!" I looked between the two of them. At the nearness of their stance and the blush in Violet's cheeks, I could only hope that the conflict had been patched up between them.

"Eddie has mentioned all you've done for him and the kids." She put a hand on her chest. "I can't thank you enough."

A new fear struck me. "Are you all returning home?" I looked at Eddie. I knew it would happen at some point, but I wasn't ready to lose them so soon.

"No," Eddie said. "We want to stay on the farm, but I wondered if Violet might stay with Annie in the house until we finish up the cabins?"

"Of course," I said. "I'd love that. Let me show you to the room."

We retrieved her suitcases from the car, and Annie helped us carry them into the house. Annie showed her through the house, but Violet turned to me in the hallway, her eyes filled with tears. "How on earth did you get him to turn around?" she whispered. "It's like my Eddie is back now, after all this time."

I took her shoulders gently. "It wasn't me. Warren and the rest of the guys were there for him, reminding him what mattered. If anything, I provided an utterly massive pile of work that perhaps distracted him from all the nightmares of the war."

Violet sniffed, wiped at a tear on her cheek. "You were a nurse, right? So you know what they faced."

I nodded, unable to speak further.

"I'm so afraid of losing him again like that. He was just a shell of himself when he came back from Europe."

I flinched, still feeling a bit like a shell of myself. "I can't guarantee it won't ever happen again. When those demons take hold, he needs you there to hold him to solid ground."

She nodded. "I never should have left."

"Your mother was sick," I said to comfort her.

"I could have come back sooner, but I was a coward." Violet put her hands over her face.

I drew her into a hug, offering what little comfort I could. "You're back now," I whispered. "That's all that matters."

Annie walked up. "Mama, are you okay?"

Violet cleared her throat, wiped her face quickly, and put on a shaky smile for her daughter. "I'm just so happy to see you again, Button."

Annie wrapped her arms around her mother's waist.

I caught Violet's eye. "Just be forewarned," I said with a light tone. "All of the animals she's adopted are going home with you if you ever decide to leave Birkstrom."

Violet's eyes widened, and I turned away, leaving them to unpack. She and her daughter had time and memories to catch up on.

I went back out to the barns to finish the evening feeds and prepare the warm mash for the toothless goat Annie had found last week.

My mind kept drifting back to Warren. It did that far too often lately. Senator Hayes. Could he help the veterans on a scale I'd never be able to imagine? What if his work meant more funding for the little Baker County hospital to care for them?

At the same time, deep sadness cut to my core. If I hadn't had a reason to put distance between us before, I did now.

If I hadn't loved him before, I did now.

Tears seared my eyelids and my vision blurred.

I loved his passion for his men, the selfless drive in him to change the world. I also loved the way he could look at me and make the world beyond fade away. How he'd swooped in and saved me and Birkstrom Ranch from ruin.

Nausea roiled in my stomach. Naming my feelings didn't change the situation. It made it even more urgent that I put distance between us. I loved him too much to let my family tarnish his bigger mission.

Something strange and foreboding sizzled in the air. Maybe a thunderstorm was brewing over the mountains.

I pushed the sense aside, along with the longing in my soul that had no place at the surface. I buried myself in the work and repetitive tasks that soothed me.

As I finished preparing the grain and mash, a hesitant footstep behind me caught my nerves, and I froze. The musk in the air was unfamiliar, the presence threatening.

Before I could turn, a hand clapped over my mouth and a strong arm grabbed me from behind. Panic rose in me as I fought and screamed against the hand that smothered me. My captor held firm and pulled me out of the barn and through the shadows.

## Warren

As I watched Violet and Eddie together, it felt like nothing could be better that day at Birkstrom. High off the regional win, a safe return trip, and now the reunion we'd all prayed for.

Violet and Eddie spoke in the aisles, their voices quiet and their hands clasped tightly.

I turned away to give them privacy, though the chores were all but done for the day. The staggering heat of the summer day meant an early start tomorrow on the construction work at the cabins.

I didn't want to leave the stables, not if there was a chance that I'd see Eva. Not that I'd seen much of her since we returned from Salem.

Peter walked up to me with his hands in his pockets and a questioning, thoughtful look on his face.

"What is it, Peter?" I would have thought the excitement of his mother's return would still be fresh.

"A man just arrived, and he said you'd called him, that he served with you and Dad. Junior let him through the gate, so I figured he must know him too, right?"

Junior had joined our unit in the last few months of the war. We trusted him, but would he have known everyone who had served in the 42nd?

My pulse pricked and I looked around. We weren't expecting any new Ghost Soldiers. "Where is he? What was his name?"

The boy suddenly looked ill. "Oh no, I wasn't supposed to let him walk about the property, was I?"

My heart now hammered. "Where is he? His name?"

Eddie and Violet walked up, drawn by the rising volume in my voice.

Peter's face clouded over with fear, the same look of a frightened boy near death after he'd been bitten.

"His name, Peter," Eddie commanded gently.

"H-he said it was Jacobs. Errol Jacobs."

My gaze snapped to Eddie.

"What is it?" Violet asked.

Eddie pushed Peter and Violet toward the stairs of the apartment. "Get up there and lock the door. Don't come out for anything."

Violet gasped. "Annie?"

Eddie gripped her shoulder. "I'll find her. Stay with Peter."

I'd already started sweeping the aisles, looking for any sign of Eva. "Eva!" I called.

The name rang through my head in terror. Staff Sergeant Errol Jacobs had died in Germany in the winter of 1944.

Whoever had shown up, posing as a Ghost Soldier, wasn't Errol Jacobs.

Eddie followed me with his pistol out and ready. Eva should be preparing grain, but we didn't see her anywhere in this barn.

Lucky saw us and immediately dropped the water bucket in his hand and pulled the sidearm from his boot. "How many?" he asked.

"One," Eddie hissed. "Posing as Jacobs."

"Eva?" I called out again.

"I'm going to find Annie." Eddie headed toward the house. "I'll clear the house."

I nodded, my gun firm in my hands as I looked for any sign of Eva—anything out of place, any scuffle of footprints in the sand.

Phantom snorted and huffed in his pen. He knew something was wrong. He always knew where Eva was—he was bonded to her.

I contemplated for a moment, then I went to the paddock gate and flung it open. Phantom whinnied and tore out of the paddock, headed straight for a small shed behind the house.

"Follow him!" I shouted to Lucky and now Mason, who had joined in the search. The rest were on gate shifts or working at the cabins. They wouldn't get here in time. "Don't shoot the horse!"

We all ran over to the shed. Phantom disappeared behind the outbuilding, and a man's cry echoed out. Phantom whinnied angrily, and Eva ran around the corner as if she'd broken free of someone's grasp.

Phantom bolted away, now clear of the scuffle. The warrior.

I lifted my gun as a man raced after Eva. "Stop right there!" I called out.

I didn't want him dead. I needed to know who he was, who sent him. I needed him to testify and put Victor and Keith behind bars. Only then would Eva be safe.

The man lifted his arm, and the metal barrel gleamed in his hand.

I launched toward Eva in a dead sprint as I pulled out my gun to return fire. But there wasn't a clean shot. If my aim was off in the slightest, I could hit someone in the house behind them.

Another body lunged at her. He was closer. Eddie, coming from the back door of the house.

A gunshot rang out.

Eddie fell, knocking Eva out of the way.

Eva screamed.

I pivoted in the same instant to tackle the shooter, jolting the gun out of his hand. My own gun went skittering across the ground, out of reach.

He swung an elbow at me, slicing me across the cheekbone. Blood stung my eye, but I hit him with a solid left hook. He dropped to the ground, dazed.

Lucky jumped on him and grabbed his hands to control him.

"Captain," Mason called out.

My racing heart screeched to a stop when I turned to see Eddie on the ground. Blood poured from a hole in the chest of his shirt.

"Warren, my bag," Eva yelled. She scrambled to him and tore his shirt at the wound.

I reacted without thinking, racing into the house and grabbing her medical bag from the kitchen table.

"What's going on?" Annie's voice squeaked as she clutched a kitten.

"Stay in here, Annie. Please, just a while longer." I held up a hand. "Everything will be all right."

I raced back outside with the leather satchel.

*Please, God, let everything be all right.*

# Twenty-Nine

## Eva

My hands shook as I tore open Eddie's shirt and looked for a way to stop the bleeding.

This wasn't just a soldier on the surgeon's table. This was Eddie. The man whose wife and children had only just been reunited an hour earlier.

Why had he jumped in front of the gun? It should have been me.

Warren returned and set my open bag beside me. "What do you need?"

"Hot water, clean cloths."

He ran back into the house. Lucky and Mason both held the attacker down harshly, though I didn't think he was waking anytime soon from Warren's punch.

My breath was ragged, my throat still sore from where the man had grabbed me, dragging me behind the shed. I didn't know where he'd come from or how he'd even made it through the layers of security.

"Eddie, hold on," I whispered. The man writhed in pain, and

while it was good that he was still alive, I needed him calm or he could bleed out before I found the bullet.

Bennett raced up to me. "What happened?"

I blinked and wiped at sweat that beaded my brow. The heat was suffocating, and my head swam. "Keep Violet, Peter, and Annie away. They can't see him like this."

What if I couldn't save him? The bullet wound was so perilously close to his heart. Was I depriving them of a proper goodbye?

*No. No. No.*

No one else would die in my wake.

I rifled through the bag with one hand and pulled out my forceps and a handful of gauze. Bullet first, stop the bleeding second. Then the hospital.

Warren returned with a pot of steaming water and a stack of folded towels from the kitchen.

Phantom stomped his hooves behind me but kept his distance. He must have smelled the blood in the air.

"Will you put him away?" I asked Warren, my voice trembling. "And then bring a vehicle as close as you can to load Eddie?"

Warren nodded. "Got it."

He stood and walked over to Phantom, who followed him away from the commotion.

My gaze locked on the wound as I felt around for the bullet. Eddie groaned and passed out.

Then I felt it at the end of my tool, the clink of metal on metal. I gripped the chunk of lead and pulled it out, then quickly stuffed the wound with gauze. "That's it, Eddie."

Warren pulled his truck to the side of the house, blocked further by the back gate.

I looked up. "Mason, I need you to help Warren load Eddie."

"Eva, I can't let this guy go."

Warren walked over. "I can get Eddie alone."

"No, we can't risk him bleeding out. We must load him carefully."

Mason looked at Warren as if unsure what to do.

At that same moment, as if overhearing the quandary, the man jerked free of Lucky and Mason, taking off toward the woods.

Lucky leveled his firearm and fired twice but only hit the dirt at the man's feet.

My heart thudded, and I saw the conflict in Warren's eyes. "Warren!" I shouted. "We have to get Eddie to the hospital."

He looked between the intruder and me, his eyes dropping to my neckline, which I knew was bruised and dirty. He wanted revenge.

There wasn't time for this, and there wasn't a question of who mattered more.

"Warren, now!" I turned to Mason. "Hurry!"

They jumped into action and Lucky held his firearm at the ready, his eyes scanning the tree line in case the man returned. Warren and Mason loaded Eddie carefully, and I crawled into the cab to rest Eddie's head on my lap and hold pressure over the wound.

Warren closed the door, instructed Lucky to get all the men formed into a search party, and told Bennett to take Violet, Peter, and Annie to the hospital behind us. Then he hurried into the driver's seat and started up the engine. His gaze locked onto mine for just a heartbeat, and I saw the same terror I felt in every cell of my body.

He tore down the roads and sped into St. Elizabeth's parking lot. He jumped out of the truck, calling for doctors and waving over a nurse for a stretcher.

Eddie's eyes opened slightly before the nurses took over. He looked up at me and offered a painful smile. "Are you okay, Eva?"

"Shh, Eddie." Tears made my vision swim. "The doctor will get you all fixed up."

I'd never, ever cried over a patient. I'd never allowed it. Yet, for the first time, I couldn't control it.

"I'll be all right either way," he said.

"Don't say such things."

"My soul is at peace." He grimaced. "I got to hold my Violet. Annie and Peter have never been happier."

"Don't, Eddie." Tears streamed down my face now. The color was slipping from his face, and the gauze was saturated. No amount of pressure slowed the rush of blood.

"You saved me, Eva." He lifted his left hand and grabbed my arm, his grip weak but his motions controlled. "You saved us all."

Nurses flooded around the vehicle, flung the door open, and helped to ease Eddie onto the stretcher.

Dr. Harrison strode toward the commotion, and I told him as much as I could—the location of the bullet, the amount of blood I estimated him to have lost. Then the doors of the hospital closed, the staff disappeared with their patient, and I staggered on the sidewalk, utterly spent.

I felt Warren beside me long before I saw him in my periphery. He gripped my arms and steadied me. Just as my knees buckled, he was there.

He caught me, and I pressed my face to his chest, unable to hold it together. He wrapped his arms around me and held me while I sobbed into his shirt.

How had everything gone so completely sideways?

What would Violet say when she found out?

Eddie's words echoed. "*You saved me, Eva.*"

I hadn't saved anyone. Death followed me like a parasite and infected everyone and everything I loved.

Who would it take next?

## Warren

Hours passed with Eddie in surgery.

Violet and the children had come to the hospital, their faces blank with shock. All of ours were.

Eva's especially.

I'd held her outside the hospital for as long as she let me. My shirt was wet with her tears, stained with the blood of my friend.

Everything whirled around me. The attacker getting away. Eddie's life hanging by a thread. Violet returning to this. Almost losing Eva.

I'd had close calls before. These were different.

I watched her, still afraid of her disappearing right under my nose.

Violet and Annie clung to each other on a sofa in the waiting area. Peter stared at the ground with his arms crossed. I'd assured him that this hadn't been his fault. He'd been tricked.

But if his father died, I didn't know if any words I spoke would set him at ease.

Eva paced down the hall, closest to the operating room and far from Eddie's family, a limp that she tried to hide visible through it all. I leaned on the wall in between her and the waiting area.

A nurse approached me again and asked to clean up my cheek and apply a few stitches. I waved her off. I wouldn't leave this room until we knew Eddie's fate.

Eva approached the nurse, took the supplies from her hands, and walked up to me. "Sit down, Captain," she said in the commanding way she'd mastered. "That needs cleaning."

We sat on the other side of the waiting room to give Violet and the kids space. Eva's expression twisted in pain whenever she looked their way.

"This isn't your fault," I said softly.

"We both know that's not true." Her focus narrowed in on my cheek as she wiped away some of the dried blood with antiseptic. It stung my skin and overwhelmed my senses.

"He's a soldier through and through," I said, my voice now gruff and angry. "Don't take that away from him. He'd have taken a bullet for anyone on that ranch a hundred times over."

She froze, her hand mid-dab on my wound. Her gaze met

mine. There was an ache in her blue eyes, and I wanted with everything I had to take that pain away from her.

I loved her.

I'd realized it the moment Peter uttered the name of a dead man and I knew her life was at risk. I'd loved her before that. The way she cared for Annie, Peter, and every tiny creature on Birkstrom ground. The way she tended to the men, encouraging them, joking with them, and hauling Eddie out of the bar when he'd slipped into darkness.

Perhaps it went all the way back to Kötzting when she'd looked upon Phantom with such wonder and care.

I'd fallen for her completely.

She finished stitching my cheek and then covered it with balm. Before she returned the items to the nurse, I took her hands gently in mine and stood. My entire being still buzzed from the adrenaline of hours earlier and from holding her when we'd arrived at the hospital.

A moment was all it took to change everything, and I couldn't afford to let another one slip through my fingers.

"Eva, there's so much I need to tell you." I closed the distance between us, cupped the side of her face with my palm.

Her eyelids fluttered shut, and she leaned into my touch, the movement turning my blood to fire. I wasn't imagining things. She felt something for me too.

Just as quickly as she'd given in, she straightened and pulled away. "No, Warren. I can't."

"Can't do what?" Talk? Be this close?

Footsteps echoed down the hall, stealing the chance I had to ask her more.

We all turned to the doctor and held our breath in that awful space between wanting to know and dreading the news. It was the stillness on the battlefield when the guns went quiet, and before counting the casualties.

I hated the unknown.

Eva slipped her hand into mine and squeezed. Pain shot through my arm. My left hand was still sore from the impact to the attacker's jaw, but her skin against mine also soothed the ache.

Violet walked up to the doctor. "Well?"

The doctor seemed to struggle to find the words. Eva's body tensed next to me.

It couldn't be. Not Eddie. Not now.

# *Thirty*

## Eva

Dr. Harrison broke into a smile and said, "He's going to be fine."

Relief nearly brought me to my knees, and Warren was quick to catch Violet, who did stumble.

Dr. Harrison was only a few years older than I was and had attended the same high school. I slugged him in the shoulder. "You should have delivered that news much faster. That's not what they teach in medical school."

"Eddie asked me to make it dramatic." Dr. Harrison held up his hands. "He's awake, so you can go back now, Mrs. Moore. Family only right now. He's pretty weak."

Violet drew in a deep breath, and I knew her ire would be directed back on her husband.

Dr. Harrison pointed at me. "By the way, Eva, that was the cleanest field dressing I've ever seen."

I swatted at his hand, still angry and buzzing from the emotional roller coaster.

Violet and the twins went back to visit Eddie. I fell into

a chair, overwhelmed and exhausted. Warren sat beside me, silent.

He had more to say. Something deeper burned inside him, but now wasn't the time, and he seemed to respect my protest. I couldn't open this door. I couldn't let him voice his feelings—the feelings I could see in his green eyes.

The same feelings I had to bury deep down.

Still, his presence comforted me. I shifted so my arm brushed his, and eventually my head rested on his shoulder.

Sleep had almost overtaken me when Violet and the twins came out. "Warren, would you take the kids back to the ranch with you?" Violet asked. "I'll stay overnight with Eddie."

"Of course." Warren stood, offered me a hand to stand as well.

Violet grabbed Peter's shoulders in that distinct, motherly way and said to Warren, "Please look after them, will you?"

"I give my word." Warren nodded. "I'll stay at the ranch house on the couch. We'll put Peter in the other room."

My stomach tumbled in knots, and I considered pushing back on that plan, but I knew it was the best, safest option.

Violet turned to me, her dark eye makeup smeared. "Eddie wanted me to tell you not to be hard on yourself. The nurses say that your triage saved his life."

I nodded my acceptance of the words. She kissed her children, thanked Warren, and then returned to her husband's side.

Warren led us from the hospital and drove us back to Birkstrom, though I hardly registered anything that passed.

*"You saved me."*

Had I?

That hardly mattered when I was the reason he'd been shot in the first place.

I should have sold the farm like Gramps had suggested. No family should have had to endure this.

No one should have to die for me.

## Warren

Annie shuffled off to her room when we reached Eva's house, a little after one a.m. Peter flopped onto the bed in another room—Bill's old room. Eva pulled a blanket from the hallway closet, draped it over the boy, and closed the door.

I handed her a small pistol, my backup handgun. "I'm going to check on Phantom and with the guys. Keep this on you."

She nodded with her eyes locked on the handgun. I saw the memories flash across her face—that hospital in the jungle and the enemies closing in.

"Eva." I gave her a gentle shake. "I'm not going far, but I'm not going to leave you unarmed again."

"No one will die because of me." Her voice was thin, hoarse.

I put my hands on the sides of her face and forced her gaze to meet mine. "I'll do whatever I can do to make sure that doesn't happen."

"You'll be gone soon," she said sadly.

Would I? How could I leave knowing Victor was now sending hit men after her? How could I leave knowing the expanse of my feelings for her?

"Let's just focus on tonight," I said. "I'll be back in a few minutes."

I checked on the horses, then with Lucky and the rest of the crew. No sign of the man who'd snuck onto the property with a smooth lie. Junior was devastated by his mistake and apologized profusely. Lucky told him to ease off or he really would slug him.

I'd worry about the assailant later. I grabbed the spare change of clothes I always kept in my truck, after the many times I'd ended up covered in manure and mud without a change of clothes for the long, humid drive to the hotel, then hurried back to the house. I needed Eva close to me, needed to know she was safe.

She stood in the kitchen, making tea.

"I thought you'd be asleep."

She shook her head. "I didn't expect you'd sleep much, so I figured I'd keep you company." She handed me a steaming mug and then walked into the living room, where a couch and love seat angled toward the radio.

Peter snored softly in the adjacent room.

Eva sat on one end of the couch, tucking her feet under her. She'd changed her clothes. I motioned to my change of clothes, and she pointed to the open hallway door on the right, the bathroom.

After washing and putting on fresh attire, I felt human again. When I emerged back into the living room, she held her tea with both hands in her lap and stared out the window into the darkness.

If she'd had nightmares before, there was no question she'd have more after today.

"So why the Senate?" she asked.

I blinked, grabbed the mug I'd set down, and then sat on the other sofa, mindful of the space between us and appearances. If there'd been rumors about us before, what would they say after I stayed overnight in the same house?

Only her safety, and that of the twins, mattered right now.

"It was Kenneth who brought it up." I leaned my elbows on my knees, holding the mug. "I'd been trying to think of a business to start or an organization that might help some of the guys. It was after—" My voice caught and I cleared it roughly. "After we lost someone who shouldn't have died."

Her jaw flexed, and she pressed her lips together.

"Kenneth has some major initiatives he wants passed through into national legislation. Our unit, they came from all over the country, so it could impact them all. I don't care for money or power," I said. "I just want to do something, anything, to help."

"I know you do," she whispered.

Did she? Why did I feel like I needed her approval? I also wanted her to talk me out of this somehow.

"I bet you always knew what you wanted to do in life," I said, motioning to the room around us. "Train horses?"

She took a sip and nodded.

"I'm jealous of that. I'd always rambled, wandered, and ducked out of whatever responsibility my father flung my way."

She smiled. "Until the Army."

"Yes. It all clicked."

"Why didn't you stay in the service?" There was no judgment or accusation in her tone.

"I wanted to find a way for us not to get into another war." I shook my head. "I don't care to be a part of so much death and destruction ever again."

"Well," she said softly, "I'd vote for you."

Why didn't I believe her? She was sad in a quiet way that I simply didn't understand.

She swirled her cup and stood as if to get more, and I followed her back to the kitchen. "Eva?"

"No, Warren," she said, refusing to turn or look at me.

"No, what?"

"No, I can't do this."

"You keep saying that," I said. I turned her gently to face me, holding on to the faintest of hopes. I brushed her cheek with my thumb and wrapped my other hand around her waist, holding her close. "Give me a reason to stay here, and I'll withdraw from the race right now," I whispered.

She melted into me, her face lifted to mine. Uncertainty raged in her blue eyes and strained features.

"I nearly lost you today," I whispered, my voice thick with emotion. "The world looks different to me now."

"Warren." Her voice was cautious, warning.

"Just tell me you feel the same," I said. If she did, I'd uproot it all. Perhaps being with her was what I was really meant to do with my life. I just needed her to confirm my suspicions. I wanted to believe, with the glances she gave me, the way her hand caught mine, the ease she had around me, that I wasn't misreading these signs.

Silence drew between us like a chain, tensioned and cracking against the pressure. If it snapped, it could shatter the illusion or open a new door.

*Eva, please.*

For the second time that day, a tear fell down her cheek. She shook her head, and my world crumpled before me.

"I don't feel the same," she whispered.

"I don't believe you," I said gruffly.

"We don't have a future together, Warren."

That wasn't the same as her not loving me. "Why not?"

"I can't tell you. Please don't ask me to."

"Do you feel anything for me?"

Her voice caught, and another tear broke free of the dam. "Of course I do."

My heart soared. "We can work anything else out, Eva."

She put her hand over mine, then pulled free and put distance between us. A wall. The wall I'd been trying to break down for weeks, further reinforced.

What could possibly keep us from a life together? What wouldn't she tell me?

"Good night, Warren."

"Please." I was desperate. "Talk to me. Don't shut me out."

"I won't change my mind about this." She paused in the doorway between the kitchen and the hallway. "We can only ever be trainer and horse owner. Soon, trainer and senator."

"Eva, I've never seen you run from anything," I said, my voice louder than I intended. I caught her waist one more time. "Don't run from me now. Not after everything we've been through."

"I wish things were different," she whispered with a tired smile. Her eyes gleamed with tears as she lifted onto her toes and kissed my cheek. The warmth of her and the smell of her soap left me intoxicated, but her words eviscerated me. "It's not meant to be."

She walked down the hall and disappeared into her bedroom. The click of her door latch echoed like a thousand munitions, demolishing the fragile possibility I had of a future with her.

# *Thirty-One*

## Eva

JULY 16

Warren was awake and brewing coffee before the sun rose. I wasn't sure he'd slept at all. I hadn't.

I'd played our conversation over in my mind a hundred times, questioning whether I should have told him the truth.

I remembered how Keith had reacted, how deeply that had hurt when I was young and hadn't even a clue what love was. Now I understood what love was and knew that Warren reacting in horror would destroy me.

Better that he never knew.

He still greeted me with a soft smile and handed over a cup of coffee.

I took it, looked through the kitchen window, and hesitated at the vehicle pulling into the driveway. "Did you call the sheriff?" I asked, my heart thudding.

"No, why?" He followed my gaze and stood beside me.

Sheriff Lowe stepped out of his cruiser in front of the house. Keith exited the other side.

Warren and I exchanged a quick look before we went to the front door and emerged onto the porch.

Lowe tipped his hat. "Miss Eva." He cleared his throat, looking between the two of us, considering the early morning hour.

I didn't care what they thought. "What do you want?" I asked.

"Answers," Keith shot back, glaring at Warren.

Warren stepped toward Keith with his fists clenched. "Me too."

I slipped into his path and put a hand to his chest. "Not now."

Warren kept his hard stare on Keith.

"We need you to come down to the station for some questioning, Mr. Hayes," Lowe said, clearing his throat again. He put his hand over his pistol. "I hope we can keep this civil."

My pulse raced and anger surged within me. "What is this about?"

"My father was killed last night," Keith said. His face was flushed and his jaw tense. "One of our staff spotted your truck on our property early this morning, Captain."

Victor Merrick, dead?

The timing was suspicious. The hit man had escaped Birkstrom last night. Did he go back to the man who'd hired him and have a disagreement that ended in blood?

"Your staff was mistaken." I couldn't let Keith and the sheriff take Warren in—he might never make it back. "Warren has an alibi, Sheriff."

"We can sort that out at the station."

"Unless you have a warrant, he's not going anywhere." I looked at Keith with ire. "Warren was with me all night."

Keith flinched as if I'd struck him. Was he still so desperate to think that I'd fall back into his arms once Warren was out of the way? In his reaction, I could see that he had been hoping for exactly that. And now he knew that wasn't the case.

"You're, um, willing to testify to that, Eva?" Lowe said.

"Of course."

Lowe looked at Keith and shrugged helplessly. "Then we have no further questions."

"Get off my property." I pushed the stunned, silent Warren back inside. His gaze had gone from antagonistic to shocked.

Once the door closed behind us and the sheriff and Keith had left, he frowned at me. "You shouldn't have said that."

"It was the truth." I lifted an eyebrow. "You were here all night."

"Yes, but they'll certainly spread rumors."

"It's happened before."

"I could have just gone to the station. They don't have any evidence to pin on me."

"You think that'd stop them from booking you and putting you on trial? Manufacturing witnesses?" I crossed my arms. "No one goes against the Merricks. Whoever did kill Victor, I'm guessing it's not someone local who can easily be found."

He nodded and looked back toward the driveway. "I'll get Reid on this and see what he can dig up."

I lowered my voice. "Could it have been the man who attacked me and shot Eddie?"

Warren's face twisted in uncertainty. "The investors don't have a deal without Victor, right? Why would they threaten him?"

"Maybe they're counting on Keith being easier to manipulate." I swallowed a lump of fear.

He met my gaze, searching for something. "You think so?"

I nodded. "He was pushed around his whole life by Victor."

"I'll look into it." He gave me a bemused smile. "Thank you for saving my neck out there."

"I'm just trying not to read into how quickly they bought it," I said.

"No one thinks ill of you like that," he said firmly. "Believe me."

I shrugged. "Gramps never cared about what people thought of him. Maybe I'm finally understanding that." I waved the matter away. "I'll get the animals fed, and then we can take the kids to the hospital to see Eddie."

He went quiet and stepped closer. "About our discussion last night." He held up a hand to stop any interruption. "No, let me finish. I just wanted to be clear that I won't press the matter further. I want Phantom to remain here, and if keeping our relationship purely professional is what it takes, I understand."

A rush of emotion threatened to choke me. It would be easier if he wasn't so good-natured about it all. If he would just get mad at me and storm off, and I'd realize that we never were meant to be.

He'd respect the lines I'd drawn. The nature of our relationship. Professional only.

Would I have the strength to do so?

"I will make sure everything is well secured before I leave for Philly in a few weeks," he said somberly. "I'll turn over Phantom's care completely to you."

That was what I wanted. Wasn't it?

## Warren

**JULY 31**

The next couple of weeks were a flurry, and each moment that passed drove my heart a little deeper into the ground.

I'd hold to my promise to Eva. If this was the only way I could stay connected to her, so be it. Maybe one day things would change. The only thing that mattered was the safety of every person and creature at Birkstrom.

Day by day, the population was growing. Eva had a handful of new clients, some of the biggest patrons in the Pacific Northwest. I watched from a distance, helping with the final touches in the cabins, as she'd interact with the clients in the barns and arena.

She was beautiful as she worked with each new horse, negotiated training contracts, and worked with Bennett to assist with some of the training tasks.

Four days after Eddie was shot, he returned to the largest of the newly finished cabins. Violet helped move the last of their items from the barn apartment, and all four of them settled into their new home.

I'd gone back to the hotel after the night Eddie was shot, knowing the gaps we'd had in our patrols were fixed.

Eva paid me for all the supplies we'd kept track of. I didn't want to insult her by refusing, but I just wished I could have gifted her that. She also let me know she could take over the salaries for Bennett and Eddie.

I nodded, covered up my disappointment. I was happy for her. She was able to relieve the looming debt and take on the staff that would keep this farm going. I'd continue to pay the rest of the salaries for as long as I wanted her farm fully guarded.

Was the threat gone now that Victor had passed? We hadn't seen a trace of the black sedans or a whisper of his associates in town. Were they gone or lying low after Victor's murder?

Eva seemed confident that the danger had passed. We hadn't seen the sheriff at all since that early morning visit. He'd called in each of my men and asked them questions, as well as Violet. Violet launched her own campaign against the sheriff for his failure to take Eddie's shooting seriously, and she rallied everyone in town to her cause. Betty called Lowe daily for updates and demanded his resignation.

I knew it wasn't the end of things. Reid was digging into Keith's whereabouts and who might have killed the elder Merrick.

Kenneth had called me a dozen times, and I hadn't been able to avoid him. I assured him that I'd be there by early August.

Now more than two weeks had passed since the shooting, and I had a mere two days until I left. I found any and every excuse to stay in the barn as late as Eva did.

She spent hours working with each of her new horses, but the bulk of her day was with Phantom in the arena as he practiced his perfect pose for the judges, trotted alongside her, and moved without her even making a visible command. It was like poetry in motion, the two of them together.

"Hey, Captain?" Junior approached me, pointing to the gates, where a small sedan sat. "There's someone here from *The New York Times*. He said he wants to talk to you about your Senate run. Should I let him in?"

I wasn't ready for that business to intrude on the few days I had left at Birkstrom. "Tell him I'll meet him at the Geiser in a few hours," I said. If I turned the opportunity down, Kenneth would have a fit. I could at least keep Birkstrom free of the press circus.

Junior nodded and ran back to deliver the message. Bennett had the man stopped and was leaning in the open vehicle window.

"Who is that?" Eva walked up beside me. Her hair was tied back, but loose strands draped around her narrow face. She took off her leather gloves and shoved them in her back pocket.

"A reporter," I said.

She froze, her gaze fixed on the car. She relaxed only slightly as the vehicle left the property and headed back down the highway toward town.

"What did they want?" she asked, her voice unsteady.

I frowned. "What's wrong?"

She drew in a deep breath and gave a little shake of her head. "Nothing."

If I'd only just met her, I would have believed her, but I knew better now. "What are you so nervous about?" I asked.

"I just don't like the idea of a reporter snooping around."

"You want to show horses in a national-level competition, but you're scared of a reporter?"

She shot me an annoyed look. "The horse world is very different than the front page of *The New York Times*." She spoke as if she knew that firsthand.

"They weren't asking about you," I said. "I'll keep them off the ranch."

She shifted her weight and looked away. "Thanks."

I wanted her to trust me with whatever lay beneath her brave front, the secrets of her past she worked so hard to hide. But my time was up. If I won the election, there wouldn't be a lot of spare time for trips back to the other side of the country. If I lost, I'd reconsider whether to reenlist and return to the only other place I'd felt like I fit in.

She didn't want me here, not as anything other than a horse owner.

She crossed her arms. "I was thinking about trying to catch the sunrise tomorrow," she said softly. "Eddie insisted I ask you to join me, for protection."

My heart lifted, and I sent my silent thanks to the ever-loyal Sergeant Moore. Always watching my back. He'd known since he returned from the hospital that something was different between us. I'd explained, and Violet jumped in to say that we needed to give Eva space and time. That didn't mean Eddie wasn't trying to engineer whatever possible scenario he could to get us alone.

"Four a.m.?" I asked.

She shrugged. "Let's saddle up at 4:30. The season is changing, sunrise and sunset are shifting."

Things were changing.

I returned to the Geiser to meet with the reporter, Michael Bass. He waited for me at a small table on the second-floor balcony in the center of the rooms.

"Kenneth Roland mentioned you'd be here," he told me as a preamble. "I'm writing a story about the wave of war veterans who are all running for various House and Senate seats this next term."

I nodded politely. "Fire away." While he ran through everything from my background to my interest in horses, I could only think of Eva and our plans the following morning. It couldn't get here fast enough, and yet I didn't want another day to elapse.

"I looked into this trainer you're working with," Michael said as he flipped to a page of his notebook. "I couldn't find anything about Eva Bryant before her time in the Army Nurse Corps. There isn't even a record of her at the Baker County schools."

"What does this have to do with my campaign?"

Michael lowered his spectacles. "I don't like unanswered questions."

I shifted my weight and leaned forward menacingly. "Well, Mr. Bass, I'll have to insist you keep your questions limited to me and my campaign, or the interview ends here."

"You don't find it odd?" he pressed.

"Do you think your readers and the voters care about a horse trainer in Baker, Oregon? I think you're looking for a juicier story than is there."

Michael tapped his pen on his pad and then nodded, returning to his questions about me and my plans once I reached the Senate.

His comments about Eva bothered me too, the same way that Reid's had when he'd mentioned finding something suspicious about her and her background.

What did it all mean?

What wasn't she telling me?

# *Thirty-Two*

## Eva

**AUGUST 1**

I saddled Acorn and Autumn as Warren pulled into the driveway a little after four the next morning. He was early.

And tomorrow he'd be leaving.

My stomach churned with nerves, and my heart ached at the same time. The reporter showing up yesterday affirmed what I'd feared. Right now, they'd want to know all about Warren Hayes, war hero. When the election got intense, they'd dig deeper into all his acquaintances, including the trainer in Oregon with the famed stallion rescued from Nazi capture. A trainer with holes in her history.

Everyone in Baker knew I wasn't Bill's biological granddaughter. What if someone dug up the adoption records?

What if Keith leaked the story to hurt me? To hurt Warren?

I was sick at the thought. The Keith I'd once known never would've done such a thing. Now I think I'd lost that version of my childhood friend.

"Eva?"

Warren was in front of me, studying me with concern etched in his handsome face. He brushed my arm lightly when I didn't answer right away.

If I had any ounce of courage, I'd tell him the truth, give him the warning so he could prepare for such a backlash. But I was a coward. The box of medals still sitting on the kitchen counter—the box I still hated to touch—was a mistake. I didn't deserve any of them.

"What is it?" He drew closer, his masculine scent washing over me and reassuring me.

I closed my eyes, fought every muscle in my body that wanted to lean into his embrace.

"Talk to me, Eva," he whispered, so earnest, so kind.

"Let's just ride." I couldn't talk with him. I was too emotional—I'd spill it all.

He studied me a moment longer and then took a step back and nodded.

We mounted the horses and set out on the trail, the stars still glittering overhead, their last sparkles before the glow of the sun overtook them. Warren led Autumn next to me, our horses keeping a steady pace as the wind brushed the trees around us.

"Any advice for me?" A smile played at the edge of his lips. "For the campaign trail?"

I appreciated the change in conversation, the levity. "What would I know?"

"Everyone likes you. Every man in my unit remembered you, and you spent all of two weeks in Kötzting."

I chuckled. "Shake hands, kiss babies."

"How is it you remember so many details about people?"

I blinked in surprise. It had always come naturally. "I sometimes pick something notable about their appearance and repeat their name a few times, visualizing that detail."

"That's a good idea."

"Perhaps you should write it down?" I shrugged. "I'd put

patient details down in my medical charts. Doctors hated it, but it helped the other nurses, and they liked to claim they just knew all those facts."

"How dare they."

I chuckled. "Gramps was good at things like that too. He tended to remember people by their horses, not so much their kids or wives."

We came into the clearing near the east gate, where EP sat in the cab of his truck. He waved to us.

"Do you think the danger has passed?" I asked. "With Victor gone?"

"No."

"Keith isn't the same as his father."

"We don't know that the investors who want this property aren't still eager for their cut."

"So, we'll keep an army here forever?"

He looked over impatiently. "Until I'm confident you're safe."

I knew that I shouldn't push back, but I couldn't afford the rest of their pay, and I didn't think it made sense for Warren to continue to do this after he returned to Philly.

"Let's see how the national show goes," he said. "Please don't make things more difficult for them while I'm away."

"I'd never."

The wooden structure came into view, so we left the horses tied to the post and hiked the small distance. Memories of the shooter were etched at the back of my mind, but I knew I couldn't let that experience steal this place from me.

The sky began to turn amber as we sat down on the ledge of the worn wooden planks.

"Thank you, Warren." My voice cracked.

He looked over. "For what?"

"For taking a chance on me." I drew in a long breath. "I'm not sure I'd still be here if you hadn't showed up with Phantom."

"You would have figured it all out and never given the Merricks an inch." He smiled. "You're as much a warrior as Phantom."

"That." I pointed to him. "That's what you need to do on the campaign trail."

"I mean it, Eva."

"So do I."

"Well, our work isn't done." He looked back at the sunrise. "We still have Mira to track down and a whole new era of horses to raise and show."

The thought pierced my heart, but I covered the pain so he didn't catch it.

I couldn't do it. Before he left, I'd need to let him know. There wasn't any horse beyond Phantom for us. I couldn't handle a future where he swooped into my life and knocked me off my feet, especially when my proximity to his career would destroy him.

The next twenty-four hours—they were the last I'd spend with Captain Warren Hayes.

## Warren

**AUGUST 2**

The following day, after I'd packed everything I'd brought to Baker and approached the registration desk to settle my bill, Betty waved me over to the phone. Kenneth, again.

"Yes, I'll be there this evening," I said into the receiver.

"You promise? No more cold feet about this?"

"I'll be there." I hung up before he went on another long monologue about his plans and where I fit into them.

It wasn't cold feet about entering the senatorial race. I wasn't ready to leave Baker, but I had no choice. I'd need to get used to the different life I'd be living in Philadelphia. Everything the opposite of this charming small town.

Betty blew her nose into her handkerchief with dramatic flair.

"There's no way we can keep you here, Captain?" she asked me as I paid the final week's bill. My suitcase was at my side, ready for my quick drive out to Birkstrom to say my farewell, and then Eddie would drive me to the airport. I'd leave my truck and the trailer at Birkstrom.

And my heart.

"You'll see me around from time to time." I picked up my suitcase and tipped my hat. I'd miss the beautiful hotel with intricate carved wood flourishes and the white stone exterior that shone over downtown Baker.

I drove to Birkstrom, dreading these final moments.

Everyone had gathered to see me off, echoes of "see you in a few weeks" ringing through the air. Most of the crew would be traveling with Eva to nationals, and I'd meet them all there.

Eddie walked forward. "I guess we should hit the road."

"I'll drive him," Eva cut in, appearing from the barn and holding her hand out to Eddie to take the keys.

Eddie winked at her and tossed them over.

She strode past me. "Shall we?"

Eddie nodded his farewell, and the rest of the group filtered back to their tasks.

What was Eva up to? She wasn't one to change plans so quickly. And while I wasn't thrilled that she'd be driving back to Birkstrom alone after dropping me off, I didn't have much choice in the matter anymore.

We drove in silence to the airfield only a few minutes south of town. A small plane would take me to Portland, and from there I'd catch commercial flights to Philly.

Her jaw tightened and her hands were tense on the steering wheel. She'd never told me what had bothered her yesterday when we'd gone to see the sunrise.

She pulled up to the small building on the edge of the little airfield and parked the vehicle, and we stepped out into the sunshine. She reached into her pocket, pulled out a small notepad and a narrow silver pen, and extended them to me. "I thought you might use this, for noting people's names and little details."

"Thank you." I took it, brushing her fingers with mine for just a heartbeat. "If I end up being good at this campaigning business, I'll have you to thank."

She didn't seem to find humor in the thought, and I braced myself for whatever came next.

"I can't keep you as a client."

Even though I'd steeled myself, every muscle in my body tensed and my teeth clenched. Those words shattered my soul.

"Eva." I set my suitcase down and stepped closer.

She held up two hands, firm. "After the show in Pomona, I'll find Phantom a trainer on the East Coast that you can trust. It makes sense so that you're better able to track his progress and be more involved in his training."

Fear shot through my limbs. I couldn't lose her—not like this. What about Mira? What about all the plans we'd discussed?

"That's not what I want, Eva. I want him to stay here."

"I can't work with him beyond nationals."

"You mean you won't work with me," I said.

She flinched, and I resented my strong words.

"Why, Eva?" I tried to soften my tone but failed.

"It doesn't matter why. I've made my decision."

"It does matter," I said. "After all we've been through these past few months, I think I deserve to know." I didn't want to imply that she owed me anything. She didn't. I hoped we'd built some level of trust. Of friendship. Even if it couldn't go beyond that.

Her expression contorted, and I regretted my words—again. I just wanted to understand. I thought I'd at least get to keep a line to Birkstrom despite her reservations.

What was more, Birkstrom was the best place for Phantom, whose progress was still fragile. Eva might not admit it, but I saw the wildness in his eyes from time to time. What if everything came undone when the wrong person pushed Phantom too far?

"I can't." Her voice cut off. "I just know that it's the best thing for you, your campaign, your career in the Senate."

"What does that mean? Why does that even matter?"

She got the same terrified look on her face as she'd had the other morning. The journalist's question popped into my head, then Reid's comment about Eva and the information I should know. Her cryptic comments about the tragic childhood she'd left buried.

What was it about her life before Bill adopted her that could impact me, right now, in a Senate race? Phantom and his well-being were the only arguments she might entertain.

"I don't trust anyone else with our horse," I said.

She pressed her lips together and looked up with a small smile. "Our horse?"

"Well." I lowered my voice, trying to salvage this conversation and get her to reconsider. "We did bring him into this world together."

Her chin trembled slightly. "We did."

"Please, let's talk about this after nationals," I said. Perhaps the distance and time would help my case.

But her gaze revealed no yielding from her steadfast conviction.

From behind the airport building, the sound of engines starting echoed.

A stewardess opened the door and called to me, "Sir, are you traveling to Portland? Your flight is leaving in five minutes!"

My pulse raced. This conversation wasn't over, but if I missed the flight, Kenneth would kill me.

As if she saw the conflict in my face, she stepped up, kissed my cheek, and whispered, "Goodbye, Warren."

The nearness of her, the lavender and hay scent of her, hovered around me and blinded me to anything other than her. The warmth of her lips against my cheek, and then—gone.

She strode away without looking back. My mind raced. Everything I'd planned on, uprooted in just a few words.

I might be out of time right now, but in another three weeks, I'd plead my case when I saw her in California for the national competition. I couldn't accept defeat. I couldn't just be another client on the wall of ribbons, another soldier she'd served with on the front lines.

Not when she was so much more to me.

# *Thirty-Three*

## Eva

**AUGUST 15**

The weeks after Warren's departure were the hottest we'd seen in the high desert in decades. It drained the animals and staff and slowed the final progress on the last cabin.

I carried on as I always had, grateful that the heat and utter exhaustion drove me into a deep sleep each night. The nightmares still raged, but I was too physically exhausted to fight them. If I worked hard enough, crashed hard enough, I sometimes didn't see Warren's face in the flashes of dreams that haunted me.

Eddie, Lucky, and I drove into Baker a few days before we needed to leave for California to buy the final supplies for the trip and enough feed for all the animals we'd leave in the care of Bennett and Junior.

I'd been asking the soldiers still left in Warren's employ to find other jobs locally. They could live in the cabins rent-free in recognition of all they'd done for me and the farm, but I couldn't be indebted to Warren Hayes beyond the show in Pomona.

They all refused. I brought it up again to Lucky on the drive.

"All due respect, Eva," Lucky said as we turned into the feed store parking lot at the end of Main. "I'll take my orders from the captain. And my orders are to stay put."

I stomped out of the cab. "Eddie, won't you reason with them?"

Eddie held up his hands. "Look, Eva, you're not going to win. They won't leave until Warren says so."

I sighed. "I'm going to the cleaner's to get my suit."

"Want me to go with you?" Lucky asked.

"No," I said over my shoulder. "I'll be two minutes." With the ninety-degree evening temperature and the tiresome argument that never died, I wasn't about to cool off anytime soon. I needed a moment to breathe.

As I reached for the door of the cleaner's, it swung open and Keith stepped out, his maroon show suit slung over his shoulder. Pain flashed across his face before he sneered, "Didn't think you went anywhere without your Captain Hayes attached to you."

The ire in his tone caught me off guard. "Well, I do," I said.

He looked around as if expecting Warren to come out of the shadows.

"He's not here, Keith." I crossed my arms. "He returned to Philly."

He blinked, shifting his weight uneasily. "Lovers' spat?"

"We were never involved like that," I said through clenched teeth.

"I'm not blind," Keith hissed. "I saw how you both looked at each other."

"Forget it." I tried to step around him to enter the cleaner's.

He blocked me. "I'm sorry, Eva. I just . . ." His words dropped away, and he stared at the ground as if he could find them there.

When the silence stretched into several moments, I shifted the conversation. "I'm sorry about your father, Keith."

"Why?" His jaw went tense. "You knew what he was like."

The words cut into my chest. "He was still your father. And I know what it's like to lose a father."

He laughed coldly, the contours of his face looking almost exactly like Victor's. "You certainly do."

Anger rose in me, along with confusion. This wasn't the boy who'd run through the fields with me and ridden horses along the fence line. The boy who'd gone from neighbor to friend to suitor despite the bitter history of the Merricks and Birkstroms.

Something sinister had taken hold of him.

"You sound just like your father." I swallowed back bile as I added, "Are you going to try to steal my land too?"

It earned me the sharp look and boiling rage that I'd expected.

"I don't want that land." He softened. "All I ever wanted was you."

The words hit me hard. The dust and warm air of the sidewalk swirled around us. Perhaps he didn't comprehend at the time, or now, how deeply his rejection had scarred me.

I hated that I hurt him now, but my heart was fixed on Warren, even though we didn't have a future together.

"I think you should come pick up Naseem," I said. "I'll refund your deposit and training fees, but I don't think we should be involved any further."

His face flushed. "The horse isn't worth much. Keep her."

"Got a problem here, Merrick?" Lucky's voice cut in as he and Eddie walked up. Eddie pushed Keith back against the brick wall of the cleaner's, and the suit in Keith's hand fell to the ground. He raised a fist to strike Eddie, but even with the recovering bullet wound, Eddie blocked every measure that Keith attempted to get free.

"Stop it," I said, bending down to pick up Keith's suit. After a few brushes of my hand, it was as clean as it had been before. "Let him go, Eddie."

He did. Keith wrenched the suit from my hand, striding away

and glaring at Eddie and Lucky. Lucky started to follow him down the street to his parked car.

"Lucky, he gets the point," I said, which drew him to a stop.

"Not sure he does," Eddie said. "Are you okay, Eva?"

I waved a hand. "I'm fine."

Keith wouldn't ever hurt me. I knew that as deeply as I'd known anything in my life.

But the pain in his eyes, the anger and vitriol that spewed from his words—I didn't know this version of Keith.

After getting my clothes from the cleaner's, Eddie, Lucky, and I walked back to the truck parked in front of the feed store.

"Hey guys?" I asked as we piled into the cab.

"Yeah, Eva?" Eddie said.

"Do me a favor and don't tell Warren about this."

Eddie and Lucky exchanged a glance but kept silent.

## Warren

"She's a mess, boss." Eddie's voice crackled over the phone line. "Won't ride, haven't seen her eat anything other than coffee. She's running herself into the ground."

I pushed aside a stack of files on the desk in front of me. In the past week and a half of this new life of mine, it had been all fancy dinners, giving speeches, and reading endless briefs from my staff. Kenneth had set everything up for me to jump right into the campaign.

The updates from Eddie had hurt worst of all.

"Today she . . ." Eddie whistled. "Well, never mind."

"If you don't tell me, I'll call Lucky and ask him."

Eddie sighed. "Keith cornered her in town."

"What?" I stood up, knocking a stack of files onto the floor.

"To be honest, I think she was the one antagonizing him."

That didn't make me feel any better. "Any sign of trouble on the property?"

"Nothing. I think it all died with Victor."

"She still trying to get the guys to find new jobs?"

"Yeah. She's wearing some of them down too."

"I'll deal with this after nationals," I growled.

A knock echoed on my door, and I hung up the phone. Reid walked in, Kenneth on his heels.

"I've got to hear this," Kenneth was saying.

I rubbed my face, putting aside Eddie's words about Eva. The truth was, I hadn't been flying high in the past few weeks either. I missed her something awful.

I couldn't sleep, couldn't eat. I couldn't hide my foul mood from the campaign team either.

At least in eight days I'd see her again.

Now I needed to know what Reid had dug up. Would it put to rest the biggest threat that Eva still faced?

I motioned the men to the two plush chairs across from my desk, and I picked up the files that had fallen. "What'd you find out?"

"Everything." Reid pulled a thick stack of papers from his bag and handed them to me.

I flipped through the stack of photos, time logs, and descriptions of movements. Each page told a more convincing story until the last few pages, which revealed the truth I had been reluctant to speculate about.

"You'll need more than photos," Kenneth said, his hand over his chin. He looked ill at the revelations on the page.

"Can you get me hard evidence?" I asked Reid. "I need it in a week."

"You'll have it. I just need to wait until Merrick drives to California. Then I'll retrieve what I can from the property and skedaddle down to meet you."

Nationals couldn't happen soon enough. Eva didn't know the

truth—she'd never believe it. I needed enough proof to convince her, let alone the authorities.

Reid left and Kenneth leaned back in the chair. "Well, at least you've solved the mystery."

"That doesn't make me feel better."

"You better put it away and get your mission straight for tonight. You know the Pulitzer family will be at the fundraiser tonight, right? The Carnegies too."

I hummed a noncommittal response, staring at the pages in front of me.

Kenneth gave a long sigh, cursing under his breath. "You're not even here, are you?"

I blinked and looked up, about to give him the automatic response that of course I was here, but he was right. All I could think about was getting back to Eva and how much I dreaded having to come back to this office, a bustling hub of campaign aides and advisers, wrapped in mahogany and cigar smoke.

"I'm sorry, Kenneth."

I didn't want to let him down. I didn't want to go back on my word. The man I was back in May when I agreed to this path—that Warren Hayes had changed into someone entirely different.

I wanted to help my fellow soldiers as much as ever. I'd seen through Eva's eyes and the impact her methods could have, one life at a time. I had people who still depended on me back in Baker. I couldn't abandon them now.

"I had a suspicion this would happen." My former commanding officer stood, putting his hands casually in his pockets, and paced the room. "I shouldn't have pushed you into this."

Disappointment swirled in my gut. As a kid, I had found humor in the many rules I broke and the endless tirades from my mother or father. Letting Kenneth down—that was an entirely different story.

Kenneth rubbed his face and sighed. "I've been thinking about this and might have an alternative. Maybe." He held up a finger.

My spine straightened. An alternative? I shouldn't have been surprised. In the field, Kenneth always had a plan B and plan C.

"I've heard some rumors that one of the senators from Oregon plans to retire once his daughter graduates from high school in two years." Kenneth raised an eyebrow. "It's not ideal for me and the support I need right now."

My heart hammered. Two years. Oregon as the home base.

"If I commit to speaking tours and building support from outside the Senate seat?" I asked. I'd do anything to make it up to him.

"That'd be the least you can do," Kenneth said, a knowing smile on his face. "And maybe this will get Adia off my back. She's been calling me ever since you ran into her in Scottsdale."

His words faded as a series of new plans and new possibilities fell into place.

But none of it would matter if Eva didn't hear me out, if she wouldn't lower her barricades.

# *Thirty-Four*

## Eva

**AUGUST 23**

"Have you seen him yet?" Violet asked Eddie as they stood down the row of stalls in the grand Pomona stables. The arena and showgrounds beyond all buzzed with activity.

"Shh," he said, knowing I was in a frazzled state and within earshot. "He'll be here."

I finished pinning my hair and looked at my reflection one final time in my compact. My eyes were dark with liner around the edges, thick mascara, and dark brown shadow that made my blue eyes stand out. My hair curled in waves and contrasted against the new ivory coat and skirt I had bought. I matched Phantom's coat so well that his bloody shoulder mark stood out like an oasis against the desert sand.

Even in the little round mirror, my cheeks were gaunt, my eyes were tired. Under the powder, there were dark circles and freckles from the summer-long sun exposure.

Perhaps it was better if Warren didn't make it. If he didn't see me like this.

Annie bounced up, her hair also curled and styled now that Violet was here and holding the children to more presentable standards. She held the copy of *Azam*, the book I'd bought her months ago. Seeing the glittering stables where the book took place had been a dream come true for the young girl. "Good luck, Miss Eva," she said. "I hope you win."

I set the compact aside and pulled the girl into a hug. "Just keep an eye on Patches and make sure he doesn't try to sneak out with us."

"It's time, Eva." Eddie walked up. "The class is starting."

My heart leapt into my throat. I straightened the exhibitor number on my arm, gave my hair one final brush with my hand, and then reached for Phantom's lead rope as Eddie handed him over to me. We walked at a brisk pace across the paved parking lot to the towering arena, where hundreds of people filled the stands for the biggest event this industry had seen since early 1941.

Phantom snorted excitedly, his eyes taking everything in around him.

I caught myself looking around in the crowd and searching each spectator's face.

*Focus, Eva. Forget about him.*

The steward waved me into the show ring. "Ah, Ms. Bryant and Mr. Merrick."

From behind me, Keith and his horse raced ahead of me in line. I knew he didn't like to be the last one in the arena—a weird superstition he had. He walked ahead of his horse rather than leading on the proper left-hand side, knocking into me and shoving me against Phantom's shoulder.

An intense pain radiated from my arm, but I shook it off, trying to find my footing again and continue my brisk walk into the arena. A moment later the gates would have closed and we'd have lost our chance.

Keith and his red stallion walked ahead of us. He placed

something shiny in his coat pocket before lifting his head and carrying on.

At that very moment, a deep shade of red in the corner of my eye caught my attention. My coat was cut, and blood seeped into the edges around the tear.

Phantom tossed his head and snorted, and his halter slid right off his nose. The crowd around us gasped.

My mind whirled as I picked up the leather halter, seeing the edges were sliced clean through. How? And then I saw a small gash behind his ear. A stream of blood followed the muscular curve of his neck and down into the bloody mark on his shoulder.

*Dear Lord*. Keith had cut the halter and nicked the horse. And me.

"Exhibitor!" a judge called to me. He was a portly man with a quick smile, but now he had a sour, stern expression as he pointed me to the gate. "You need to leave."

"Give me one chance." My words came out before my brain even processed what they meant. I put the lead around Phantom's neck to show I still had control. "We can present without the halter. If he steps out of line once, you can dismiss us."

The judge glanced back at his two other colleagues, who both shrugged. "You get one chance."

That was all I needed.

## Warren

"Eddie, she's bleeding," Violet said, her hand flying to her mouth.

Eddie, Violet, and the twins had found me in the stands moments after I'd arrived. Another ten-minute delay and I might have missed it all. But I'd needed to ensure that every piece was in place.

Eddie glanced at me, and I dared not look away from Eva as she walked the arena—with no halter to restrain Phantom.

The crowd murmured in confusion. Several people nearby thought her cut and stained coat were just a costume to match the horse's unique markings.

Eddie and I knew better.

"I'll kill Merrick," Eddie growled under his breath.

"Not if I get to him first." Anger churned deep inside me. As Eva and Phantom circled the arena and passed in front of us on the perimeter, I saw the extent of her injury, and it took everything in me not to call a stop to the class.

I'd mapped this day out a hundred times over and never once considered Keith would make such a vicious move. I'd never expected him to hurt her.

That made the next part of my plan a bit easier to stomach.

Phantom kept pace with Eva as if she still had a firm hold of his halter rather than a loose line around his neck. I'd known from our own adventures wrangling horses at Hostau that horses were difficult to control unless you had the ability to point their nose in the direction you wanted them to travel.

"Is it normal for a horse to behave like this?" Violet asked her husband. Her gaze was glued to Eva and Phantom, as was every other one in the entire building.

"No." Eddie smiled. "That girl is something special."

She was. Seeing her again after just those few weeks apart, I felt the broken part of myself was now whole.

She held the broken halter and lead rope in her left hand, tucked against her side, while her right hand pointed and moved in subtle cues for the horse to walk, trot, and stop.

The three judges hardly looked at the other competitors. That didn't mean her win was guaranteed.

Cheryl squeezed through the crowd around us and stopped beside me to whisper, "Everything is arranged. Let's meet at the office after." Then she looked at Eva and froze. "Is she bleeding?"

"Yes."

"Keith cut the halter?"

"Who else?"

"That doesn't make any sense." Cheryl shook her head. "Why would he risk this?"

I chuckled. "He didn't know she'd still be able to compete."

Eddie's chest inflated with pride. "He underestimated her."

*"You're not the first to underestimate me."*

I could hear her voice from Kötzting, and I loved her even more. She'd overcome every obstacle thrown at her, and this was no different.

The horses and handlers lined up in the center of the arena for the judges, and Eva glowed as Phantom stood without a single piece of tack attached. Then the class standings were announced.

Eva and Phantom won second place.

The crowd booed as a result, startling most of the other horses in the arena, but Eva kept her calm and kept Phantom's attention on her.

The grand prize went to Keith and his chestnut colt. The displeasure of the crowd heightened as he did a celebratory lap.

Eva and Phantom, as the next to exit the arena, stepped out of the line and then paused. It would be improper for her to do a lap like the grand champion, but she froze a few horse lengths away from the other competitors and lifted her right arm into the air.

Phantom jumped high into the air so his back legs extended parallel to the ground, reminiscent of the stallions of Lipizza, the horses of the Spanish Riding School in Vienna.

The crowd erupted. The other horses startled and nearly got loose in the arena, and Eva led Phantom out before facing a reprimand from the steward or judges.

At least she'd solidified her place in the industry by reputation. As unforgettable as their performance was a few weeks ago in Salem, this was even better.

Now it was time for Eddie, Cheryl, and me to act.

I nodded to Eddie, and he pushed through the crowd to set the plan in motion. Cheryl and I headed toward Eva and Phantom.

She stood in the warm-up arena as spectators flocked around her and competitors tried to wade through the sea of people to return to the stalls.

I saw right away she was unsteady on her feet. I pulled my handkerchief from my suit pocket and reached for her as we closed in on the horse. Eva had looped the leather lead rope around Phantom's neck, careful to keep it away from the three-inch gash there. It wasn't deep and the blood had already crusted over.

Cheryl took the lead rope from her friend's hand. "I'll get him to the vet."

I caught her good arm and searched her face. She was blinking against dizziness or unconsciousness.

"Eva?"

She straightened and seemed to force herself back into consciousness. "Warren?"

"I'm here."

I looked at her arm, tearing the fabric slightly more to see through to the wound on her skin. It was also about three or four inches and a clean slash. From a sharp knife. I pressed the handkerchief to her arm and tied it around the wound. Getting her to a doctor would have to wait.

She winced.

"Eva, you need to come with me." I nodded to Cheryl. "She'll get Phantom treated and safely to his stall, but we have a few things that need to be sorted."

"What are you talking about?"

I took her hand and led her through the crowds, toward the show office. Stuart Davis, the organization's president, and two other board members we'd met in Seattle sat inside.

The room was no more than sixteen feet wide and ten feet deep and full of tables of papers, ribbons for distribution, and typewriters. A few secretaries sat in the back, looking up in confusion. They were about to get quite the display.

"Miss Bryant? Captain Hayes?" Stuart said. "Can we help you? What happened to your arm?"

"We have a few concerns to address," I said. "Cheryl Jenkins will join us shortly, along with a few other key persons."

"This is hardly the time or procedure to redress concerns."

Eddie and Lucky burst through the door with Keith and tossed him to the floor.

"What in the devil!" Stuart cried.

Cheryl followed closely behind and then gave me a nod to confirm that my other guests were also on their way.

"Eddie?" I asked.

He produced a knife and handed it to Stuart. "Found this on him." He kicked Keith's leg. "Too stupid to throw it away before we got to him."

Stuart opened the blade, where blood had dried on the edge. He looked at Eva. "He did this to you?"

Eva nodded. "He slashed the halter and cut me and my horse."

"I'm so sorry." Keith looked up from the floor, his eyes wide and his mouth open in horror. "Eva, it was an accident. I swear. I didn't mean to hit you or Phantom. I just wanted to keep you from entering the class. I'd never hurt you. You know that, right?"

She looked down on him with pity.

"There's more," I said.

Eddie reached down, pulled Keith to his feet, and shoved him into a wooden chair. "Don't move."

The office door opened and two men in suits walked in, followed by Reid and Harold Jefferson.

"These are two detectives from the state police and Harold Jefferson from the FBI," I said, watching Keith's reaction. "We brought them in and provided some key evidence, since Sheriff Lowe hadn't gotten to the bottom of your father's murder."

"To cover up your involvement, Captain?" Keith said with weak bravado.

"Not quite," I said. "My friend here, Reid Erickson, is an

investigator who followed you around for several months and has dozens of sworn statements from your own staff as to your whereabouts."

The color drained from Keith's face, and his body tensed.

"The physical evidence doesn't lie," I said. "You pushed your father down and he hit his head on a boulder. It was an accident, wasn't it?"

Keith's head bobbed slightly.

"Covering it up and trying to pin your father's death on me," I continued. "That makes it manslaughter and obstruction."

"I had no other choice," Keith growled. "He was going to kill Eva. I had to protect her."

# Thirty-Five

## Eva

Impossible.

This was all impossible. Harold Jefferson, the investigators, the detectives.

My arm throbbed, my head swam, my stomach wanted to heave.

I stepped past Warren and knelt beside Keith. "Keith—how could you?" My voice trembled.

Eddie held Keith's arms tightly, and Warren stood a short distance behind me. But I wasn't afraid of the small, frightened boy before me.

"He hired someone to kill you." Keith slumped against Eddie's hold. "He wasn't going to stop. I couldn't reason with him. He wasn't ever going to stop until he had Birkstrom. I was so angry. I shoved him, and he fell."

The president and staff from the breed organization all stared in amazement.

Something deep inside me had considered it after that day outside the dry cleaner. The moment I'd seen a helpless, wounded boy who had given in to his hatred.

In the first moment Keith had ever stood up to his father, he'd accidentally killed him.

The buzz around me intensified, and the room felt ready to explode.

Harold crossed his arms. "We tracked down the men who were colluding with Victor and his son to purchase your property, Eva. They've been detained on a few smaller crimes, but you should rest assured that your farm is safe from any further mob intervention. We also found the hit man who tried to abduct you and shot Eddie."

I'd wanted to hear nothing more. Except it meant that the Merricks' dynasty had been completely upturned.

The room fell silent. I saw the two officers exchange a knowing glance, and I could sense the relief in Eddie and Warren that the truth was out.

Keith looked up at me and whispered, "I've always loved you, Eva. I never wanted to see you hurt."

Pain shot through my body, along with the smallest thread of relief. The man who had been desperate to take my property, my livelihood, my life—the man who had hurt my dearest friends—was gone.

I never would have wanted this. Victor might not have been an innocent bystander or guiltless party, but he didn't deserve the fate he'd earned, at the hands of his son.

Warren took my elbow, pulling me gently to my feet and away from Keith. He must have noticed I was swaying and about to fall over.

I'd lost a lot of blood. I hadn't eaten anything, and the news was all too much.

The officers pulled out their handcuffs and went for Keith as I pressed my face into Warren's chest. He wrapped his arms around me gently, careful not to squeeze my injured arm.

"Eva, I did this for you," Keith said as the metal cuffs clicked into place. "He wasn't going to stop until he killed you. I saw it in his face. He'd never have stopped."

"It's better for you to stop talking now," one of the officers said somberly. "Let's go."

Footsteps shuffled.

"No, wait," Keith protested. "I love you, Eva."

"You love her, so you cut her horse's halter and her arm?" Eddie growled.

"I never meant to hurt her." His voice went frantic. "I just needed one more win. Father left a financial mess for me too. I wanted more time to convince you that we could combine our properties, our efforts. I just wanted to be together, and he was in the way."

Victor was in the way? Or Warren? I slammed my eyes shut. My throat constricted. Would Keith have hurt Warren if he hadn't gone to Philadelphia weeks ago?

The officers pulled Keith out of the small room.

Stuart let out a long breath. "I've never—" He cleared his throat. "Um, of course the grand prize standing will be awarded to you, Miss Bryant. Mr. Merrick will be stripped of all his awards and membership. What horrible business this is. I trust, Miss Bryant, that we can keep this matter under wraps. Rumors spread so quickly . . ."

Warren led me out of the office, perhaps as equally annoyed by the pretentious man who had lost sight of everything that had been revealed.

A man's life was gone.

A young man was now condemned for the rest of his.

Two lives, lost.

The echo of my parents' sins returned once more. I would never be free of them.

The next few hours were a flurry of police, spectators, and show officials covering each inch of the show grounds. Violet and Cheryl helped me clean and bandage my wound, and by the time I'd changed my outfit, the veterinarian on-site had treated Phantom's cut as well.

The final classes had ended, and competitors, horses, and law enforcement officials slowly filtered away from the grounds. A calm and quiet settled over what had been chaos.

Darkness wrapped around the barns. Lucky and Warren were the only ones left, and while they were talking quietly at the end of the aisle, I took Phantom from his stall and led him to the large arena. Where he'd won the champion title but not in the moment. Where we'd put on a good show and overcome the hardest obstacle I could ask of him.

His neck had a neat row of stitches and thick smear of ointment to keep it soft while it healed. The blood had been cleaned from his pearl-white coat, but the dark red spots that painted his bloody shoulder mark remained as brilliant as ever.

The mark of a warrior.

In the arena, I took off his halter again and walked with him silently. We hadn't had the chance for our victory lap. So I'd take this small, quiet one and say farewell to the horse I loved.

The time had come to find him a new home. If ever I was sure of it, it was after seeing the ripple of destruction in my wake earlier that day.

Eddie wouldn't have been shot. Peter wouldn't have been bitten. And Keith . . . I couldn't let Warren get caught up in the bad luck that seemed to follow me.

After a lap, I looked up to see Warren leaning along the railing, his gaze tender as he watched us. As Phantom and I drew near, the horse walked over and sniffed him.

Warren rubbed the horse's face affectionately and then asked, "Mind if I join you?"

I motioned to the empty arena, and he climbed over the wall and landed next to me in the dirt. We resumed walking, and Phantom, who knew from my lack of cues and focus that he wasn't in a lesson, wandered off and sniffed the ground.

Now it was just Warren and me.

I missed him. I missed this. The walks we'd taken late at night, the pre-dawn trail rides, and sitting together as the sun emerged.

"How's the campaign going?" I asked, my voice strained.

"Your notebook has been helpful," he said, though that didn't really answer my question. "That jump was amazing. Was this another Bill trick?"

"No." My chest inflated with pride. "That was one of mine."

He chuckled warmly, kicking a dirt clod aside as we circled the arena in tentative silence. Small talk didn't become us.

It was also time for me to tell Warren the truth. His words before he'd flown back to Philly had echoed in my heart every day. He deserved an explanation.

After today, my soul was fractured enough as it was. Why not tell him and face the inevitable cringe and repulsion—the way Keith had responded when I'd told him my parents' identity. Then he'd have no aversion to finding Phantom a new home. He'd probably be angry I'd let it go so far. What if the press of this day caught wind and it damaged his campaign?

He'd know now what a fool and coward I truly was. He'd leave me in the rearview mirror and never look back.

And that was for the best.

## Warren

Eva came to a stop and turned to me, her eyes glassy as she looked up. "Warren." Her voice caught. "You were right, at the airport. That you should know why our relationship, business, whatever this is"—her lips curved into a smile for just a heartbeat—"why that needs to end here, now."

No, this couldn't end. My breath came short and my chest constricted. I hadn't expected this—not here, not now.

I'd hardly processed all that we'd learned from Keith in his confession—that he'd killed his father in his effort to save Eva.

My blood still boiled at the stains on her coat and the droplets in the dirt because of Keith's greed and carelessness.

I faced her, took her hands in mine, clamping my molars tight to keep from interrupting.

She grasped my hands, her body trembling. This wasn't the fearless woman I knew.

"Remember in Seattle, how Elaine Hartford thought I looked like Irene Chalmers?"

I blinked, trying to place the names. Elaine was the older woman at the banquet?

"I wasn't honest with you about my past." She searched my face as she spoke. "I look like Irene Chalmers, because she was my mother. Raymond Chalmers was my father."

At first, my mind didn't process the weight of her words.

"My name isn't Bryant. It's Evelyn Chalmers."

Eva, short for Evelyn. But Chalmers?

Then the memories rushed in.

The bank robbers. The murderers. The husband-wife duo who died in a shootout with police at my father's bank in Philadelphia. Their six-year-old daughter—the girl with haunting blue eyes—in the car when they'd battled it to the death.

The flash of an image on *The New York Times* front page came to mind. A young girl, led from the shattered and bullet-ridden remains of a black sedan, and her sorrowful, captivating innocence. The photo had been reprinted thousands of times, and Evelyn Chalmers had become as infamous as the Lindbergh baby. The Lindbergh case had ended in tragedy, but the absence of Evelyn Chalmers from public knowledge had only deepened the lore.

Because she'd escaped to Oregon. Where kind stranger Bill Birkstrom took in the broken, terrified little child and adopted her as his own.

It all made sense now.

Her tragic childhood that she never wanted to explain.

Her comments about the publicity of a national show championship and how different it was from the front page of *The New York Times*. She'd known that firsthand.

As my thoughts settled into place, I absorbed the shame in her eyes. The guilt and regret that poured from her twisted features.

Compassion rose from deep inside me, and I pulled her closer, holding her back with one hand, cupping her face with the other. "Eva," I whispered. "Is that why you thought we couldn't be together?"

She blinked, the angst in her face morphing into confusion. "It's not a trivial thing, Warren."

"It must have been horrible for you." I brushed at a tear that escaped the corner of her eye. "You were a child. You're innocent in all of that, Eva."

She searched my face, still surprised by something.

"Why didn't you tell me sooner?" I asked.

"It changes everything."

"It changes nothing."

"Your campaign?"

"If I can't win on my merit, so be it. Your past is your past. You're not responsible for those lives."

"You have no idea," she said. "The frenzy."

"I have some idea." I squeezed her arm gently. "It happened at my family's bank. But I don't care. I will face that a thousand times over with you."

Tears flowed freely down her cheeks. "I've only ever told one other person." She sniffed.

"Keith." My jaw might break with how hard I bit back what I thought about that, about him. She'd indicated after Seattle that he'd been the one to convince her she never wanted to marry or start a family.

She nodded. "He broke up with me when he found out."

"He was a fool," I growled. "He never deserved you."

"It just never seems to end, Warren." She closed her eyes, her forehead crinkling in pain. "Everyone around me ends up hurt or dead."

"You've saved more lives than you're willing to see."

She drew in a shaky breath, seeming to struggle to accept my words. "I won't ask you to suffer in this too. I can't let you."

"We can work through this, Eva."

She shook her head.

I wished she'd told me sooner. Perhaps then I could have talked through more of this with her before it became so heavy on her shoulders.

Her mind was made up. I felt it deep in my core.

I pressed my forehead to hers, my heart splitting into a thousand pieces.

"I have what I wanted—Birkstrom Ranch. I can't ask God for anything else."

"What if God wants more for you? What if this is our moment to choose a path together?"

"I won't sabotage your life the way my parents have haunted mine." Her jaw flexed, those beautiful blue eyes clearing of tears. She was resolute. "I want to see you as the leader I know you are. You'll do amazing things in Washington, DC. I can't let my name tarnish that future."

"There's nothing I can do to convince you, is there?"

"I'm sorry, Warren. I should have ended this after Seattle, when I realized—" She stopped herself.

But I knew the words she was going to say.

I pulled her closer, gently lifting her face. She didn't resist, her lips meeting mine with tender exploration. She lifted her good arm around my neck, and her other hand pressed against my chest as she melted into me.

Her lips were warm and sweet. The smell of lavender, hay, horse, and sweat lingered in the air. She sank deeper into our kiss, and I'd never known anything so right and true.

And yet, it didn't feel like the kiss of a sunrise, full of a bright future.

It was a sunset. A goodbye.

She broke the kiss, her eyes bidding me farewell.

I was breathless, my skin still on fire with her nearness, my mind fuzzy, and my lips yearning for more of hers. I brushed her cheek with my thumb. I wanted to tell her that I loved her, that I only cared about a future with her by my side.

I couldn't find the words, and neither could she, it seemed.

She stepped back, took my hand from her cheek, kissed my palm lightly, and let go.

She left the arena, not letting Phantom follow her out of the gates. She disappeared into the night beyond. Phantom trotted over to me and nudged me, seeming anxious and uneasy now that she was gone.

"I know, buddy." I rubbed his broad forehead and wished I could reassure him further.

This was the end of our business arrangement. Of whatever else we were beyond that.

But I had other plans and new ideas forming. Words might not sway her, so I'd have to set the rest in motion. Whether it took one year or a hundred years for us to be together, my heart belonged to her.

Yet even with all my scheming and every resource at my disposal, a prick of fear deep in my gut said it might not be enough.

# *Thirty-Six*

## Eva

**OCTOBER 24**

I bolted awake in the dark and turned to look at the clock on my nightstand. Two a.m. The rain of bullets mixed with the memories of Eddie taking the bullet that had been meant for me.

I wiped the sweat from my brow and tossed my blankets aside. How much longer could I fight this?

In the past two months since nationals, with the stables so empty of everyone who had brought so much life—Phantom, Patches, Lucky, EP, Warren—my nightmares and insomnia had only gotten worse.

I saw Victor's face, Keith's rage.

In the dim light of my house, too quiet without Annie, I walked to the kitchen and filled a glass with water. My hand, steadying myself on the counter, brushed the metal box that Annie had brought me all those months ago.

Tears stung as I held the water in one hand and ran my fingertips over the metal lid with the other. Why couldn't those memories just stay trapped inside that stupid tin?

I carried the box over to the dining table and turned on a floor lamp in the small area between the living room and kitchen. A dull glow was cast over the table, and I swallowed the lump of fear that choked me.

I lifted the latch and the hinges creaked open.

Ribbon and brass, all tangled in a heap.

And to one side, dog tags.

Bill Birkstrom from his service in 1917 through the end of the Great War. He'd never talked about his time in the trenches. I understood why.

I lifted the awards out, piled them on the table, and pulled out a small brown book. I flipped it over to see a cross and the words "New Testament—Army and Navy Edition" on the cover. The edges were worn and tattered, mud stained and stiff.

Gramps didn't go to church each Sunday, but when I closed my eyes, I could see him sitting on the platform at Beacon's Bluff. One morning, I'd asked, "What do you think about out here, Gramps?"

"I thank God, honey. And anything else that's bugging me, I give it all to him. Each morning, anew."

Was that the true secret to all his tricks? The reason he could so effortlessly tame a horse with just his words and gentle hands?

I pressed the small book to my forehead, and my heart cried out for release. "I can't do this alone," I whispered.

I had held tightly for so long. The more I gripped my past, my failures, my uncontrollable dreams, the more I fell into a pit that I couldn't escape.

I knew what happened to horses that learned to pull and never stop, like Stormy. Gramps had every trick in the book to teach them to yield to pressure. But I hadn't even realized I was one of those stubborn horses that wouldn't give in.

I was going to break if I didn't yield. I'd fall with no soft landing behind me.

*God, I give it all to you.*

The cross, bullet casing, and dog tags strewn across the table glittered at me, and somehow I felt their barbs soften. My heartbeat slowed, my breathing calmed.

I picked up Gramps's tags, that .45 casing, and the Bible and got dressed, then slipped into my boots and a coat to ward off the fall morning chill. I left Eddie and Violet a note in case I didn't return before the start of morning chores.

Passing the barns, I set out to walk the familiar trail to the platform, using the extra time to feel the ground beneath my feet, smell the pine and cedar in the air, pick up on the distant smell of rain and thunder.

I hadn't ridden to the bluff since that last ride with Warren.

The memory of him brought goose bumps to my skin. Eddie had stopped mentioning him, stopped asking if I would call him.

We'd all accepted the truth—it was over.

Phantom was doing well at Mountain View Stables in Virginia, and their head trainer wrote to me often about his progress. That was the only involvement I could allow.

Anything else was too painful.

I missed Warren. I still loved him. I wondered what life would have been like if circumstances were different. What if I hadn't said goodbye to the other man who had saved me?

I shook the what-ifs away.

The past month had been rough enough with Keith's trial. I hadn't attended except the time I was required to testify. Warren had been a witness too, but our paths never crossed.

The little boy from next door, the teen I'd once envisioned as my future, would be in prison for at least twenty years with the possibility of parole. The jury took into consideration the threat against my life and Keith's actions to protect me from his father, but the dozens of witnesses and reports of his behavior in Pomona had worked against him.

Keith's family property had gone to auction, and the horses had scattered to Arabian breeding facilities across the country. I didn't know anything about the new property owners. No one knew, not even Betty with all her town connections.

The neighborly feud was over. Ater all, there wasn't a true Birkstrom or Merrick left on these lands.

The end of a bloody and terrible story.

Branches snapped under my boots as I walked the worn path. The smell of pine floated around me and soothed my soul.

A little under an hour later, I reached the platform and scaled the ladder as the hints of black sky turned to dark blue. I set the Bible and dog tags on the platform and flung the bullet casing into the distance. It would no longer haunt me.

It was October. In early November, Warren would win the election for his Senate seat. A new era would begin.

The sunrise passed before my face, but I only thought of him.

*God, I give you my pain and regret and my yearning for Warren.*

I crossed my legs and pressed my face into my knees. I would never be free of loving him, but I couldn't fight it. Like Gramps had said, I needed to release it, give it to God. Each day, anew.

Until maybe one day, it wouldn't hurt so much.

## Warren

The air was brisk, not like the summer months in the high desert.

I carried wire cutters, a hammer, a fence post, and my thick leather gloves to the edge of my property to repair a gap in the barbed wire I'd noticed a few days ago. It happened to be along the part of the fence line that I shared with my new neighbor, and I didn't want to add to her plate.

The sun had just risen, but Beacon's Bluff blocked the full impact from my side of the fence.

I set about the task, pounding in the metal post to reinforce the section of barbed wire some deer or elk had twisted. The noise echoed through the hills, but I focused on not smashing my thumb with the sledgehammer. I wasn't as skilled as Eddie when it came to this stuff.

I had finished the last of the wire when soft footsteps drew near.

"Warren?"

I looked up at Eva's voice. My heart tripped all over itself, like I was some teenage boy staring at his longtime crush. If she was out here this early, that meant she was catching the sunrise. That was a good sign.

"Where's your horse?" I asked, looking for Acorn. "Did you fall off?"

Her hair was unbrushed, wild and windswept, her face clear of makeup and her eyes wide. She was even more beautiful than I remembered. I wanted to jump the fence and sweep her into my arms.

"I didn't ride out here," she breathed. "I walked. What are you doing here?"

"Fixing my fence." I motioned to the wire.

"Y-your fence?"

"The property went up for auction." I wiggled my eyebrows. "I got it for a steal."

She covered her mouth with one hand. Bewilderment, wonder, horror, sorrow, confusion—every possible emotion flashed across her face.

My pulse raced with uncertainty. I'd been looking for the right time, and there was no turning back now.

"Do you want to come over this morning?" I asked. "I have something I need to show you."

"Um, in an hour or so?" she said hesitantly. "After I feed the horses?"

"I'll see you then." I turned and left. The fence was finished for now. If I lingered here for too long, I'd lose control and take her into my arms. I needed her to see the rest of what I'd spent months working on.

I returned to the main barn as dozens of men tended to the stream of construction projects all over the grounds. Merrick Stables was no more, but the new property had a long way to go before it would match my vision.

Lucky approached me with a perplexed look. "You all right, boss? You look like you've seen a ghost."

"I ran into her on the fence line." I took off my gloves and shoved them into my pockets. "She's coming by soon."

Lucky elbowed me in the ribs. "Don't mess it up this time, Captain."

I punched him in the arm but knew his words held merit.

It wasn't in my hands anymore. I'd worked for two months to prepare for every contingency, but there were no certainties ahead.

An hour later, Eva pulled up in her truck and stepped from the cab, looking around at the activity with her mouth ajar. EP and Junior ran to her, and she gave them a long hug. I could see her asking them how they were doing and probably asking how their extended families were back at home.

I walked toward her after a few minutes. Her gaze landed on me, and my nerves coiled like a rattler.

"What is all this?" She motioned to the construction.

"An overhaul," I said. "Shedding the past." I pointed to the manor, which didn't suit our needs anymore. "That's becoming a boardinghouse, and we're adding a few small ranch houses in the flat meadow behind it. No one person needs a house that ghastly."

"Boardinghouse?"

"For veterans who need work." I shrugged. "I want to replicate what we had at Birkstrom. Bring in the horses that need the most help, pair them with former soldiers who need the same."

She pressed her fingertips to her lips again as if she were going to cry, turning her body to absorb the sheer volume of the work. This property eclipsed Birkstrom several times. We'd be able to house more than thirty soldiers and up to a hundred horses.

Mason appeared carrying several wooden beams, nodding at us as he walked by. Eva gasped and laughed in amazement.

"You've been busy," she said to me.

"We've gone to the local auction a few times and are in need of a trainer for some of those we rescued."

"Oh, really?"

"Step into my office." I motioned to the barn, where my half-finished office sat next to the few horses that we'd moved in last week.

Two horses, their heads hanging over the half doors, turned as we entered.

Eva gasped. "Mira!" She ran to the gray mare and looked her over, petting her cheeks and putting her own face to the mare's.

The weight of the past two months, the moments when I missed her so much it hurt, the dead ends in searching for Mira, the long travel days of campaigning for Kenneth—it all lifted. The future was still uncertain, but the joy in her face was the most treasured sight I had ever beheld.

She looked over with wide eyes and a huge smile, which thrilled me to the core. "Where did you find her?"

"A tiny farm in Oklahoma. Her name had been mislabeled as Mirror."

"How did you even . . . ?"

"I put Reid on it, and Adia tracked down some records from Kötzting." I'd made the farmer an offer of five times what he'd paid for her, and he handed her over without hesitation.

"I thought you were in Virginia." Eva moved to Phantom, who nuzzled her affectionately. She put her hands on his cheeks and kissed the bridge of his nose.

Patches bleated as he walked up the aisle and sniffed the ground for anything to nibble.

I kept a few steps back, allowing Eva space for a reunion she probably had never expected. I'd moved Phantom a few weeks ago and asked the trainer at Mountain View not to let her know.

"I don't understand." She shook her head and turned to me. "What is all this? What about the Senate race?"

"I withdrew from the Pennsylvania race."

She took a few steps closer to me. "What?"

"I have my eye on a different seat." I pointed to the ground. "In Oregon, in two years. That means I return here in between legislative sessions."

Her expression went somber again. "Oh, I see."

For her, this meant that nothing about her resolve had changed. There was still no future for us—not with what she believed about her past and her family's reputation.

I picked up a handful of papers on the desk in my office and brought it out to her. It was a typed report that my campaign staff had worked on for a solid eight weeks.

"Read this." I extended the stack.

"What is this?" she asked, taking it from my hands. She held my gaze a little longer, searching my face for any sign of what was to come.

"Read it," I said. "Please."

She turned away, pacing slowly as she read. After the first few pages, her jaw flexed, her eyes filled with tears.

"I knew nothing I could say would convince you," I whispered. "I had my team run scenarios and talk to focus groups about the public perception of a potential US senator married to the daughter of Raymond and Irene Chalmers and the electoral implications."

She blushed and arched an eyebrow. "Married?"

That pink on her cheeks was a good look. I needed to see more of it. "Thought I'd shoot for the stars."

She frowned, waving the sheets at me tauntingly. "So, is this a proposal, then?"

"Only if your answer is yes."

She rolled her eyes, turned the page.

The conclusion of the report was clear. Overwhelmingly, the public sentiment was either positive or neutral. The Chalmers child was of interest, but in the same way I didn't blame her for her parents' actions, neither did the public we'd surveyed.

Her deepest fears and insecurities were unfounded. And I had more than just a gut feeling to reassure her.

After I knew she'd absorbed the highlights, I stepped up to her. I couldn't hold back anymore.

I tossed the papers onto my desk and took her hands in mine. "None of that really matters to me. You won't face the frenzy alone, Eva. The only last name I care about is you taking mine."

She closed her eyes, and I expected her to shake her head and dig in further. Instead, she smiled and brought her hands up to hold my face. "And what if the report is wrong?" she breathed.

"I'm by your side, regardless." Chills shot to my toes. "We'll deal with whatever comes our way."

"What if it does derail your political plans? Would you come to resent me?"

"Never." I slipped my hands around her middle and pulled her to me. "If God closes that door, so be it. I can't go back to life before you. You changed everything for me, Eva. I'm a better person when I'm with you. Our dreams are stronger together."

"I missed you so much." She pressed her forehead to mine.

Her words filled me with relief, and her nearness overwhelmed my senses. I brushed her hair back, put my lips to her ear. "I love you, Eva."

Her breath caught. "I love you too."

She pressed her lips to mine, no hesitation and no reservation. Her arms tightened around my neck, and she deepened the kiss. The distant noises of construction and conversation faded around us. All that existed were the two of us. Fire sparked and exploded between us, consuming me body and soul.

This wasn't the slow, farewell kiss we'd shared two months ago in the arena in Pomona. This was one of new beginnings, of hope.

This was a sunrise kiss.

Distant whistling, hooting, and cheering drew us apart. Mason, Junior, Lucky, and all the rest were watching us from the driveway.

Eva laughed, a musical sound that set my heart on fire.

"Get back to work," I growled, but their shouts and whistles were slow to fade. I wondered who had won the ongoing betting pool about us.

I pulled her closer to me again. She smiled and shook her head. "There's no hiding anything from them, is there?"

"You don't have to hide anymore, Eva."

"I'm not running anymore." A tear slipped from the corner of her eye, and she lifted onto her toes to kiss me again.

"So, about that proposal," I said against her lips. "I know you don't like impractical things." I stepped back and held up an intricately etched gold band. No frills, no diamonds.

Her eyes went glassy, and she took the engagement ring, hesitating.

Had I overstepped? Should I have waited a bit longer?

"Are you sure about this, Warren?" she asked. "You're completely certain you want to weather the storm to come?"

I slid the ring on her finger and kissed her again. "I've never been more certain."

# Epilogue

## Eva

NOVEMBER 6, 1947
NEW YORK CITY

"Introducing Phantom, the stallion with the famed bloody shoulder mark from Janów Podlaski in Poland, liberated by our fine American soldiers, led by trainer Evelyn Hayes."

I followed the announcer's cue, and we ran into the cavernous expanse that was Madison Square Garden. Thousands of people clapped for the horse that had survived terrible odds.

I only cared for the man behind the stadium, waiting for our exhibition to be done. The man who had brought me from the shadows of the past and into the world of full sunlight.

It had been chaotic at first. Reporters, stories, radio reports. Everyone wanting to know the truth about Evelyn Chalmers and who she was today. And the fact that she was engaged to the war hero Warren Hayes, aspiring senator.

Warren offered an exclusive interview with Michael Bass from *The New York Times*, which endeared America even further to him. The article covered my life in hiding and my sterling military career. Instead of letting others tell the tale, Warren and I set the record straight from the start.

My fears that had grown so wild after Keith's rejection when we were teens had been misplaced. While Keith had been terrified of the press, of the rumors, Warren met the conflict head-on. He never blinked, never shied away from what had driven Keith to betray me.

It turns out I hadn't shared my secret with the right man.

Warren had been by my side through every article, phone call, and unexpected visitor. It hadn't been easy. I'd wrestled with the never-ending guilt and the photos from the shootout that had been so troubling and captivating to the public. Everything I'd worked so hard to forget, resurfaced and raw. But I held to Warren and the rest of my new family at Birkstrom. After nearly a year, the fervor died down.

Now, I wasn't often recognized or noticed. Especially since my last name had changed to Hayes.

I led Phantom into the arena, removing his halter to show off what had become a crowd favorite. Phantom running without my hold but obeying my every command. In the past year, he'd grown more muscular, and his mane now flowed well down to his shoulders like dancing grass in the wind.

We finished our routine and left the arena for the next exhibit to enter. Gramps would have been so pleased. I felt his words and affirmations from deep within.

Warren met me in the tunnel under the stands as we went back to put Phantom in his stall. My husband slipped an arm around me, kissed the top of my head. "Beautiful," he said.

I knew he meant me and not Phantom's performance. My neck and face flushed.

He chuckled, enjoying the way he could draw color to my cheeks.

There had been a lot to do after Warren came back. His work at the Merricks' farm transformed the property and buildings into an entirely new campus of barns and facilities. We then built connecting roads and outbuildings across the former property lines.

Eddie and Violet moved into the old Merrick manor to oversee the veterans and run the boardinghouse as a family. Eddie was also building his own carpentry shop, and he taught soldiers these skills too. Gramps's patterns were used daily now, something he'd be proud to know.

Annie stayed at the Birkstrom Ranch house from time to time and grew her collection of animals big and small from across both ranches. Peter had turned his grades around in school and worked often with the horses.

In springtime, Warren and I married at sunrise at Beacon's Bluff, with nearly the entire staff of the two farms and half of Baker crowded onto the hill. Yellow arrowleaf, purple lupine, and orange tiger lily bloomed all around us.

Eddie had presented us with a wedding gift like no other. The wooden sign destroyed by Victor's fire, rescued and crafted anew. It was glued, honed, and sanded to perfection, with a few of the charred marks remaining. A reminder of the flames we'd endured.

I hadn't even realized Eddie had taken the lump of wood, and until I saw it restored, I didn't know just how much that sign meant to me. A piece of Gramps's legacy, the name forever tied to the sliver of land. The hope and redemption in something pulled from the ashes.

That morning in October, I'd given everything over to God, and he delivered a life that I'd never imagined.

As incredible as it was to showcase Phantom in front of the global audience in the stadium seats, I itched to get back to our little corner of the world—the little house Warren and I had turned into our own, and the stables that now spanned more than five thousand acres and bustled with soldiers turned cowboys.

Instead of rescuing horses, we'd found the secret to bringing souls broken from wartime into touch with nature and the creatures that somehow connected with them beyond just transportation or sport. In just these few months, lives had been changed, word had spread. Bennett, Lucky, Mason—they'd all called in more of their fellow soldiers who needed work or homes.

"Do you want to catch the rest of the show?" Warren flipped open the program. "Looks like the hunter jumper class is next."

I slipped my arm in his and leaned my head against his shoulder. "How about a walk through the city?"

He put his arm around me and held me close.

It was the thing I'd miss while he was in DC, though with Captain Johnson on standby to fly me for visits, I figured I'd be taking more trips out east with my husband.

There were so many hands at Birkstrom, I didn't need to be there day and night. And I caught Warren's passion for bigger-picture changes, for some of the plans he and Kenneth had been working on. Broader veterans' programs, better medical care, more funding to rural areas like Baker. Veterans' farm loans that didn't get caught in endless loops when the farm owner was an unmarried woman. Perhaps even nationwide programs that connected soldiers with horses in need.

What if Gramps's tricks could reach more people with the healing power of horses? What would the world look like then?

Our dreams had mingled, merged, and become something entirely more than we'd ever predicted. The paths that seemed so vastly wide had snaked together in the most surprising ways.

My husband held me close as we strolled the bustling city streets and the sun sank on the horizon. Lights flickered on around us.

He'd been right about a lot of things. My distaste of sunsets, my disinterest in flowers—all of that had changed once Warren came along. I had needed the right man to help me appreciate things differently.

I still refused any jewelry other than my gold wedding band.

The only shine I wanted was the silver or brass fittings on my horse's tack.

"Tired?" He kissed the side of my head as he noticed my pace slowing.

I nodded and closed my eyes gratefully. He rubbed my arm gently and turned us back to the hotel.

For the first time in my life, I didn't fear sleep. Didn't fear the ghosts and spirits that had haunted my dreams. Ever since I released what I'd held so tightly, the nightmares had faded.

The other dreams I'd long given up on—becoming a mother, having a family—those looked different now.

A pang of nausea hit me just as we reached the lobby of the hotel, and I drew to a stop and closed my eyes again.

When I opened them, Warren watched me with suspicion. I had my own theory, but I wasn't certain. There had been subtle signs for weeks. Exhaustion, sickness, dizziness. I didn't want to get his hopes up. Not unless I was sure.

"Eva?" he asked softly.

The shadow of the old me didn't dare hope for such things. The Eva who didn't believe I deserved any measure of happiness. I'd been gifted so much in the year since I'd lost Gramps. How could I ask God for anything more?

We had a bustling ranch across thousands of acres and dozens of former soldiers running cows, training horses, rehabilitating all types of animals. It was the operation I'd always dreamed of.

Dare I hope for a child on top of it all?

I didn't need to say anything. Warren knew me so well, he could read my thoughts. He drew me in, kissed me warmly, and brushed the side of my face tenderly.

"Oh, Eva," he said. "That's wonderful."

A tear slid down my cheek, and he caught it with his thumb.

"I don't know for certain," I said.

He pulled me close, his arms steady and strong around me. Neither of us had known exactly what marriage was supposed to look like, but the partnership and companionship we'd found in each other surpassed our wildest expectations.

"I think you do," he said with a smile. "And I think this means you'll need to learn how to rest every now and then."

"As long as I don't have to give up our sunrise rides." I looped my arms around his neck.

He chuckled. "I'm guessing our child will be born knowing how to ride and train horses."

I leaned my head against his chest. From the presentation of Phantom in the National Horse Show—the most prestigious stage for horses across the globe—to the seismic news that would forever change our lives, this day was more than I ever imagined.

But like with the view from Beacon's Bluff, I treasured the beauty of each moment and released everything I couldn't bear any longer.

The past was buried, the pain healing.

The weight of all we'd carried home from the war was now cast free to make way for the love, life, and sunrises to come.

# Historical Note

The information about Operation Cowboy in this story is true, and readers can learn more about that incredible mission in my book *Until Our Time Comes: A Novel of World War II Poland*. A few of the details about the postwar auctions and the timing of those have been altered to fit this story. The impact these horses, including the prestigious stallion Witez II, had on American breeding programs cannot be overstated.

A disclaimer about the Arabian horse organization and judges on the show circuit: I heavily implied that there were bribery and manipulation of the show results. This was for dramatic purposes only, and I do not want to cast the real Arabian horse organizations or horse show industry in a negative light. I grew up showing my horses, and these groups are essential in education and advocacy for this unique breed.

The name of Baker changed periodically and is currently Baker City, Oregon. But during the time of this story, it was Baker.

The power of horses to touch the soul is a long-established truth in the rich history between humans and beasts. The therapeutic value of horse training and riding is now a more established treatment for post-traumatic stress disorder and so much more. There are hundreds of programs across the country and a lot of information available for anyone in need of these resources.

# Acknowledgments

There would be no Eva and Warren without the family stories of Billy "Bomp" Miller and his unique horse training methods that have filtered through the generations. From the sack full of horseshoes to the water bucket trust exercise, the ways of "horse gentling" or "horse whispering" are ones of wonder and lore.

My thanks and reverence go also to the many trainers who have brought these methods into the mainstream and inspired me from youth: Tom Dorrance, Ray Hunt, Monty Roberts, and Buck Brannaman.

To my dear friends who have cheered on my writing from the start: Heather McLendon, Darci Andrews, and Michelle Martin. The notes we passed in high school were the first and my most treasured book reviews.

To my critique group of fifteen years who never fails to catch all the little things and big things: Melanie Dobson, Julie Zander, Jana Kaye, and Tracie Heskett. Thank you all for always being so honest and thorough.

To my generous beta readers: Dyana Worthington, Hannah Lanphear, Sarah Frost, Caitlin Anderson, Gloria Tome, and Angela Chunn. You all offered such valuable edits and encouragement. I'm so grateful for you.

An extra special thanks to my niece and beta reader, Samantha Lanphear, for her incredible literary analysis of this manuscript that helped hone the story direction and deepen many of the characters.

To my amazing agent, Wendy Lawton, who has been a steadfast coach, cheerleader, and adviser through all my writing ups and downs. You are the best. Truly.

To my wonderful editors, Rachel McRae and Jessica English, and the entire team at Revell. I am so blessed that my debut novel found its home with you, and that I have the chance to bring more horse stories to the world. You all are the dream team.

To my husband, John. I wouldn't have been able to do it without your love, persistence, and thoughtful edits. Your insights brought new dimensions to this story. You have always pushed me to be the very best version of myself, and I see all of the best features of Bomp in you.

To my boys, Anthony, Aiden, and Charlie. You all bring so much joy and inspiration to my life. I love being your mom.

Finally, this book is for my father-in-law, John Miller Sr., aka "Old Fat Grandpa," who left us far too suddenly in July 2024. It was his father, Bomp, who inspired the horse training stories, and his family's deep history in Baker City that brought the beautiful high desert town to life for me. John, you were the biggest champion of my writing career and the loudest salesman when my debut novel released just a few weeks before your death. I'm so glad you got to read some of it and that we got to talk about the book. I hope this tribute to Bomp makes you proud. Thank you for the boys I now call mine and the legacy you left behind.

Read on for an excerpt
from Nicole M. Miller's

# UNTIL OUR TIME COMES

Available now wherever books are sold

# Prologue

**JULY 23, 1939**
**WYGODA, POLAND**
**FIVE KILOMETERS NORTHEAST OF JANÓW PODLASKI STABLES**

The movement was swift. The fingers light. The absence of his pilfered pocket watch barely noticeable—and yet it was as if a blaring siren sounded through his skull.

Bret Conway whirled and spotted a small, short frame slipping through the crowded marketplace. Despite the summer heat, the afternoon shoppers fresh from Sunday picnics and church mass filled the town square. Vendors called out wares as the smell of spices and hot cobblestones filled the air.

Bret followed the little thief's path, a glimpse of the boy's tattered fedora popping in between the sundresses and tan shirt jackets.

Polish conversation drifted around him. After his three years in Warsaw and now six months in this quiet town, it was almost as natural to his ears as the conversations on the streets of London.

He kept at a distance, watching the boy, no more than six or seven years old, as he stopped at Babka and Ludwik's fruit stand. The slender child stood beside a woman in pale riding breeches with a grass stain on her right thigh. Was the boy going to steal something from this unsuspecting victim too?

Her back was turned to Bret, though the angle of her head and her elegant stance sparked something in the back of his mind. She had the recognizable, practiced posture of an equestrian—something he recalled from his own time on horseback and among Olympians.

Ludwik and the woman leaned over the harness of a cart horse, lost in their discussion. The leather straps were crisp and new, and it appeared the woman was helping fit the cart to the small, chestnut-colored mare. Babka was sorting through the fruit and helping old man Pieter with his purchase. The thief stood in their midst casually, his relaxed posture almost seeming bored.

Bret needed that watch back—it was too priceless an heirloom to lose so embarrassingly to a little pickpocket. And yet the scene intrigued him.

"Amerykanka? Can we go now?" the boy said in heavily accented English. He reached up and tugged her sleeve impatiently.

The woman turned, her features fully in Bret's view now as she smiled brilliantly while speaking with Ludwik. She stroked the horse's neck confidently, kindly. "Yes, soon," she assured the boy before resuming her conversation with Ludwik.

Something tightened in his chest. He knew of this Amerykanka. Everyone in Wygoda knew of this woman. She was a rarity. An outsider beyond what even he, a Brit, could boast.

The American horse trainer. Adia Kensington.

She tightened up the final harness strap and patted the horse's rump as if about to say her farewell, and Bret's feet compelled him forward.

The boy peeked over his shoulder in Bret's direction, and his eyes widened. Ducking behind the American, he put his hands over his eyes as if it would make him invisible. "No, Amerykanka, I am sorry. I did not mean to do it!"

"Do what?" Adia asked, looking down at the child.

Bret stepped up beside her and cleared his throat.

"Przepraszam," she said. Then she seemed to recognize that he wasn't a local. "Oh, excuse me," she said in English, her American accent more unfamiliar than the slurry of Polish.

He'd spotted her a dozen times in town but had never stood so close. At this distance, the curve of her lips and her long, dark lashes caused his heart to speed up. Her dark hair shimmered in the brilliant midday sun. Momentarily, he forgot what had even brought him over.

"My apologies for the intrusion." Bret cleared his throat. "I believe the boy"—he nodded to the little thief—"has something of mine."

She frowned and narrowed her gaze at the boy. "Myszko," she said firmly, "we talked about this."

"I am sorry, Adeeea," the boy she'd called mouse whimpered.

She crossed her arms, standing as a confident barrier between accuser and accused. Her long hair was pulled into a cascading chocolate ponytail that curled in soft waves at the ends. Her shoulders were narrow, her hands cut and blistered but radiating strength. The dirt under her nails and the natural creases in her work shirt set her apart from the high-society women Bret's mother had thrust upon him. None of those girls had the natural beauty or presence this woman had.

Ludwik, within earshot, harrumphed and pointed a finger at the child. "And I'm still missing my set of playing cards, little one."

The boy, wide-eyed with unkempt brown hair poking out from his hat, ducked his head and whimpered again. He pulled Bret's brass watch and a deck of cards from his pockets.

Adia took the watch and held it out to Bret. He took it from her flattened palm, his fingertips sizzling at the touch of her skin.

"I'm so sorry." She smiled. "He's compulsive about . . . collecting things even though he knows it's wrong. Please forgive him."

"Perhaps the lad should not be so easily forgiven," he said.

She captured his gaze with her deep brown irises, and a fire seemed to spark inside her. "He's only a boy."

Babka, the heartbeat of Wygoda and the chef of the best pierogi in all of Poland, wandered over and smiled at Bret. She had deep wrinkles and wiry gray hair but always exuded energy and warmth. "Ah, so good to see you, Mr. Conway. What is all this commotion?" She looked to Adia. "You surely have met before, yes?"

Adia's gaze remained skeptical.

Who was this street urchin to the American horse trainer? How had the lad commanded such loyalty of her?

"The boy took something of mine," Bret explained to the matron of the town square.

Babka waved a hand. "Harmless, harmless. All little boys go through rebellious times."

"It's a dangerous world," Bret countered. "He could pick the wrong pocket and face far more severe consequences."

Adia crossed her arms, angled her head. "Would you have the boy flogged, Mr. Conway?" Her voice deepened as if she were digging a trench and burrowing in for a fight. "Sent to prison? His hand cut off?"

"I'd settle for far less." He grinned.

She drew back as if sensing a trap.

"And what is that?" She crossed her arms.

"Dinner. With me."

Her lips fell into an O as Babka clapped her hands and squealed excitedly. "That's a wonderful idea! I'll prepare my best table for you both. Ludwik, haven't I said for months now these two should meet?"

Ludwik grunted distractedly, still messing with the horse's harness.

"And how would that help Ewan's bad habit?" Adia protested.

"What does that matter?" Babka elbowed her sharply and

smiled with crooked teeth. "You need a night off. As I always tell Filip, you work too much in those stables of his."

Adia shook her head and rolled her eyes. Clearly, she'd had this discussion with Babka before, and it was a tired one.

"I should have started with a proper introduction." Bret put a hand to his chest apologetically. "My name is Bret Conway. I'm a correspondent for the *Daily Express* in London." The lie slid easily off his tongue. He'd perfected it in his three years in Poland and two in Spain.

Her eyebrows, slender and arched, lifted ever so slightly. Skeptical or surprised? She was tough to read. And reading people was his true occupation.

Babka looped her arm through Bret's, beaming. "Oh, he's just being modest," she crooned. "This fine man here also helped Ludwik and I when we were renovating the kitchen a few weeks back—finding us all the supplies we needed and wielding a hammer or two. He's a jack-of-all-trades."

Bret chuckled at the compliment. Truth was, Charlie had gotten them into that to earn a few extra meals from Babka, since good cooking was sparse in their line of work.

Adia glanced down at the boy. "I'm still unsure of how my accompanying you to dinner will teach little Ewan the dangers of stealing, Mr. Conway."

"Well, we could discuss that very thing over Babka's unforgettable pierogi." He smiled and tucked his pocket watch away.

She chuckled softly, a musical sound like that of a sea siren. He needed to hear more of it.

Babka beamed and poked Adia's arm. "I can vouch for the man. It's just one dinner, after all."

"I do have a weakness for your pierogi," Adia said to her. And then to Bret, "But I also have a history of relying on the wrong men."

"Just a dinner." Bret put a palm to his chest. "Nothing more, nothing less. I give you my word."

Adia bit her lower lip, and her eyes slid to meet Babka's expectant gaze. The older woman nodded firmly.

Hope soared within Bret.

Adia turned slowly, holding Ewan's shoulders as if he were a shield. "Fine. Tomorrow at seven o'clock," she tossed over her shoulder. "I'll meet you at the restaurant." She waved farewell to Babka and Ludwik and slipped away.

Hope crashed into dismay. Tomorrow?

He and Charlie were to meet one of their contacts outside Warsaw tomorrow night. How on earth would he manage this?

Charlie emerged from the crowd, crunching an apple loudly. Bret's redheaded friend, partner, and brother-in-law watched Adia's disappearing form. He nodded a greeting to Babka and Ludwik and then leaned in to whisper to Bret. The smirk on his face indicated he'd overheard it all.

Babka and Ludwik both turned to a group of shoppers to help fill their orders, out of earshot of Charlie and Bret.

"My, my," Charlie droned in his thick Irish brogue. "Dare I believe my eyes and ears? The avowed bachelor, going on a date?"

Bret ignored the barb. His fingers curled around his grandfather's watch in his pocket. The engravings were worn, and a familiar dent on the edge served as a reminder of the time and war it had endured. Colonel Harold Conway had always claimed it was lucky. It had deflected a bullet in the trenches of France back in 1914, saving his life.

Bret had never believed in such superstitions—until now. Had his grandfather's luck endured in a different form?

"This is a mistake." Bret shook his head. "What am I thinking?"

Charlie lifted a bushy eyebrow, his green eyes sparkling in jest. "From the looks of her, I know exactly what you were thinking. She the lass who works at Janów?"

"I'll send a message to the farm to cancel with her. We meet our new contact tomorrow and there's no time for distractions."

Charlie fed his half-eaten apple to Ludwik's cart horse, then took Bret's shoulders, staring him down. "I can handle the contact alone. Trust me, mate. You can't pass up this particular distraction. You won't get another chance with her."

No, he wouldn't. Nor would they get another chance at a rendezvous with this contact claiming to have access to high-level German intelligence. A source like this had been three years in the making.

Charlie elbowed him in the ribs. "Come on, let's go."

Bret followed his partner in the opposite direction that Adia and Ewan had disappeared.

They went through the motions of checking in with their various sources and embedded spies for the rest of the afternoon. Bret's mind constantly darted back to Adia and the lie he'd so easily shared about his occupation. His cover as a reporter was easy to repeat, but she'd seemed almost skeptical about it. Sparring with her over dinner would be far too fascinating—he could already predict as much. His mind worked through a hundred different scenarios on how the dinner might go. It soothed his mind to war-game every possible outcome.

At dusk, Charlie drove them back to their small safe house south of Wygoda. The sun was deep into the horizon, and yet the dim lighting did little to hide Charlie's toothy grin. Apparently, Charlie had been thinking about his upcoming date as much as Bret had. Since they'd known each other nearly all of their respective twenty-seven years on this earth, it didn't take much to communicate between them.

"Shut it," Bret fired over.

"I'm just tickled I can wire yer sister and give her a little bit of hope. She's been praying for years you'd find someone who might tame yer wild ways."

Elizabeth—Charlie's wife—certainly would be happy to hear even the possibility of a romantic interest. She hoped for anything to anchor Bret and Charlie back to England. It was Bret, after all, who'd convinced his friend to join British Intelligence instead of becoming a boring old lawyer or doctor.

"It's just dinner."

"So you say," Charlie said, glancing in the rearview mirror and hesitating. His brow furrowed slightly.

Bret knew that look. All humor fled between them. He reached for his pistol and turned in the seat. "We have a tail?"

"Coming fast." Charlie pressed the accelerator, and the car lurched forward.

The headlights behind them grew larger, brighter.

"In front!" Charlie shouted. Bret turned to see a car barreling toward them. They were pinned. And neither threat slowed or veered off path.

This wasn't an accident or wayward driver. They'd been targeted somehow. Their cover blown.

"Brace yourself," Bret called.

Everything flashed through his mind in the span of a heartbeat.

The information and potential leads he'd be unable to pass along.

The obvious leak in their network he'd be unable to rectify.

The trouble he'd be in with Elizabeth for putting her husband in danger.

The realization that he'd miss his dinner with the elusive and mysterious horse trainer. And he'd have no way to let her know.

And then glass shattered, metal screamed, and pain pulled Bret from the sea of his regrets. Darkness overtook all.

**Nicole M. Miller** lives in southwest Washington State with her husband and three sons, along with her Arabian horses, chickens, dogs, and cats. As a longtime horse owner, she's been involved in many horse organizations, including serving as a Clark County Fair Court Princess and Miss Teen Rodeo Washington.

When she's not writing or tending the animals, Nicole works in human resources. A journalism major, she's received several national and regional awards for her nonfiction writing from American Horse Publications and the Society of Professional Journalists. See more of her horse and animal stories in *The Horse of My Heart*, *The Horse of My Dreams*, *The Dog Who Came to Christmas*, *Second-Chance Horses*, and *Consider the Birds*. Her debut novel, *Until Our Time Comes*, was a Christy Award finalist.

Follow her on Facebook or Instagram @NicoleMillerWriter and learn more at NicoleMillerWriter.com.

# Connect with Nicole

NicoleMillerWriter.com

NicoleMillerWriter